"Lacey Alexander's books … of us. Unforgettable in an 'Oh, yeah, do that again please' sort of way."

—Romance: B(u)y the Book

"Thoroughly tantalizing, with magnetic characters, a sizzling plot, and raw sensuality, this book will have you fanning yourself long after the last page!"

—*Romantic Times*

and for
Lacey Alexander

"Ms. Alexander is an exceptionally talented author who, time after time, takes us on extremely erotic journeys that leave us breathless with every turn of the page. . . . This author pens the most arousing sexual scenes that you could never imagine."

—Fallen Angel Reviews

"Lacey Alexander has given readers . . . hot, erotic romance with no holds barred."

—Romance Junkies

"Ms. Alexander is probably one of the most talented, straightforward, imaginative writers in erotic romance today."

—The Road to Romance

"Lacey Alexander just 'wowed' me! Incredibly hot!"

—Romance Reader at Heart (top pick)

"Lacey Alexander is a very talented writer."

—The Romance Readers Connection

"Lacey Alexander is an intoxicating erotic writer using sensual and sexual prowess to embrace your inner passions and desires. Sexual discovery at its best."

—Noveltown

"Lacey Alexander's characters . . . are so compelling and lifelike."

—Coffee Time Romance

"Sooo romantic and sexy!"

—Cupid's Library Reviews

"Lacey Alexander takes blissful hedonism to a whole new level in this blazingly brazen, passionately erotic love story!"

—Ecataromance

ALSO BY LACEY ALEXANDER

Voyeur

Seven Nights of Sin

The Bikini Diaries

What She Needs

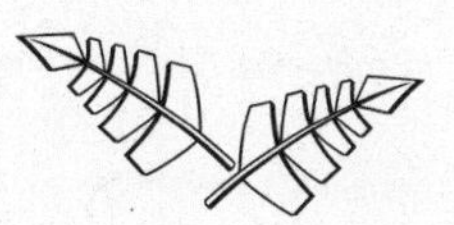

LACEY ALEXANDER

HEAT

HEAT
Published by New American Library,
a division of Penguin Group (USA) Inc.,
375 Hudson Street, New York, New York 10014, USA
Penguin Group (Canada), 90 Eglinton Avenue East, Suite 700, Toronto,
Ontario M4P 2Y3, Canada (a division of Pearson Penguin Canada Inc.)
Penguin Books Ltd., 80 Strand, London WC2R 0RL, England
Penguin Ireland, 25 St. Stephen's Green, Dublin 2,
Ireland (a division of Penguin Books Ltd.)
Penguin Group (Australia), 250 Camberwell Road, Camberwell,
Victoria 3124, Australia (a division of Pearson Australia Group Pty. Ltd.)
Penguin Books India Pvt. Ltd., 11 Community Centre,
Panchsheel Park, New Delhi - 110 017, India
Penguin Group (NZ), 67 Apollo Drive, Rosedale, North Shore 0632,
New Zealand (a division of Pearson New Zealand Ltd.)
Penguin Books (South Africa) (Pty.) Ltd., 24 Sturdee Avenue,
Rosebank, Johannesburg 2196, South Africa

Penguin Books Ltd., Registered Offices:
80 Strand, London WC2R 0RL, England

First published by Heat, an imprint of New American Library,
a division of Penguin Group (USA) Inc.

First Printing, November 2009
1 3 5 7 9 10 8 6 4 2

Library of Congress Cataloging-in-Publication Data:
Alexander, Lacey.
What she needs/Lacey Alexander.
p. cm.
ISBN 978-0-451-22801-7
1. Hotels—Fiction. I. Title.
PS3601.L3539W46 2009
813'.6—dc22 2009023653

Set in Dante

Printed in the United States of America

This book is dedicated to Lindsey Faber,
assistant extraordinaire!

What She Needs

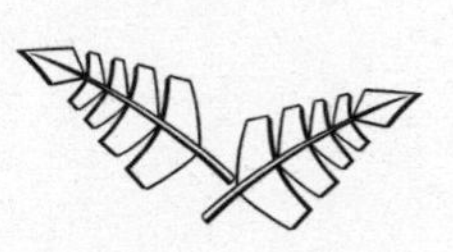

Prologue

"Seriously, Jenna, when was the last time you got laid?"

Jenna Banks looked up from the slice of pizza in her hand, across the room to her best friend Shannon's husband. She loved Kevin—he was like a brother to her—but when she'd been invited over for pizza and a movie, she hadn't expected to be grilled on her sex life. Or lack thereof.

"And I should tell you this *why*?"

Kevin tilted his head as if to say, *Come on—it's me, your buddy, Kev.* "I just think you need to . . . have more fun, that's all. You're an attractive single woman and you're letting life pass you by."

At this, Jenna laughed. "Unless I happen to step in front of a bus or something, I have plenty of life left."

"But maybe not a lot of . . . you know, *youth*," Shannon chimed in, her blond curls bouncing as she settled on the arm of Kevin's easy chair. They both flashed expressions that made Jenna think of the Spanish Inquisition.

Yet she merely rolled her eyes. "I'm twenty-nine. According to the experts, I won't even reach my sexual peak until thirty-five."

"But don't you want to be in the game when it happens?" Kevin asked.

"And what if your peak comes early?" Shannon added. "What if you miss it?"

"My God, you two, get a grip. It's not as if I never have sex. I'm just . . . selective about my partners. Which I happen to think is wise in this day and age. I mean, you guys are married—you don't have to worry about that stuff anymore. And besides, if I'm happy with myself—*and I am*—what's the problem?"

"We just don't want you to have any regrets later in life," Shannon said.

Kevin leaned forward in his chair then, a challenging look in his eye. "And since you claim you *do* have sex, when *was* the last time?"

Fine, she'd take the challenge, if it would stop this silliness. "When I was dating Todd Rogers."

"Todd Rogers!" Shannon exclaimed—as Kevin's eyes fogged over in horror.

"That was how long ago?" he asked.

Jenna let out a breath and did the math. She and Todd had been together on the Fourth of July last year, but had broken up by Labor Day, and now it was August, so . . . "About a year ago, I guess."

"A year," Kevin repeated, appearing dumbfounded.

Next to him, Shannon simply let out a sad sigh. "A year of your life when you could have been indulging in good sex."

Jenna finally dropped her pizza on the plate in her lap—it had gone limp and cold in her hand anyway—and lowered it to the coffee table in front of her. "You two make it sound so easy. Like there are decent, eligible, good-looking guys just lining the streets. But that's not how it is. And sure, I could hang out in bars and try to pick up men for one-night stands, but . . . why? That sounds so . . . yucky."

Shannon shrugged, and Kev said, "Back before Shannon, I had some pretty good one-night stands in my day."

Jenna thought Shannon would smack his arm for that, or at least scowl a little, but instead she simply said, "Me, too. Surely you remember."

Certainly Jenna did. Shannon had been a lot more wild than her back in college at the University of Michigan—and come out none the worse for it. "Look," Jenna finally said, "just because that sort of thing worked for you guys doesn't mean it's right for *me*. When I have sex with a guy, I want it to—"

"Please don't say 'mean something,'" Kevin interrupted. "That's such a *girl* thing."

Jenna sat up a little straighter, thoroughly irritated now. "I *am* a girl, thank you very much, and that's how I feel. And even if it isn't *always* deep and meaningful, I at least want it to be with a guy I sincerely like, and respect, and feel comfortable with. Otherwise, it's just—"

"*Pleasure*," Shannon finished for her. "For your information, there can be a lot of *pleasure* involved regardless of like, respect, and comfort. And sometimes you just have to think . . . well, like a guy. Sometimes you have to be in it for the pure physical enjoyment. And there's nothing wrong with that, by the way. This is the twenty-first century—women are allowed to seek their own pleasure. Sometimes, my dear Jenna," she said as if she were very wise, or Jenna were very thick, "a good orgasm has to be enough to satisfy you."

Jenna paused, turning the words over in her head. She was loath to admit it, but she *almost* saw what they were saying. She wasn't particularly aching for an orgasm—but the point was, if she couldn't find a guy she really *liked*, maybe it was better to at least take some pleasure from one she could . . . crave. One of those really hot, sexy guys who probably *did* hang out at meat market bars looking to get lucky. She could fix herself up—wear something short and tight from Shannon's closet, put on more makeup than usual—then go out and pick up a guy. Before she got old, like they were saying. In case Mr. Right never came along. So that she would at least have a few wild nights, a few hot romps to look back on in her later years.

Except . . . *wait a minute*. What was she *thinking*? She couldn't do what they were suggesting—ever!

"The problem is," she began in rebuttal, "I don't think a good orgasm *would* be enough to satisfy me. In fact, if that's all I got out of it, I'm pretty sure I'd be depressed afterward, and feel empty inside. *Blegh*," she concluded, making a face.

Kevin just shook his handsome head, clearly sad for her. "We just worry about you, Jenna."

"Well, don't. I have a perfectly full life without casual sex every weekend. I have my work and my family, both of which I love. I have my friends, whom I also love—*most of the time*," she added, raising a reproachful eyebrow. "I have a great condo, my book club every other Thursday, my weekend getaways with Shannon each summer—face it, I have a great life. If I sometimes have a nice guy and some sex added to the mix, all the better. And if I don't, I'm still perfectly satisfied."

. . .

Three weeks later, Jenna burst through the front door of Kevin and Shannon's house without knocking. *"I'm going to kill you! I'm going to kill you both! With my bare hands!"*

Kev looked up from where he sat on the floor in front of the TV fiddling with the remote—just as Shannon entered the room, jostling the bowl of popcorn she held to send a few fluffy kernels scattering to the carpet. "Happy movie night to you, too," she said.

"Movie schmovie," Jenna snapped. "You're both dead."

"What did we do?" Kevin gaped at her, the remote resting forgotten in his hand.

"I got a phone call a little while ago," Jenna informed them, so livid she could barely speak, "from a place called the Hotel Erotique! They tell me I've won the grand prize in their annual 'singles sweepstakes,' a two-week stay at a resort where *sex* is the main amenity! Well, you can imagine my shock," she said, trying to calm down, but segueing into complete sarcasm, "since I've never heard of the place and certainly never entered their sweepstakes. And when I acted confused, they then said it had been an e-mail entry—from an address that happens to be *yours*!" She pointed a threatening finger at Kevin, who now dropped the remote altogether.

Kev and Shannon exchanged glances and Kevin said, "Uh-oh."

This somehow managed to make Jenna even *more* angry. "What the *hell* were you thinking? What on earth *possessed* you? Are you out of your freaking mind?"

"I was just, uh, playing around on the Internet one night," he began uncertainly.

"You mean looking at porn," Jenna corrected.

"Whatever," he said, shaking his head. "And I came across this website for this place that, well, sort of helps people live out their sexual fantasies, and . . ."

"And?" repeated Jenna, querying him. Because surely he had more of an explanation than *that*.

"Well, I called Shannon into the room, just because I thought it seemed pretty cool—and then we saw the form to enter the sweepstakes and . . ." He trailed off again. *The coward.*

"And," Shannon picked up for him, "Kev thought it sounded like exactly what you needed."

Jenna gasped, and Shannon cringed, and Kevin hung his head in shame. "I didn't mean that in a bad way," he explained, cautiously raising his gaze back to her, then slowly lifting himself up onto the couch—presumably to put some distance between them. "I just thought something like that would . . . bring you out of your shell. Make you like sex more."

At which she gasped again. "I like sex *fine*, for the trillionth time. And I am not in a shell! But I might soon be in a *cell*—after I murder you."

"So . . . what did you tell them?" Shannon asked. She set the popcorn down and moved to sit beside Kevin on the couch—probably to protect him, Jenna concluded.

"Well, I was completely flustered—I've never been so caught off guard in my life! And I was going to say no, flat out, that they should give it to someone else—but then they told me the prize was worth *fifteen thousand dollars*! And *that* threw me so much that I said I was in the middle of something and would have to call them back."

"Are you gonna go?" Kev asked with a small, speculative head tilt.

Jenna simply blinked, nonplussed. "I'd rather be tarred and feathered."

"But think about it," Kevin said, apparently overcoming his fears and getting back to his usual confident self. "You *won*. Out of probably thousands and thousands of entries. I mean, what are the chances?"

"I don't know, but next time, enter me to win something I *want*, please. A tour of Tuscany maybe. A week in Paris. *Not two weeks of sex with strangers paid to give it to me.*"

"But wow," Shannon said, still obviously dumbstruck by the price tag, "a fifteen-thousand-dollar value. Are you going to just give that up?"

Jenna drew a deep breath, trying to think it through. For crying out loud, why couldn't it be a fifteen-thousand-dollar trip to somewhere she felt passionate about, like one of the many places she'd researched for the historical biographies she wrote for a living. But no—*she'd* won a trip to some sort of crazy *sex palace*. Just her luck.

"I have an idea," she said, pinning Kevin in place with her stare. "Why don't *you* go? Since you thought the place seemed so cool and all?"

"Well, because I'm not single. The prize was for a single, right?"

A technicality, Jenna decided. "Yes, but I checked out the website, too, and I see couples are welcome. I bet they can give you a slightly less deluxe package for two of the same value. *You* entered—*you* go."

"The thing is," Kev said, "I'm not the one in need of a, uh . . . sexual outlet. Shannon and I are perfectly happy with our sex life."

Jenna let out a huge breath. Why did he not get this? "*So am I*, for God's sake! I don't need this any more than you do. I'm a happy woman. When my friends don't butt into my life in weird ways, that is."

"Okay, okay," Shannon soothed her. "You're right. We went too far. It was just a spur-of-the-moment thing, sort of a joke. We never dreamed you'd really win."

"Well, ha ha, very funny."

"Listen, though," Kevin added, clearly trying to sound reasonable, "why don't you go anyway? Not for the sex, but for the other stuff."

"What other stuff?"

"Well, if you went to the website, you saw the pictures. It's an upscale beach resort—pools, a spa, restaurants, you name it, and I'm sure all that stuff is included in your prize. So why don't you just go and sit on the beach—soak up the sun and relax."

She let out a sigh. "I could *use* a little relaxation after this." And then the irony hit her—that she might have fewer people pressuring her to have sex at a sex resort than she did here at home. "Do you think they'd mind my turning down the sex part of the prize?"

"I don't see why," he said with a shrug. "That's what the amped-up price is for—mostly. According to the site, they do this big analysis of each guest to design the perfect sexual experiences for them, and I'm sure that takes a lot of time and planning. So they'd be getting off cheap if all you want is the room and the pool and the spa."

Jenna looked to Shannon, who said, "I think you should go for it. What do you have to lose?"

"But what if I get there and it's . . . icky? I mean, what if there are people having sex all over the place, out in the open, and it creeps me out?"

"Then you get on a plane and come home," Kev replied.

Okay, easy enough. They couldn't *make* her have sex, after all. And they couldn't make her stay if she was uncomfortable there. And though it was a far cry from the castles and battlefields of Europe, a tropical vacation sounded nice. "All right then. Hotel Erotique, here I come." But that didn't keep her from casting Kevin one last glare. "And you'd better hope this doesn't blow up in my face, or you're a dead man."

Chapter 1

While everyone at home in Michigan was busy carving pumpkins and munching on candy corn, Jenna was stepping off a plane at the Miami International Airport. Miami—seemed like a probable-enough place for a hotel specializing in sexual gratification. Although the website made a big deal about the Hotel Erotique being in an undisclosed location—probably because the very concept was so kinky and "out there." And if customers were more or less paying for sex, well, wasn't that illegal? So no wonder the hotel's address was a Miami PO box and the site was so cryptic about the exact locale.

That still didn't prepare her, though, for what happened next.

She'd been told an escort would meet her at baggage claim, and sure enough, there he was—a man in his thirties, blond and mildly handsome with an endearing smile, holding up a card with her last name on it. And the moment they made eye contact, a horrifying thought struck her: *He thinks I'm here for sex! He thinks I've come to live out hedonistic fantasies with strangers! Ugh.*

She thought about defending herself, explaining the situation—but that would just seem childish, and even prudish, to a guy who delivered people to the Hotel Erotique for a living. Still, as she identified herself and he said, "Hi, I'm Gabe," smoothly taking her bags, her face heated with embarrassment.

Oh brother. This was not a good start. *How are you going to spend two weeks at this place if you can't look at anyone without blushing?* Unfortunately, though, this was the first moment she'd thought about the other people she would encounter there, or how they would perceive her. She'd—stupidly—envisioned herself sunning and swimming all alone, in complete solitude. Damn Kevin and Shannon for getting her into this.

The part that really threw her, though, was when she followed Gabe through the airport, traversing hallways, going through doors, until finally he led her out into the hot south Florida sun—not to a limo or shuttle bus, but onto a tarmac, where a small private jet waited, suspiciously devoid of color or markings.

"Um, where are we going?"

Gabe didn't appear taken aback by the question—she must not be the first guest to get confused at this point. "To the Hotel Erotique, of course," he said with a carefree smile. "It's just a short flight away."

"How short?"

"Once we're in the air, thirty minutes."

"So it's . . . on an island?"

He nodded easily over his shoulder as they approached the plane, then bent to stow her luggage in an open compartment, which she noticed was empty but for hers. Well, that much was good. She didn't want companions on this flight—people going there for sex who also thought *she* was going there for sex. Yuck.

"A private island between the Keys and the Bahamas," Gabe clarified. "Self-contained. The whole staff lives on the island full-time."

Wow. A private jet and staff accommodations. She was starting to get why this place was so high priced—even if a large portion of the fees did go to executing sex fantasies.

"We'll have you soaking up the sun in an hour or two," Gabe said with a wink that made the juncture of her thighs tingle. Just a little. Because of all the thoughts and worries and concerns about sex surrounding this trip, she supposed. Even if she wasn't partaking, the whole concept made it difficult not to have sex on the brain. And Gabe *was* cute. Tan. Well built. "Then, after you get a chance to unwind, you'll meet with your guide over dinner."

Her guide. She'd read about that in the folder of information they'd sent her. Each guest was assigned a guide to orchestrate his or her "experience" at the Hotel Erotique. The guide was always the same gender as the guest and served not only as confidant and advisor, but also analyzed the guest to design his or her sexual fantasies. Of course, as Jenna had read more of the resort's literature, it had sounded less like a place where you lived out your fantasies and more like a place that came up with the fantasies *for* you. Which seemed, to her, even weirder. But each guide also possessed a degree in psychology, so maybe it made sense to have someone like that to sort of . . . *direct* one's casual sex.

Geez—casual sex. Gabe still thought she was here for that. Upon remembering, she found herself mumbling a noncommittal, "Oh, okay," and again feeling embarrassed.

"You'll love Mariel," he went on as he followed Jenna up the small jet's stairway. "She's great. Really easy to talk to." She'd already been given the name of her guide, and apparently so had Gabe.

"Wow, seems you're in the know about everything. Next, I'll find out you're the pilot," she teased, stepping onto the luxurious plane.

"Co-pilot," he said with a shrug, and she turned to him in surprise. Was he kidding? "Really," he added, as if reading her mind. "As soon as I get you a drink from the bar and get you buckled in, we'll be ready for takeoff."

A few minutes later, Jenna sat in a plush chair next to a window, peering out over aqua Caribbean waters, sipping a fruity drink Gabe had called "erotic rum punch," and getting more and more nervous as she approached her final destination. Odd, she hadn't been nervous before meeting Gabe and climbing aboard this plane—but somehow that had made it all real to her. Lord, she was going to the Hotel Erotique!

But stay calm. You're just going for the beach and the sun.

Only now she was regretting a few things, such as the online questionnaires she'd filled out at Mariel's request. She wasn't sure why she'd done it. Maybe she was curious to find out what her answers meant. Although some of the questions were about sex and fantasies, mostly they had been about less risqué subjects, from her childhood to her current hobbies, and seemed to point toward something like a personality profile.

She supposed she'd also feared if she told them up front she didn't want the sex part of the prize that maybe, despite Kevin's theory, they'd take it back. And by that time she'd made firm plans to go, even buying some new beachwear—slightly sexier than her usual wardrobe, just to kind of . . . fit in and not feel like a freak among the sex-seekers.

Now she wished she hadn't completed the forms, nor been so honest on them. Not that she'd had all that much to share. Maybe that was part of the regret. Maybe she would appear to be a classic case of someone who needed help in the sex department, just like Kevin thought. When she'd been sitting at home, looking at her computer screen, it had felt like a game—something to do when she needed a break from work. Now it was feeling very real.

But stop worrying—this will be fine. Nothing had actually changed, after all. Tonight at what the brochure called her "orientation dinner," she would tell Mariel her decision—not to partake in the sex—and surely the woman would understand, especially if she was as great as Gabe claimed. Then she'd perhaps, out of curiosity, ask Mariel what the analysis had revealed about her. Because who didn't want to know stuff like that about themselves?

After that, she would embark on two full weeks of sun and relaxation. She was already looking forward to some of the spa treatments, and she'd packed a few books she'd been wanting to read. All this would turn out . . . okay. Better than okay, in fact. It was a free vacation, after all. In a tropical paradise. What more could a girl ask for?

Four hours later, Jenna actually felt relaxed.

Of course, maybe that had to do with the numerous "erotic rum punches" she'd consumed throughout the afternoon. But better to be a tiny bit intoxicated and relaxed than strung out and nervous.

She'd found that, in keeping with the pictures on the Internet, the hotel and grounds were immaculate—luxurious with just a hint of casual island flair that meshed nicely with the tall palm trees swaying in the breeze. After landing on a private airstrip, Gabe had loaded her baggage into a lavish golf-cart-for-the-rich-and-famous, complete with a polished wood dashboard and leather seats. Then he'd driven her up a meandering stone pathway lined with lush tropical foliage to the open-air lobby, where checking in had been surprisingly . . . normal, like at any other hotel.

Her deluxe suite, she soon discovered, came with an enormous bathroom and balcony, along with a spacious sitting area. And after unpacking, she'd put on a new bikini—leopard print, and a bit more scant than what she wore at home—and nervously made her way down to the pool. Because even if the lobby and room seemed normal, she'd decided that surely there'd be some heavy sexual vibes at the pool.

Yet as she stretched out on a lounge chair beneath the sun and started reading some more literature the desk clerk had given her, she learned that the main pool was a sex-free zone, one of many areas at the resort where guests could retreat during their stay to have an experience like they'd find at any ordinary beach destination.

She couldn't have imagined more welcome news. And *that* was when she finally quit being nervous—delighted to learn she could indeed bask in the sun here every day without worrying about sexual . . . *creepiness* invading her space.

And to celebrate, she started indulging in more of the same drink she'd been served on the plane, even if it embarrassed her just slightly at first to order "erotic rum punch." But her handsome poolside waiter, Josh, quickly put her at ease with his friendly manner, soon explaining that the punch was a trademark Hotel Erotique concoction.

Josh kept the rum flowing all afternoon, until Jenna was *so* relaxed she even napped a bit. Then went for a dip. When, for the first time, she grew brave enough to look around her at the other people at the pool—some couples, other singles—and had that same odd feeling as when she'd met Gabe: *They think I'm here for sex.* But then she remembered *they* were here for sex, and that suddenly seemed a more interesting thought. Walking up the steps out of the lagoon-type pool in her leopard print bikini, water sluicing from her body, she found herself wondering if anyone saw her and wanted to have sex with her.

That was when she realized she'd had too much rum punch—and she quickly tried to banish the thought. But it stayed with her—and was suddenly a lot easier to ponder under the influence of rum. It was easier to look at the attractive couple a few chairs away and wonder what *their* fantasies were. Easier to surreptitiously spy a hot blond surfer-looking guy stretched out under a small palm tree and wonder if he'd noticed her bikini, if anything about *her* meshed with the reasons he'd come here.

And when Josh delivered another drink, she couldn't bring herself to turn it down. "But this is the last one," she told him with a smile—maybe even a *flirty* one. Unintentionally, of course, because unlike everyone else at the Hotel Erotique, she wasn't here for sex. And she didn't want to send Josh the wrong message. Yet at the same time, she wondered if he might be admiring her body at all. Because, according to Shannon and past lovers, it was a *good* body. And one not normally this much on display.

"I mean it," she added when Josh cast a doubtful grin.

"If you say so," he'd replied teasingly. "But you know where I am if you change your mind." The cute waiter had pointed to a thatch-covered tiki hut bar on the opposite side of the pool before departing with a wink that—just like talking with Gabe earlier—had made her a little wet.

Now, she'd just showered in the luxurious marble bathroom in her suite and was off to dinner with her guide. Following the map she'd been given upon her arrival, she took in the beach to her right, the sky turning blush-colored as the sun began its descent. And as she started across a long wooden boardwalk, sea oats sprouting up from the sand beneath, she spied a gazebo in the distance—which her trusty map marked as the spot for her orientation dinner.

She'd worn a pretty pink sundress with a low-cut halter neck—like the bathing suit, sexier than what she'd choose at home. Because she didn't want Mariel to think turning down the sex part of her prize meant she was prim, or repressed, or anything else. She wanted Mariel to see her as a confident woman who had made the right decision for herself.

She walked slowly to ensure not losing her balance on her sexy, strappy cork wedges—and again couldn't stop herself from thinking about sex. How many people were having sex right now somewhere on this island? She felt warm in her panties, imagining, wondering, as vague, shadowy images of sweaty bodies moving together wafted through her mind.

Damn—she'd finished her last rum punch nearly an hour ago, but she still felt it. Otherwise, she surely wouldn't be thinking about sex so much—or suffering the response between her thighs.

But don't worry—this really will *be okay.* Eating would help sober her. And after dinner, she could turn in early, then get up tomorrow and enjoy a lazy day on the beach.

The setting sun cast shadows over the interior of the gazebo as she approached, but she stepped boldly inside, ready to show Mariel how self-assured she was. Until she saw a completely scorching-hot guy sitting at a table for two—and flinched, halting in place on her wedge heels. "Um, sorry—wrong gazebo."

His dark hair was thick but well kempt, contrasting slightly with the sexy stubble on his chin—and a slight smile made him even more handsome. Everything about him looked strong, confident, powerful—like she wished *she* really felt right now. "No—right gazebo, Jenna."

Oh, shit—he knew her name. She stood up straighter, her spine going rigid. "I'm supposed to meet Mariel. And you're . . . not her."

His smile deepened—he looked amused at how flustered she appeared—and she couldn't help noticing, even in the dim light, that he possessed deep gray eyes, sexy and captivating. He stood and walked around the small table—set for dinner, complete with ensconced candles and wineglasses—to pull out the chair on the other side. "Sit down," he said, "and I'll explain over some pinot grigio." Her favorite wine. Had that been on a questionnaire somewhere?

She couldn't figure out a graceful way to *not* sit down, even though her impulses immediately told her to run, to extract herself from this situation. *But for heaven's sake, calm down—he's only an incredibly hot guy, not a demon from hell or anything.*

Although she feared she was probably looking at him as if he were indeed Satan himself. Because she'd had a plan, and whatever it was he had to explain, this changed it. And suddenly everything felt different. Despite how calm she'd been through the afternoon, now she sensed sex all around her, in a pervasive way.

But then, wait, no—maybe it was only . . . him. His eyes. His body. He dripped sex. He made her tingle between her legs even amid her unaccountable fear. He looked like a guy who could steal a woman's soul.

"Sit," he urged her again. "I won't bite. Promise." Then he winked.

And there it was again, that undeniable pulse at the juncture of her thighs.

Jenna sat, but only because she didn't know what else to do. And since she'd already acted totally weird in front of Mr. Soul-Stealing Hottie, she now experienced the urge to make him see what she'd wanted Mariel to see—a confident, in-control woman. With Mariel, it had been to prove she didn't need the sexual offerings here—yet with this guy, it was simply to redeem herself.

After pushing in her chair, he returned to his own—which meant they were face-to-face again and it was time to meet his gaze. Her chest tightened as she forced herself to do so. She simply wasn't accustomed to dealing with a man so attractive. In a world designed for sex. Where had her pleasant sense of intoxication gone? Its departure left her feeling vulnerable, for reasons she couldn't understand.

"First," he said, still smiling that sexy smile, "congratulations on winning our grand prize, and welcome to the Hotel Erotique. I hope you're enjoying your stay so far."

"Thank you, and yes, it's lovely." *Get to the point already.*

Before continuing, though, he paused to lift an open bottle from an ice bucket to pour two glasses of wine. "Second," he finally went on, "I have some unfortunate news. Your guide, Mariel, has just been called away on a family emergency."

Oh God. *I know I should feel bad for Mariel, but right now, I'm more worried about* me. "I'm . . . sorry to hear that. Nothing too serious, I hope," she managed to add.

"Her father had a heart attack, and he's expected to have a complete recovery, but she still needs to be with him."

"Of course," Jenna replied, nodding.

"And as luck would have it, the only other female guide on-site this week is already very overbooked. We have two more, but both are on vacation."

"I see," was all she could say. So what did that mean? Well, maybe she should simply go ahead and tell him her decision and this wouldn't even matter since she didn't actually *need* a guide. But before she could figure out how to broach the topic of sex, he went on.

"I know our literature promises a same-gender guide for each guest, but these are unusual circumstances, so I apologize and hope you won't mind being stuck with *me*." His enticing grin widened, making her thighs melt even as her jaw went slack.

"You," she repeated numbly.

"Brent Powers," he said, extending a hand across the table.

She forced herself to shake it. It was big. Strong.

"And I can assure you that, despite this being unusual, I'm committed to ensuring your stay with us exceeds your expectations," Brent went on. "I've been with the Hotel Erotique for fifteen years and have spent ten of those as a guide. I have a BS in social psychology and a PhD in clinical sexology. I'm also part owner of the resort, so I hope all that will convince you you're in safe hands."

Clinical sexology, huh? And he even had a doctorate in it—which she supposed made him an official doctor of sex. It was strange to know she sat across from a man who was not only hot as hell but who also knew more about sex than she could possibly fathom.

But none of that mattered. What mattered was . . . "Actually, I was planning to tell Mariel that . . . I'd like to decline the, uh, sex portion of my prize. So I don't really need a guide. I'd just like to enjoy the rest of what the resort has to offer."

Across from her, Brent Powers blinked, looking truly surprised. "May I ask why?"

She sucked in her breath. This part would have been easier with a woman. Or even with a less-attractive man. She found she couldn't quite meet his eyes as she spoke. "Well, I simply decided I'm not comfortable having sex with strangers. No offense—I'm sure it brings many people a lot of, um, pleasure—but I just don't think it's right for *me*."

Only when he didn't answer right away did she manage to lift her gaze from his white button-down shirt to his face—to see him appearing unduly concerned. So she rushed on. "Maybe I should have given the prize back—I'm sorry if that's what you would have preferred. But I really could use a vacation, and when I discussed this with some friends, they suggested I simply enjoy the other aspects of the prize—like the pool, and the spa." She decided to blame at least part of it on Shannon and Kevin since this was actually *all* their fault. "Is that okay? Or should I leave?"

At this, Brent Powers reached out to touch her hand where it rested on the table near her untouched glass of wine, and—yikes, the simple connection sizzled through her like electricity, skittering all the way up her arm. "Jenna, we would never ask you to leave. But I'd like to talk more about your decision."

Oh boy. She finally took a drink of her wine. A big one. She needed it. "What's to discuss?" she asked, trying for an easy, confident expression.

Brent lifted his wine for a sip, too—then smiled that killer smile again. "Well, to begin with, what we do here is more than 'sex with strangers.'"

Oh? Could have fooled *her*.

He went on. "People come here for a lot of different reasons, and we welcome them all, but by and large, I see what we do here as being therapeutic."

Hah! Was he serious? It was truly hard to hold in a sarcastic laugh, but she contained it somehow.

"There are many reasons people seek out new sexual experiences, and I'm sure you know we design a series of individualized fantasies based on what we've learned about each guest from our questionnaires. And we usually fine-tune it a bit after the guest arrives. If we saw our job as nothing more than supplying 'sex with strangers,' we wouldn't go to so much trouble, nor would we have a full staff educated and trained to give our guests the optimal sexual encounters while helping them attain their sexual needs and, in some cases—like yours—resolve their sexual issues."

She hadn't thought about that, she supposed—they truly did seem to take great care in creating each person's fantasies. Except . . . *wait*. Sexual issues? What was he talking about?

"If people just want casual sex, there are other resorts that offer that, with less-expensive price tags. When people come *here*, we know they desire more—we're unique in the service we provide. And I'm not telling you this to change your opinion of the Hotel Erotique so much as to suggest you reconsider your decision."

Okay, so it was official—he was trying to talk her into going through with the sex part. Which she really hadn't expected. Kevin had been so sure they'd be happy to let her skip it—damn him.

"The thing is," she began, "I don't *have* sexual issues. I think you just said I do, but I don't." Maybe clarifying that would make Mr. Sexology back off.

Across from her, though, his eyelids lowered slightly, shading his gaze and making him look even more seductive. "Jenna, I've read your questionnaires, as well as the profile Mariel prepared after receiving them. I was under the impression you realized . . ."

"What?" she asked when he trailed off, her heart beating too fast.

He tilted his head, peering at her as if they shared a secret. "I know you haven't had sex in more than a year," he said, his voice so smoky he made even *that* sound alluring. "Although you characterize the sex you've had as 'good,' nothing in the way you described it was very convincing. And I know, too, about your parents' view of sex—and also about your cousin."

All the blood drained from Jenna's face. Sexy voice or not, she couldn't have been more dumbfounded. He, or Mariel, or both of them, had taken bits and pieces of information scattered throughout those online forms and cobbled them together in such a way that . . . oh God, they thought she had sex hang-ups! They thought that was why she'd come here, why she'd entered their stupid contest. If she'd felt vulnerable a few minutes ago, it was nothing compared to now.

Just then, a handsome, dark-skinned waiter entered the gazebo bearing a large tray, and Brent looked up. "Good evening, Rico."

"Mr. Powers," the waiter said with a nod, then also smiled politely in Jenna's direction—which made her blush. This was one more person who thought she'd traveled here for sex—and now it was worse; now it was assumed she'd come here to solve sexual *problems*!

Rico lowered two dishes—fine china from the look of it—overtop the larger plates already on the table. Glancing down at hers, Jenna saw chicken cordon bleu and didn't remember choosing it from a menu at any time, despite it being one of her favorites. Unless it had been on some questionnaire she couldn't remember—she'd filled those out weeks ago.

By the time Rico departed, Jenna's irritation finally superseded her nervousness with Mr. Hottie Sexologist and allowed her to look him squarely in the eye, ignoring her food. "You think you know a lot about me, don't you?"

She was beginning to get the picture here. He not only thought he knew about her in sexual ways—he was also showing her he knew what she liked to eat, to drink. Were they meeting here because he'd somehow discerned that she found gazebos quaint and loved sunsets? She felt . . . utterly invaded.

"You *told* me a lot about you, Jenna," he reminded her matter-of-factly. "In the questionnaires."

"I told *Mariel*," she corrected him.

"And I've apologized for not having another female guide available right now, but that's not really what this is about."

"What *what* is about?"

"Your anger."

"I'm not angry," she snapped—then realized that she, indeed, sounded pretty angry.

"We consider it a large part of our job to learn as much about you as we can, in order to provide the experience you need here. And you freely gave us the information necessary to do that," he pointed out.

Which pissed her off even more, because he was right. She'd stupidly filled out the forms, not thinking anyone was going to analyze them *that* closely—simply thinking it would be fun to find out if she was more type A or type B, more creative or analytical, that sort of thing. "True, I did. But you keep using the word 'need,' and I assure you I don't *need* anything. If I *needed* it so badly, why would I be turning it down?"

"Because you're afraid of it, Jenna," he answered without missing a beat. "Which is perfectly understandable, considering your profile."

She lowered her chin derisively. "So just what is it you think you learned about me? What is it you think I need so badly?"

Her sexy guide simply tilted his head, the move making him appear almost arrogant. "If you don't know, then I can't tell you, Jenna. You have to find out along the way."

"Along *what* way?"

"By experiencing the sexual fantasies we're going to create for you here over the next two weeks."

"That's another thing," she said, her dander rising even more. "You and your brochures call them fantasies—yet *you* design them? That doesn't make any sense."

"Sure it does," he claimed. "We use only data you give us to design your fantasies. Many people tell us that what they experience here mirrors their own fantasies exactly. Others say we help them live out fantasies they weren't bold enough to create in their own minds. Either way, we feel the term 'fantasies' is a good way to describe the experiences."

Jenna simply gave her head a short shake. She couldn't believe this. Getting out of the sex part had sounded so easy. But Brent Powers was making it pretty challenging—and upsetting her in the process.

Until she suddenly remembered: It didn't matter what he said, or what he thought he knew, or even if some little part of her wondered if, or feared, he could be right—she didn't have to do anything she didn't want to. So that's what she told him. "I don't have to do anything I don't want to."

"Of course you don't," he said smoothly. "But you *will* want to, Jenna."

She sat up a bit straighter, unnerved. "What makes you so sure?"

"Because I'm going to *make* you want to."

For a second she couldn't breathe. Because she was pulsing in her panties again. Just from looking into his dark eyes and listening to his seductive voice and oversure words.

But then she pulled herself together—again. Damn it, this man possessed the ability to make her come undone at a glance. "I don't think so," she simply said.

And at that, a small smile formed on her guide's face. "Tell you what," he suggested. "How about you just eat dinner with me, and if I haven't proven to you I'm right by the time it's over, you win—you're free to just enjoy the beach and the spa, and I won't bother you with this again. How's that sound? Fair?"

Frankly, it sounded unsettling. Since it meant he'd spend the next hour trying to talk her into something she absolutely wouldn't, couldn't do. But she was a big girl—she could just keep saying no as she had so far. And if she stormed out of the gazebo in a huff, it was going to make it difficult to stay here and have a relaxing, all-expenses-paid vacation. She could put up with the arrogant "sexologist" over dinner if it meant she could enjoy her vacation with his blessing. And besides, she was determined to convince him he didn't know as much as he thought. And whatever *needs* he thought she had . . . well, he'd clearly *over*analyzed her. "All right," she finally said. "Fair."

"Good," he said with a short nod. Then he lifted his wineglass in a toast. "To . . . what I suspect will be an enlightening meal."

Chapter 2

"I read in your profile that you write historical biographies for a living," Brent said. Having always liked smart women, he found her occupation fascinating. "How does someone get into that line of work?"

Across the table, pretty Jenna Banks arched one brow and looked completely suspicious as she cut into her food. "You mean you don't know? After all, you know what kind of wine I enjoy and how I like my chicken—I figured I had no secrets left."

He couldn't resist a grin. "I know a *lot* about you—but not everything. Not yet anyway." He concluded with a wink, just before forking a thick chunk of filet mignon into his mouth.

Despite himself, he found her attractive—not only her brain, but also her body. A little obstinate, a little underconfident—but he could go a long way toward helping with those issues once she started seeing things his way. And though it might make him a pig, he found her annoyance at him rather cute.

"I have a passion for history," she explained of her work then, suddenly sounding much *less* annoyed, "and a gift for storytelling. But I'm not especially good at making things up—I'm better at retelling the facts in an engaging way. Or that's what the reviews say anyway." She shrugged as she took a bite of chicken—yet he could see, that quickly, that when it came to her work, she *was* confident. And he instantly liked seeing the truly self-assured version of Jenna. It made him all the more determined to improve her life through what the Hotel Erotique could give her in the coming two weeks.

She didn't get it, of course. She honestly didn't see how negative sexual attitudes and events had shaped her into who she was, both socially and emotionally. And that was the challenging part for him.

Of course, whenever someone arrived with bigger problems than a guide felt could be solved here, the guest was counseled and sent home. But Jenna didn't fit that profile. She wasn't unhappy; she wasn't ruled in any way by sex or lack of it. Yet—whereas most people arrived here either knowing they had sex issues to resolve or simply wanting some out-of-the-ordinary fun—Jenna was in denial about what she wanted, needed, deep down inside. He'd never been faced with a guest who *refused* the very sex they'd come here for.

But then again, she'd won a prize—not paid for it—so that changed the circumstances. Still, why had someone so in denial about her sexual hang-ups even entered the contest?

"I Googled you," he admitted, watching as she cut into her baked potato. "Not as part of the job, but because I was curious about your career. Your books look interesting, and very successful."

She smiled—still showing that confidence he liked in her so much. "*New York Times* bestseller," she said with an appealing pride. "And I'm fortunate to be in that small sector of the population that truly loves its work."

So was he, but this didn't seem like the time to mention that. "Who have you written about?"

"A wide variety of people—Marie Antoinette, Thomas Jefferson, Anne Boleyn, Cleopatra, and I'm currently working on an anthology about some of the more famous pirates of the Golden Age. Basically, I write about people who are already pretty well-known, but I try to dig deeper than most biographies and find the really human, emotional sides of their stories."

"It doesn't surprise me at all," he said, "to hear you find emotions compelling."

"Something you got from my profile, I presume," she replied dryly.

Her attitude made him chuckle. "True enough," he admitted. "And it fits with everything else I know about you."

She gave her head an irritated tilt, back to being annoyed. "So you can tease me about that, but you can't *tell* me about it?"

He shrugged, biting into a dinner roll. If he told her everything he knew about her—about the way sex had shaped her psyche, her reactions to people, to men, the world—she wouldn't believe him right now. She had to be shown. Changed. But he could tell her . . . a little. "Let's just say people who place a high value on emotions are people who tend to feel things deeply themselves. Meaning that every good thing—or bad thing—that happens to you affects you perhaps a little more than it would most people."

She simply blinked at him, still clearly just as aggravated. "You just told me I'm emotional—which I could have told you myself. That doesn't get to the heart of the matter."

"As I said, you need to be *shown* the heart of the matter, Jenna. And I promise if you let your guard down enough to experience what the Hotel Erotique has to offer, you won't regret it."

Across from him, she simply rolled her eyes. "Look, I know you think you're very suave and persuasive, but I'm afraid it would take a hell of a lot more than that to make me . . . do what you want me to do here. Speaking of which," she said, "dare I ask how someone gets into *your* line of work?"

He smiled. "It's simple, really. I like sex."

She was obviously waiting for him to expound upon that, and when he didn't, she said, "That's it? You like sex? *Lots* of people like sex."

"But most of them don't like it enough to get a PhD in the study of it and make it their life's work. I like sex enough that, when I was young, I realized I wanted to be in an environment where I was surrounded by it, but where it was . . . treated like an important part of life. Then, later, I decided I wanted to help people experience sex to the fullest, so they could learn to love and revere sex as much as I do."

"Revere," she repeated. "That's an interesting word to describe sex." She took another sip of wine and he realized she might be getting slightly drunk. He took it as a cue to refill her glass. Her profile indicated that alcohol often relaxed her and helped release her inhibitions—and that was exactly what he needed to happen tonight.

Only . . . hell. It was a long leap between getting her to talk about sex and convincing her to indulge in the resort's sensual offerings over the next two weeks. He'd simply had no idea she'd show up for dinner as anything but a compliant guest, ready to begin her fantasies. So he wasn't entirely sure how to accomplish this. But one thing he knew was—her denial complicated everything, and when she did agree, he'd have to toss most of Mariel's plans for her out the window and devise his own.

In the meantime, he needed to focus on the conversation here—it was all important. "You wouldn't say sex is something you hold in reverence?" he asked.

She drew in a deep breath, obviously thinking it over, and suddenly not seeming as argumentative as a moment ago. Good—maybe the wine *was* doing the trick—urging her to drop her guard. The problem with emotional people was that sometimes they stumbled upon emotions so deep they couldn't face them, so they turned them off. That was clearly what Jenna had done—with many of her feelings surrounding sex—and his job was to take those bad emotions and memories and replace them with good ones.

"When I'm with a guy I really care about," Jenna finally replied, "sure, I revere sex. Only it's . . . the intimacy I'm *really* holding in reverence then. Because . . . if it were just the sex, it wouldn't need to be with a guy I care about, right?"

"Right," he said. "So you revere intimacy, but not just sex itself."

She nodded. "And you . . . you value sex alone that way, without intimacy?" she asked as if sincerely trying to understand.

"Yes," he replied easily. "Humans were built for sex—our bodies were designed for it. It's one of our most basic instincts and among life's greatest pleasures. Everything about sex—every nuance, every physical response, every little kink or fetish—fascinates me. I've never seen the point in trying to hide that or be dishonest about it."

"You know," she said, pausing to take another sip of wine, her meal now appearing long forgotten, "maybe I *wish* I were like you. But I'm not. And the trouble with people like you—and with my friends Shannon and Kevin—is that just because *you're* satisfied by the act of sex without emotion, you think everyone else should be, too."

At this, however, he shook his head in firm disagreement. "I never said that. And I'm in no way suggesting you shouldn't feel emotion with sex. That's how you happen to be put together and it's fine."

"Then what *are* you suggesting?"

He considered his answer—how could he make her understand? "Sometimes," he began, "there are bigger issues at work than intimacy and emotion. And if you let me design two weeks of fantasies for you, I guarantee that every time you have sex after leaving here, it will be *better*, even *more* emotional, with *more* intimacy."

Her eyes went wide with doubt. "That's a bold claim, Mr. Powers."

"Damn right." And he wasn't backing down from it a bit. "What I'm suggesting, Jenna, is that if you can temporarily push aside the idea of romantic intimacy, you'll leave here with a much clearer, healthier, happier view of sex, which will make you a happier person more likely to find healthier, longer-lasting relationships."

She peered across the table at him as if maybe she was actually thinking it over. Her blue eyes sparkled in the candlelight now that dusk had fallen over the gazebo. The sunset painted the sky to the west in shades of vibrant pink and orange, but he didn't bother looking because he found himself liking the view of Jenna more. He *knew* her. In a primal way. He understood her so much better than she thought. And beyond the obligations of his job, he was struck with the surprising urge to rescue her . . . from herself, whether she liked it or not.

Jenna could scarcely believe the promises Brent Powers was willing to make. They were ridiculous. And he must think *she* was ridiculous if he expected her to believe them. Given how weirdly personal the conversation now felt, she decided to come completely clean. "You want to know the whole truth, the reason I'm here?"

"Very much so. Because like I said, most people don't come to the Hotel Erotique to turn down the sex."

"I didn't even *enter* the contest," she confessed. "My friend Kevin entered my name—because *he* thinks I'm not having enough sex. I wanted to kill him when I found out, but then I decided I could use a free beach vacation. I filled out the forms online on a lark, just for fun, and also figuring if I admitted up front that I didn't want the fantasies, maybe I'd lose the trip. So there you have it. I didn't enter. I don't want more sex than I already have. I'm a perfectly happy, content woman. So what do you think of that?"

Brent's eyes nearly burned a hole through her, but he didn't look angry. So far he had *never* looked angry; in fact—he simply looked like . . . a sexy, presumptuous know-it-all. And ever since the "presumptuous know-it-all" part had been added to "sexy," she'd felt much less intimidated by him. Even if the way he looked at her right now still had her breasts aching and the crux of her thighs throbbing. But that was just . . . the whole sexual aura of this place, of this discussion. It meant nothing.

"What I think," he finally said, soft, low, his voice almost intoxicating, "is that this means it's fate."

"Huh?" she mumbled in disbelief.

"Maybe fate brought you here, Jenna, to help you face your sexual issues."

At this she rolled her eyes. "For the last time, I do not have sexual issues. The way I see it is—just because someone like me chooses to be selective about my sexual activity, someone like *you* thinks that makes me some kind of prim and proper Little Mary Sunshine. Basically, you think *your* way is right and *my* way is wrong and that I need to be . . . liberated or something."

"Not true," he said, still calm and smooth, despite the fact that she'd just ranted a little. "Someone like me knows there are reasons—valid reasons, by the way—that someone like you is overly careful about sex. All I want is to change that, change the negative perceptions that were ground into you over time."

She didn't answer for a long moment. Why had she been so freaking honest on those forms? About her loving yet superconservative parents always acting as if sex were a dirty word, acting as if everything about it were wrong. About her older cousin, Donny, who had, on more than one occasion, made obscene remarks to her when she was an adolescent, and had once rudely grabbed her between her legs at a family picnic when no one else was around—and, of course, she'd been too mortified to tell her mother, afraid it would seem like her fault somehow. And—oh Lord, this meant he'd also read about that time she'd been in a crush of people at an amusement park when she was fourteen and a man's hand had snaked out of the crowd to squeeze her breast, leaving her to feel helpless and violated. She'd never even seen his face.

Sitting there across from Brent Powers, she hated that this man had gotten such a close look into a private window of her life. She was long over all those things now—she'd written them down in response to pointed questions, thinking only a woman would ever see her answers. And never expecting anyone to think they'd . . . scarred her, for heaven's sake.

"Just so you know," she finally said, wondering if she appeared weak after thinking back on unpleasant things, "I'm a well-adjusted adult who is perfectly capable of overcoming a few less-than-ideal situations in my youth."

"Less than ideal? That's a mild way to put it."

"I disagree. Much worse things happen to people all the time. I'm a grown-up—and I got over all those things a long time ago."

"I don't believe you, Jenna," he said, his voice as dark and smooth as melted chocolate.

God, the man was insufferable. "Then what *do* you believe? And don't give me this 'You have to show me' crap. Tell me what it is you believe about me."

"All right," he finally said.

Their gazes met and locked across the table, and her heart beat harder than she thought it should. She felt tense, a little tipsy, and still struggled against the fluttering sensation in her panties every time she looked into Brent Powers' eyes.

"I believe you want, value, crave, and even revere sex a lot more than you think. But I also believe that, deep down, you fear that all but the tamest forms of sex are, on some moral level, wrong. I believe there's a very sensual, sexual woman inside you, hiding behind a bunch of negative messages you received as a kid. I believe you're in serious denial and that you need to be shown how amazing, how really *phenomenal*, sex can be. And further, I believe you need to trust me here—just take it on faith—that I know what I'm talking about, because your denial is thick enough that you won't be able to see the truth without my help."

She took it all in. Absorbed it. Felt a little abused. Embarrassed. Angry. Because none of that was true. Yeah, those bad things had happened—but most people, girls especially, had to deal with stuff like that at some point in their lives, didn't they? It was awful at the time, sure, but it didn't mean she was screwed up because of it. "You want to know what *I* believe?" she asked.

"Sure."

"That you're the most arrogant man I've ever met. And that you have a serious God complex."

"No," he said, "I don't think I'm God, Little Mary Sunshine. But I do think I can save you."

His words settled deep down inside her. They were too much. Too overwhelming of a promise for her to take. And why on earth did it make the juncture of her thighs throb even harder?

She couldn't look at him anymore, just couldn't. In fact, she wanted to run away—just like when she'd arrived here.

Instead, though, she simply stood up and walked a few steps to the gazebo's railing to peer out on the beach. The sun had sunk below the horizon now, but the sky remained awash in color, and it was much easier to face the sunset than the man who was making her feel such conflicting emotions.

Lust. Fear.

Curiosity. Regret.

And the strange sensation of wanting to . . . somehow be possessed by him.

Oh Lord. That last part made her shake her head. Where had it even come from?

The wine, surely.

But she couldn't keep attributing everything to alcohol. Something strange was taking place inside her—some of the most intense sexual feelings she'd ever experienced swirled and swam there, clashing with everything else she was. Jenna the historical biographer. Jenna the conservative dresser. Jenna the dependable friend, the academic, the library volunteer, the college wallflower, the student council president, the eighth-grade girl with braces . . . It went on and on, all the way back to her youth. None of those Jennas knew how *this* Jenna—this Jenna whose breasts ached with longing and who thought she might die soon if she didn't have an orgasm—had suddenly come into being.

God, it had been a long day. A long day of thinking about sex. Of feeling it in the air here—even if it hadn't been "in her face," as she'd worried about. No, it was more subtle than that. It lingered in corridors and wafted among the palm fronds, being blown to and fro by the sea breeze. It had . . . soaked into her skin, she feared. How else could she explain the raw lust coursing through her veins now?

Wine and rum punch? Sure, maybe. But there was more. The aura of what this place was about. And then had come this man—this hot-as-hell, smooth-as-silk man who unnerved her, irritated her, and excited her all at once. This man who had somehow made her talk about sex and who thought she *needed* it. And worst of all, now she did. Now—because of *all* this—she needed it.

But she couldn't have it. To agree to what he was suggesting would be insane.

All you have to do is turn around and tell him you still don't want the fantasies—then walk away. That was the agreement—it's all that's required of you.

So do that. Do it now. Put an end to this. Get on with your vacation, and your life.

She sensed his presence behind her just before his hand closed warmly over the curve of her waist. His breath warmed her neck as he leaned close, speaking low. "What'll it take, sunshine, to prove I'm right? To prove to you how much you want all the sex you're not having?"

She tried to breathe evenly, think clearly. "I can't imagine *anything* would convince me of that." *Go now. Walk away.*

"Really?" he whispered. "Nothing?" His hand moved slowly around, sliding onto her stomach, and the warmth of his body cocooned her from behind.

And still she heard herself say, "Nothing."

Yet—oh God. *Oh God.* What was happening? He was . . . touching her. At first, she'd tried to believe it was . . . not sexual, just supportive. But *this* was sexual. His thumb, gliding along the underside of her breast, was sexual. His breath on her ear was sexual. His body, pressing gently, seductively into hers from behind was sexual. And God knew the way her body yearned, the way the mound between her thighs practically hummed now—that was sexual, too. More sexual than she'd even known she could feel.

And she wasn't walking away. She wasn't moving at all. Except for the pounding of her heart. And that outrageous pulse in her panties.

And then—oh God, oh God, oh God—she felt . . . his arousal and gasped. She wasn't sure if it shocked her more to know she was capable of that—arousing this man—or to feel the stunning hardness stretching upward against her rear. She'd begun to tremble.

His hold on her tightened gently, anchoring her as he whispered low again into her ear. "It's all right, sunshine. Relax now. I've got you. And I just want you to feel good."

In front of him, she bit her lip. How could this be happening? But . . . maybe that didn't matter because—oh, it felt amazing. Especially after aching and tingling all damn day. It felt like . . . lush, intoxicating relief.

Finally, she gave in to it, *sank* into it, into his large, sturdy male body.

The next thing she knew, he was kissing her neck, making her feel it where she throbbed, each kiss like a tiny explosion between her legs—and she instinctively bent her neck to give him easier access.

And she knew she had to stop this before it got out of hand. Well, any *more* out of hand. Because she'd just told him she wasn't comfortable having sex with strangers. And she wasn't.

But when his hand eased up higher under her breast, when his thumb stroked upward, over her nipple—she couldn't get the words out. Just another gasp. She wasn't wearing a bra under the halter dress, leaving one less barrier between her chest and his touch, and the sensation had shot through her like a rocket soaring toward the heavens. A glance down revealed *both* her nipples, erect and poking through the cottony fabric of her dress, and she wondered if they'd been like that all through dinner. And then his thumb stroked the same hard, beaded peak again—and *seeing* it this time in addition to feeling it made her let out a tiny sob of pleasure.

Say something. Because you can't just let this happen. You can't. "I . . . I thought I read . . . that guides . . . are never involved in sex with their guests."

"They're not." Now his voice came like a low growl in her ear.

"Then what are you doing?"

"I'm breaking a serious rule, sunshine."

"Wh-why?"

"Because I need to show you," he murmured, stroking his thumb across her breast yet again, making her shudder within his grasp. "I need to make you see how bad you need it."

At the moment, she didn't think she'd ever needed anything more in her life. But she wasn't about to admit that. Instead, she insisted, "This means nothing. This is . . . seduction. You're a sex expert—you know how to seduce girls."

"This means everything," he replied. "Because you're not telling me no. And I'm not even sure you like me. But you can't stop because it feels so good. Because you need it so bad. You need me to touch you." With that, he moved his hand full onto her breast, massaging the soft fullness, leaving her helpless, unable to summon more words. Her breath grew thready and her only response was to melt a little deeper into his arms.

Yes, not just one arm now, but both—he wrapped around her from behind and she stayed agonizingly aware of his erection at her rear, pressing deeper now, even as his other hand slid, slow and seductive, downward over her stomach.

"You need me to stroke your hot little pussy, Jenna," he breathed fervently.

And again, she shuddered at the promise as her legs grew weak and her cheeks flushed with heat, shock.

She held completely still as his fingers sank lower, lower, finally easing between her legs over the cotton skirt of her dress. She sucked in her breath as that part of her seemed to swell—she suffered the odd sensation of growing larger and larger in his hand.

Oh God, he was touching her there. Her eyes fell shut, her head dropped back. He caressed her fully—her breast, her crotch. She heard her own breath—she was panting for him now and hadn't the power to stop it.

Without ever taking his hand from between her thighs, he began to gather the fabric of her dress in his fist. He was going to touch her. *Really* touch her. Thank God. *Thank God.*

Finally, he'd bunched the full length of the skirt in his fist, allowing him to slip his hand underneath—and straight into the lacy edge of her panties. His fingers moved surely, smoothly, over her pubic hair and down into her very core, making her let out a ragged cry of pleasure.

And then she began to move—her moisture against the solid pressure of his fingers. Yes, *yes*.

"Ah, God, you're so wet. That's how bad you need it, honey." Another deep, sexy rasp came warm on her ear as a tropical breeze lifted her hair from her shoulders and somehow made her feel even wetter.

And part of her wanted to deny what he'd said, about needing it, but she couldn't think of an argument that made any sense. All she could think of was sensation. And moving against his big fingers as they stroked, stroked, ever so capably through her feminine folds.

His smooth voice was like another form of touching her. "That's right, honey, move against my fingers. Fuck them," he whispered more gently than she'd ever heard that word uttered before.

Jenna had never felt this way in her life: blinded by lust. She held on to the railing in front of her with both hands, bracing herself, moving more vigorously against him. Against his fingers in her wetness, against the incredibly hard column that slid up and down through the center of her rear.

She would come soon—she knew it. She bit her lip and thrust herself at his touch with sheer abandon. She kept her eyes clenched tight—she wasn't sure why but didn't examine it; maybe she'd always done that when approaching orgasm. And she was pretty sure she'd have climaxed already if she hadn't been fighting this so hard, but she was unable to fight any longer. Oh God, she *was* wet for him, dripping wet, and for a brief, startling moment she allowed herself to revel in that, in how wet he'd made her and the knowledge that she was getting his hand *just* as wet.

"That's so good, baby," he purred in her ear now, "so damn good. But you need more, sunshine, and you know it. You need my hard cock in your tight little pussy."

And—dear Lord—she did. The dirty promise vibrated through that very part of her, making it ache—for more than just his skilled touch, for . . . fullness, something thick and sturdy inside. And she knew she should end this—because sex was a big step beyond touching—but she felt almost paralyzed, stuck between two extremes, both nagging at her. Her instinct was to say *stop*, but if she did, he would, and that wasn't what she really wanted.

Now both his hands were up under her dress, pulling her panties down to midthigh. And then his touch was gone and she knew he was undoing his pants. Her paralysis grew worse—stark, raging lust warred with something that ran nearly as deep: her common sense, her lifelong morals, the sense that having sex with a stranger was insanely wrong.

His hands closed warmly on her exposed bottom now, and—dear God—his erection pressed into the valley there, his hard, hard flesh nestling where she was soft. She bit her lip and gripped the rail tighter, nearly torn in half with conflicting emotions.

"Tell me you need it, baby," he purred, low and demanding. "Tell me you need my big cock."

Unthinkable. She didn't know how to talk that way. And she couldn't admit to needing it—she just couldn't. "I can't," she whimpered, hating how weak she sounded.

Now his fingers dug slightly into her hips, and his rigid length began to . . . move up and down again, sliding, as if sawing into her defenses. "Then tell me you want it," he whispered more softly, seductively. "Tell me you want this, sunshine."

She let out a breath. Faced the cold, hard truth. "I can't do that, either."

Behind her, he tensed slightly—she heard him breathe in deeply. God, she was frustrating him. But she couldn't help it. This was entirely new territory and she wasn't even sure how she'd gotten here.

He leaned back in, slow, warm, and at the same time slid one hand back around to the crux of her thighs, letting the tip of his middle finger come to rest on the spot where she felt most swollen and needy. "What *do* you want, Jenna?" Despite what she'd feared, his voice remained entirely gentle, understanding. He was really asking her, asking her what she wanted.

It forced from her . . . a shocking, unshrouded truth. "I want . . . not to decide. Because no matter what I say, yes or no, I won't be happy. I want . . . the decision taken away from me." Her eyes bolted open then to peer out on the dark, empty beach in the distance, across the dunes, to the stars now dotting the night sky, and the world felt surreal. She wasn't sure what she'd just admitted, but it felt . . . like a confession of epic proportions. It left her more drained than anything else that had happened here—her limbs felt weak; her *soul* felt weak.

But Brent still held her up. His hands eased around her in a warm embrace from behind, settling at her waist. He leaned over and gently bit her shoulder—barely letting his teeth press into her flesh—and the unexpected affection jolted through her, straight to where he'd been touching her, forcing a sigh from her throat. "All right then, Little Miss Sunshine," Brent murmured against her neck, "I'm going to give you what you want." Then he leaned closer and spoke even lower. "What you *really* want."

Her lips trembled as she found the quiet strength to turn her head toward his, bringing them face-to-face, their eyes, mouths, only a few inches apart. "Which is?"

"Just like you said. You don't get to decide. I do. And I'm going to fuck you *so deep*," he promised, his teeth clenching lightly, "*so good*, that it's gonna be the best you've ever had. Because that's what you want—*and* what you need, baby. To be fucked."

Their eyes still locked, Jenna parted her lips to speak, having no idea what she intended to say. But Brent stopped her anyway, with a short shake of his head. "No words, Jenna. No more decisions or choices. You just do what I say now. You just be a good girl and turn around and hold on tight to that rail."

Jenna drew in her breath and slowly did what he instructed—looked straight ahead and gripped the railing. And felt guilt and worry slip away, like a silk gown falling from her body. It was a game of words, but that didn't matter—somehow, never telling him she wanted it made it less heinous. Forcing him to make the decision washed away the conflict inside her.

His hands locked on to her hips less gently now and her body tensed with strange pleasure as she waited. He pulled her closer then, making her re-situate slightly on her heels, her back arching. And then—God—his fingers were there, behind her, moving between her legs, parting her, and at least two of them pushed up inside her, making her cry out. Yes, *yes*! At last—something there, inside her. She bit her lip, her breathing ragged. *More, please.* She wanted to beg—but she couldn't. She didn't *want* to want it. She just wanted him to take it.

His fingers thrust inside her and she heard her own wetness and wondered briefly what she looked like bent over a handrail, her dress lifted to her waist—but she pushed that thought aside. In fact, she shut her eyes again since that made it all easier. To just feel. To just pretend she was dreaming or something.

And then Brent's fingers were gone and Jenna knew what would come next, so she bit her lip, bracing herself, and then there he was—so, so hard—positioning himself, and she instinctively arched deeper, lifting her bottom higher, and then—*oh*!—he was inside her, entering slow and, as promised, so very deep.

Thank God she held on to the rail or she'd be on her knees now. The sob that left her rose from her gut. God, he felt big—it had been so long since she'd done this. But he also felt *good*, delivering that incredible fullness she'd yearned for.

When he began to move in her, it was slow, thorough, his strokes stretching all through her—from head to toe. Big, so big. He filled her. And she gradually began to push back against him, meeting his long, sensual thrusts, taking him deeper still.

"Open your eyes, Jenna," he purred over her. She'd turned her head to the side at some point, so he knew they were closed. "Feel this. Experience this. All of it."

Biting her lip, she did as he said. She took in the beach again—a glimpse of white foam as waves broke over the shore in the moonlight. He was right. She felt it more this way. And it made it . . . dirtier. To be forced to remember she stood in a gazebo, fully dressed, being . . . *fucked* by him, a total stranger. She never used that word, but *he* used it a lot, and as he drove up into her wetness, again, again, she knew that's what this was—fucking.

She pushed against him, harder, harder. She heard her own labored breathing.

And then Brent's hand snaked around from her hip to the front, and when he sank his fingers there, she moaned. *Yes, yes, God, please.* More words she couldn't bring herself to utter. With some other lover in some other place and time, maybe—but not with this stranger, this man who insisted he knew what she needed. It was impossible.

So instead she simply moved with his touches and heard her heady moans waft up into the warm night air. Like before, each hot grind gave her pleasure from the front *and* the back, only much more intense now. His other hand rose to cup one breast through her dress, finger and thumb toying hotly with her nipple and making her undulate more wildly against him.

His heated breath behind her fueled her, exciting her more. Soon he released her breast—only to thrust his hand inside her dress and warmly recapture it, flesh to flesh. She cried out at the new connection, and when he caught her sensitive nipple between two fingers, squeezing it as he began to massage—oh God. She bit her lip and thrust her wetness more insistently against his hand. And he whispered, "That's right, baby, that's so good." And he began to drive his erection into her harder, harder, and she looked out on the beach and—oh my—spotted a couple, naked, doing exactly what *they* were: fucking.

She took in everything Brent delivered as she focused, stunned and incredibly aroused, on the couple in the sand. The man lay on his back and the woman rode him wildly, her arms over her head like some sort of erotic cowgirl. They were far away, small from where she stood, but she could still make out the movements clearly, could still see the woman's large breasts swaying in the moonlight. And she could sense the woman's pleasure, stark and *guiltless* pleasure—and that was when the orgasm exploded through her body like an earthquake, the crux of her thighs the epicenter.

She heard her cries—couldn't begin to suppress them; she clutched the rail as tight as she could, feeling the rolling waves of pleasure echo through her from head to toe, a release so powerful she could barely withstand it. The world shifted; everything inside her spun and tilted crazily.

When it was over, every part of her body tingled, all the way out to the tips of her fingers and toes—and somehow she and Brent were on their knees now, both of them. She'd sunk there, unable to keep standing, and he'd descended with her—still inside her.

His arms circled her waist as she collapsed against him, trying to come back to herself, and he was whispering in her ear, "Aw, *baby*, that was *so* good. You did so fucking good, honey."

And somehow, it helped. A moment when she might have suffered in anguish over what she'd just done, was *still* doing, instead became one where she felt . . . comforted, cared for, praised. So she rested against him, trying to regain her strength—but she stayed aware, too, that he remained inside her. And when that grew to be the sensation she felt more than her recovery from orgasm, she found herself biting her lip in raw pleasure.

"We're gonna shift now," Brent said, his breath warming her neck, "and you're gonna move to your hands and knees."

Oh. My. She'd never . . . But then, she'd never done it standing up before, either. And . . . and . . . she'd given him the power, told him she didn't want to make any decisions. So . . . she moved with him, slowly, leaning forward until her palms pressed into the wooden plank floor of the gazebo, and she arched her bottom just like before and felt a little obscene, but when he began to thrust into her again with those slow, deep, thorough strokes, it took everything else away.

The position was hard to maintain in her exhaustion, but each drive traveled all the way through her, out through her limbs. And when he began to move harder, faster, grunting his pleasure with each plunge, even her face began to tingle hotly and she once again couldn't hold in her cries of pure lusty joy. Oh God, he felt so good, so big, thrusting, thrusting, so deep, so hard. She sobbed. She moaned. She felt utterly taken, possessed, just like she'd wanted—although she still didn't understand why on earth that was a good thing.

And just when she feared her arms would give out and she'd collapse to the wood beneath her, he muttered, "Fuck yeah, baby, I'm gonna come. I'm gonna come so fucking hard in your sweet pussy. Here I go." And then his low, masculine groans filled the night—and seemed to fill her *soul*, too. To know she'd made this insanely sexy, powerful man climax so fiercely. The sex expert. The sexologist. It was a unique delight that had her smiling secretly in the darkness, for just a brief moment, before their bodies slowly crumpled to the gazebo's floor.

They lay silent for a few minutes, during which Jenna tried not to feel anything inside. Just the physical part. Because—for whatever reason—she *had* needed sex tonight. So she tried to enjoy the afterglow. And she tried really hard to forget the weirdness of where she was and whom she'd just had really amazing sex with.

Until Brent—lying on his back next to her, peering up toward the gazebo's rafters—said, "Sorry, sunshine, but looks like I win."

She sucked in her breath and turned her head toward him. "Win what?"

Next to her, he sat up, then reached for her hands to draw her upright, too. "I proved my point," he said, back to being the smooth, matter-of-fact "sex doctor." "You agreed that if I did, you'd let me take you the rest of the way, through the fantasies you need."

Ugh, there was that icky word "need" again. "This proved nothing except that apparently I *can* have sex with a stranger."

He grinned, lowering his chin indulgently. "However you want to look at it. But we both know you want this now. We both know you'd take enormous pleasure from it."

Her cheeks filled with heat. *We do? We know that?* She had no idea how he'd made that leap—since one occurrence of sex with him, however hot and scintillating, did not equate to going through the whole series of fantasies, with *more* strangers.

"What—what would it entail?" She heard the words leave her mouth, but she couldn't believe she'd actually asked. As if she were considering this. Because that was insane.

"I'm sure you've read the literature," Brent replied. "As your guide, I prepare a series of scenarios designed especially for you and your individual needs and desires. By the time you've completed them, your sexual inhibitions will be a thing of the past and you'll be a happier, healthier person."

Sexual inhibitions. Did she really have them? *Could* he know what he was talking about? And yet . . . she needed to rephrase her question. Because she wasn't asking about what he thought she needed as much as she was asking about . . . the man she'd just had sex with. Although she tried to sound casual about it. "No, I meant the sex itself. The fantasies. How do they work? Would . . . you be there?"

Their eyes met in the dim candlelight from the table above. His filled with reservation. "I'm not *supposed* to be."

Jenna pulled in her breath, nodding lightly, not quite able to meet his gaze anymore. It had been crazy to even ask. What difference did it make if he was there? She supposed some small part of her had begun to think: *Maybe if I can do* this *with him, I could do* that *with him.* But since when did she want *this*—sex with a stranger—anyway?

Placing one bent finger beneath her chin, he forced her gaze to his. "Would it make you more comfortable if I were involved?"

Jenna blinked. Tried to wade through her tangled feelings. "The total truth?"

"Absolutely. I'm all about the truth, sunshine."

She drew in her breath—and fought to be honest with him. "The truth is that I can't believe I did this with you and I can't believe I'm sitting here with my panties still around my knees—because this is not the kind of thing I do, which I'm sure you understand by now."

"And that's exactly why you needed to do it."

Need again. *Shut up about that already.* "The very notion of . . . of doing what you're suggesting, going through these fantasies you want to create for me, is . . . mind-boggling. I can't believe I'm considering it for even a second. But I suppose I was thinking that since I've now been . . . like *this*, with you, that maybe, just maybe, it would make future such . . . *experiences* easier for me . . . if you were there."

Brent sighed. "It's a pretty big fucking rule, Jenna. It's there for a reason."

She didn't ask the reason, just stated the obvious. "You just *broke* a big rule, which I presume was there for a reason."

"True," he said.

And Jenna knew she should accept that, because it was her Get Out of Jail Free card—a damn good reason to say, *Okay then, sorry, but I can't do this*. That was what she'd planned on in the first place. And one round of sex with him didn't change that. Or it shouldn't anyway. So it was simply beyond her understanding when she instead said, "Look, I've been honest with you, far more honest than I intended to be, so here's more honesty. I truly didn't come here for the sex, so I'm not mentally prepared for this—in fact, I'm absolutely scared to death of it. So I think the only way I could possibly do it would be if . . . if you *were* there."

He looked at her in the shadows, his expression quiet, even kind. "If you're scared to death, why are you considering it?"

"More truth? I don't know," she whispered. "I really don't."

He pursed his lips, looked troubled, and then . . . conceded. "All right, sunshine. If you'll agree to this if I'm involved, then I *will* be."

Oh God. She wasn't sure she'd expected that. It had been like the sex itself—she hadn't been able to bring herself to say no, but she hadn't been sure she wanted the answer to be yes, either.

Yet Brent looked almost . . . proud of her. And for some reason, she liked that. It was much better than having him insist she was a needy woman in denial.

"How does it, um . . . start?" she asked.

"You'll receive instructions prior to each fantasy about time, place, and what to wear. You'll be given a safeword, something you say only if and when you want out, if you want the fantasy to end—if it's truly not bringing you pleasure. But I'll be working very hard to make sure it *all* brings you pleasure," he said with his usual seductive smile. "Still, sunshine, I should warn you—sometimes you might have to be patient for a little while and trust me on that. Don't say the word out of fear—only say it if something has begun to happen that's bringing you true *dis*pleasure. And I promise, the pleasure will *always* come. *Always*."

Oh Lord. What had she put into motion here? She tried to catch her breath and be brave. "All right."

"There are a few other things we need to go over, too," he said. "First, about the other people you'll meet here. Sometimes we build fantasies for our guests that can . . . overlap. That means you might meet someone during a fantasy who is actually in his or her own fantasy at the same time, even though the goal of that fantasy might be entirely different than the goal of yours. And, conversely, you'll interact with other participants who are employees of the Hotel Erotique. We request that you not ask anyone whether they're a guest or an employee—simply because it decreases the sense of fantasy."

"Um, may I ask . . . what if you put someone in my fantasy who I'm, uh, not attracted to?"

He grinned. "No need to worry, sunshine. Do you remember when you went through a long online page of photos clicking next to those you found attractive?"

She nodded. She'd known it was telling them something about her preferences, but she hadn't thought any further ahead.

"Many of the people you saw are our actual employees. We use your response to others to fill in the gap—for instance, we would never put another guest in your fantasy if they didn't fit the parameters we gathered for whom you're physically drawn to."

Dear God—this was strange. She knew it made sense to populate her fantasies with people she found attractive, but she'd never thought about the actual logistics of how it would work, since she hadn't been taking this part seriously.

"And we also ask that you remember—most of our fantasies are designed to be just that. You'll be traveling to other places in your fantasies, maybe other times. You and I and everyone else involved will all be playing roles, and even if that feels odd at first, just do your best and I promise it'll be okay. We won't be just Brent and Jenna anymore—but if you need me, or if you need to invoke the safeword, just find me with your eyes and I'll be there. Otherwise, the idea is to immerse yourself in the setting and situation as much as possible.

"And finally," he continued, "I need to address sexual safety."

Oh, shit. He hadn't worn a condom! Combining the intensity of the moment with the fact that she was out of practice, it had totally slipped her mind. Then again, how was a girl supposed to remember a condom in a situation as freaky as *this*?

But Brent seemed cool as a cucumber. "Every employee who takes part in our fantasies is tested monthly and the documentation is in our offices, should you wish to see it. We have yours on file, too."

As luck had it, she'd recently been tested as part of a screening process at a community college where she'd applied to teach a history course to earn extra money between book advances—and she'd even gone so far as forwarding the results via e-mail when Mariel had requested them, all to keep up the appearance that she was planning to take the whole prize. And now she was. Unbelievable.

Jenna had also reported to Mariel that she was on birth control—even if most of the time the only purpose it served was keeping her periods regular. So he surely had that information, as well.

Yet still, despite all that, she swallowed uncomfortably. "How do I know, um, *you're* safe?"

To her surprise, he looked amused. "Mine's on file, too, if you want to see it."

She blinked. "Why do you need one? If you don't normally participate in guests' fantasies."

"I don't participate in the fantasies of the guests to whom I'm a guide. That doesn't mean I don't take part in those of *other* guests."

"Oh." Hmm. He had sex here, with strangers, on a regular basis.

It didn't change anything—she'd known it all along really, but somehow maybe she'd hoped he'd outgrown that part of the job upon becoming a guide. Now pictures filled her head: *him*, in the center of orgies, naked, thrusting, the way he'd just thrust into *her*. And it reminded her that she'd just agreed to do whatever he chose for her. With him. With other people. And for all she knew, *she* might end up in the center of an orgy! Oh God, had she lost her mind?

Just then, as sanity was about to return, Brent reached out to touch her, his fingertips curving over her cheek. "Thank you for trusting me enough to do this, sunshine."

And that brief glimpse of sanity forced her to ask, "Why . . . *do* I trust you? I just met you. And as you said, I'm not even sure I *like* you." Even if her sarcastic tone hinted otherwise.

In reply, he leaned close and whispered in her ear. "Maybe it's because I just gave you the best orgasm of your life." Then he pushed smoothly to his feet, said, "Goodnight, sunshine," and walked away, leaving Jenna to wonder just what the hell she'd gotten herself into and why.

Chapter 3

When a bright blast of morning sun woke Jenna, her first response was to roll over and pull a pillow over her head—which happened to be pounding. But then she realized she wasn't at home. And she remembered where she was. And that she'd had a lot to drink throughout the day and evening yesterday. And that she'd . . . oh boy. Oh God.

She'd had sex with a big, hot, sexy hunk of a man she'd never met before last night.

She'd had the best orgasm of her life, as he'd accurately pointed out.

And she'd agreed to . . . *yikes*!

Jenna bolted upright in bed and looked around the room. Was she remembering all this correctly?

She found herself hoping desperately that it had all somehow been a dream. A really big, long, drawn-out, amazingly detailed dream. Maybe she'd just returned to her room after an awkward dinner with her decidedly very *male* guide and fallen asleep in a rum-punch-and-wine stupor, inventing the whole thing in her subconscious mind.

Of course, the dress tossed unceremoniously on the floor in a heap near the bed wasn't a good sign—she was normally neater than that. And . . . ugh, she was a little sore. *There*. Which meant she hadn't just fabricated wild sex with Brent Powers. Uh-oh.

And this also meant she'd agreed to something absolutely . . . *insane and unthinkable* in the afterglow of what had clearly been mind-altering sex.

Well, too bad. She'd just have to call Mr. Powers and tell him she'd come to her senses, that she'd been drunk last night, and that the deal was off, so if he was busy mapping out sexual adventures for her, he could stop, or use them for some *other* guest. One who'd actually come here for sex.

Just then, a soft knock echoed through the door, and before Jenna could even react, a male voice said, "I'm leaving your breakfast outside, Ms. Banks."

Breakfast? Was room service every morning part of the deal? She didn't recall reading that anywhere. Still, giving the server time to walk back down the hall, she pushed back the covers, tried to move slowly to keep her head from hurting any worse, and eased out of bed. Quietly opening the door in just a cami and panties, she peeked outside to make sure she was alone, then pulled a bamboo breakfast cart inside.

Atop it, a covered plate sat next to a vase of fresh-cut tropical flowers with a crisp white envelope tucked amid the blooms. First, she lifted the lid to find pancakes—which, again, she didn't remember placing an order for, but they were exactly what she was in the mood to eat. Recovering the plate to keep it warm, she turned her attention to the envelope, plucking it up from the flowers. Her first name was written on the outside—and ripping into it, she discovered a handwritten letter on Hotel Erotique stationery.

Good morning, Jenna.

I thought after last night you might enjoy a quiet breakfast in your room. I know what took place between us was a big step for you, so I wanted to tell you again how proud of you I am.

And if you've woken up this morning regretting anything that happened or sorry you agreed to my plans for your stay, remember what you told me last night. You wanted the decision taken out of your hands. Consider this my way of taking it. Last night you committed to experiencing the sex I think will be the most pleasurable and beneficial to you, so you're going to experience it. You may recall, too, that I spoke of what's to come as being a leap of faith for you. Rest assured that I fully intend to see you take that leap, even if I have to push you.

The events of the next two weeks will transform you, Jenna, and as your guide, I'm now invested in ensuring that happens. So there's no going back—only forward. Take that leap of faith and keep making me proud.

Feel free to use the morning as you wish—at the pool or beach, or at the spa—but return to your room by 2 p.m. when more instructions will await you.

Brent

Huh. Jenna just stared at the piece of paper, the breakfast practically forgotten.

He was proud of her. He'd said that last night, too, and she'd liked it. She still did—even without quite understanding why. Maybe she liked the idea of being a bolder sort of woman, more like Shannon. Although she didn't think even Shannon would ever have done anything like what Brent Powers was suggesting.

Or was that *demanding*?

She knew he couldn't make her, of course. Yet he'd very firmly taken the lead she'd given him in that weak moment when she'd admitted she wanted the decision removed from her hands. Meaning—*I want to have sex with you, but I can't* bear *to want it or to* admit *I want it, so I want you to take over and make it happen*—which he'd definitely read loud and clear. What a hell of a thing to confess.

And so he thought that confession stretched into today, too, and the rest of the trip, did he? The truth was, something about the way he took charge—both last night and now—turned her on a little. She'd never liked bossy or controlling men, but . . . somehow this appealed.

Because it does exactly what you need it to? Because it takes the accountability away from you? At least in a technical sense. And last night that seemed to have been good enough.

But today . . . well, to begin with, she wasn't intoxicated.

And her body wasn't humming with lust.

Well, not much anyway. Now that she was forced to think back on last night, and on Brent Powers and everything so hot and seductive about him, it was making her a little warm in the panties again. "Sheesh," she scolded herself, "knock it off already."

Here's what you're going to do. You're going to sit down and enjoy these pancakes. Then you're going to put on your bikini, head down to the beach, and find a relaxing spot to soak up some sun and clear your head. After which you'll send Brent a little note just like the one he sent you, thanking him for last night but telling him you've decided to stick to your original plan—the beach, the pool, the spa. No more sex with strangers, Brent or otherwise.

Brent walked along the shoreline in the morning sun, berating himself. He ran the place—he should know the damn rules. And the biggest? Never fuck your own guest. *Never.* Guides just couldn't. It threatened to fracture the whole system.

And in all his years, he'd never broken that rule. Until now.

Of course, it helped that until now, he'd never been guide to a female guest. One he was attracted to at that. And one whose need he'd felt in an almost tangible way. Somehow, over the course of dinner, he'd begun to feel responsible for fixing everything that was less than perfect inside her when it came to her sexual self.

And he was pretty sure her sexual issues ran deeper than even her questionnaires implied. He strongly suspected she'd absorbed every bit of negative sexual reinforcement more profoundly than some people might, just because that's the kind of person she was; she felt things intensely.

Not that seducing her had been part of his grand plan. Turned out it worked well enough in convincing her to go through with the fantasies, but nothing had pulled him up out of his chair and over to that railing other than pure desire. The entire time he'd sat across from her, he'd been admiring the way her dress hugged her breasts, the lush inner curves on display, her nipples jutting provocatively against the fabric. He'd found her blue eyes bright, pretty, expressive—and her lips had looked downright kissable. Not that he'd actually gotten around to that, kissing her—he'd been too busy touching her, persuading her, fucking her. He got a little hard again now, just remembering.

And now he'd agreed to take part in her fantasies. Shit.

Unfortunately, he really cared about giving the girl what she needed. And since she'd come here under false pretenses, not even knowing she needed anything . . . well, that still complicated things immensely. That was why, despite all these rules he was breaking and should probably *quit* breaking, he'd sent her that little breakfast greeting. Checking his watch, he suspected she'd gotten it a few minutes ago.

How was she reacting? Was he winning her over, convincing her not to go back on the agreement? Or was she packing her bags and heading toward the airstrip at this very moment?

And why the hell did he care so damn much?

God knew he'd fucked a lot of women here, taken part in a lot of fantasies. It was almost all he knew. His whole adult life had been spent helping people find sexual fulfillment, and through that, finding his own—along with professional fulfillment as well.

He'd never set out to be a sex expert, as Jenna had called him last night. No, he'd set out to be a garden-variety psychologist. But somewhere during his last year of undergrad, he'd realized his goals weren't focused enough. He'd been unsure whom he even wanted to help—mainly just fascinated by learning about the human mind, behavior, and how it all worked together.

And then, as graduation approached, he'd lost what little focus he'd had to begin with. That's when another psych major, his buddy Chris, had told him he knew where they could both get what he'd called "a dream job." Brent had soon become a facilitator at the Hotel Erotique, which was what they called the employees who weren't qualified to be guides but took part in the fantasies. Some facilitators actually had acting aspirations and enjoyed that facet of it, but *all* were required to have some sort of background or education in psychology and were carefully screened to ensure they possessed healthy, mature attitudes about sex. At the time, it had been a good distraction from some recent pain—and he'd discovered that finding people who shared viewpoints on sex similar to his had felt kind of like . . . coming home in a weird way.

As it turned out, Chris had worked here for only six months before meeting a girl on a weekend trip to Miami whom he'd soon married, and now he was a respected psychiatrist and happy father of three. Brent, on the other hand, had never left.

Sure, he'd gone home to his family in Pittsburgh on holidays, but that had lasted just a few years. Now he only sent gifts and actually spent Thanksgiving and Christmas here with friends who, again, had come to feel more like family to him over time.

A weird lifestyle? Sure, he supposed it probably seemed that way. But he knew his work here truly helped people lead more fulfilling lives, and he took pride in it—enough that after three years as a facilitator he'd taken an extended leave of absence to get his PhD, allowing him to return as a guide. And he'd become so enmeshed in the resort that when the older couple who'd originally opened the place—Charlie and Madge—were ready to retire, they'd kept twenty-five percent of the business for themselves, selling other equal shares to Brent and two of the other longtime guides, Mariel and Dave.

So what did Jenna Banks think of him—a guy who chose this as a way of life?

And . . . hell, why did he give a crap? He'd met literally thousands of women here and seldom thought about their views of him. He could only attribute this to the oddity of having to perform the more personal guide duties to a female guest.

The peculiar part was—designing a plan for her should have been harder than usual, but it was easier. Guys were more difficult to analyze, because they often had a hard time being open, even on a questionnaire. With his usual guests—who could be cocky jock types, forty-year-old virgins, newly divorced men, guys having midlife crises, you name it—it was always a challenge digging into their psyches and figuring out what was missing in their sex lives, why it was missing, how it affected them beyond sex, and many other questions. With Jenna, she'd kindly put it all out there on the forms she'd completed, making it startlingly clear-cut—and then she'd simplified matters further by showing him last night that she was in denial about it all.

And while it had been tricky to get her to agree to the fantasies while being in denial, now that she had, the rest seemed . . . incredibly simple. So simple that as he walked along the water's edge, hands in the pockets of his khaki shorts, he devised her fantasies, one after the other, all in about twenty minutes. There'd be more details to work out as they went along, and as he saw how she responded to each—but his job here was plain: Take her from being a woman who desired sex but inside feared it was dirty and wrong . . . to being a woman fully in touch with her sexual self, fully at ease expressing her sexuality; a woman no one would ever call Little Mary Sunshine between the sheets.

"Get ready, Jenna," he whispered to himself as the surf rushed up over his feet, "because the first thing we need to teach you is how to follow my instructions." She'd already let him know last night that putting him in a position of control worked for her—so that was a central tool he'd use to get her through this process. Once she grew accustomed to obeying his commands, half the battle would be over—she'd soon be rising above her past and accepting her true sexual nature.

Jenna had found a quiet, secluded spot on the beach not far from her building where a few umbrellas stood lodged in the sand—padded lounge chairs dotted the area as well. She'd taken a book, a Civil War memoir that would normally hold her interest, but she found it hard to concentrate. God, she wished she could call Shannon and tell her all that had happened—but Shannon worked in a busy office where she couldn't take personal calls, even one about the most freaky occurrence of her best friend's life.

So she stretched out on the beach chair and struggled to stop replaying the unbelievable memories of last night over and over in her mind. She enjoyed the sun and sea air and peaceful views and tried to quit stressing over the unexpected turn her trip had so quickly taken. She attempted to focus on the pleasant sensation that her skin was beginning to tan beneath her coconut-scented sunscreen. But all she really kept thinking was, *I still can't believe I had sex with that guy last night. Really* hot *sex.*

When a waiter who introduced himself as Ryan arrived out of nowhere, descending the dunes behind her to ask if she wanted a drink, she nearly fainted. Since this expanse of beach lay nowhere near the pools, restaurants, or main public buildings, she'd thought she'd found an isolated area to be alone—and that had been the idea, to get away from the Hotel Erotique for a while.

"How did you even know I was here?" she asked, dumbfounded.

The waiter, a good-looking, muscular guy in his early twenties who had surely been a jock in high school, just smiled. "Any place you find an umbrella on the beach is an area where we provide service. As a guest here, your pleasure is our business."

She drew in her breath, slightly flustered. "Oh. Well then, how about one of your, um, erotic rum punches?"

"Coming up," he said with a wink, then walked away.

And for the first time, Jenna wondered—did people who worked here in other capacities, such as waiters, ever take part in the fantasies? Like this guy? Or Josh, her waiter from yesterday? What about Gabe? She shivered a little, despite the heat of the Caribbean sun, just curious, just beginning to cautiously imagine what a Hotel Erotique fantasy might be like.

Of course, maybe a waiter here was only a waiter, and a . . . sexual partner was a sexual partner. But now, suddenly, she remembered the couple she'd seen on the beach last night—while Brent was inside her, touching her, making her come. Had the couple been living out a fantasy—of one, or the other, or both of them? Or were they just . . . fucking, as Brent would have called it, on their own, no fantasy attached?

And . . . what sorts of ways would Brent concoct to fix whatever problems he thought she had? What kinds of fantasies was he perhaps creating for her this very moment? To her distress, she got a little wet just thinking about *him* planning sex for *her*.

Of course, it still irked her that he thought there was something *wrong* with her. Just because she wasn't wild or kinky, he thought she'd been damaged by her parents' prudish attitudes and those other negative incidents in her youth. But what was wrong with not being wild and kinky? She supposed in *his* world wild and kinky were normal, but in hers, normal was . . . in the eye of the beholder. And she thought she was normal.

Even if she tended to close her eyes through most of sex.

Even if she sometimes had a hard time admitting she *wanted* sex, even to a guy she wanted it *with*.

She was just . . . well, maybe a little more shy about sex than she'd been willing to confess to Shannon and Kevin—or even to herself, up to now.

She bit her lip, remembering an instance last night when Brent had been behind her, touching her, and she'd had the urge to reach back and touch him, too—his thigh, or his butt. But as soon as she'd thought about it, she couldn't do it. Even though she'd been responding to his advances, she'd been unable to . . . advance things any further herself. She'd been unable to be bold—even when that simply meant reciprocating a little.

God, what if there *was* something wrong with her?

Well, even if there was, Brent Powers couldn't fix it with a bunch of kinky sex in two short weeks.

So no matter how she looked at it, the smart thing was to write that note as planned. And she was going to do it early—she would return to the room by one, write and send the letter, then exit again quickly so that she'd be gone when his "further instructions" arrived. Even if she still remained curious about what exactly those instructions would be.

And then she gasped. Oh dear—what if they were instructions she might actually *like*? Maybe he'd plan some sort of softer, gentler sex—something romantic or beachy perhaps. Or even a little *wilder* and beachy, like the naked couple last night. Either way, what if it turned out to be a fantasy she might honestly concoct on her own, as he'd said was often the case?

She couldn't deny having enjoyed last night—although *enjoyed* was a mild way to put it. She'd never had sex like that before, sex so utterly steamy and mind-numbing. And what she'd admitted afterward was true—the stark intimacy had made her comfortable with him. And he was undeniably a sex god in the flesh—the most gorgeous man to ever look her way. So . . . maybe the whole reason she'd begun entertaining the notion of going through with the fantasies was simply . . . because she wanted to be with him again. And that had seemed like the only way.

Well, if that was the case, all the more reason to write that note and put an end to this once and for all. She couldn't have sex with God knew how many people just because she might have gotten a little attached to Brent Powers last night. The very idea sounded insanely . . . destructive. And this just proved her point anyway—she wasn't cut out for casual sex; she couldn't *take* it casually.

So even if she might risk losing out on some perfect beach fantasy with her perfect, hunky fantasy guy—too bad. No more sex for her at the Hotel Erotique.

She'd just reopened her book, finally ready to resume being normal Jenna, when her waiter returned, colorful umbrella drink in hand.

"Here you go," he said with a grin.

Before she could take it from him, a large drop of moisture dripped from the glass to plop wetly on the exposed ridge of her breast, making her flinch from the cold.

"Oops, sorry."

"No biggie," she assured Ryan, taking the drink from him. "I was kind of hot anyway."

"You can say that again," he replied with another sexy wink. "Anything else you need? Just say the word and I'm your guy."

She swallowed. At the compliment and that word again—*need*. It was everywhere lately, it seemed. *Was* there anything else she needed?

A strange, reckless part of her was almost tempted to ask him if he ever took part in guests' fantasies—but then she came back to her senses, despite the wetness now also surging between her thighs. "I'm good for now, thanks," she finally replied.

And as he walked away, she promised herself she'd *stay* good. She really *didn't* need anything here, no matter what Brent Powers said.

After a light lunch on the beach—courtesy of cute jock waiter Ryan—Jenna made her way back to her lavish room ahead of her self-imposed one o'clock deadline. She spent the walk back composing her note to Brent in her head and keeping an eye out for any random sexual activity she might spot from the path along the way. She saw nothing, but as usual, her chest still tightened and something in her sizzled when she wondered what sorts of naughty activities might be taking place all around her.

She dug her room key from her straw beach bag, thinking: *All right, get in the room, find some paper, write the letter, then head back to the beach—dropping the note at the front desk on the way, with strict instructions that it must be delivered to Brent Powers immediately.*

Then she pushed through the door and—oh, hell. Damn it. He'd already been here. Or *someone* had anyway—and not just the maid. A pink envelope sat atop the freshly made bed, and next to it rested a small pink shopping bag with pink tissue paper billowing up from inside.

Of course, she could just ignore that and write her letter as planned.

But curiosity quickly got the best of her. If the letter and bag contained information about the first fantasy he'd designed for her, how could she not at least look? Because how often did she end up at a sex resort, of all places? Even if she wasn't into it, it still drew her attention in that morbid fashion, like a wreck on the highway: She expected to be horrified by what she saw, but still she had to peek. And *unlike* a wreck on the highway, this would actually serve a purpose, surely shoring up her decision not to ride the Hotel Erotique merry-go-round.

Sliding her finger under the pink envelope flap, she drew out a card of white vellum printed in formal black script, like a wedding invitation. Only this was a different sort of invitation altogether.

You Are Invited to a Fantasy

Where: Room 222 (map enclosed)
When: Today, 5:30 p.m.
You have always been an apt student,
but you've just enrolled in a tantalizing new subject.
Wear the lingerie provided.
Put anything you like over it to walk to the room.
More directions await you in the bathroom—follow them exactly.
Remember, obedience is key in the classroom.
(Your safeword is Marie Antoinette.)

Jenna would have smiled about him choosing the topic of one of her books as her safeword if she hadn't been so eager to reach into the bag and see exactly what kind of lingerie Brent had selected for her. And—oh my!—she couldn't have been more pleasantly surprised to find a sexy yet utterly classy white lace bra and thong set. It was exactly the sort of thing she would buy if planning a romantic evening that might lead to the bedroom.

So . . . wow. Did this change things? Her decision? Because if Brent had indeed designed some sort of simple, sexy, white-lace fantasy for her, then . . . hmm, that might be nice. She wouldn't have thought so yesterday, but given that she'd already had sex with him and that it had been freaking *amazing* . . . would it be so awful to indulge once more?

Sure, it meant risking a deeper attachment to a guy with whom she had nothing in common and certainly no hope for a future, but . . . maybe this would be good for her. Maybe the whole experience *would* help her get better at casual sex. Not the kind he surely had planned for *later* in her stay, but . . . maybe the kind Kevin and Shannon had been pushing her toward. In one sense, it still sounded unappealing, but in another . . . well, last night had proven, if nothing else, that casual sex wouldn't kill her. And in reality, it hadn't even left her suffering any real regrets.

Still holding the lacy bra in her hand, she checked the tag: 34C. Yep, right size. Just like the right wine and the right chicken.

And, of course, if she went through with the sex tonight, Brent would surely be pissed when she announced it was the last time after all, and he'd try to cajole her into more—but the decision would remain hers. She could do what she wanted here—take none of her prize, or part of it. And if she desired one more—and only one more—night of hot, knee-weakening passion with the sex doctor himself, then that's what she would have.

"Wow," she murmured, her cheeks flushing with heat. Because apparently she was doing this—entering into one of the fantasies. She'd never imagined she could be so bold, and despite lingering fears, she found herself peering down at the lace in her hands with a mischievous smile.

Now, to get ready for her white-lace evening. Dropping the bra on the bed, she stripped off her bikini on the way to the spacious bathroom. Stepping inside, she reached to turn on the water in the marble shower—then spotted some items on the wide countertop. Again, not things the maid had left—she'd been so enraptured by the lingerie and her decision that she'd completely forgotten more instructions waited here.

She was unsettled *enough* to see a feminine-looking can of shaving cream and two pink disposable razors, but she nearly fainted when she picked up the card propped next to them and read the words printed in more fancy black script:

Shave your pussy completely smooth.

Oh boy. Feeling light-headed, she pressed a palm to the sink top for balance and tried to catch her breath. She knew guys liked that. She knew Shannon did it for Kevin—although she got the area waxed instead, making Jenna cringe every time she thought about such pain. But she'd certainly never done it herself. No guy she'd ever dated had asked her to. And why *else* would a woman do that?

She saw several choices before her. She could just ignore this part. Or she could change her mind altogether and refuse the fantasy.

Or she could shave.

She bit her lip, staring down at the words on the card again.

Then she drew in a deep breath. What would be the harm? It was hair removal, not amputation. It would grow back. And if Brent was into the bare look, well . . . what did she care? She *wanted* to excite him again, didn't she?

And thus began the process, which, to her vast shock, succeeded in arousing her as she worked.

Then again, didn't *everything* arouse her here? From the waiters to the rum punch, from the co-pilot to her bikini—so what did it matter if revealing a little more of her own skin turned her on?

Although, as she removed more and more hair, she began to think maybe she understood why it aroused guys, too. Usually, it was almost as if the vagina were *hiding* behind the pubic hair. *This* put it completely on display—she could truly see it, everything about it. Although, she didn't shave *all* the hair off. She decided to leave an oval patch above the slit. She wasn't sure why—but while she could understand the merits of baring herself, leaving a *little* hair somehow just felt . . . safer, or maybe more normal.

A mere glance in the mirror after she wiped the remnants of shaving cream away made her more aware of the way she was built, of the split in the center and what it opened to. And when she ran her fingertips over the skin to either side—wow, she'd never felt anything softer. Yeah, no wonder guys liked it this way. Would Brent like *hers* this way? She shivered in anticipation, then oozed with moisture.

As she stepped into the shower, she felt . . . new. Or maybe just different. She was a woman who shaved her intimate area, a woman who was preparing to meet a lover for an evening of hot sex. The very act of running the soap over her freshly tanned skin—over her shoulders, breasts, stomach, and lower—made her feel sexy, ready. She could be like other women. She could be like Shannon. She could surprise Brent even more—and maybe show him she didn't need as much help with her sexuality as he thought.

Twenty minutes later, she stood before the mirror in her sexy new lingerie—part lace, part sheer white fabric. Her nipples, clearly visible, shone darkly through, and the panties left her denuded mound noticeable as well. The bra was cut low and built to shove her breasts upward, making them look high and round.

Usually, she thought she looked pretty in an average way. Right now, dressed for sex in a sophisticated bra and thong, with her long brown hair falling in soft waves around her shoulders, with her face tanned and her eyes and lips freshly made up—she thought she looked like a knockout, like a woman any man would be lucky to be with.

Last night, she'd thought *she* was lucky to be with a man as gorgeous as Brent. But tonight, she felt much more his equal.

Smiling to herself, she slipped into a pair of shorts and a baby blue tank, then stepped into her beaded flip-flops. And by the time she walked out the door, the map to room 222 clutched in her hand, she wasn't even nervous anymore. She couldn't wait to see what Brent had in store for her.

Chapter 4

The map led Jenna along a series of winding paths across the grounds that soon felt like a maze. But each path was marked with small signs that told her she was going the right way. As she walked, she felt herself becoming more and more isolated—she heard no voices or movements other than the occasional bird in the palm and banyan trees overhead. And with each step, the lace of her thong rubbed against her, heightening her arousal.

Finally, she emerged from a foliage-lined path to find herself face-to-face with a non-descript brick building that didn't seem to fit the surroundings. Consulting the map, she saw it labeled simply as SCHOOL—and her fantasy was to take place inside it.

Pulling open the heavy front door, she followed a dark hallway lined in old-fashioned green tile, passing numbered doorways, then made her way up a set of stairs to the second floor, finally reaching room 222.

Biting her lip, her stomach churning a bit, she twisted the doorknob and stepped inside—only to find herself in a tiny room, not larger than a walk-in closet. It contained a padded bench, a row of hooks on the wall above, and a large oak wardrobe. As well as another door.

A white card rested on the bench, so she snatched it up.

Change into the items in the chifforobe, leaving the lingerie on underneath.
After you've dressed, come inside, prepared for class.
Don't be afraid. Be ready.

Jenna sucked in her breath. So there were more props here. She began to get nervous again.

At the same time, though, the juncture of her thighs still tingled and she suffered the sense of having come too far to turn back, the sense that whatever pleasure he'd laid out for her, she owed it to herself to experience.

Still, when she opened the wardrobe, she gasped—at the sight of a small white blouse and short plaid skirt, à la naughty Catholic schoolgirl.

Okay. So she'd been wrong, as in ridiculously naïve. This wasn't a soft, romantic fantasy. This was . . . kinky. And she clearly should have paid more attention to the emerging school theme. What was *that* about?

Yet he'd told her there would be costumes involved and roles to play, so maybe she shouldn't be so surprised.

And it could be worse. He only wants you to be a sexy schoolgirl. And at least she'd *been* a schoolgirl before, even if not a sexy or Catholic one.

As she reached for the skirt, she started to wonder why she wasn't stopping this now, why she wasn't backing out and changing her mind, screaming, "Marie Antoinette!" through the door and running like mad in the other direction.

But she didn't allow herself to go there. Since something was telling her to put on the outfit.

Lust, she decided. It was lust. It was wanting to be with Brent Powers again. It was the way her feminine mound pulsed from all the anticipation, the way desire stretched all through her now, the same as last night at dinner. And maybe, just maybe, it was . . . realizing that she'd never again in her life have this unique opportunity, at a place where no one knew her or would judge her, and maybe she actually wanted to have the experience.

Of course, she knew what happened at the Hotel Erotique wouldn't really *stay* at the Hotel Erotique—it would come with her and be a part of her for the rest of her existence. So if she ended up with regrets . . . well, she'd had very few in life so far. So if that happened, she would simply push it aside and consider it an honest mistake.

Thus it was lust and curiosity and the invisible sense of arousal permeating everything here that had her zipping up the scandalously short skirt, which began well below her navel yet barely covered her butt, and tying the tight white, short-sleeved blouse—no buttons—under her breasts.

Then she spied the shoes on the floor of the chifforobe—white strappy platform heels like strippers wore. Oh my. She'd never even thought about putting on such a pair of shoes before, and she questioned whether she could walk in them, but . . . she'd decided to do this, right? So she sat down on the bench and slid her feet into the ultra-sexy heels, then stood to look in the long mirror inside the wardrobe's open door.

Whoa.

She blinked, studying herself from head to toe, trying to adjust to this new image of herself.

She looked downright sinful. Naughty indeed.

And . . . oh God, she *liked* it.

She'd just become . . . every man's dirty fantasy. Fresh moisture pooled in the area she'd so recently shaved, and she was stunned to discover she could get so hot looking at . . . herself.

And she knew instantly, she wanted Brent to see her this way. She wanted him to know she could look like this.

Not that she didn't remain nervous as hell. She was nearly as nervous as she was turned on. But in this moment, she wanted to find out what waited on the other side of that closed door more than she could have imagined a few hours ago. Brent had seduced her again, it seemed—this time with risqué clothing and written commands. But that was who he was—a wildly seductive man. She'd accepted that about him quickly and surrendered to it. And she felt like Alice in Wonderland as she reached for the doorknob, gently turned it, and stepped through the metaphorical rabbit hole.

She found herself in a large schoolroom. She could even smell old books, aging wooden desks, and the scent of chalk. Moving farther into the space, she glanced down at the teacher's desk to find props that made it feel all the more real: a teacher's gradebook, a pencil holder, a couple of history textbooks, and a wooden bin filled with tests, marked with red ink. When she noticed the one on top bore the name Jenna and had received an F, written in angry red strokes, she fought to conceal a smile. She was beginning to understand her role here.

Except that it still surprised her to walk around the front of the desk in her sexy heels, clicking loudly on the tile floor with each step, and see a nameplate that read: FATHER POWERS. "Oh," she murmured, discovering his role as well.

"Do you know why I made you stay after school today, Jenna?"

At the sound of the deep, sexy voice, she looked up with a start to see Brent had entered the room through another door in the back, wearing the black suit and collar of a priest. And—oh God—if it was possible, he looked even hotter than he had last night, a mere glimpse of him making the mound beneath her short skirt flutter. But maybe it was just because she hadn't seen him since then—maybe she'd forgotten exactly how good-looking he was.

"Answer me!" he snapped. "Do you?"

"Um . . . no." Lord, she was flustered. She'd never been much of an actress and hadn't had a chance to think about this aspect of things.

He proceeded up an aisle between rows of desks until he stood only a few feet away, after which he gave her a once-over that told her he liked what he saw. When their eyes met again, her breasts seemed to swell within the tight cups of her bra. "You're consistently late for class," he said without breaking the gaze, "you fail all your tests, and you try to tease and distract me with your body. You're a very naughty girl, Jenna."

Again, she felt the response between her thighs, even if she didn't quite understand why.

"Do you have anything to say for yourself?" he asked, eyebrows raised. And wow, he was good in his role, since she actually felt a little intimidated by his brusque manner—nothing like the man she'd met last night.

"Um . . . I'll try to do better?" she managed.

"Not good enough, Jenna. I'm going to have to teach you a lesson—you're going to learn who's in charge here once and for all. You need to be punished."

Punished. She swallowed, not sure what he meant. "How?" she whispered.

He never took his eyes off hers. "Bend over my desk," he said. Then he stepped past her and used one arm to sweep half the desktop's contents to the floor in a loud clatter that made her flinch—which she felt in her panties as much as everywhere else.

God. Despite her arousal, well . . . this changed things. It was a far cry from the romantic sex she'd hoped for. And maybe the schoolgirl outfit had made her anticipate something . . . well, at least playful—but they'd just left playful behind. "Seriously?" she asked.

He looked positively outraged by the question, his expression actually making her take a step back as her heart pounded against her ribs. "When I give you an instruction, you do it. Do you understand? *Now, bend over!*"

Jenna sucked in her breath and slowly moved to where he stood. Biting her lip, she leaned over the big desk until the upper half of her body rested on it. She turned her head sideways, toward him, to try to see what was coming, not at all sure she was ready for it.

"Lift your skirt up over your ass," he demanded.

In response, even in her subdued position, lust continued to flow through her veins. After all, she'd *wanted* to show him—all through her preparations, she'd *wanted* him to see her. And despite the weirdness of being bossed around this way, as she reached behind her to flip up the tiny skirt, revealing the strip of lace there, her arms felt heavy, warm.

Upon seeing her bottom, he let out a low sound of approval that ran all through her.

But when he brought the flat of his hand down on her rear for a stinging slap, she cried out, stunned. Maybe she should have understood that was coming, but somehow she'd gotten too caught up in the moment to really expect it.

"Tell me you're a bad girl, Jenna," he instructed her from above.

She let out a breath and said the words. "I'm . . . a bad girl." But it sounded so odd coming from her throat, in a voice too meek, disbelieving.

He brought his palm down to deliver another slap. "Again," he commanded.

"I'm a bad girl." Better this time. Stronger. Not that she was sure why that mattered to her. But at the moment, she found herself compelled to appease him.

Another hard, spanking blow—and again, she yelped slightly. He wasn't being gentle and it hurt. "Tell me you like showing me your ass."

"I like showing you my ass." As she said it, though, her eyes fell shut. She just didn't usually think of her rear as her *ass*. And to tell him such a truth, because it *was* true . . . felt strangely difficult.

He spanked her again, and this time, his voice deepened slightly—she could hear the stark lust in it. "Tell me you want to show me your tits."

Another word she never used. And another truth she felt at her core but found it painful to admit. Yet as a writer, she knew words were only words—she wasn't offended by them, just not accustomed to using certain ones. She knew guys liked that particular word, so if he wanted to hear it, if it would keep him from being angry, fine. "I want to show you my tits."

An additional slap of his hand made her wonder if her . . . *ass* was turning red, and if that turned him on. "Tell me you want me to play with your wet pussy," he instructed—and for some reason, she felt that one in her gut.

"I—I never talk that way, so . . ."

"You do *now*. What I command, you do. Now say it!"

She let out a breath. She'd realized he was a know-it-all, but she hadn't foreseen him being so . . . mean. Words so foreign-feeling had never left her mouth, but she focused on getting them out in a calm, obedient manner. "I . . . want you to play with my pussy."

Behind her, he went quiet and she wondered if her acquiescence excited him. She wondered what the hell all this was supposed to accomplish in terms of her sexual education. And she didn't want to be aroused anymore—she wanted to be angry. But despite her wishes, her crotch still throbbed against the desk as she waited . . . for something, and sort of wished this were over. Her heart beat too hard.

This wasn't what she'd hoped for when she'd put on the bra and panties—at all. She even considered using the safeword—just to end it.

Yet she didn't. Maybe *because* her crotch throbbed. And her breasts felt full, needy, pressed against the desk. Part of her was appalled by this, by what he thought qualified as a fantasy for her . . . and yet, wasn't she aching for more? Wasn't she excited?

So she lay there, nervous, pulsing, anxious, torn.

That's when he eased one finger inside the narrow band of lace stretching downward over the center of her bottom. She bit her lip at the touch—and sharply pulled in her breath as his fingertips moved slowly over her anus. They felt damp, as if maybe he'd moistened them first. She tensed, waiting for the pleasure of his fingers stroking lower, through her wetness—so it shocked the hell out of her when his touch didn't stray from the small fissure and he instead slid one finger smoothly, firmly inside it.

A startled cry lurched from her throat at the strange, uncomfortable sensation. "Wh-what are you . . . ?"

"Punishing you, naughty girl."

"B-but . . ."

"Quiet," he told her, and began to move his finger in and out.

Jenna had never felt anything like it. She wanted to think it hurt—the initial entry had been distressing—but . . . it didn't. In fact, she began to squirm, almost involuntarily, and she heard her own breath growing ragged. With pleasure? She couldn't figure that part out, but *something* was definitely making her hotter inside. She suffered the sense of being invaded, never having expected anything to enter her there, yet she never said the safeword or anything else that equated to asking him to stop.

Then he used his free hand to spank her again—harder now, in a faster rhythm. Jesus God. She yelped at each strike of his palm, overcome by the combination of odd feelings vibrating through her. Did it hurt? Or did it feel good? She couldn't even tell. But each unyielding slap echoed through her body, seeming to heighten every other sensation: the finger moving in and out of her anus, the hardness of the desk beneath her hips and breasts, the pulsation between her legs.

"Have you had enough?" he finally asked.

"Yes," she burst out. Because her bottom was sore, and inexplicable feelings wracked her from head to toe.

Yet even as he withdrew his finger, making her yelp yet again, he said darkly, "I don't think you have. I think you need to be punished *much, much* more, Jenna." And with that, he grabbed her hip and rolled her to her back on the desk.

It shook her to see him again, face-to-face, after what he'd just done to her, yet his expression held nothing but intense desire mingled with power. Stepping between her legs, he leaned over, brusquely curled the fingertips of both hands into the cups of her bra, and yanked them down, causing her breasts to tumble free.

"Damn," he murmured then, for a brief second sounding more like the Brent of last night than Father Powers, and his reaction reminded her it was the first time he'd actually seen them. His response warmed her cheeks and made her glance down to where the two mounds emerged from a frame of white knotted blouse and askew lace, large and round, nipples pointed.

His eyes remained locked there, too, as he closed his hands over them, massaging roughly. A moan escaped her throat when, below, his hardened length connected with her crotch through his pants and her thin undies. Her body felt supercharged now, as if everything up to this moment, from the shaving to the spanking to the anal play, had all been priming her . . . for whatever happened next.

Brent aggressively twirled her nipples between his fingertips, then pulled on them, gentle but firm, the move seeming to elongate them further. Soft cries and mewls left her and she suddenly felt out of her head with pleasure—and the need for more.

Next, he bent over her, taking one turgid peak in his mouth, sucking it in hard. "Oh!" she cried. "Oh God!" It hurt—and yet it didn't. Because it made her throb still more wildly below. He rubbed against her there now, and her head dropped back in abandon. She felt her back arching, urging him to take as much of her breast into his mouth as possible. She'd had no idea she liked things a little rough.

She wanted to protest when he released her breast and stepped back, disconnecting their bodies completely, but she held her tongue when he reached under her tiny scrap of a skirt to pull the lace thong down and off, over her sexy shoes.

Once it was gone, he moved back between her legs and flipped the skirt up again to look at her—there. She tingled madly, pulsated almost violently. But then—oh no—he looked furious. What on earth was wrong?

She didn't have to wonder long. "You disobeyed me again, Jenna! I instructed you to shave your pussy completely, yet you didn't."

She simply blinked, surprised—and still crazily aroused, as well as a little freaked out because he seemed so upset again. "Yes, I did. Mostly," she insisted, realizing he was referring to the small thatch of hair she'd left, despite its being located well above the area that mattered. "I mean, I just thought . . ."

"You just thought you'd do what *you* wanted to do," he boomed at her. "How many times do I need to make this clear? When I tell you to do something, you do it—or you suffer the consequences. Do you understand that?"

Quietly, she nodded. She didn't know how else to reply.

"I don't think you do," he groused. "And I think I need to teach you a lesson the hard way!"

Lying half dressed yet fully revealed before him, she shuddered. "How?"

"I'm going to fuck you until you scream."

Oh. My. That didn't sound much like punishment.

But then she got it . . . sort of. He was *pretending* sex was punishment. He was doing what she'd asked him to do last night—take the choices away from her, and at the same time give her what they both knew she wanted.

Why did that make it so much easier?

And yet, for her, it did. It felt so much more instinctive to act dismayed at the words than show her delight. She even managed a gasp and drew her knees up, closing her legs tight.

Their eyes met and she realized he understood—all of it. That it was her natural, normal reaction, even when she desired sex. That all her life, it had felt easier to *make* a guy part her legs than to do it willingly. And that's what felt better now, too—as he placed his hands firmly on her knees to briskly pry them open.

She let out a breath of excitement, surging with still more moisture when his gaze dropped again to where she'd shaved for him.

His palms skimmed swiftly up her inner thighs, coming to rest where they met, framing the part of her that glistened wet and open there. It was another way in which she'd never quite seen herself, but like him, she was looking. His expression made her feel obscenely beautiful. And she almost wanted to beg. *Please, please touch me.* But she didn't. Because she couldn't. Because it was just like everything else—so much easier if the guy just *did* it, if she never had to worry about letting him know her desires.

That's when Brent stroked two fingers down through her moist folds—thank God—making her whimper and quake. He smoothly pushed the same fingers into her drenched opening and a low sob left her.

Rather than move his fingers in and out then, he instead began to turn them in a slow and more circular motion, as if reaching around inside her, exploring her inner walls. The odd sensation gave her chills, despite the room being comfortable, and she breathed unevenly, audibly. With his free hand, he reached to undo his pants, his zipper, and she bit her lip when his erection burst free.

Oh—oh God. She'd not seen it last night, only felt it. Long and straight and undeniably hard, the straining veins along its length made it look like a powerful, dangerous tool. Even having taken it into her already, the sight made her nervous now—because he looked bigger than any other guy she'd been with.

"Get ready to take your punishment, Jenna," he said, his voice low and threatening.

In response, she lay back more completely on the desk and shut her eyes.

Yet as Brent's hands closed tight over her bare hips, he leaned over and rasped, "No. Open your eyes and watch me fuck you."

She forced them wide in response, but focused on the ceiling.

And then felt him waiting—waiting for her to do what he'd said.

So she lightly clenched her teeth and drew her gaze slowly, uncomfortably downward, until she met his—and he said, "Lower. My cock."

She sucked in a breath, felt her chest heave. Dragged her gaze downward, over the priest's collar and the black fabric of his suit. Until she again saw the large male appendage jutting from it like a steel girder.

She watched him close his fist around the base. She watched him guide the engorged head, a dot of shimmering moisture at its tip, to where her pink folds lay parted, ready. She watched him push the head inward—her body braced for the impact, which came, hard.

As his length drove slowly, deeply, into her, they both let out long, low groans, and Jenna continued witnessing the amazing way her body swallowed that part of his. Until her eyes fell shut again, out of pure pleasure, fullness—and this time he didn't insist she open them just yet.

With his big hands back at her hips, he began thrusting in earnest. He didn't go slow like last night—instead he found a brisk, hard rhythm, and she felt every stroke at her very core. Each made her cry out as it jolted her body—her breasts jiggled within the tight lace still outlining them, and she found herself gripping the bottom edge of the desk with both hands to hold herself steady.

"Open your eyes, Jenna," he said, his voice warm, dark.

She obeyed, meeting his as their bodies collided, again, again.

Then he released one of her hips and reached down for her hand, removing it from the desk's edge. He drew it up over where he entered her—hard, so hard—and pressed her fingertips to her clitoris, holding them there. "Touch yourself while I fuck you," he said, his gaze still steady and commanding on her.

Impulsively, she tried to pull her hand away, but he wouldn't allow it. He pushed her fingers back down, even moving them over the sensitive nub to send an unbidden pleasure expanding outward.

"I don't want it to happen that way," she protested as he continued to pound into her flesh below. "I want *you* to do it."

He simply gave his head a short, definite shake. "Rub your clit," he insisted. "Do it!"

But the second he began to remove his hand, she did, too—so he shoved her fingers back down, rougher this time, forcing her to feel her own wetness.

She bit her lip, their eyes still locked. "This . . . doesn't . . . make me . . . feel good," she managed between the hard strokes of his erection.

"It will if you let it," he assured her. "You can even close your eyes if you want." He suddenly sounded a little more like Brent than Father Powers, and she immediately accepted the offer to shut her eyes, shut out all the shocking, erotic images assaulting her. But she still didn't want to touch herself. It wasn't that she never did—she did sometimes; it was that she couldn't bear to do it in front of someone. Even during sex. It felt so . . . private, personal.

Yet Brent still held her fingers down into her folds, and even just the friction created by his thrusts succeeded in moving her clit against her hand. And soon she heard her breath begin to change, deepen, felt her chest begin to expand and contract as she bit her lip and lifted her hips to better meet his hard drives—and her own fingers.

Oh God. Oh God, it would happen soon. Still, Brent flattened his fingertips over hers, moving them in a hot little circle that made her begin to moan.

And as his touch grew gradually lighter, she wanted to lift her hand away, too—but she didn't. *Couldn't* really. Because—dear God—she was so close, everything inside her pounding, pulsating, reaching. And then she exploded in orgasm, crying out, lifting to meet his big erection and her own wet fingertips, again, again, again.

Oh God.

When the hot waves passed, she felt spent.

Above her, Brent was saying, "That was good, baby. So hot. You did so well." And she opened her eyes to find his gaze on her—and it somehow made her thrust harder against him, wanting more and more of him, deep inside her, wanting him to make her feel *everything*, everything there was to feel in the *world*, in *sex*, in *passion*.

Until he was moving in her so violently, fucking her so hard, that she couldn't think straight, screaming at every powerful plunge, and he began to growl, to groan, and then his eyes fell shut and he began murmuring, "Fuck, aw fuck, I can't stop. Here I come, baby, here I come."

And the thrusts he delivered then, accompanied by still more fierce growls, nearly nailed her to the desk—and she liked it.

Soon he fell forward onto her, collapsing in exhaustion, and she noticed for the first time that her legs were wrapped tight around him, the tall heels of her shoes digging into his ass. And as she lay there beneath him, she realized in pure horror that somewhere along the way she'd begun to think in the terms *he* used: ass, fucking, clit. How the hell had *that* happened? It made her feel like . . . someone else, someone she wasn't. Or at least she didn't *think* she was that person.

She could smell him, the musky male scent of him, and suffered the urge to wrap her arms around him, too, or maybe run one hand through his thick hair, his head resting gently on her shoulder now—but she didn't. Because she wasn't sure how this part worked. And she wasn't *at all* sure she should let him know, that despite the fantasy situation here, she was feeling a little connected to him just from being so close, so weirdly personal.

Finally, he rolled off her, onto his side on the desk, withdrawing his erection—a move that left her feeling oddly abandoned.

"You okay?" he asked, suddenly back to being Brent now.

She hesitated, weighing her answer. "I think." Then she gave her head a soft shake. "It . . . wasn't what I expected."

When she found the will to meet his gaze again, he'd propped up on one elbow. "What were you expecting?"

The question made her shift her eyes back away, embarrassed by the more innocent visions in her head. "It was silly, really."

"Tell me."

She took a deep breath and tried to be honest. "Something . . . softer. Satin sheets and violin music, maybe? Some kind of romantic beach tryst. Something I might . . . really fantasize, like you said." Then she sighed. "Something that, now, I don't think you'd *ever* arrange for me—since your goal here is fixing whatever you think is wrong with me, not just making me feel good."

"My goal is to do both," he clarified.

Jenna found herself blinking uncomfortably. "I'm just not sure this was . . . me." She motioned around the room, then peered down at the clothing she only half wore.

"You *came*. Hard," he pointed out, sounding just a bit arrogant.

She pulled in her breath, unable to deny it. "I just don't know . . . what all that was about."

Brent couldn't explain it to her—too much information, too much detail, would only screw up the effects of the sex. Still, he found himself wishing he could, because she'd been brave coming here today and he felt a little bad for her now. He probably should have anticipated an uncertain reaction—but again, he just wasn't used to fucking anyone who wasn't thrilled to be here. Usually, people were happy after fantasies—sometimes exhausted but replete, other times delighted and giddy, and everything in between. "Remember I said you have to trust me," he reminded her.

"I did—and I'm not sure I liked what happened."

He thought about going soft on her, but the truth would be better for her in the long run. "You just don't *want* to like it. Because it's a lot dirtier and more complex than satin sheets and violins."

She tilted her head. "Are you implying there's something *wrong* with satin sheets and violins?"

"Not at all. But you wouldn't have felt half as much. And you wouldn't have come nearly as hard."

"It would help if I knew what I was supposed to take away from it."

Maybe, maybe not. She might not appreciate knowing that a big part of this was about making her obey him—so that he could get her through her fantasies without her balking at his every instruction.

He'd also wanted her to start playing with the concept of being a bad girl. Girls like Jenna, who'd absorbed a lot of negative sexual content growing up, usually went one of two ways—all the way bad or all the way good. Jenna had been a hard-core good girl, the kind who would be mortified if anyone ever thought she was bad—but he'd just shown her that she *could* be a bad girl and the world wouldn't stop spinning, the sky wouldn't fall. Right now, she saw things too much in black and white, not appreciating shades of gray—and there were *lots* of shades of gray in sex.

"I can't go into it with you," he explained. "But you need to loosen up and feel what it made you feel. Not the I-wanted-satin-sheets part. Forget what you wanted and feel what you got. Not just the orgasm. All of it."

Next to him, she took a deep breath and he could sense how hard she was thinking. Finally, she said, "I . . . wanted you to make me do it. I didn't . . . *want* to want it."

"I know that," he said simply.

"Well, isn't that a *bad* thing? I mean, I'm smart enough to know that probably isn't the healthiest sexual desire in the world."

"It's one of the things we're going to be working on," he told her, then heard himself confiding a little more than he probably should. "But for now, it's something that satisfies you, so I used it to help get you . . . into the game." Part of this had indeed also been about making her take what she subconsciously needed him to give her. She'd made it clear last night that she wasn't comfortable admitting what she craved, that she wanted the guy to take the lead, so if that made her do what he wanted for a while, he would play to that. Then later, he'd make her advance beyond that attitude.

In the meantime, though, if it pleasured *her* and allowed *him* to take her in new directions, he'd be the dominant lover she required. And he'd enjoy it, since being dominant in bed came naturally to him. "The main thing, sunshine, is what I keep telling you—you need to trust me. And you need to do what I tell you. You need to understand that anything I demand of you is ultimately going to pleasure you."

"Maybe you make me do things that actually pleasure *you*," she suggested, switching on her argumentative side, "but they really won't pleasure *me*. Maybe people don't take pleasure in the same things."

He only sighed. Did she really think he was that dumb? "Of course they don't—we all have certain things that get us off more than others. But again, everything I'm doing is for your own good."

"Making me talk dirty? That's something that turns guys on—but not girls."

At this, he couldn't contain a small laugh. Poor Jenna—she was so naïve in some ways. "Sunshine, I can assure you plenty of women are excited by dirty talk."

She pursed her lips and looked him in the eye, appearing to weigh his words, deciding if she believed them. "Maybe it does a little more for me when *you're* doing it—but *I* don't enjoy doing it."

He considered it progress that she'd even admitted *that* much. But she was missing the point. "For your information, making you talk dirty doesn't have much to do with whether or not you enjoy it—maybe you will and maybe you won't. Right now, it's about getting over stigmas."

She looked skeptical. "Stigmas? What do you mean?"

"You *know* you avoid certain words, sunshine."

"Maybe I just don't find them appealing," she argued.

"Or maybe you're afraid there's something wrong with saying them."

She rolled her eyes. "That's stupid."

"Then say them."

"Why?"

"Because I said so. Because if you can't even say certain words, how are you ever going to attain real sexual freedom?"

"I can say them. You told me to say them and I said them."

She had. But it had been a strain for her. And purely mechanical. "Well, from now on, I expect you to say them a lot more. I want you to start thinking of having sex as fucking, of my penis as my cock, and of your vagina as your pussy—or your cunt."

She flinched, visibly.

And he said, "See? You're afraid of the word."

"I'm a writer, Brent, and for *your* information, words don't scare me. But I happen to think of that *particular* word as a very derogatory term for women."

"Then that's a problem," he said matter-of-factly, "because you *should* be thinking of it as what's between your legs." He reached down and flicked a fingertip through her slit for good measure, enjoying it perhaps a bit too much when she gasped in unbidden delight. "This is another example of how you've let one negative perception color your whole view. It's a body part—a fucking *beautiful* body part. That's all. You've given the word more power than it deserves, Jenna. Turn it into nothing but a body part and you've taken the power *back*."

She said nothing, looking both stunned and as if—maybe, just maybe—she was realizing the truth in what he'd said.

"Tell me what's between your legs," he instructed.

"My . . . cunt," she whispered.

"Very good," he said softly in reply.

Just then, she drew in her breath, knit her brow. "Were you really mad at me for not, you know, shaving the very top, too?"

He grinned, conceding. "No. It looks incredible, by the way."

She smiled as if she'd just caught him at something. "Aha! So that part *was* for you."

He laughed at her sureness, then shook his head. "No. That, too, is for you. To make sure you're very familiar with your body, comfortable with that part of yourself, fully in touch with the parts that bring you the most pleasure. And by the way, *keep* it shaved while you're here."

"Fine. But if you like it this way, how can you be sure it's not at least *partially* for your benefit?"

He tilted his head, thinking it was cute as hell the way she argued these points, seemingly forgetting she wasn't all that comfortable talking about such things. "Okay, to be fair," he confessed, "let's say it was for both of us."

He thought she'd look happier about that—instead, it appeared she already had something else on her mind.

"What?" he asked. "What's going through that head of yours *now*?"

"I guess I was just wondering . . . do I . . . excite you?"

She had to ask? "Of course, honey. Did you not feel that hard dick?"

She flushed slightly, prettily. "I mean, you've been with a gazillion women and this is your job, so . . ."

He couldn't help reaching up, brushing a long wisp of hair back from her face. He hated that he'd somehow made her doubt his true attraction to her. "If you think this is work for me, sunshine, think again. When I walked in and saw you, I nearly came in my pants, right then and there."

"Really?"

He simply tilted his head and gave her a look. Could she honestly not know how appealing she was, how hot? Then again, maybe she'd never let herself be in many positions to find out. "You make a *bangin'* naughty schoolgirl, honey. And it's important to me that you know just *how* fucking sexy you really are."

"Important professionally or personally?"

"Both," he said, without elaborating. Because it was true, and he knew she needed to know that—but there was a damn fine line here and he couldn't cross it or they'd both end up regretting it. Even beyond this fantasy, he was the teacher here and she was the student. That was all there could really be. So he changed the subject. "I'm going to give you some homework."

She lowered her chin. "What makes you think I'm going to continue with this?"

She could argue if she wanted, but he'd seen enough to know without doubt—she'd come too far not to want to keep going. "Because you're starting to trust me. You're starting to figure out that maybe you *do* have a few issues to work out and you're willing to let me help you do it. Now, homework."

She simply rolled her eyes again, so he went on.

"I want you to spend some time thinking back over everything that happened today, all of it, and examine how you felt at each point. Figure out the things that excited you and those, if any, that didn't. If they truly *didn't* physically excite you, ask yourself why? Think about what made you feel sexy and hot. Think about what made you nervous or afraid. Then make a list of the positives—one list of things that made you feel sexy, and another of things that turned you on. Even if they don't seem PC—it doesn't matter. Be honest with yourself. Lesson number one—sex isn't supposed to be politically correct, sunshine. Pleasure is far more complex than good taste allows for, so you have to let go of all that when you're in bed."

"Is that it, on the homework?"

"Before you go to sleep tonight, call the front desk and tell them you have something to deliver to me. Put your lists in an envelope—

there should be some in the desk in your room—and someone will pick it up."

"Ah, so you're going to *see* the list. I thought maybe it was just for my own self-awareness."

"Afraid not, sunshine. It'll help me know where we stand in your, uh, tutorial. So, again, be honest. There's nothing you could say that would shock me or change my opinion of you. Believe me, I've heard it all."

She grinned. "I'll just bet you have."

He returned the smile, then began to push to his feet and finally zipped up his pants. After which he took her hands and pulled her to an upright position on the desk. "I'm gonna go. You can stay here as long as you want, take your time. No one will be in to tidy things up for a few hours." Then he leaned a little closer and lifted his hand to her face. "I'm proud of you, sunshine. For letting yourself do this."

She looked so pretty just then, so strangely innocent. At some point while they'd talked, she'd pulled her bra back into place, but she was still the naughty Catholic girl sitting there with her pussy nearly on display—looking as pure as the driven snow. "Can I ask you something?"

His voice came out too soft. "Sure—anything."

"Are . . . we allowed to kiss? Because I've noticed we haven't."

He drew a deep breath. How could he explain this? "It's not against the rules, but . . . given how many rules I'm breaking here already, I don't know if it's the best idea."

"Okay," she said, clearly trying her damnedest to sound as if it didn't matter at all—but he felt in his gut how much she yearned to be kissed right now, how much she needed what had just happened on this desk to matter, even just a little.

And he *shouldn't* validate it, because he couldn't ever let her believe the sex between them was more than what it was—a phenomenally pleasant time between two people while one of them educated the other. Yet something about the expression on her face made his chest feel like it was caving in.

He started to go, but after two steps, heard himself mutter, "Hell—fuck it." Then he turned back, stepped possessively between her thighs, and slid his hands around her slender waist. He lowered his mouth to hers and kissed her hotly, passionately.

Though after a minute, after that initial kiss or two, the connection of their mouths slowed, their lips lingering together for a long, still moment—which drove him into a drawn-out, deliberate, deeper kind of kissing.

When his spine began to tingle, he knew it was time to stop, so he pulled up, gently backing a step away.

Their eyes met and he once again felt like he was seeing all of her: the sweet girl inside; the girl who was frightened sexually but standing openly before him, exposed, both physically and emotionally; the hot, dirty girl he knew hid within, wanting to come out.

"Sweet dreams, sunshine," he said, then turned and exited the room.

Chapter 5

Jenna lay on her bed in a cami and cotton panties, hugging a pillow to her chest, feeling too dreamy after Brent's kisses. *But you have to stop it. You can enjoy sex with him—and kissing—but you can't get any more attached to him.* For one thing, she'd known him for just over twenty-four hours. For another, in two weeks, he would be history, a memory. No matter how hot and soft his kisses had been.

Getting up, she gathered pen and paper, then stepped out onto the balcony. Anyplace else, she might worry about putting on more clothes, but here, she considered being seen in underwear the least of her worries. It was dark out, getting late, and she hadn't composed her lists yet.

She'd returned to her suite to find dinner waiting—a chicken salad plate and some fruit. Damn him, how did he know she'd been in the mood for something light after all the weird sex and weird talking?

After eating, she'd taken a long bath and started on her homework, rethinking the sex, bit by bit. Parts of it still freaked her out a little—but sometimes, she discovered, the things that had freaked her out were also the same things that had turned her on. And as she replayed it all in her mind, she tried her best to start thinking the way he wanted her to think—in dirty words. Instead of remembering the moment she saw his penis, she remembered the moment she saw his cock. Instead of remembering how he'd moved in and out of her, she remembered the way he'd fucked her. She still thought that was . . . silly at best, but for some reason she couldn't quite determine, she wanted—more and more—to be a good student for him.

Maybe it's because of the kisses.

Peering out over the sea, where a nearly full moon shone down to make the water sparkle, she tried to laugh that off as a ridiculous reason, but the truth was—the man knew how to kiss. He'd kissed her better than anyone ever had.

Quit thinking about kisses and make your lists.

Half an hour and lots of lusty, tingling memories later, she had compiled them, and though it had been difficult to be totally honest, especially knowing he'd see them, she'd succeeded. Admirably so, she thought.

Things That Made Me Feel Sexy (Not Necessarily a Complete List)

The way I looked in the bra and thong in my room

The way I looked in the schoolgirl outfit (which surprised me and makes me feel a little weird, actually)

Wearing such sexy shoes (another surprise)

Seeing in your eyes that you liked the way I looked, too

The way you looked at my breasts

The way you looked at my pussy (not when you acted mad, but other times)

Hearing you moan and groan because of me

Having you kiss me after you pretty much just said you shouldn't kiss me (and now that I've written this down I hope it wasn't some sort of pity kiss)

Things That Turned Me On (Also Not Necessarily a Complete List)

Shaving my cunt (very big surprise)

Your voice, when you walked into the room

Looking at you

Being spanked (but I'm not sure why)

When you put your finger in my ~~anus~~ asshole (is there some dirtier word for that I should be using?)

When you sucked my nipple into your mouth so hard

When you forced my legs apart

The first time I saw your ~~penis~~ cock

Watching you put it inside me

Right now, writing the word cock for you, sort of (but that still doesn't mean I'm into talking dirty)

The way you kissed me at the end

She knew she probably could have thought of more, but she was tired—such strange sex had worn her out—and she wanted to go to bed. After folding the lists and putting them in an envelope, she wrote Brent's name on the outside, called the front desk as instructed, then slid the envelope partially under the door, so she wouldn't have to bother getting dressed to open it.

As she closed her eyes, she thought once more about the day. Had it changed her inside? Sexually? In other ways? It had certainly shown her a few unexpected things about herself, but in her mind, it was far too soon to recognize any far-reaching results. As for how on earth she'd been sucked into going forward with more of this, she wasn't sure. As much as she'd loved his kisses, she would have liked attributing her cooperation to that as well—but she'd agreed, or not argued anyway, *before* he'd kissed her.

And maybe that was all the proof she needed to know this experience *had* already changed her, more than she could have conceived of just a day or two earlier—that seemed like a lifetime ago. Lord, how changed would she be after two full weeks of Brent's fantasies?

. . .

You Are Invited to a Fantasy

Where: The Sheik's Palace (map included)
When: Tonight, 8:00 p.m.
You are a newly acquired slavegirl in the sheik's harem.
Appropriate attire will be provided at the palace, as will an evening meal.
Do as the sheik instructs and unthinkable pleasures await.
(Your safeword is Amelia Earhart.)

Brent sat on a large ruby red throw pillow in the harem room, reading the invitation he knew Jenna had received a few hours ago—guides were always given a copy of their own invitations as a matter of course, allowing them to make sure everything was right.

The large area was draped in colorful satins and silks, jewel-tone draperies spilling down walls and drooping from the ceiling like waves. Thick carpeting covered the floor, which was home to mounds of various-size pillows in more rich, saturated colors, taking the place of furniture. To give a sense of greater dimension, the room had been built on two levels; three steps descended into a square "pit" to one side and stretched along its length. And Brent's clothing, of course, fit the setting—he was the sheik, complete with a small white turban and billowing white pants. For this particular fantasy, he wore no shirt.

Around him, people bustled about, arranging pillows and adjusting lighting. He looked up to see two pretty girls enter the room in their harem costumes. The taller one, a shapely blonde, met Brent's gaze and playfully jiggled her tits within the sky blue chiffon bikini-type top that held them. "You like?" she asked.

Yes, he liked, very much, and gave her a wink in reply. "Very nice, Sasha." Sasha was twenty-eight and working at the Hotel Erotique while she wrote her thesis—she'd soon have a master's in social psychology with a focus on sex roles. The girl at her side, Barbie, was in her early twenties and had a BA in psychology, but was busy rebelling against her parents for a few years—after which Brent expected she'd get a job in counseling, a plan that had been sidetracked when her rich father cut her off unless she pursued a more lucrative position in the field.

Just then, Ryan came in bearing trays laden with finger sandwiches, chocolate-covered strawberries and chunks of banana, and a ceramic jug filled with wine—he lowered the tray to the wide step just above where Brent sat. Brent had heard Ryan had waited on Jenna at the beach yesterday. "Food and drink for the new slave girl," Ryan said with an easy wink. "Kirsten's bringing the cups."

"Good man," Brent said with a nod. Ryan wouldn't be participating in this particular fantasy, but Brent would likely pull him in later if he found a role he thought fit. For tonight, it would be only he and a number of female facilitators.

And it was good that he'd already planned to bring more people in on this second fantasy, since . . . shit, what had he been thinking, kissing her last night? He'd always been in full agreement on the rules about guides and guests, but now he understood why more than ever before. It was easy to get too involved, to start caring on a personal level. Worse, he was realizing just how easy that made it for the *guest* to get attached, too.

So what had he done? Kissed a girl who he knew was already prone to getting attached to people she had sex with. *Smooth move, Powers.* He gave his head a disgusted shake.

Just then Kirsten entered, carrying a tray of small ceramic cups without handles, designed with colorful Middle Eastern flair, which she lowered to the carpet. She looked stunning in red chiffon, rows of gold coin-shaped medallions draping from the bottom of her revealing top, her long dark hair pulled up in an *I Dream of Jeannie* ponytail. At thirty, she was one of their most skilled and experienced facilitators and would soon likely advance to being a guide. "Anything else we need?" she asked.

He looked around, then shook his head. "Nope, the sheik is pleased," he answered teasingly.

When Kirsten walked away, though, his mind returned to kissing Jenna—and it forced him to remember the way those kisses had figured into her lists.

Otherwise, though, she'd done well, and a number of the entries had made him smile. *No, sunshine, calling it an asshole is fine.* Other list items had relayed to him in subtle or not-so-subtle ways that much of what he'd hoped to achieve last night had worked. She was learning to more boldly take pleasure from her own body, and to *recognize* taking that pleasure. She'd enjoyed aspects of the kinkiness involved—even though she might not fully realize it. She was learning to talk more frankly about sex, without shying away from language, and he was pretty sure she *did* get off on dirty talk—she just didn't know that yet, either. And—key for right now—she was adapting well to obeying his instructions. She hadn't even balked about making the lists—and he'd fully expected her to. Despite her general protests and arguments, she was becoming a much more malleable, docile Jenna very quickly, and that would aid his work immensely.

Tonight's fantasy would expand on what they'd accomplished yesterday. The activities would again rely on discipline—on him taking a controlling role, compelling her to obey. And it would once more be about him *using* that control to make her take what he needed her to experience—but this time he wouldn't be the only person delivering pleasure to Jenna.

So tonight she'd have to open up *a lot*, trust him *a lot*. He wasn't sure she'd do everything he asked, but he hoped she'd find the boldness inside her that he knew was there—she'd greatly enjoy the harem fantasy if she could just let go of her inhibitions.

Moments later, the other players in Jenna's carefully designed fantasy came in, greeting him and one another as they took their places. Music that fit the scene wafted softly from hidden speakers, adding to the sensual setting. Wine was poured into cups, and he saw Kirsten getting in the mood by rubbing her curves playfully, provocatively against Amira, a lovely Palestinian girl who was probably the most extreme case of a rebellious facilitator he'd seen in all his years here. She'd come as a guest while attending college at NYU, and she'd soon returned as an employee.

Nearby, he noticed Sasha settling her head into Barbie's lap, both stretching out on plush pillows. Across the room lay a sensuous redhead,

Lola, and a petite but busty blonde, Candy. Candy was new yet eager, and the more-experienced Lola had been a good teacher for her in the few months since her arrival.

In total, ten women lounged around the lush room in scant chiffon outfits, looking completely fuckable and making Brent's cock begin to harden. Only a few would engage directly with Jenna, but all were necessary to set the tone and fully acclimate her to the fantasy.

Soon, the lighting dimmed—a signal from Ryan, hidden from sight, that Jenna had reached the dressing area to read her instructions and would soon enter the room. In response, Lola and Candy began to gently touch and kiss—falling easily, he noted with amusement, into their roles. Other girls lounged about, beginning to lazily run fingertips over the shoulders or hips of a fellow female facilitator. Sasha turned to playfully lick Barbie's belly button, which happened to be encircled with a curling scrollwork tattoo. And Kirsten took a place beside *him*, hanging casually on his shoulder, her ample breasts rubbing against his arm.

When Jenna entered the room, however, his full attention shifted her way. She wore a pale yellow chiffon bra top, the bottom edge sporting draped rows of gold coinlike beads, and a matching skirt that rode low beneath her navel and sported side slits all the way up to the thick row of gold coin beads that served as a waistband. Numerous gold bangle bracelets circled both wrists and an elaborate gold necklace lay about her throat and the expanse of skin below. From her heavily made-up eyes to the way her curves peeked so enticingly from the bits of chiffon, she looked like a true harem girl—except for the shock in her expression.

As she glanced around the room at the girls touching one another, she appeared taken aback—but no one acknowledged her presence in any way, and Brent let her use the moment to begin adjusting to the setting, hoping like hell she could handle it and wouldn't go running away. Her safeword tonight was, like all safewords, something that would never be uttered during this fantasy for any other reason than wanting out. He prayed she wouldn't say it tonight—and realized he felt that perhaps a little too strongly. Besides wanting her to reap pleasure and proceed toward full sexual freedom, he also wanted to *deliver* that pleasure, see her *feel* it. The very thought hardened his dick still more, making it rise to create a tautly stretched tent in his loose pants.

When finally she looked to him, her eyes brimming with trepidation, he didn't smile. As much as he would've liked to put her at ease, it was time to take on his role. Tonight he owned her. And she needed to understand and accept that if they were to move forward.

Becoming the sheik in mind as well as appearance, he studied her body unabashedly, noting that she might be afraid but her nipples pointed prominently through the soft top, and that while her cunt was covered by a curtain of chiffon, he could see she'd followed the instruction not to wear anything underneath. He summoned her, his voice low but exercising great authority. "Come sit beside me, slave girl."

Timidly, she came toward him across the plush carpet on bare feet, and he hoped the chiffon gliding against her thighs as she walked added to her unwitting arousal. She knelt on the opposite side of him from Kirsten—who still clung sensually to his shoulder, watching the scene unfold.

Brent motioned to the step rising just above the pit, to the wine and food tray. "Eat," he told her. "Drink." And as she began to obey, reaching to pour herself some wine, Kirsten poured some for *him*, and even lifted a strawberry to his mouth in an example of unbidden slave girl subservience. He watched Jenna observing, trying not to react, and hid his amusement while willing *her* toward such eager submission, too.

As she ate one of the small sandwiches provided, he said, "I own you now, Jenna. You are bought and paid for, and your only purpose for existence now is to do my bidding. Do you understand?"

She drew in her breath, and he realized what he'd said was harsh, but for tonight, it was entirely necessary. Tonight they took a big step forward. *Each* night would be a big step forward—he had only two weeks to undo a lifetime of negative impressions, memories, and ingrained beliefs about sex.

When she didn't answer immediately, he went on. "You are lucky I noticed your beauty and rescued you from the life of squalor you would live as one of my regular slaves. Here, in my harem, you will have every luxury. All that's required of you is to serve and pleasure me in whatever way I demand."

Meeting his gaze, she said quietly, solemnly, "I'll try."

And damn, he wanted to go soft on her then—but he couldn't afford to. "No, *you'll do it*," he snapped. "You are a sex slave now, like it or not." Only then did he allow himself to go a *little* soft. "However, there is much pleasure in it for you, too. Tonight, in fact, I am taking mercy upon you, planning to initiate you into my harem gently."

"That's . . . kind of you," she replied, still cautious, but he could see her warming to her role now, just a bit—which pleased him greatly, both as her guide and as the lusty sheik who intended to force her into pleasure with or without her consent. Given his dominant tendencies, he'd always gotten into the sheik fantasy, perhaps too much.

"This evening," he said, his tone still imparting full power, "all that will be demanded of you is to relax and let me enjoy you, however I see fit."

He watched her suck in her breath, then whisper, "All right."

So far, she'd eaten only two little triangle sandwiches, and he wanted her to have energy for what lay ahead, so he now did as Kirsten had done for him—he picked up a piece of chocolate-covered fruit and held it to her lips. She bit into the chunk of banana, sighing her pleasure at the taste. After she swallowed, he fed her the rest, gently slipping his index finger between her soft lips. She met his gaze and he knew they both felt it between their legs until he extracted his fingertip.

Normally, as sheik, he wouldn't lower himself to feeding a harem girl, but Jenna was different. As a facilitator, he'd taken many women through the harem fantasy, and for most, now would be the time to push them to their backs and take them or to instruct the other girls to pleasure her, but Jenna required just the right care: hardness tempered with a pinch of softness, authority tempered with a hint of affection. And he knew from the look in her eyes that he'd just hit the right note to make her pussy surge with moisture beneath that sexy chiffon.

In response, Jenna reached toward the fruit tray herself, plucking up a strawberry and lifting it for *him* to eat. Despite himself, he could have sworn it tasted better coming from her. After swallowing, he closed his grasp warmly on her wrist, using his other hand to take the stem from her and cast it aside. Then he drew her index finger slowly, deeply into his mouth, sucking. Their eyes stayed connected the entire time, allowing him to see her pleasure.

Finally, he released it, saying, "Good little slave girl. You please me."

"I'm glad."

Next, he brought her hand back to his mouth to flick his tongue through the soft, sensitive valleys between her fingers, one by one—and he loved seeing that it excited her unexpectedly. He heard her breath catch; he felt his stiff cock tighten further.

Reaching up to gently stroke her cheek, now tanned from a few days in the sun, he soon let his fingertips skim downward, his touch just grazing her neck, then passing over her heavy necklace and onto the bared skin below. His fingers swept tenderly between her breasts, the flesh there also on lovely, curving display.

Raising his attention back to her face, he found a blush staining her bronzed cheeks. Maybe she was embarrassed to be touched in front of other girls. Or maybe she was just pleasured by his caress. Most likely both. *But you have to get over the first, Jenna, to really experience the second.*

So he pressed on, intent on forcing the pleasure to overpower the stigma of having strangers in the room. Intent on overcoming many *other* stigmas, too, but this was the one on his mind as he gently cupped the sides of both her breasts, raking his thumbs over those beaded nipples, a hint of their dark color visible through the layers of pale yellow. She sucked in her breath, sighed audibly. The fact that she willingly met his gaze the whole time caused a soft pride to swell inside him.

"You have perfect tits," he said, not sure if he was being himself or the sheik. Another instance when the answer was: most likely both. Despite the staggering number of female breasts he'd seen in his life, he'd fallen in lust with hers last night. Although he'd known her bra size from her profile, they'd appeared plumper, rounder, than he'd expected, and now, it was important for *her* to know how lovely they were.

She flushed a bit more, but managed to say, "I'm . . . glad they please you."

And he smiled darkly, gratified that she was getting into this, slowly but surely. "They'll soon please me much more. *You'll* please me much more. *Won't* you, slave girl?"

"Yes," she murmured, appearing breathless, still nervous—but that was okay. "I . . . *wish* to please you."

"Good little sex slave," he fawned.

Then he tweaked her nipples lightly, making her let out a pretty whimper, and glanced to his right. "Barbie, Sasha, come here." It was time to turn things up a notch and hope she didn't freak out.

Both girls complied, one kneeling on each side of him so that they all faced Jenna.

"Look at our new harem girl. Isn't she lovely? Doesn't she have beautiful tits?" His hands still framed them loosely.

Barbie answered first, casting Jenna a warm smile. "Very lovely indeed."

"Mmm, sumptuous," Sasha purred.

"I wish to kiss her neck," he announced then. "Move beside her and draw her hair back from her shoulders."

Sasha and Barbie obeyed—and Jenna's eyes filled with uncertainty.

Yet as he placed one palm at the curve of her waist and leaned in to lower a gentle kiss to her neck, he felt her relax. In reaction to the second kiss, she even sighed. Inwardly, he smiled, sizzling with anticipation now—and despite her shyness, he began to feel more assured she would let his will be done.

As he skimmed his touch over her shoulder, her arm, he delivered more kisses—and she leaned her head back to accept them, letting out more pretty sighs in response. Did she notice when *more* light caresses came on her shoulders as his own descended, grazing over her breasts to the soft skin below? Did it dawn on her that he couldn't touch her in that many places with only two hands?

Her eyes had closed, but he didn't reprimand her, not yet—because she was doing surprisingly well, his Little Miss Sunshine.

When he relinquished kissing her neck and shoulders, he said, "Sasha, Barbie—last night, our new slave girl indulged in activities that might have left her back aching, so I want you both to massage her."

Jenna didn't even appear dismayed when the girls did as instructed, Barbie beginning to knead her neck and shoulders as Sasha's palms molded to lower areas of her back. But she did open her eyes, meet his gaze, appearing languid and acceptant.

"Relax and enjoy, slave girl. Let this soothe your tensions," he said. Then he turned to Kirsten, who sat waiting behind him. "Pour Jenna more wine."

A moment later, Jenna accepted the ceramic cup willingly, taking a sip.

Good, he thought. This was going *extremely* well. It should, of course—he had years of experience at this. But given that Jenna was such an unusual case, he hadn't been as confident of the outcome as he normally would.

When Jenna finished her wine, he motioned for Kirsten to pour still more. Sasha and Barbie continued rubbing her back, deeply, occasionally causing a small moan to erupt from Jenna's throat. And elsewhere in the room, his other harem girls persisted in entertaining one another as well.

Finally, he took the cup from her hand and said, "Go lounge amid those pillows," pointing toward a stack of cushions a few yards away. Sasha and Barbie withdrew their touches, allowing Jenna to lie back among the cushions, a sensual vision in yellow. Her eyes said she was ready for more, and if it was possible, his dick got stiffer. "Very nice, slave girl," he told her when their gazes met again—as he, too, reclined, leaning back against a large red bolster, propping himself up on his elbow.

That's when she realized. "You're not coming? Over here?"

He gently shook his head. "There's more than one way for me to enjoy you, and right now, I wish to do it with my eyes."

Jenna drew in her breath. Things were changing here, too quickly. And it had already been so very much to take in: the rich colors and shadowy air; Brent's cock standing at attention for all to see beneath those pants while a gorgeous woman clung to him; and, of course, all these girls making out and touching each other. At first sight, her stomach had squirmed. But at the same time, she'd been drawn to watch even while embarrassed by her interest.

Once she'd started getting used to that, it had seemed like . . . wallpaper, like something that blended into the background after a while, and things had grown easier when he began to caress and kiss her. Even when he'd had the two pretty girls massage her, she'd not freaked out—she'd had occasional massages at home and had told herself this wasn't really any different. That was a ridiculous lie, of course, but it got her through it.

And now . . . oh God, what was going to happen? Was he expecting her to do what those girls across the room were doing? Just then, she let out a silent gasp because a glance at two women on the room's higher level revealed that it was more than just kissing now—one was eating the other. And a glimpse of yet another pair shocked her just as badly—both were topless now, kneading each other's breasts.

"Spread your legs and reveal your cunt," Brent said. She returned her gaze to him to make sure—and yep, he was talking to her.

She felt much as she had at moments in the schoolroom yesterday—like maybe it was time to say her safeword. But then she remembered—Brent had urged her to say it not from fear, but only if she was truly displeasured. Of course, being asked to reveal her vagina to a room full of other girls could be viewed as something that displeasured her—but did it? Really?

She sucked in her breath at the answer.

At any other moment of her life, it likely would have repulsed her. But right now, in this room, with all these beautiful, sexual women . . . there was an unforeseen part of her that wanted . . . to be like them. Be one of them. So sensual and carefree. Following urges. Seeking pleasure. And besides, she still found herself wishing to please Brent.

So she tucked away the safeword in the back of her mind and met his gaze, a place where she always found . . . not solace or safety exactly, but something that gave her courage, urged her onward. Then she took a deep breath, reached down—still keeping her eyes only on him—and slowly drew the front draping of her skirt to one side, revealing first her thighs, then the juncture above.

She didn't look down, though, because if she did, she might stop. *Just keep watching Brent. Keep pleasing him.* His masculine gaze truly fueled her. Enough to make her pull the swath of yellow chiffon completely away. Enough to make her slowly part her legs for him.

His eyes narrowed at the sight and he looked more lust-filled than she'd ever seen him. She prayed she wasn't imagining it, because without that, without honestly believing he desired her, she couldn't do this. His heated expression made her spread farther, and farther still, until she knew she was fully displayed, not only for him, but for any other woman in the room who cared to glance over.

"Barbie," he said, "place this tray between Jenna's thighs." He motioned to the fruit-and-chocolate tray, and Jenna accidentally held her breath as the delicate, dark-haired girl approached a moment later, carrying out Brent's command. She felt like . . . an obscene dessert.

"Now, girls," Brent said, looking to both Barbie and Sasha, "I want you to taste her. I want you to stroke the fruit through her wet pussy and eat it."

Jenna began to shudder lightly, unsure if it was from repulsion or the bizarre excitement of such an utterly kinky command. But she still didn't say the safeword—and instead, it was Brent who began to speak, in a surprisingly soothing tone. "Jenna, I will take immense pleasure in this. And so you will do this for me, your master." He arched one dark eyebrow, like a firm nudge, and somehow—*somehow*—convinced her to let this happen. Oh Lord, she truly *was* an obscene dessert.

As the blond girl in blue picked up a strawberry, Jenna kept her gaze riveted on Brent, but he gave his head a short shake. "Look down. Watch."

With her knees slightly bent, she made herself glance downward as the pretty girl slowly raked the chocolate-dipped fruit through her most intimate folds. Jenna had mostly stopped shuddering now, but the new sensation made her tremble again, in—*oh my*!—a strange sort of pleasure.

She bit her lip, cautiously raising her gaze to see Sasha sensually bite into the moistened treat, then close her eyes, letting out a long, "Mmmm," looking as if she were savoring it.

Next, the dark-haired Barbie, just as pretty and lithe, stroked a piece of banana through Jenna's pinkness. Again, she watched. Again, she quivered lightly. God, it felt good. *Shockingly* good. But then, maybe *any* touch would right now. The way Brent watched her increased everything she felt.

Although she'd been tense and nervous when this had started, as the two harem girls continued to drag the strawberries and bananas through her cunt and eat them, purring in delight, Jenna began to relax more with each piece. She simply watched now, simply tried to accept the pleasure, shutting her eyes lightly each time it struck, then opening them again to see the girls eat the odd delicacy and let out soft moans. Soon, she was oozing with new moisture, especially when the girls swept the fruit over her clit. It had grown swollen; she felt the touches more and more each time.

Peering down, she saw that now Sasha's fingertips, too, touched her, from the particular way she held the fruit. Was Jenna getting the girl's fingers wet? And—oh Lord, why did that thought excite her? She'd never desired another woman in her life. And yet a stark, forbidden sort of arousal struck—coursing through her veins, and her pussy. Her own impassioned sighs now added to the sounds in the intoxicating room.

When she sensed movement nearby, she shifted her gaze to see Brent coming toward her. Her gaze locked on his, but in her peripheral vision, she couldn't help noticing the size of his erection through those thin pants, and it compounded her yearnings. Her pussy pulsed now—she felt her heartbeat there.

Kneeling between her legs, beyond the tray, he didn't smile as he plucked up a strawberry of his own and smoothly glided it deeply, oh so deeply, through her sensitive pink creases and over her clit in a way she felt even more than before. She watched him bite into it, chew, swallow. "Mmm, sweet," he said, gazing into her eyes.

She wanted, more than anything in that moment, for him to kiss her, to fuck her, madly. Now her whole *body* pulsed, every cell suddenly screaming to be taken by him.

But that wasn't what happened.

Instead, he simply lay back next to her in the colored pillows and said, "That was lovely to watch, my little slave girl. And now, I want *you* to learn the pleasures of watching, too."

With that, he pointed across the room to where the rest of the girls made out and caressed one another. "Watch," he said again, because she'd lowered her gaze automatically. "Your master demands it, Jenna."

Jenna took a deep breath. She knew she didn't have to do this—she could leave at any time—but, God help her, she *still* wanted to please him, give him what he wanted, make him proud, prove herself worthy of his attention and desire. And so she focused on a group of three girls, all with their breasts bared, softly touching each other.

"That's right," Brent whispered low and deep. "Just watch, honey."

That's when a buxom redhead bent to lick the nipple of an equally well-endowed blonde. And just as Jenna began adjusting to what she was seeing, a dark-skinned girl clearly of Middle Eastern descent crawled nearer to take the blonde's other hard nipple between her lips. The woman being pleasured let her head drop back in ecstasy for a moment, but then resumed watching the ministrations the same as Jenna did, beginning to stroke the hair of the two women suckling her. Jenna could have sworn she felt the suckling between her legs.

Especially when Brent, already leaning against her, slid his hand onto her thigh, gently caressing. Her pussy went crazy, just from that, and it was all she could do not to squirm and beg.

"Keep watching, Jenna," he had to instruct her again, and she realized her eyes had dropped to where he touched her—and at the same time she noticed something new: a small tattoo on his upper arm, the initials D.L.

When she looked back across the space, though, the view left no energy for wondering what the tattoo meant. Now the dark-skinned girl had backed away and the redhead suckled the blonde harder, using both hands to squeeze and mold the woman's large breasts. Soon the red-haired woman stretched out on her hands and knees, her face still buried in cleavage, the move encouraging the Middle Eastern girl to caress *her* now. Dark hands glided over the redhead's slender stomach, until finally the Middle Eastern girl situated herself behind the redhead to sensually massage her ass through emerald green chiffon.

At some point, Barbie pressed a fresh cup of wine into Jenna's hand and she began to drink, simply because it was there. Brent's scintillating caresses continued on her thigh, making her crazy, but her gaze remained riveted on the unfolding scene across the room.

The redhead kissed her way down the smooth stomach of the blonde as the darker girl kneaded her ass, finally pushing the green chiffon aside to deliver tender kisses there. Soon, the redhead was pushing aside *another* chiffon panel, this one fuchsia, to lick between the blonde's parted thighs. The blonde flinched and cried out her pleasure, and Jenna's stomach swirled with strange, forbidden excitement as she took another drink of wine and felt her cunt throb. Brent's hand caressed her mere inches away, but it felt like miles. Her swollen breasts ached for attention as well, and with every subtle move she made now, her chiffon top moved against her nipples, creating friction where she'd not noticed it before.

Across the room, the redhead ate the blonde vigorously, and the other girl now thrust two fingers into the redhead's pussy. Moans filled the room, and Jenna realized—remembered—that there were yet other women pleasuring each other among the pillows. The one that had hung on Brent's shoulder before now kissed another girl in a corner of the room, having pushed aside the girl's top. And another group of three convened near the steps that led into the pit—one girl lay between the other two, having her pussy rubbed by a petite girl with long, coppery hair while another busty blonde bent to dangle a bared breast into her waiting mouth.

It was so much to take in, Jenna barely knew where to look. Yet now, somehow, she wanted to see. She wanted to somehow . . . wallow in the wonders of it, trying to understand *why* she wanted to watch, trying to understand the excitement it produced inside her.

She drank more wine and feared her pussy would explode if it didn't get some attention soon. Brent's slow, confident caresses were driving her mad. She still suffered the urge to beg him, but simply could not. She scarcely understood why—this was by far the most sexually free she'd ever felt, *and* the most aroused, but she remained unable to ask, to let him know what she desperately craved.

Still, her breath grew labored, and whereas her legs had naturally closed after the fruit eating had stopped, now they'd parted again, just as naturally, so that when she glanced down, she saw she'd put her pussy back on display.

She almost snapped her thighs shut at the realization—but she stopped, forced herself to keep them open. She couldn't tell Brent what she wanted, yet . . . if she could just keep her legs spread for him, well, that alone seemed like a victory right now. Seeking a distraction from her own thoughts, she took another large drink of wine, draining her cup—and like an on-call servant, Barbie was right there, leaning over Jenna in her pretty chiffon to pour more.

It was as Jenna took the first swallow that Brent's caresses finally—finally!—advanced toward the juncture of her thighs. Oh God, *yes*! She parted wider, instinctively, hungry—*so* hungry—to be touched there. Her whole being ached and she took another large sip, this time trying to drown her need somehow, slow it, weaken it. But it made no difference—she needed sex like she'd never needed it in her life.

When Brent's fingers finally sank into her denuded pussy, she let out a guttural moan. At last. *At last!*

Brent's pleasure flowed through his lusty gaze. "Does that feel good, slave girl?"

"Yes. Mmm, *yes*."

As he began to stroke her, she moved against his hand, never even thinking to squelch the urge. *Yes, yes, yes*.

"Keep watching my other harem girls," he reminded her, and so she stared as the dark-skinned girl bent to eat the redhead from behind even as the redhead continued feasting on the blonde. Jenna thrust rhythmically at Brent's hand, and she discovered she also liked looking down, seeing his large fingertips buried in her pinkness, seeing the wetness she left on his hand. She would come soon, so soon.

But then—oh Lord, damn it, no—he drew his touch away!

She instantly whimpered, to which he responded, "Relax, slave girl—I'm not going anywhere." Thank God!

And already he was repositioning himself between her legs, stretching out on his hands and knees—after which he met her gaze to say, "Spread wide, so I can eat this pretty pussy until you come screaming."

She sucked in her breath, but didn't hesitate to do what he said.

And then came the hot joy that permeated her being. He licked her from bottom to top, slow, thorough, ending at her clit, which he sucked into his mouth briefly before letting it go. She cried out from the powerful pleasure bolting through her—then watched him do it again, again. Each lick produced a wild burst of heat inside her, so intense she could barely absorb it before the next arrived.

As her own moans mingled with those of other girls, she glanced from the beautifully obscene sight of Brent's face between her legs, wet now, to the forbidden liaisons taking place all around her. She thrust at his mouth, hard. And then she grew aware of . . . other hands . . . soft, feminine hands . . . on her arms, shoulders. Like earlier, Sasha and Barbie were gently caressing her, adding to the myriad sensations already assaulting her senses.

And then one of those small, feminine touches slid to her breast and she glanced to see Sasha skimming the back of her hand across Jenna's hardened nipple through the chiffon. She wanted to be appalled—instead she was thrilled. Her breasts ached, needing affection, and it didn't seem to matter where it came from at this point.

When Jenna didn't protest, Sasha lightly cupped her breast and stroked her thumb across the sensitive peak. *Oh God*—it felt different than when Brent or another *guy* touched her there; it was very clearly the touch of a woman. And it excited her to take pleasure in that, so much that she gushed with fresh moisture for Brent below.

More, please more. She needed more of *everything*. She couldn't ask for it—*still*, damn it—but she needed it badly.

Soon Sasha caressed one of Jenna's breasts while Barbie fondled the other, and finally, Sasha pulled aside the chiffon, sighing in delight. "So pretty," she murmured, sweeping the other chiffon cup away as well.

Below, Brent's licks sliced through her wildly, and their eyes met over her bared breasts, and she saw in his gaze the fiery pleasure he took in what she was allowing to happen. It made her thrust harder against his mouth—*hard, hard, hard*—still taking in the gentle caresses the girls delivered to her tits, lightly touching, tenderly twirling her nipples between their fingers.

And then, oh God, it struck—the wildest orgasm of her life. As

Brent had promised, she screamed as it barreled through her. She pumped at his mouth and thrust her breasts upward, still hungering for more sexy touches. She shut her eyes and let every hot pulse assail her, infuse her being, make her forget everything but coming, coming, coming.

And when finally it faded, she was ready to relax, recover—but before she could even process what had happened, Brent rose from between her thighs, his handsome face sticky from her juices, to say, "You did *so* fucking good, baby. Now get ready for more."

Chapter 6

Oh Lord, *more*? Right now?

And then it hit her—he was going to fuck her. With that big, hard cock that had been jutting through his pants like a missile through the entire fantasy. Thank God!

"Sasha," he said then, "come lick this sweet cunt, since I know you want another taste of it."

Just barely over her orgasm, Jenna's body went numb. *Sasha*? He wanted *Sasha* to eat her? Moreover, he wanted her to *let* Sasha eat her? *Enjoy* Sasha eating her? Above her then, she saw Sasha lick her lips and cast Brent a naughty grin while Barbie hovered on the other side.

Her eyes must have looked crazed, since Brent gazed down and lowered his voice in that commanding way. "Now you're going to please your master by letting lovely Sasha go down on you." Then, to her shock, he winked. "Who knows—you might like her tongue even better than mine."

Jenna said nothing, but sucked in her breath as Sasha and Brent quickly traded places, Sasha now on all fours between her parted thighs. Despite her orgasm, her pussy still pulsed, her heartbeat still pounding there. Barbie eased one arm around her shoulder and used her free hand to again lightly caress her breast. And—*mmm, God*—her cunt vibrated harshly; she was somehow truly excited again, that quickly.

So when Sasha's small tongue flicked over her clit, Jenna simply shuddered and sighed. Oh—oh, it felt good.

Sasha's next naughty lick was longer, like Brent's, traveling all the way up through her pink flesh, then running in a heated little circle around her still-engorged clit.

"That's so hot," Brent murmured, watching Sasha's ministrations closely. Then he used both hands to reach between Jenna's thighs and part the lips of her pussy even wider for Sasha's next oh-so-deep lick.

"Unh." Jenna heard herself groan as the sensation snaked through her, and despite herself, she was aroused by it *all*—by the way Brent held her open, wanting her fully exposed; by Sasha's eager, sensuous feasting; by the fact that now Barbie bent over her to massage her breasts, looking enraptured by her task.

Soon, though, Sasha stopped delivering licks and instead sucked on Jenna's swollen clit. Like before, with Brent, she couldn't help thrusting as moans of delight echoed from her. Nothing happening here made sense—this couldn't be her, this couldn't be real, it was all too strange—but the onslaught of pleasure made her forget all that as she simply sank into it, soaking it up.

As Sasha sucked her clit, Brent, now using only two fingers to part her pussy, dipped to lick her erect nipple. Barbie still squeezed and massaged both tits and it gave Brent the opportunity to draw Barbie's index finger into his mouth as Jenna watched. Once it was wet, Barbie extracted it, using it to dampen Jenna's other hard, pointed peak—after which she bent to lick it as well.

Oh—oh God. Jenna sighed her pleasure—it was too much, literally coming at her from all angles. It felt as if her body floated on an ocean wave as she thrust in a smooth, even rhythm, undulating between Sasha's mouth at her cunt and Brent's and Barbie's on her tits.

The whole room seemed to moan with her—she sensed pleasure all around her. She lifted her arms above her head in sweet abandon and let herself simply feel it, simply take it, everything Brent wanted her to have. "Oh . . . *oh,*" she heard herself groan deeply. She couldn't believe it, but just like last night, she was going to come *again.* From a woman's mouth this time. It seemed impossible.

But then the climax hit, shorter than the first—yet still harder, too. She didn't hold back—she couldn't, her pelvis jerking against Sasha's mouth of its own accord. But Sasha held on through the whole orgasm, during which Jenna heard herself crying out, "God, yes—oh, yes!"

When it passed and she opened her eyes, she spied Sasha between her legs, smiling lasciviously, then lowering a soft kiss near Jenna's belly button, above the row of gold medallions still holding her harem skirt in place. Likewise, Barbie gently kissed the side of her breast, smiling sweetly. And Brent hovered next to her, whispering, "So fucking hot, my little slave girl."

Then his voice took on a slightly more ferocious quality. "Now I'm going to give your hungry little pussy the last thing it needs tonight. Do you know what that is?"

With more boldness than she'd have believed she could show, she reached out and wrapped her hand around the thick column still poking at his pants. "This?"

He growled lightly at the touch, then said, "Mmm, yes, slave girl—*that.*" Then he yanked open the front of the thin white pants with one hand and his big cock burst free.

She gasped, and Barbie let out a hot sigh.

Jenna wasn't sure she'd ever wanted anything as much as she wanted that incredible appendage inside her right now, and she bit her lower lip in eager need.

Within mere seconds, Brent and Sasha had switched positions again, and now it was Sasha who held Jenna's pussy open with two hands—while Barbie reached boldly out, closed her fist around Brent's cock, and guided it to Jenna's opening.

When the head pushed in, Jenna moaned, feeling the entry in her gut. Then he drove inward, to the hilt, and she cried out as he groaned. Oh God, he was big! But good—so, so good inside her.

"How's that cock feel, my little sex slave?"

She could barely speak, so her words came out breathy. "Huge. Amazing. Like it fills every inch of me."

"It does," he promised her. "Your pussy is fucking *tight.*"

She drew in her breath as he began to move in her. Short, slow strokes at first that made them both let out heated sighs. Sasha caressed Jenna's inner thigh as he fucked her, while Barbie moved behind her, soon reaching around beneath Jenna's arms to resume fondling her tits.

When Jenna's eyes met Brent's this time, he didn't tell her to look anyplace else. In one sense, she could almost forget the other two girls were there, a part of their sex—but on the other hand, she stayed startlingly aware of their presence and excited to be sharing something so forbidden with Brent.

Soon he thrust harder, plunging deep, as he bent forward to nibble her breast. Barbie automatically lifted it for him, releasing Jenna's other tit to run her fingers through Brent's hair. While Sasha caressed Jenna's hip with one hand, she used the other to caress Brent, his back, his leg, eventually even grabbing on to his ass.

After a long while of kissing her welcoming tits, Brent rose back upright and resumed fucking her wildly. The girls still touched them both, heightening every sensation, and Jenna cried out at each body-wracking plunge. "So damn tight and wet," he rasped, teeth clenched, and she lifted to meet the brutal ramming of his rock-hard erection. She heard his cock moving in her wetness—the *slap, slap, slap* into her female juices—and knew she must be more drenched than ever before.

And just when she thought she'd felt everything there was to feel, she realized her clit was tingling hotly again—Sasha had reached down between her and Brent to rub it. Jenna's every upward thrust met Sasha's naughty touches as well as Brent's length—until Jenna exploded into orgasm yet again!

She screamed it out in earnest—there was no stopping her cries or holding them in. She screamed and screamed—until finally her body went so weak she feared she couldn't move another muscle.

And that's when Brent said, "Aw, baby, I'm gonna come. Gonna come in your sweet pussy—hard." His orgasmic strokes nearly lifted her from the pillows upon which she lay and she found herself reaching out, holding on to the cushions at her sides, trying to find purchase as he emptied into her.

Oh God. Oh wow.

Then he collapsed gently forward onto her body.

Over his shoulder, she saw Sasha and Barbie exchange lusty looks, as if maybe they finally needed some pleasure of their own—which in fairness, she could easily understand. And then they were gone, just like that, and Jenna sensed the entire room quietly emptying of all but her and Brent.

The fantasy was over. And she'd survived it.

Except—oh God, she truly couldn't fathom the things she'd done.

She'd thought sex with Brent had felt like sex with a stranger—but it measured nothing compared to the things she'd done here tonight—or had done *to* her.

And yet . . . she had responded. With orgasm after amazing orgasm. Three. Dear God. She hadn't known she could do that. As she rested her head more deeply in the plush pillows, she couldn't quite decide how she felt about it all.

A long moment later, Brent rolled off her onto his side. He propped one fist beneath his head and rested his other hand on her stomach. It made her look down at her askew harem girl outfit, her breasts and pussy still on display. She felt brazen. But she liked the way his hand looked on her skin.

"How are you?" he asked, gazing down.

She tried to sort through it. "Aghast," she finally replied.

"Don't be. It was a beautiful thing to watch and take part in."

She found herself shaking her head. "I've never . . . even thought about . . ."

"Shhh," he said. "Doesn't matter. It felt good. For you, tonight, that's all that counts. Accepting that it felt good. And that you're still the same person and that there was nothing wrong with it—no one got hurt; it was all about mutual pleasure."

She took in his words—all were true. Her life would still go on. She was the same person she'd been before this.

But . . . was she? Or hadn't something intrinsic changed inside her tonight? The real question, she decided, was how she felt about that and how she dealt with it. With secret shame or . . . secret satisfaction.

Brent opened his eyes to see Jenna in lovely disarray, curled against his body, her bare breasts pressed against his side.

Jesus God, she'd aroused the hell out of him. Sure, he could credit some of it to the other girls—any facilitator at the Hotel Erotique was super hot—but he knew himself and his body, and he knew most of his excitement tonight had come from Jenna's willingness. He'd always enjoyed watching girls together, but other girls who came here *wanted* what they were getting. To watch Jenna open herself to pleasure like that, to think of how far away that openness had been just a couple of days ago—shit, *that* was what had had his cock about to explode like a stick of dynamite.

He liked this too much, being both a guide and facilitator at once. Or maybe it was having her within his command that was getting him so worked up. Usually when he was in this position, it was with a woman who liked being submissive and wanted to play out that fantasy. But with Jenna, he was *making* her submit. His dick hardened further just to think about that: her trust in him, the way she liked pleasing him.

Of course, he couldn't make her be this submissive for long. The ultimate goal was to give her sexual freedom, and taking her through a light domination/submission process was only a means to an end.

And maybe that was why—when she opened her eyes, looking so fucking . . . ready to give, ready to submit some more—he left behind his plans, his scripted fantasies for her, and did something totally, completely selfish.

Or . . . maybe it *wasn't* a hundred percent just for him. Maybe it was simply the next step in her journey. Maybe he was just taking a cue from her that would pleasure them *both*.

Either way, nothing could have stopped him in that moment. Right now, he wanted what he wanted. To dominate some more. He'd made her *take* tonight—now he wanted to make her *give*.

So when she gazed up at him so pretty and open and innocent, he took her face in his hands and said, unsmiling, voice low, "Suck my cock, slave girl."

It stiffened him almost painfully when sweet Jenna didn't even hesitate. She simply moved down his body until she reached his already erect shaft, gently closing her hand around it. He sighed, drew in his breath. God, he *really* wanted this, really wanted to see and feel her mouth on him. "That's right," he urged softly. "Suck it."

And . . . mmm, that's what she did, sinking her warm mouth over the tip of his cock, then taking him farther, deeper, soon beginning to slide her lips up and down his rigid length.

He watched her, felt the power of her affections moving through him, and . . . *fuck*. What the hell was he feeling? Something too . . . tender, too soft. He ran his hands through her hair, felt the slow passion inside her as she found a steady rhythm, heard himself whispering, "So good, baby. So good."

Such sweetness wasn't what he'd intended when he'd told her to suck him—but something about her pulled at his heart. Even during the harem fantasy, there'd been moments when he'd let himself feel more gentle than he'd intended—and of course, he knew, again, this was exactly why guides never fucked their own guests. *But you're in this now, and you'll just have to work it out, that's all.*

As she sucked him some more, he remembered again how incredibly hot and beautiful she'd been with the other girls, all of them in their chiffon costumes looking like any man's dream come true. She was beginning to change, his Little Miss Sunshine, beginning to let go of her old sexual ideas. Even though they had a long road ahead, she was already experiencing things, because of him, that she never would have otherwise. And *that* made him feel powerful.

So when she looked up, her mouth stretched obscenely around the circumference of his thick shaft but her eyes still remarkably innocent, giving—hell, it pushed him over the edge in a way he hadn't seen coming. "Oh God, Jenna," he moaned, then did his best to physically lift her from his cock without being forceful—he didn't want to come in her mouth; he didn't think she could take that and it wasn't important to him.

"What?" she asked, looking worried.

"I'm gonna come," he growled. "Push your tits together for me."

Again, without hesitation, she did it.

And he took his throbbing cock in hand and helped himself the last bit of the way there, then groaned his pleasure as his hot semen shot onto her pretty breasts in three intense bursts.

She was breathing hard, looking down at her come-spattered tits as well, and it dawned on him that maybe—probably—no one had ever ejaculated with her like this before and she likely thought it was kinky as hell, like everything else he did with her. Releasing his dick, he cupped her breasts in his palms and said, "They look amazing this way."

"They do?" All innocence.

He simply nodded. "Hot. Dirty. It turns me on sometimes to come like that." Then he met her gaze. "And it would turn me on even more to watch you rub it in."

She sucked in her breath. And he almost thought of rescinding the request—this wasn't part of the plan, after all, and she surely needed some downtime, some safe time, without his sexual demands.

But he didn't. Because even if it wasn't part of the original strategy, this was no time to start letting her make choices or feel less submissive to him—it was too early for that and could cause her to regress.

So he simply looked at her, prodding her with his eyes.

And she slowly reached up and used both hands to gingerly massage his semen into her skin. It practically gave him another hard-on already to see her chest, tits, wet and shiny with his juices. "Sleep with it that way, me *on* you," he told her.

Again, she visibly pulled in her breath—but he said no more, growing quickly drowsy again. His eyes fell shut, yet that naughty vision of Jenna wet with his come stayed in his mind as he slept.

He awoke the next morning still in the harem room, still with Jenna cuddled against him. Damn, he must have been more tired than he'd thought. He guessed when the cleanup crew had peeked in to find them still there, they'd gone away, and he was glad. In all the evenings he'd spent in the sheik role, this was the first time he'd woken up the next day still amid the scattered pillows with a sexy harem girl in his arms.

"Morning," she said, those blue eyes easing open.

"Morning," he returned, trying not to put any particular emotion in his voice.

But then her arms looped around his neck and she proceeded to kiss him, and just like in the schoolroom, he couldn't resist. So he kissed her back for a long, hot, pleasant minute, even lifting his palm to cradle one bare breast—but when the kisses ended and she smiled into his eyes, he knew he had to put a stop to this. Because she was looking sort of . . . romantic. And in some other setting, some other world, he might have been inclined to do the same, but he had to snap out of it. He was her guide, her tutor. That was it.

So he sat up, out of her grasp, and pulled his pants together in front while making small talk. "You should go get some more sleep," he said, "since you'll need to stay well rested for your upcoming fantasies."

She sat up beside him. "Do I have any homework this time?"

He held in his smile. It didn't surprise him to learn Jenna really *was* a good student—apparently, once she committed to something, even "sex school," she intended to do a good job. And she was doing a *very* good job already. "Homework," he said, pondering it. "Let's keep this simple. I just want you to think about the various pleasures you experienced last night, and I want you to quit being *aghast* about it. You did admirably well—you were fucking amazing, actually—but we still have a long way to go and you need to be ready for it."

Meeting her gaze, he could see his last words clearly concerned her a little. And maybe that was good, given the next fantasy he had slated for her.

"The next one won't be so soft, sunshine. You should prepare yourself for that."

Jenna lay stretched out on a wicker chaise on her balcony that afternoon, doing her homework, even if it was all in the mind. But what she kept coming back to was his warning. Not so soft? He'd thought the harem fantasy had been *soft*?

Well, she understood that in a way—all the female curves, the lulling music, the soft fabrics and equally soft touches—but it had been a lot to handle at once. So it hadn't *felt* soft. Utterly *seductive*, maybe, but not soft. So what was coming tonight?

Although maybe she shouldn't worry so much about what was coming as what had already been. *Concentrate on your homework.*

She still couldn't quite believe she'd fooled around with other girls. Or let *them* fool around with *her* anyway—she hadn't exactly taken an active role. Still, even Shannon had never done that—other than one drunken bump-and-grind fest with a stripper in New Orleans at Kevin's prodding. Shannon had been red-faced telling her about it afterward, but had finally summed it up with, "What can I say? Something about it was really hot."

Jenna had concluded that a drunk Shannon was not a great judge of what was hot—but now she got it, sort of. Probably far more than Shannon did, actually. There was a world of pleasures to be experienced out there, and many of them simply weren't . . . traditional, not what anyone in her suburban neighborhood growing up had been raised to think was normal, by a long shot. But that didn't mean it didn't feel good. It had. And she supposed that here, at the Hotel Erotique, it *was* normal. Maybe Brent really *did* know exactly what she needed.

So as she peered out over the vast Caribbean waters in the distance, sparkling in the sunlight, she made herself a vow. Whatever was coming, she would take it. She wouldn't use her safeword. Whatever sex Brent thrust upon her, she would endure it. For him. And even for herself. If she could do what she'd done last night and come out feeling better, stronger, for it—instead of just freaked out and ashamed like she probably would have a few days ago—she could do anything he wanted her to. She would show him just how sexual she could be.

Not that she was sure when this had become about Brent. From the beginning, she supposed, at that first dinner. But if getting a little caught up in him was necessary to make her break out of her sexual shell, so be it. In fact, that was probably the only way this *could* happen. And when she left here, maybe she'd surprise herself and discover she *could* have casual sex more easily now; maybe she'd find she could appreciate it solely for the physical pleasure it brought, not the emotional part. Maybe.

Just then, a knock came on her door. She barely heard it from the balcony, but rose on bare feet to go answer. She opened it to find only a small black gift bag, which she picked up and took inside. Reaching into black tissue paper, she found a velvet jewelry box with a white envelope—and being a girl, she couldn't resist opening the box first.

But, lifting the lid, she didn't know what she was seeing. The little pieces of silver jewelry came in a pair, like earrings—but they weren't earrings. Although they were circular, open-ended, and unadorned. She sighed. God, she should have known a box from Brent wouldn't contain anything simple.

Which left her no choice but to rip into the white envelope, seeking answers.

Jenna,

These are nipple rings, which I picked out especially for you. Presuming you've never worn such jewelry before:

1. First, make your nipples hard if they're not already—although I've noticed with pleasure that yours are usually erect.

2. Slide on the nipple ring and overlap the ends, squeezing with your fingers until they're tight. They shouldn't be painful, but tight enough to feel them.

3. Wear them until the next time I see you.

Brent

P.S. I hope you weren't expecting earrings or a bracelet. ☺

Oh boy. *Just when you thought things couldn't get any weirder around here.* Nipple rings? Was he serious? *Oh, what are you thinking—of course he is.*

And, of course, he'd never know if she didn't put them on yet—she could keep them in the box right up until the next fantasy and he'd never know.

But . . . maybe she was curious.

And maybe she was truly starting to trust him more—at least about what brought her pleasure.

Hell, when else in her life would she have a good reason to put on *nipple rings*, for heaven's sake?

So, taking a deep breath, she carried the box into the bathroom to stand before the large mirror atop the sink. Then she reached up, drawing down the straps of the cami she wore and the bra underneath.

It struck her then how everyone had seemed so taken by her boobs last night. They weren't the perkiest pieces of her anatomy, which had always bothered her, but . . . they *were* ample and round, with large pink nipples that, as Brent had noticed, often stayed erect whether or not she was consciously aroused. So maybe they were . . . more striking than she'd ever realized.

In fact, now that she thought about it, some of the harem girls' breasts hadn't been as firm and porn-perfect as she might have expected, either, so . . . hmm. Maybe it meant breasts didn't have to be perfect to be appealing.

But she hadn't come in here just to analyze her tits.

Tits, she thought then, a little surprised at herself. She really *had* adapted to Brent's way of talking—shockingly fast. She could only blame it on the aura of lust and debauchery in the air here.

Finally, she reached into the small velvet box and drew out one of the nipple rings—a simple silver circle with tiny round balls on each end. Playing with it a bit, she discovered it was flexible, as he'd implied, and could be adjusted. As usual, her nipples were already pointing prominently, so she slipped the ring on her right nipple, then squeezed it enough to make it cling there.

After which she looked in the mirror, then bit her lip.

I look kinky.

Amused by the thought, she put on the other ring and looked again, unable to deny that feeling kinky was kind of *hot*.

Although she didn't think feeling kinky was the sole goal of the jewelry—the idea, he'd let her know, was to be physically aware of it. So she reached up, squeezing each ring a little tighter, until she suffered a soft pinching sensation that echoed through her pussy. That's when she realized the constant pressure of the rings probably *kept* a woman's nipples hard for as long as she wore them. Which likely kept her just slightly aroused for the duration. And that was probably the *real* purpose behind them.

Hmm. Well, she would see about that.

Jenna waited all afternoon to get a fantasy invitation—but it never came. And the whole while, her nipples stayed beaded tightly in the rings, keeping her very aware of them, making her wish she had Brent here to play with them or suck them like last night.

Finally, she put on a sundress, deciding to venture to one of the resort's restaurants for dinner. Given that she *was* at the Hotel Erotique, she wore one of her thinner, prettier bras underneath—and felt unduly sexy to leave the room with her nipples jutting through the pale blue fabric of her dress, knowing she still wore the nipple rings. Her pussy tingled within her lacy thong—not her usual undies, but another of the items bought specifically for her trip. Her only disappointment was knowing Brent wouldn't see them.

She chose a casual restaurant located on a deck overlooking the ocean, complete with tiki torches. The sun was just beginning to set as she arrived at the Paradise Grill, and a calypso band played on a small stage in the corner.

It was strange to sit down and look around at the other people—couples, friends, again knowing they were all here for extreme forms of sex. But she felt less embarrassed by it now than she had before.

She drank an erotic rum punch while she awaited her food, having chosen a simple barbeque sandwich with coleslaw and fries. If she had the night off, she was going to be low-key about everything, just relaxing and enjoying the downtime. Even if she continued to remain more aware of her body than usual. She wasn't sure whether to blame it on the nipple rings or on three successive nights of hot sex. But she tried to take pleasure from the awareness more than push it aside—because that's why she was here, right? To learn to enjoy her body. And besides, she knew more sex was coming, even if it wasn't tonight.

The food was good without being too filling, so she indulged in a piece of key lime pie for dessert, enjoying the Caribbean music and the vibrant colors left behind in the sky when the sun sank past the horizon.

When the band played a particularly upbeat instrumental tune, heavy on the steel drums, the lead singer—a tall, handsome black man with a light Jamaican accent—encouraged the crowd to dance. "Up on ya feet—everybody."

One couple took the floor, then another, soon joined by a group of three girls who looked a little tipsy on their heels but appeared to be having a good time. Probably because Jenna happened to be the only person dining alone, the singer—who bore a striking resemblance to Blair Underwood—wove through the tables to offer a smile as he held out his hand. "Dance with me, pretty lady."

She instinctively waved him away.

But then he cast a teasing look, an *enticing* look, and said with that soft island lilt, "Come now, lady—don't break my heart." He laid a dark hand across his chest. "Share a dance with me tonight."

And suddenly it hit Jenna: She wanted to dance with this man. Because it was a beautiful night and a warm tropical breeze wafted over the deck. And because the music was intoxicating and fun. And because she had on a pretty dress and there was simply no reason not to.

So this time she put her hand in his and pushed back her chair. He led her to the dance floor, where she found the beat easy to move to and realized she was truly enjoying herself. A few days ago? She never would've done something like this, simple as it was. Maybe with Shannon, but never by herself. She would have feared looking silly, tripping over her feet or dancing badly, people staring. But somehow, now, none of that mattered.

She danced with the handsome man for the remainder of the song, occasionally daring to smile up into his eyes—which were always on her when she checked, it seemed—and when the music ended, he gallantly kissed her hand and said, "Thank you for the dance, my dear."

A bit flushed but energized from the exertion, she headed back to her table—only to see Brent sitting there grinning at her.

"How long have you been here?" she asked, sinking back into her chair.

"Long enough to see a side of you I didn't know was there."

She lowered her chin thoughtfully. "Maybe I didn't, either."

"I like it."

She smiled, feeling a bit self-indulgent. "I think I do, too."

"I was afraid last night might have sent you swimming for the mainland, but it looks like you survived quite nicely."

"Oh ye of little faith," she shot back at him coolly, as if she hadn't indulged in ultra-kinky, near-orgy type sex last night.

"I have all the faith in the world in you, Jenna. And I'll have even more if you assure me you're no longer aghast."

She tilted her head, weighing how she felt—for some reason, Brent always made her want to be as honest as possible. "Yes, less aghast. Although . . . it seems surreal. Like something I could have dreamed—even though I've never had a dream like *that* before. I guess I've begun to learn that . . . I can find pleasure in things I never would have thought possible."

He gave a solemn but satisfied nod. "Very good, sunshine. And speaking of that, are you wearing what I sent you?"

The mere question made her pussy quiver. "Yes."

"Good," he replied simply.

"So . . ." she ventured, "do I have . . . plans tonight?"

He gave his head a short shake, and despite having already feared as much, she suffered a twinge of disappointment. "You get the night off to rest. I just happened to see this vision in blue dancing as I headed home, so I thought I'd stop and say hi."

She smiled. "I'm glad you did. But where's home? You live *here*, on the island, right?"

He nodded. "I have a private bungalow up the beach."

"Wow—sounds nice. I hadn't thought about what staff accommodations might be like."

"Only the other owners and I have houses," he explained. "Everyone else lives in apartments or dorms, depending on tenure."

She nodded, then let herself smile in amusement. "Tenure. Who knew the Hotel Erotique thought in such lofty terms?"

He chuckled warmly, but changed the subject. "You *will* have some more light homework, though. You'll find your assignment when you return to your room."

For some reason, that thought actually pleased her, but she didn't examine why.

Just then, Brent pushed back his chair, clearly preparing to go. "By the way, just because I saw you accidentally tonight, that doesn't mean you can take off the special jewelry I sent."

Hmm. "So you're saying you want me to wear it until . . ."

"Until I see you again. Tomorrow evening."

He looked arrogantly content with his answer. But her dance with her new Jamaican friend had her feeling a bit bolder than she sometimes did with Brent. "I *could* just take it off, then put it back on before I see you."

"You won't," he said, completely certain.

She tilted her head. "What makes you so sure?"

"You're an obedient little student, Jenna," he said, his voice still all confidence as he met her gaze, "and you do what I say."

She still wanted to fight back. "Maybe I'll surprise you."

"You already have. Every day since we've met. But you'll still do as I tell you." Then he leaned in and spoke lower. "Because you've begun to figure out that I know what I'm doing and that it all brings you more pleasure than you've ever known. Plus—you like pleasing your master," he added with a wink, then stood and walked away.

. . .

Dear Jenna,

Tonight and tomorrow, I want you to think about cock. Every cock you've ever had, or ever even seen. I want you to think about what a hard cock feels like inside you—in your hand, in your pussy, in your pretty mouth. I want you to think about the way it fills you and satisfies you in a way nothing else can. I want you to let yourself crave it.

And if anything about that is difficult, consider this: A woman's body was made to take a man's cock, to want a man's cock. It's far more natural to crave it than not to.

Tomorrow, the day is yours. Go to the beach or the pool—whatever you like. But keep thinking about cock. ☺

And be back in your room tomorrow by five.

Brent

P.S. I'd remind you to keep the nipple rings on, but I know I don't have to, my obedient slave girl.

Jenna followed Brent's instructions, and such bold, naughty thoughts came more easily than they would have before her arrival here. She thought through the sex partners she'd known in her life—a handful of guys, all of whom she'd felt deeply about. And she'd loved the way their cocks had felt inside her, yet . . . she'd often felt timid around the appendage, too. It was so . . . foreign compared to anything on a woman's body. And she'd been utterly shocked the first time she'd seen one—in a movie actually, as a young teenager, with Shannon, who'd insisted on watching R-rated films on cable when her parents were away one winter day.

Of course, she'd long since learned to appreciate the merits of a penis. But the truth was, she'd honestly felt more enamored of *Brent's* cock in the few short days she'd known him than in any she'd had before. It was so big, downright majestic looking, like one more ultra-strong, sure part of him. And he used it so damn well, too.

When he'd demanded she suck it in the middle of the night, the command had excited her and she'd instantly embraced her task. Which, now, struck her as odd since going down on a guy had never been her favorite activity. It was something she'd done to please her lovers, and she'd taken satisfaction from their pleasure, but she'd never taken *personal, physical* pleasure from the act—until last night. She'd *wanted* to get up close and personal with Brent's magnificent shaft.

In addition to thinking about cocks, though, Jenna also found herself thinking about breasts, nipples. Her own. She'd felt ridiculously erotic showering in the nipple rings—which seemed content to hug the pink peaks pleasantly tight without ever growing uncomfortable.

And sleeping in them—in a cami and boy-short panties—kept her in a slight but constant state of arousal all night. She had vague dreams—of Brent, and harem girls, and hard cocks—and she woke more often than usual, repeatedly finding herself reaching up to touch, to see if the tips of her breasts were *still* hard, *still* encircled, and they always were.

The next morning, as she donned her bikini, she found herself again enjoying the kinky look of her tits in the mirror. And as she took a lounge chair at the pool, it titillated her to know she wore the rings beneath her leopard print, and that they likely made her nipples protrude even more than usual through the tight Lycra. Every time she spoke to an even remotely attractive man—a waiter at the pool or anyone else—her pussy surged with the mere thought of how hard the guy would get if he knew about her hidden jewelry.

She tried to read more of the Civil War memoir, realizing she'd barely read thirty pages in five days. Yet she simply couldn't concentrate. Her pussy tingled too pleasantly from the effect of having worn the nipple rings for nearly twenty-four hours now—and from simply feeling sexy in her bikini, her body stretched out across the chaise in the sun.

So she simply soaked up the rays, drank a couple of erotic rum punches, ordered a sandwich for lunch from her spot by the pool, then returned to her room by five, as Brent had instructed.

Walking in, she found a large black gift box on the bed, tied with red ribbon. A black envelope rested on top.

As usual, she couldn't bear to open the envelope first, going straight for the box. Standing there in her bikini, she briskly untied the ribbon, yanked off the lid—and gasped. Inside rested an elaborate outfit of black leather. The main item: a boned leather corset with thick shoulder straps, but the molded cups for her breasts looked tiny. Next she encountered a pair of black fishnet stockings—then realized the corset possessed garters. Digging deeper in red tissue paper, she drew in her breath upon discovering a pair of high leather boots with the same stripperlike platform heels she'd worn with her Catholic schoolgirl outfit. And then—oh, dear God—she came across what appeared to be a black leather . . . collar, decorated with silver rings, and two matching . . . cuffs, to be worn on her wrists perhaps? Underneath it all lay a black vinyl trench coat—to wear over the naughty outfit when leaving her room, she supposed.

The truth was—by the time she'd examined the whole outfit, her heart beat like a drum against her chest. Despite Brent's warnings, she'd not thought much about what lay ahead—which was just as well, since she couldn't have imagined . . . this.

Barely able to think straight, she tore into the envelope to extract an invitation, this one on thick red paper, printed with black ink in a rather menacing-looking font.

You Are Invited to a Fantasy

Where: The Dungeon (*map included*)
When: Tonight, 10:00 p.m. *Don't keep the Master waiting.*
You are to be the Master's new sex slave tonight,
coming to him in a state of complete submission.
Eat before you arrive—a meal will be delivered to your room.
Then prepare yourself for a night of bondage, domination, and submission—
resulting in brutal pleasure.
(Your safeword is Susan B. Anthony.)
(But a submissive slave wouldn't even think about saying it.)

Chapter 7

Brent sat on the master's throne in the resort's dungeon, wearing black leather pants and a black leather vest with slashes in the fabric, awaiting Jenna's arrival. Tonight was make-or-break. Either she'd survive this fantasy and go all the way, or she'd use the safeword and end it all. Brent's only worry: Would it be too much for her?

The goals were the same as last night's—but more intense. Tonight she would be instructed not only in taking, but in giving. Tonight she would be exposed to rougher sex—and other partners, not just women this time. Tonight he would teach her that sex didn't have to be gentle to be good. *No silk sheets and violins for* you, *sunshine.*

He hoped like hell she'd stick this out and keep trusting him. It had to happen for her to make the leap to true sexual comfort and freedom. She might never do anything this wild again, but she had to do it tonight if she were to be truly, deeply happy in her sexuality. It was just her bad luck she'd gotten ugly impressions of sex in her youth—but since she had, and since it had affected her lifelong outlook on the activity, she had to take big, definitive steps to alter those perceptions.

Despite himself, he would take it personally if she opted out. Not only would he fear he'd failed her—but he would fear for the rest of her sexual life. Oh, he knew she'd be okay—not miserable or anything—but he wanted more than that for Jenna. He wanted her to know every possible pleasure, every joy. And besides, he'd be sorry to see her leave, since he was enjoying this particular challenge—as well as the guest who'd challenged him. His cock was already stiff, not only because playing the dominant came so easy to him, but because he ached to see her nipples wrapped with those tight silver rings.

Glancing around the room, he thought briefly through his plans for her. BDSM tools and toys hung on the pegboard secured to the fake stone walls across the room and lay upon the black wooden bench in front of it. Nearby, adjustable-length chains for securing slaves extended from the pseudo–rock wall, along with a variety of cuffs and harnesses. Various padded tables dotted the space, some with chains attached, others with leather restraints, still more with cuffs at each corner or steel rings for slipping ropes or other tethers through. Far to his right stood the whipping post and what the facilitators casually referred to as the pommel horse, an apparatus for bending someone over for spanking or fucking. And near the door hung the black bands of the room's two sex swings, and beyond that, the stocks and cage.

The room was specially designed to make visitors feel they'd gone underground—even though that would be impossible on a small island. Jenna would soon be entering a building on the ground floor, following her instructions toward a set of dark, winding stairs that led downward—but the structure had been built on a slope, and the entrance just happened to be on a higher piece of land than most of the island.

Throughout the room, facilitators stood chatting, ready to take their places when she arrived. For tonight in particular, he'd chosen people who fit everything he knew about what appealed to her on both a conscious and a subconscious level. And while he'd told her it was possible other guests could show up in her fantasies, mostly, Jenna would encounter only trained facilitators—given her trepidations, he couldn't risk including someone he didn't know. Especially tonight.

Now he had to hope he had it all *just right*.

He sighed, thinking ahead to the evening. If it went well, he would enjoy it tremendously, as he had the previous fantasies he'd created for her—but even if she didn't use the safeword at any point, she still might be angry with him when this was over. So be it. Going soft on her wouldn't give her what she needed now.

So tonight, everything coming her way would be very *hard*.

Trust me, sunshine. Be a good little submissive and trust me.

. . . .

Jenna walked the distance from her room slowly. Despite feeling weirdly on display—black coat or not, it was pretty easy to tell she was on her way to a fantasy—she didn't want to twist an ankle in the high boots. Thankfully, it was dark and she didn't encounter anyone along the path, and by the time she reached the stairway with a downward-pointing sign that said DUNGEON, she thought she'd mastered the boots.

The fact was, after checking herself out in the mirror, she'd felt like a sex queen. A dominatrix. A woman far bolder—sexually—than she could ever be. If the ensemble had come with panties, she was sure they'd be soaked by now, especially when she added her ongoing arousal from the nipple rings and other less obvious stimuli from the last day and a half. So she was very ready for sex.

She was just scared to death about what she'd find at the bottom of these stairs.

Please let it be only Brent. More slave play she could handle, even though it would obviously be darker than last night's. Domination, submission—she thought she could handle that, too—so long as Brent was the only other person involved. And maybe he was intuitive enough to realize that. God knew he'd been intuitive enough about her so far.

She still couldn't believe she was *starting out* the evening pantyless, though—that her cunt was completely bare beneath the coat, without even the sheer covering her harem skirt had provided. The corset itself extended to her hips, but not beyond—and the boning made her feel very *bound* already. Which was the idea, she supposed. As she'd suspected, the leather cups for her breasts were small, just barely covering her nipples, and the corset shoved her breasts high, making them look plump and sexy.

Yet, of everything she wore, as weird as *all* of it felt, the most unsettling accessories were the collar and wrist cuffs. They weren't uncomfortable, but in her mind, they lifted the kinkiness of the outfit to a whole different level. Even so, she'd tried—for Brent, and for herself—to embrace this as much as possible, even applying exaggerated eyeliner in some attempt to look a little more daring than usual.

Reaching the bottom of the steps, she encountered a heavy wooden door. Taking a deep breath, she turned the knob and stepped inside.

But this clearly wasn't the dungeon—this was some sort of entryway to the dungeon, just like she'd gone through for her other fantasies. Although she'd dressed in her room, she could see the same clothing hooks and closets she'd encountered en route to the schoolroom and harem room.

Just then, the door on the opposite wall of the small space opened and in stepped a beautiful . . . *porn star*. That's all Jenna could think, since that's what the girl looked like. The blonde was gorgeous and topless, with large, perfect boobs. She wore a miniscule leather skirt with black stockings and black patent-leather stripper heels. Both the skirt and shoes possessed lots of silver buckles. "You must be Jenna," the girl said as naturally as any party hostess.

Taken aback, Jenna could only nod.

"I'm Serena," the petite but buxom blonde said. "Let me take your coat."

Jenna could barely breathe as she untied and unbuttoned the long trench—and when she slipped it off, she was trembling with nerves.

Serena noticed. After tossing the coat on a wall hook, she turned back to Jenna with what looked like genuine concern. "I know you haven't played any BDSM games before, but there's nothing to be afraid of—I promise."

"Okay," Jenna managed to eke out, yet she knew she didn't sound convinced.

Serena held up one finger. "I'll be right back," she said, and not thirty seconds later, she returned with a glass of white wine. "Here, drink this. It'll help."

Jenna took it, sat down on the padded bench near the door, and sipped. She'd downed half the bottle of pinot grigio that had come with dinner, but that had been hours ago. It just now occurred to her that Brent had probably sent it to relax her before the fantasy. So she drank more from her glass, eager to take the edge off her anxiety.

Serena sat down beside her, shifting to face her. "About the BDSM—let me assure you no one here would ever do anything to cause you real pain unless you specifically requested that, and even then, we have our limits. Your fantasy tonight isn't about pain—it's about discipline and obedience. I hope that helps assuage your fears a little."

"Actually, it does." Deep down, she knew Brent wouldn't hurt her, but given the setting and lack of control involved, it was a little scary. "Brent always says that everything he designs for me will ultimately bring me pleasure." She supposed she was reaching out to Serena for even more reassurance.

"Completely true. After all, that's what we're all here for," she added with a smile as she squeezed Jenna's hand.

You seem so nice, Jenna wanted to say. *Why do you work here?* Why did *anyone* work here? But then, why was she here herself? Maybe the circumstances that brought someone to the Hotel Erotique were too complex to be tackled in pre-fantasy small talk.

"Drink up," the topless Serena said, then widened her eyes playfully. "And let yourself get excited about this!"

"Okay," Jenna said, finishing the wine and setting the glass beside her.

Then she watched as Serena reached into the nearby chifforobe and pulled out a long, thin length of leather—which she then smoothly snapped onto one of the decorative rings on Jenna's neck collar.

Oh God. Oh shit. They weren't just decorative. "Um . . ." she said nervously.

But Serena acted as if it were nothing. "Just a little leash," she said. "Remember, you're Brent's new slave tonight—and it's my job to deliver you. And . . . I might not seem as friendly once we're inside, but that's just part of the game. Don't be afraid. Let your body love this."

With that, she opened the door and pulled gently on the leash, and Jenna literally had no choice but to follow her through—into what looked like a true dungeon, complete with curving rock walls and ceiling. Except, glancing around the room, she could see this wasn't a place where people were banished to die—it was clearly where people came to be punished.

Brent sat in a large black chair atop a small pedestal, but Jenna was so busy taking it all in—the strange, scary equipment and the other men and women in the room, all wearing more domination-style black leather or shiny vinyl—that she didn't even look at him at first. He'd been right—the harem fantasy had been a walk in the park compared to this. She wished she were back in the harem room in her flowy chiffon right now.

"The new sex slave, master," Serena said, leading Jenna to Brent's perch.

Their eyes met, only for a second, before his gaze swept down her body. He didn't smile, but she wasn't surprised. She wasn't expecting many smiles here. "Chain her to the wall," he said.

The wine had just hit her and she went light-headed. *Chain her to the wall?* But when Serena tugged, she followed—what else could she do?

Say Susan B. Anthony, a little voice in the back of her mind answered.

But a submissive slave wouldn't even think *about saying it.*

Never use your safeword out of fear.

And this is only fear. Calm down. It will all be okay.

She stood obediently, trying to relax her breathing, as Serena pushed her back to the wall directly across from Brent, from which chains protruded at various heights. Serena secured one of the chains to her collar, after which she removed the leash. Then she hooked chains to each of the cuffs on Jenna's wrists. Thankfully, their length left plenty of room to move around if she chose—but she still felt trapped. Why on *earth* did that make her pussy spasm?

"Get her tits out," Brent commanded then, making Jenna flinch atop her impossibly high heels. "But be careful—she's wearing nipple rings."

With movements still as smooth as silk, Serena reached up to draw down the leather cups covering Jenna's breasts. And there she was, as topless as Serena—and bottomless, too—in a room full of strangers.

And, of course, her breasts, nipples, remained sensitive and aroused from the rings—and a glance toward Brent told her he knew it. "The nipple rings suit you, slave."

Jenna wasn't sure how to reply. "Thank you," she answered feebly.

"Master," Serena whispered next to her.

"Huh?"

"Thank you, *master,*" she said softly. "You must always address him as master."

"Thank you, *master*," Jenna repeated, but the words came out light, barely audible, because this felt so strange.

"Attach a nipple chain, Serena," he instructed, and while Jenna waited to see what the hell *that* was, she realized her breasts were heaving a bit—still from nervousness, but also from the stark arousal she'd been suffering. Nothing here should *be* arousing her—and nothing *was*, mentally—but after so much unanswered lust, her body seemed to be responding to the hard sexual aura of the setting: the clothes she wore; the men and women staring at her breasts and pussy right now; and knowing that whatever Brent wanted to give her here, she had to take. Unless she ended it all with the safeword. She'd decided unequivocally not to use it, but this fantasy had her reconsidering that.

Serena returned from a nearby cabinet with a much smaller chain in hand—thank God—than those that held Jenna to the wall. Carefully, she slid one link at the end of the silver chain onto the overlapping end of one nipple ring, then repeated the process at the other breast, leaving the length to dangle in a semicircle between Jenna's boobs. Glancing down, she noticed black beads decorating the chain, like a necklace—except it hung from her nipples.

"What's it for?" she asked Serena.

"Did I give you permission to speak, slave?" Brent boomed from his chair.

Jenna flinched, but no one else seemed surprised. "Um, no," she managed timidly.

"You do not speak unless spoken to. You are here for *my* pleasure, to do *my* bidding—nothing more. Do you understand that?"

She swallowed nervously around the lump rising in her throat and forced a nod. She couldn't speak at will? That made her uncomfortable.

"Serena," he said, still sounding brusque, "you may tell the new slave the purposes of the nipple chain."

Serena looked to Jenna and said, "Two purposes. It looks sexy. And this." She reached up, curled the tip of her index finger under the dangling chain, and gave a light tug.

Which sent a burst of sensation that straddled the line between pleasure and pain shooting through Jenna's breasts and outward.

"Ooooh," she sobbed lightly, noting the dark amusement on Serena's face.

After this, Brent left his chair, moving in a leisurely manner, not meeting her gaze as he walked past to take something from the wall at her left. Then he came to stand in front of her—looking frighteningly handsome tonight, she realized—holding on to a tool which she recognized, sort of, from her studies of Medieval times. Designed to look like a cat-o'-nine-tails—a torture device—this was smaller and constructed of thin leather strips, both black and red. It resembled a limp leather pom-pom—but would clearly inflict pain. "Have you ever seen a flogger before, slave?"

Now he met her gaze, but it didn't feel like she was looking at Brent—she was actually a little frightened of him right now, and so far, she didn't like this fantasy very much. She shook her head, afraid to answer audibly.

"A flogger can be used in *soft* ways," he said, his voice growing slightly more gentle as he dragged the leather strips across her breasts, making them tingle and ache, then down her arm in a caress that left her burning for his touch.

"Or," he went on, "it can be used to *punish*." She feared he might strike her, but instead he snapped the tool harshly against his own thigh. "Be a good, obedient little sex slave and you won't have to suffer the latter."

She wasn't sure whether to nod, so she didn't—simply suffered the unexpected ribbons of pleasure that fluttered through her in response to the flogger's fingerlike strips.

"Now," he said, turning back to Serena, "take that to the new slave." He pointed to a small, round stool, the seat padded in black leather, like so much else in the room.

Serena situated the stool against the wall beside Jenna.

Brent then pointed at it again. "Sit, slave."

Jenna sat, made aware of the chains that bound her, when she moved—and of her bare ass, when it encountered the leather.

"Now spread your legs wide."

The demand caught her off guard and the very idea left her feeling horribly exposed. So much that she considered refusing. But that was fear talking, and Brent's words echoed in her head once more. *Never use your safeword out of fear.*

So Jenna took a deep breath and slowly parted her legs—mostly covered with her boots and fishnets—as wide as she comfortably could, putting her surely glistening pussy on full display for everyone in the dungeon. The move made her swallow nervously—yet again, she oozed with unexpected, unbidden excitement. God, how strange.

Brent now passed his flogger to Serena. "Tease her cunt," he instructed simply.

So Serena knelt between Jenna's thighs and gently began brushing the flogger up and down through her pussy as if it were a feather duster and Jenna's crotch needed tidying.

And—oh God—it was hard not to react. The fact that her cunt was shaved left the soft skin there ultrasensitive to such a light touch. Not to mention the effect the tender strokes had on her clit, which she suspected had been protruding from her slit long before she'd parted her legs at Brent's command.

Again and again, Serena swept the flogger between her thighs, and it was impossible for Jenna to hold in her sighs, impossible not to thrust ever so gently against it.

She didn't look at Brent—for some reason, she didn't want to acknowledge to him how much pleasure this particularly kinky act was bringing her. At moments, she looked at Serena, but that felt odd, too, and at other moments, she simply looked down, at the flogger and her pussy—but again, weird. So finally, she just closed her eyes—and then, oh God, she *really* felt it, even letting a soft moan escape her lips.

"Gabe, Zack, secure the new slave's arms tighter to the wall."

Brent's voice briefly interrupted Jenna's pleasure to make her glance up, but her pussy felt so swollen and hot now that even this command didn't frighten her the way it might have just minutes ago. Maybe she was starting to get accustomed to the game here.

In fact, rather than worry about what was happening, she found herself more interested to see exactly who was joining the festivities—

and, oh my, her whole body warmed further at the sight of the two strapping, muscular guys heading her way through the dim lighting.

She decided the one with the large Z—like the mark of Zorro—tattooed on his arm was surely Zack. Sporting long, dark hair and a silver hoop earring, he looked like . . . a biker or someone equally as dangerous. Gabe, on the other hand, was—oh shit, how had she forgotten? Gabe was her greeter and co-pilot! He looked scruffy but sexy tonight, his dark blond locks messy, a light, stubbly beard shading his face.

She stayed utterly brave as the two men positioned themselves on both sides of her and pulled on the chains attaching her to the wall—simultaneously hoisting her arms from her sides to an outstretched position, as if she were being crucified. The move thrust her breasts forward, jiggling her nipple chain lightly, and though it was far less comfortable than before, the cuffs supporting her wrists were soft, and the flogger at her cunt continued to deliver delectable sensations. The position somehow left her feeling even more on display, but despite herself, that only upped her excitement.

When a large shadow moved over her, she looked up to see Brent—easily lifting one leg over the kneeling Serena to bring his bulging crotch eye level with Jenna. She leaned her head back to peer up at him—and oh God, he felt powerful and ominous looming over her, muscular and hot.

But she instantly drew her eyes downward when he began working at the front opening of his leather pants, and a few seconds later, his big cock came free, somehow appearing more enormous than usual just an inch from her face.

He took his hard shaft in hand, bending it toward her, and said, "Suck it, slave." Then he smoothly fed it to her.

She accepted it willingly, at once stunned but not, at once embarrassed at performing such an intimate act in front of others . . . but not. Pure, hot, animal lust overrode every negative emotion and in that moment, she became—truly—his willing slave in a way she had not before now. Something about that strange pleasure, the heat of sucking his cock mixed with having no choice, no control, enslaved her to him. She suddenly didn't mind that her arms were being stretched and that she had no use of them. She didn't mind the harsh setting, her harsh master, the strangers surrounding her. Nothing else mattered in those moments but sensation, both physical and mental.

Brent moved his rigid length in and out of her accepting mouth like a piston, emitting low sounds of pleasure with each steady thrust. Soon, he held her head with both hands, threading his fingers through her hair. As Serena pleasured Jenna, Jenna pleasured Brent, and she found a primal joy in being a tool for his gratification. Part of her, her logical self, thought she should have felt devalued, degraded—and yet . . . there was something deeper at work here. Because she felt completely the opposite. She felt vital, giving, like a fully realized sexual being, as she'd yearned to feel in the harem room last night. She was surrendering to him everything he asked—demanded—of her, and with it came an undeniable freedom she'd never experienced.

She felt free to suck his hard cock with unbridled enthusiasm, even as Gabe and Zack watched closely. She felt free to accept the pleasure Serena's flogger delivered so gently, along with the more brutal pleasure of having Brent drive his cock repeatedly toward her throat. She felt free to be sexy and dirty in front of everyone in the room. She felt free to give herself over to whatever Brent wanted.

"That's good, baby, so fucking hot," Brent murmured above her in the darkest voice she'd ever heard from him. He *sounded* like a master and she loved pleasing him. "Suck that big cock, my nasty little slave. Let me fuck your warm, sweet mouth."

Something about it all, about being restrained yet confident, forced yet pleasured, left Jenna feeling shockingly empowered—so that she sucked Brent's shaft still more vigorously, no matter how stretched and tired her lips became, so that she moved her pussy against the strokes of the flogger almost involuntarily now.

Until she came—*hard*, so very *hard*, sobbing her orgasm around Brent's erection, letting it all flow through her, rocking her body, her very soul. She'd never been so entranced and freed by any sexual act in her life.

As the orgasm passed, Brent pulled back, extracting himself and using his hands to tilt her face upward. "You did *very* well, Jenna," he told her, sounding somewhat like the Brent she knew but still in master mode. She didn't care, simply glad to have satisfied him, her body still winding down from the intense climax.

And then it hit her—oh God, oh wow, *that* made her come. Being restrained. Forced. And she suddenly wasn't very sure she liked it.

It's the two-day arousal, she assured herself. That's all. She'd just needed to come so badly.

She took a deep breath and got hold of herself, still a little stunned by it all. Then she looked back up into Brent's eyes. Yes, still in master mode. But despite herself, she *remained* aroused. On some level, it excited her even *more* just to know she *could* be pleasured by what had just taken place here.

"Nicholas, take Amira to the swing and fuck her," Brent said then, surprising Jenna by focusing on someone other than her. She felt almost relieved, watching as a cute blond guy grabbed on to the hand of a dark-haired girl—whom Jenna recognized as the Middle Eastern girl from the harem—and led her to a contraption of black bands sewn together and hanging from the ceiling. As Amira reclined among the bands—which did indeed form a flexible sort of swing—she shimmied out of a pair of leather panties.

"Gabe," Brent added, "tie Serena to the horse and fuck her, too."

As Serena was escorted away, toward something that looked like a gymnast's pommel horse minus the handles, Jenna's pulse kicked up. Because of all the new, rough sex beginning to take place around her and because, oddly, she felt as if she'd lost her one comrade in the room with Serena's departure. Brent *should* be that, but tonight, he wasn't—even when he approved of her.

With her arms still stretched, she watched fair-haired Nicholas pull a string that brought his cock lurching forth from his pants. She noticed it was smaller than Brent's and possessed a slight curve—right before he drove it between Amira's thighs. She cried out and Jenna flinched, her breasts jiggling.

She was just getting accustomed to watching Nicholas and Amira when a female moan drew her attention across the room. She expected to see Serena being fucked, but instead she was simply being tied—and apparently taking great pleasure in it. Her body straddled the horse, as Brent had called it, her rear elevated at one end, peeking from beneath her tiny leather skirt—apparently, she hadn't worn panties, either. Gabe wrapped a rope around her body, circling it and the horse repeatedly, and with each length that crossed her back, she emitted another sound of pleasure.

Within moments, Gabe revealed a sizable cock that looked red and formidable in the brief seconds Jenna glimpsed it before it plunged into Serena from behind. Then both girls were crying out at the rough thrusts being delivered, the guys grunting and groaning their pleasure, and Jenna barely knew where to look—but her pulse raced still more wildly, her pussy already swollen and sensitive again.

Oh Lord, how had she gotten excited again that quick? But she supposed it was like with the harem—if the stimulation kept coming, her body kept responding. Now the stimulation was all visual and audible, stunning her with how powerful that could be.

Only when she looked for Brent did she realize he'd returned to his thronelike chair, lounging there like a well-satisfied prince of darkness. His cock still jutted from his pants, magnificent as ever, and she wondered how he looked so satisfied without having come. He seemed so in control of his body that she was beginning to find it intimidating. Especially since she seemed so . . . *lacking* in control.

"Zack, go to the cabinet and get the newest glass dildo."

Jenna sucked in her breath. A glass dildo? And they had so many that one was clearly the newest? Could this get any kinkier?

Another two girls and a guy still hung in the shadows of the room and Jenna waited with odd fascination to see what happened next. Who would this glass dildo be used on? And when she saw the other faces, would there be more she recognized?

Meanwhile, her eyes were drawn back to Amira and Nicholas and their naughty sex swing. Amira's boobs bounced, her body jerking with each stroke from Nicholas, and Jenna's cunt pulsed harder still. She felt caught in a porn movie. Not that she'd ever seen one—but she couldn't imagine them being any wilder than *this*.

When she found herself switching her gaze toward Serena on the pommel horse, she instead spotted Zack with—oh my—a shocking, clear dildo that made her gasp. Probably ten inches long and considerably thick, it came with a ball-type knob on the tip, and the handle, as lengthy as the phallus-shaped part, consisted of a succession of smaller glass knobs. Brent looked to the bizarre tool in Zack's fist and smoothly commanded, "Fuck our new slave with the glass cock."

And all the blood drained from Jenna's face.

The second Zack knelt before her, she instinctively snapped her thighs shut. Because that *couldn't* go inside her. It was too strange. Invasive in a whole new way. Brent was pushing her too far.

But the defensive closing of her legs brought him instantly to his feet—he looked like an angry god, fury blazing in his gray eyes. *"Do you want to be flogged, slave? The hard way? If not, spread your legs—now!"*

The threat silenced the room—the couples having sex went still as Jenna's whole body tensed.

Could she? Do this?

Despite herself, her pussy ached for more attention.

But . . . this kind?

"Do it!" Brent demanded, and their eyes met.

And she knew she had two choices. Say her safeword—or part her legs.

Slowly, she spread her thighs, again making her pussy available for viewing—and fucking.

Still kneeling before her, Zack moved closer and lifted the glass tool, gently sliding the shockingly unyielding tip up and down against her folds—letting her get used to it, she realized. It was so amazingly hard, with no give or flexibility, that it scared her. So she held very still, focusing on the Z on his arm as he inserted the head—making her let out a small noise—then slid it deeper.

I should be horrified. I have not exchanged even a word with this guy. And if I thought everything else I've done was kinky . . . well, this tips the scales. A glass dildo. Being inserted into me by a hot, dangerous stranger.

But the *truly* horrifying part, it turned out, was how her excitement escalated with the glass toy inside her. Watching it move in and out was . . . amazing. Inside the walls of her cunt, the head was so unforgivingly rigid, rubbing against her with each gentle stroke, that she almost thought she could come without clitoral stimulation. She heard her own breath as she drew it in, let it back out, awash in astonishing pleasure.

Zack began to whisper to her, too low for Brent to hear. "What a hot, wet pussy," he breathed, peering up at her with dark, seductive eyes. "I love watching the glass glide in and out of your pretty pink flesh. Mmm, I bet it's warm in there. I bet it's fucking *hot*. I wish I could slide my cock in and find out." And like everything else happening in the dungeon, Jenna wanted to be appalled, but instead she was involuntarily aroused. God, maybe Brent was right. Maybe dirty talk *did* turn her on.

Without quite meaning to, she began to lift her pelvis ever so slightly toward the inward thrusts Zack delivered.

"That's much better, slave," Brent said from his throne.

Then, casting a mischievous smile Brent still couldn't see, Zack leaned forward, bit down on the chain dangling between her nipples, and gave a slight pull.

And, oh God—what a hot burst of pleasure / pain! She moaned. Met his gaze. Felt they shared some sort of obscene secret now.

"Jason, Decker, go watch the new slave take the glass cock," Brent said.

So Jenna lifted her gaze to see two more men exit the shadows and head her way, both sporting dark hair and muscles. The one who'd responded to the name Jason wore his hair short and looked like a tough guy, and Decker was . . . a more devilish version of Brent himself—midthirties, but with slightly longer hair, curling at the ends, and a goatee. Both dripped with an undeniable sexual energy she felt. Or—who knew—maybe it was just the glass dildo in her cunt skewing her thoughts, turning every sight, every person, into something lust-worthy.

"Jason, kneel on one side of her—Decker on the other," Brent instructed. "Then suck her tits. But don't suck the rings off—I want those left on."

Oh shit. Three guys at once? Doing unthinkably intimate things to her?

Maybe, all things considered, it was no more shocking than anything else she'd done, but it felt that way. Three. All strangers. She suffered the urge to cover her breasts, but of course, her arms were chained to the wall. She drew in her breath, suddenly feeling vulnerable again, more than at any point so far.

Damn it. Should she do this? Or should she end the madness and say Susan B. Anthony, once and for all?

But she couldn't think straight because Brent had sensed her reaction and was back on his feet, pinning her in place with his gaze from across the room. "Remember the flogger, slave. What I give you, you take. Now take it!"

You should say it. Susan B. Anthony. Just say it.

But her pussy throbbed with pleasure, even amid her fear and indecision. Her breasts ached. And when she envisioned what Brent wanted to see—three guys pleasuring her at once . . . oh God—was she crazy? Wicked? More sinful than she could have imagined? Because despite her trepidation, a part of her wanted it. Wanted to see it. Wanted to feel it. Wanted to be that dirty, that brazen.

So she said nothing. Just took a deep breath, looked briefly from Jason to Decker, then faced forward, closed her eyes, and leaned her head back. With her arms still outstretched, she surrendered—crucifying herself in a whole new way.

Her breath caught at the first new sensation—a light chafing of whiskers against the flesh of her breast, then a wet tongue flicking over her nipple. Her pussy spasmed, and she let out a moan when Zack chose that exact second to begin moving the glass toy again.

Next came a warm breath on her other breast, then a light nibble on the peak that made her sob. *Jesus God, the pleasure.* Already, it was nearly unbearable.

And then they did what Brent had told them to—each man began to suckle her in earnest. Gently, she noticed, so as not to dislodge the rings and chain, but the sensations still stretched through her like taut rubberbands connected directly to her clit.

She opened her eyes to watch then. And, mmm, the sight was positively obscene. She *was* the porn movie now. The porn *queen*.

It was unbelievable to realize she was being so deeply pleasured by three total strangers. Yet she had no choice but to finally let herself sink into it—the sensations were too powerful not to. She had to do what Serena had advised: Enjoy this. She had to take the pleasure Brent always promised—and always delivered. Would she prefer it come from him? Yes. But he was watching, just like last night, and moving closer to her now, and somehow that was the next best thing. She wanted to be hot for him, nasty for him, wanted to be what he wanted to make of her—a submissive slave.

She no longer made any effort to squelch her moans, letting them flow forth at will. It was like exhaling after holding her breath—the whole new level of freedom she'd just given herself increased her pleasure still more. "God—oh God!" she heard herself cry.

Her only frustration was that her clit got no attention. And it *needed* some—badly.

And then, Brent—only a few feet away now—said, "Zack—remove the dildo and fuck the slave."

Oh Lord. Oh no.

Just like a few minutes ago—despite all her pleasure, the command froze something inside her. Maybe it made no difference at this point—a guy's real cock versus a fake one—but to Jenna, it was an enormous leap. Zack remained a stranger, and it was one thing to do all this other stuff, but to be *penetrated by another guy, someone other than Brent*—the very idea made her panic. Brent kept pushing her tonight, further and further, too far too fast, and she'd just reached her breaking point.

When Zack smoothly extracted the glass toy, time seemed short, so without a plan, Jenna cried, "No! I can't!"

Like before, everyone in the room went still and she could have sworn she heard her own heartbeat.

Clearly enraged, Brent took a step closer. "You dare defy me, slave?"

Lips trembling now, Jenna peered up at him, trying to figure out her next move.

Brent had always brought her pleasure and maybe this would be the same; maybe she should apologize and let this happen. Based on everything that had taken place in this room so far, she'd probably be screaming in ecstasy soon if she went along with his demands.

But he *had* pushed her *so* very far tonight. And as she met his gaze, her disobedience became about more than protesting sex with Zack. There was a part of her—a dark part, perhaps brought to life just tonight, since arriving in the dungeon—that wondered what would happen if she *did* defy him.

"Yes, I dare defy you," she said recklessly, then added sarcastically, "*master*."

He narrowed his gaze on her, his silence forcing her to recognize the obvious fact that hung between them—she was openly defying him, but she wasn't saying the safeword. She wasn't . . . ending this. Even *she* knew it was a challenge. To see what he'd do. Would he dish out *real* punishment? He wouldn't *really* hurt her, would he? Serena had said no one would. Yet her heart pounded violently as that new, darker part of her waited to see what happened next.

Finally, Brent's expression hardened even further and he sounded angrier than ever. "*You refuse to be fucked? Fine then—that wet, hungry pussy will not be fucked.*"

It wasn't what he'd said so much as his tone that made Jenna's blood run cold. He'd sounded so heartless—as if her insolence had crushed any bit of kindness he'd held for her tonight.

"But you *will* be punished. *Ruthlessly*," he said with just as much rancor. "Zack—attach the clit chain to her."

She sucked in her breath. Oh God—what the hell was a clit chain? How much would it hurt? Was it too late for the safeword? But when Zack left and returned quickly, she saw that what he carried didn't appear as frightening as it sounded. Thank God.

Her legs remained parted—they'd been that way so long they'd simply stayed in the position without thought—and now no one touched her, but the other guys in Brent's command knelt around her, watching as Zack closed a small clip over her swollen clitoris, from which hung a short, thin chain, black beads dangling from the end. It was like the nipple rings and chain: sexual jewelry.

The pinch of the clip was so light that it inflicted no pain . . . just a certain pressure. Which increased her need for release almost immediately. She felt her features scrunching slightly as she tried to get used to it. And she quickly figured out that—damn it—it was more than mere jewelry. It was a torture device. It was like a horrible itch that couldn't be scratched—inflicting a constant, gnawing need.

"Decker, Jason—release the slave's arms, but don't let her have use of them. Zack, grab a strip of leather and tie them behind her back."

Being a sex slave had already felt surreal, but it was now that the term took on a whole new meaning. Feeling completely at Brent's mercy, she was so caught up in everything happening to her that she forgot the safeword existed altogether. It was as if challenging him had stripped away her last bits of courage and independence and now she was lost to the situation she'd created, left to suffer the consequences.

"Now tie her to the kneeling rail," Brent said.

Chapter 8

When Jason and Decker pulled her to her heels, she almost thought she'd faint. She could barely walk, fearing whatever apparatus they'd chosen to call by a religious name, having no idea what would happen next. A minute ago, she'd wanted to know. But now she wasn't so sure—she couldn't think straight, couldn't reason.

A slight bit of relief echoed through her when they approached a simple piece of furniture, the main surfaces padded in black leather. She was put on her knees on a small steplike platform approximately a foot off the floor and her torso bent forward over a larger slanted surface. Her bared breasts, complete with chain, protruded over the top.

Brent had said she was to be tied, so it didn't surprise her when Zack and Decker pulled connected leather straps from beneath the padding where her stomach rested. One was stretched across the backs of her upper arms where they'd been pulled behind her, and another was drawn tight across her waist, under her tethered wrists but over her corset. Bondage, she thought. Maybe if she'd been a good slave, the only bondage she'd have suffered would have been the chains on the wall, but now she was learning about being restrained in a whole new, utterly subduing way.

Gathering the courage to look around her, she realized Serena and Gabe no longer occupied the nearby horse, and judging from the lack of moans and groans in the dungeon, she was back to being the main event.

As a large, warm body leaned over her from behind, Brent's voice came low near her ear. "Unfortunately for you, now you must endure the rougher use of the flogger." His erection nestled at her ass, and despite herself, she longed for it, inside her. Her clit ached maddeningly.

Then his warmth was gone—and the next sensation was a stinging blow on her bare ass that made her cry out. But it also vibrated through her breasts and cunt, like a harsh echo.

A second lash from the leather flogger delivered yet another stinging sensation—even while, oh God, somehow heightening the arousal in other parts of her body. It was like when Serena had pulled on the nipple chain, delivering pleasure and pain at once—but now it came on a much more consuming level.

She clenched her teeth, preparing for the next blow—which hurt but simultaneously dispensed that strange, permeating pleasure, a heat that moved all through her, stretching down through her fishnet-covered thighs and up through the small of her back. As she flinched against the bands strapping her to the kneeling rail, somehow even *that* brought a hint of unexpected excitement.

Again and again, Brent brought the leather flogger down on her flesh, allocating the snapping lashes to one side of her bottom for several blows, then switching to the other. As she suffered the nearly paralyzing sensations spreading through her being, she wondered if her skin there was turning red. She sobbed, as much from pleasure as from pain—all of it soon drowning out thoughts and leaving only reactions. "Oh!" she cried out. "Oh God! God!" And once she even heard herself yell, "Please!" but she didn't even know what she was begging for: more, or less; to be fucked, or freed.

Just when she wondered how much more she could take—of *any* of the overwhelming sensations—they quit coming. And her body went limp within the ties that held her. Was it over? Her punishment done? And oh God, her clit still pulsed like mad, making her crazy inside.

"Bring me the glass dildo," Brent said, and she let out a slight moan. The weirdest part was—even *she* couldn't tell if it was a moan of dread or needful anticipation. She'd never been so emotionally torn, so confused about her own responses.

Then she remembered Brent saying her pussy wouldn't be fucked—but maybe he thought the sex toy didn't count. And just as she tried to puzzle through that in her depleted mind, she experienced the oddest sensation—then gasped. Oh Lord. He was pressing the glass knob at the fissure of her ass.

She sucked in her breath in disbelief—and fear. It had felt surprisingly good when he'd inserted his fingers during the schoolgirl fantasy, but the glass dildo was much larger—and so incredibly hard.

Yet . . . he didn't push it in—he simply rested the round end against her and twisted it back and forth, almost as if teasing her. And—mmm, God—*that* felt good. *Too* good. She tried to be completely still within her bindings, lest she follow the urge to lift her ass against the toy and make him think she *wanted* it inserted.

"Lubricant," Brent said—and she sensed, in her peripheral vision, someone going to get it. She swallowed nervously.

A moment later, something slippery was smeared at her anus, perhaps Vaseline. And then—again—came that same pressure from the round knob.

Almost in disbelief that he was going to do this, she found the strength to crane her neck, to look over her shoulder. The angle was difficult—and impossible to hold—but she was even more stunned by what she'd caught a glimpse of. He wasn't preparing to fuck her ass exactly the way she'd thought—instead, he held what she'd thought of as the *handle* of the glass dildo toward her, with its row of smaller glass knobs, and suddenly the penis-shaped part had become the piece he held.

Part of her was relieved—the knobs were a lot smaller on this end, so getting them inside her ass didn't seem as inconceivable. And yet—how would it feel? How deep would he go? It would surely be a much more extreme experience than when he'd used only his fingers.

"Arch your ass toward me, slave," he said deeply, "and brace yourself."

She could have ignored the command, but she didn't. It was only smart to give him an easier angle.

And then came the pressure—and the first knob entered the tiny opening. She sobbed lightly, but . . . it wasn't from pain. God. Oh. It was . . . it was like before, with his fingers. It was a most odd but certain pleasure.

He pushed again and another glass knob slipped inside. Her breath came heavier as her ass began to feel more filled.

A few seconds later her asshole swallowed another of the knobs, and then another. She cried out, from pure amazement—and the consuming fullness. Her scalp tingled and began to pulse. Her nipples ached and her breasts heaved. Her clit felt huge—and abandoned, deeply in need.

And just when Jenna thought maybe that was it, all that would happen, Brent began to slowly fuck her ass with the toy, pulling it part of the way out, then pushing it back in.

She let out a long, low, "Ohhhhhhh." that sprang from her gut as the smooth knobs moved through her. She could barely understand the overwhelming pleasure he delivered—she'd broken out into a sweat and, oh God, one touch to her poor clit and she knew she'd explode in orgasm, but there was still no way to stimulate it.

Oh God, oh God, oh God—she trembled, teeth clenched, as Brent fucked her ass with the glass balls. So much profound pleasure, as if the toy stretched through her whole body—and yet still so much need, too. Oh damn it, she needed that chain off her clit! How much more could she take?

Just then, the flogger came down on her ass again, making her flinch and yell—and then she sobbed more deeply as her own movement jarred the glass toy. She heard herself begin to whimper and couldn't stop—she'd lost complete control of herself.

"Take over with these," she heard Brent softly instruct, and she hardly even cared who he was handing his torture devices over to at this point—she only wondered what the hell would happen next.

Brent walked around in front of her, which brought his still stone-hard cock back to her eye level. Oh God, he was hot. Even now, amid everything else, she could comprehend *that*. He was hot and dirty and made her wild inside.

She watched as he stepped closer and without touching himself or her, he raised his erection behind her nipple chain and used it to pull slightly outward. She cried out yet again—oh God, more pleasure/pain, more insanely intense sensation. With each second, she grew more crazed. So much pleasure but no release, just that teasing clit chain—how was she supposed to stand it? Perspiration still poured from her skin as heat echoed through her with every smooth glide of the glass knobs in her ass, with every hot sting of the flogger.

In utter desperation, she leaned her head back, straining to look up at Brent. She had to find some way to relieve herself of the crushing frustration. "Can—can I ask you for something, tell you what I want?" She'd never heard herself sound so helpless, almost despairing.

She wanted—needed—for him to fuck her, the *normal* way, and to rub her clit, to let her come. She needed it like she needed air to breathe. Nothing else mattered but sweet release.

She peered up at him, not breaking eye contact even when the dildo plunged into that tiny opening and made her sob with hard pleasure.

She couldn't read his expression. Clearly lust drove him, yet his eyes appeared pained as he leaned down close—and when he spoke, he sounded partly like her master but also like Brent. "Not tonight," he whispered. "Tonight you have to obey. It's the only way."

She thought she would die. She found herself wriggling against her leather bindings, as if that would do any good. More whimpers left her throat.

Brent gently touched her face. "Open your mouth now," he said, still low but soft, almost as if ignoring her pleas were as hard on him as on her. "And suck my cock."

Jenna simply did as she was told. All choice had been taken from her. Brent *was* her master now. He pushed his erection slow and deep and she accepted it—even welcomed it, since at least it was another form of being fucked, and right now, she *needed* more, more, more, even if the "more" wasn't what would make her come.

He moved gradual and steady between her lips, fucking her mouth fully, unapologetically. And Jenna closed her eyes and simply *felt*. Every sensation. Even the clawing, nagging pressure on her clit. Her face flushed with warmth even as she attempted to calm herself and just be a good slave, just serve him.

Finally, he placed his hands on her head and drew back, leaving her lips stretched and sore. "Have you had enough torture?" he asked, still sounding more like Brent than the angry, controlling master.

"Yes," she breathed, aware that the glass toy had gone still in her ass and the leather strips of the flogger now rested unmoving on her flesh.

"Apologize," Brent instructed her solemnly.

"I'm sorry, master."

"More," he insisted.

She didn't hesitate. "I should have taken what you wanted me to have, master. Please forgive me. I'll be good from now on."

"Tell me that whatever I wish for you, you wish it, too."

She took a breath. "Whatever you wish for me, I wish it, too."

"Tell me you want to be fucked however I deem you should be fucked."

"I want to be fucked however you deem I should be fucked."

Now Brent crouched down before her, looking her very closely in the eye. "Jenna, tell me you mean it. Tell me you're truly prepared to take what I decide you need. Tell me you want it. Tell me it's real."

As she peered into his dark, beautiful eyes, something caught in her throat. He was . . . himself now. Brent. Still all-powerful, but also Brent. Asking her to truly trust him, and to truly choose to please him in a deeper way than she'd experienced thus far. And unable to break her gaze from his—so persuasive, full of emotion—oh God, it became real and profound. The deep need to do as he bid. To please him unconditionally, no matter what it required. Her words came out barely audible, but heartfelt and sincere. "It's real. I mean it. I want it. Whatever you want *for* me, *from* me. If *you* want it, *I* want it. I'll take it. For you."

Their eyes stayed locked—and his softened. "That's very good, baby," he murmured, reaching to stroke his fingertips across her cheek. He raised his voice then, to be heard, but his gaze remained soft on her as he said, "Untie the slave. Strap her to the examination table."

Jenna didn't know what to think. Things were changing, but she didn't yet know how. Would he relieve her frustration or just deal out more?

When the glass knobs exited her ass, it felt odd, uncomfortable, but she couldn't concentrate on that for long since she realized she was being unbound—both the leather straps around her back and the tie around her wrists loosened. She didn't even know who helped her up from her knees—she felt like a robot as two men escorted her to yet another apparatus, this one a simple table. Yet she could see more straps and chains attached to it.

She was laid on her back—and went willingly. She'd meant every word she said to Brent, so even as her pussy ached maddeningly, she let herself be guided.

From the bottom of the table, two extensions were drawn out—sort of like a doctor's table, they supported her legs, yet left empty space between them. Thick leather buckles were fastened at her ankles, over her boots. Her arms were stretched over her head and she heard something—metal or steel—being fastened to the cuffs still on her wrists. She waited for more, but no further bindings came.

"Zack, fuck her," Brent said, and though she sucked in her breath, this time it was no longer in fear or repulsion or moral concern. That was all gone now. Now it was a strange combination of numb obedience and anticipation. More. She would get more. More pleasure. More sensation. And it would please Brent. And that would please *her*.

Zack stepped between her legs, his erect cock already in hand. He wasn't as big as Brent—but he rivaled the glass dildo. And she wanted him between her legs now.

Positioning himself, he closed his hands over her bare hips and pushed smoothly inside. He groaned and she sighed. He began to thrust—smooth, steady—and she found herself meeting his drives, *excited* to be fucked by a stranger now, for Brent, who stood at her side watching her cunt accept and respond.

"Serena," Brent said—calling Jenna's attention to the fact that Serena again stood nearby, "remove the clit chain and suck her there."

Jenna made no attempt to hold in her sounds of joy at what he'd just commanded. Finally, *finally*, she would come! She couldn't imagine needing to climax any worse than she did at this moment.

As Serena followed Brent's instructions, soon closing her lips around Jenna's swollen clitoris, she cried out. And Brent stepped closer, leaning over to cup her breasts and begin massaging them in the same rhythm as Zack's strokes below. "Tell me when you're gonna come," Brent said.

And as she'd known, it didn't take long—mere seconds, in fact—from Serena's soft suckling. "Now," she said, then louder. "*Now.*"

And as the powerful orgasm roared through her body like a tidal wave, Brent yanked the chain between her tits, pulling the rings from her nipples, and she yowled even louder, the move stretching the climax to what seemed an impossible length. The wild pulses in her cunt rolled on and on as she sobbed her release, eyes shut in an unbelievable ecstasy she couldn't have anticipated. *Oh God—yes, yes, yes, yes, yes!* Pleasure had never been wrenched from her body in such a profound and intense way.

After that, things went quiet in the dungeon; she sensed the other players leaving, and thank God—because it was as if her body simply shut down. It had been through too much. Part of her basked in elation at such an amazing orgasm, thrilled she'd survived this, and thrilled she'd done what Brent had wanted and that it hadn't been so awful, after all—it had been undeniably pleasurable and she had to start *accepting* that, accepting that he truly *knew* what she needed. But she felt so physically spent that she nearly dropped into a deep sleep, just like guys often did after they came.

She forgot everything else and just rested—and though it briefly crossed her mind that Zack had not ejaculated, she didn't belabor it, figuring he would get his satisfaction with someone else now.

Soon, the cuffs at her wrists were turned loose and she stretched her sore arms slowly down to her sides. She eased her eyes open to see Brent move to her feet, silently unbuckling the straps that held her ankles.

Finally, when she was freed, he raised his eyes to hers. "Are you pissed at me?"

He was totally Brent now. He'd even zipped up his pants, and though she had a horrible thought—he hadn't finished either, and if they were done here, who would *he* come with?—she pushed it aside. There was far too much else to ponder right now.

She considered his question and bit her lip. "I'm not sure *what* I am right now. Besides overwhelmed."

"I'm sorry," he said, sounding completely sincere, "that I had to put you through that—but I did. For you to really move forward. I know it seemed harsh, but with only two weeks and one of them nearly over, it felt necessary to make you take a big leap. And now you know some things you didn't this morning. You know that being fucked by a total stranger can bring satisfying pleasure without any emotional connection, whether you wanted to believe that or not. I'm not saying that's always the case, but it can happen, it can be enough—even for you. And now you know sex doesn't have to be soft or sweet to be good. Sometimes really hard, rough sex can be fucking *great*, and you understand that now. And sometimes it can feel freaking fantastic to just let yourself be totally dirty—even though I'm sure you don't like that idea, either. But it's true, and there's nothing wrong with it. You came an incredibly long way tonight if you'll admit it to yourself."

Jenna took a deep breath, let it back out. "As usual, everything you're saying is true. And as things went on, I understood . . . about submission and obedience—I really did want what you wanted, no matter what it was. But at this moment, now that I'm no longer desperate to come, it's all freaking me out a little. Even if I *do* know all these things I didn't know this morning, I'm not sure . . . it's me."

He stepped up between her still-spread legs and rested his hands on her thighs, the move more comforting than sexual. "It doesn't *have* to be you. It's you *tonight*. It's you for the coming *week*. It's a hurdle you're jumping, and on the other side you're going to find yourself a lot more at ease in and in control of your normal sex life—whatever you choose to make it."

She sighed and leaned her head back on the table. "It's hard to imagine my sex life ever feeling normal *again*."

When she met his gaze, he cast a small grin. "It will, sunshine—and all this will just seem like a dream, the dream you had to have to get where you needed to go."

Then something hit her—something she hadn't thought about before, and it felt important. "What if . . . what if I meet a guy and he's the *one*? But . . . well, what if he's a lot more like *me* than like *you*—what if it would change his opinion of me to know the things I did here?"

"Then maybe he needs to come here, too," Brent replied with raised eyebrows, his look half teasing, half sincere.

She propped up on her elbows. "Not everyone who doesn't indulge in kinky sex with multiple partners needs help, Brent."

To her surprise, he actually appeared contrite—an expression she'd never seen on him before. "Fair enough, and very true. So . . . maybe when you find this Mr. Right, you just don't tell him."

"Then there's a huge secret standing between us."

"Not one he needs to know if it'll fuck up your relationship. What you're doing here has nothing to do with any future guy you're going to meet and it's no reflection on who you are as a person, Jenna. It's just about making you enjoy the sex you choose to have to the fullest. In fact, Mr. Right should be *glad* you came here, because I guarantee it'll make *his* sex life a lot better, too."

Brent suddenly found himself trying to envision Jenna's future Mr. Right—probably some Ivy League academic type, somebody who wouldn't be nearly what she needed in a man. Maybe there was a reason no guy she'd ever dated had gotten her very excited about sex—she probably picked boring guys.

So he added, "Do me a favor. Don't pick a boring guy."

She grinned. "And exactly what kind of guy should I pick?"

He shrugged, then teased her. "Somebody more like me."

She tilted her head, arched a brow. "Not likely. You have sex for a living."

"Again, fair enough. So . . . somebody like me but who *doesn't* have sex for a living."

She flashed an expression he couldn't quite read. "I'm afraid I've never met anybody quite like you before." And he wondered how she meant that but didn't ask. Maybe he didn't really want to know. Maybe, after tonight, she was starting to think he was a pretty awful guy.

Not that he knew why he cared.

But he did need to retain her trust in him—now more than ever.

"You were fucking amazing tonight, Jenna," he felt the need to tell her.

She looked surprised. "I . . . didn't feel amazing. I felt like . . . a plebe. Ignorant, out of place. Silly."

He lowered his chin in doubt. "You didn't look too silly when you were excited and coming. You were . . . smokin' hot, babe. I really need for you to know that."

She appeared to be thinking back over the evening. "Okay, maybe I mostly felt like a silly plebe at the beginning. I was pretty scared."

"But you still managed to go along with the fantasy. And I enjoyed every minute of it," he assured her.

She sat up a bit more, leaning back on her hands, and bent her knees, her legs still spread before him. "What did you enjoy? In particular? It would help me to know."

His cock still ached in his pants—he'd actually been through a lot of arousal himself tonight without getting off. And thinking back on it all made him begin to throb—but he still met her gaze as he answered. "The way you look in leather. Your tits, with the rings, and the chain. That you're able to let a woman touch you now without flinching." His voice deepened. "How you let yourself accept pleasure when you were chained to the wall. The way you looked . . . bound. The way your ass closed so tight around the glass. The way you whimpered and moaned."

Her skin flushed and he tightened his hold on her thighs, squeezing lightly. He found himself watching her eyes, then her mouth—her lips pouty-looking from stretching around his dick for so long. He felt the urge to kiss her. But he resisted. It was best he start doing that more—resisting.

Remembering the period of time when she'd been strapped to the kneeling rail and how intense it had all gotten, he felt a little bad. But he wasn't going to keep apologizing. Instead, he said, "What were you going to ask me for at the kneeling rail?"

"I was going to beg you to fuck me," she said. Little Mary Sunshine no more. A perfect good girl gone perfectly bad. He wanted her like hell. "It turned out you were right, like always—what you wanted *did* bring me pleasure. I wasn't repulsed by it—it was . . . more than I could have dreamed. But . . ." She lowered her eyes then, looking strangely bashful for a girl who wore a revealing corset and dominatrix boots. "I still find myself wanting now," she went on softly, "what I wanted then."

For him to fuck her. Him. No one else.

Brent lifted his hand from her fishnet-clad thigh, leaning over to touch her pretty face. He *should* resist. But he wasn't going to. "Beg me now, sunshine."

Looking beautifully needy but determined, she sat up fully and ran her hands through his hair, making his scalp tingle. "Please, Brent. Fuck me." Her breath was shaky, audible. "Please, please, please—fuck me hard and deep. I'll beg you all night if you want—I just need you inside me. Please."

Damn. He'd begun to think she didn't have it in her—the ability to let a lover know what she desired so honestly, so frankly. And this was another major step—a triumph—in her journey toward sexual freedom. But mainly, he heard it with his cock. And with his heart, which was beating way too rapidly. "I love hearing you say that, baby. Say it some more," he rasped.

"Fuck me, Brent. Fuck me, fuck me, fuck me," she pleaded in a hot, breathy voice that nearly buried him. "I want you to make me come. And I want to make *you* come, too. *Please*."

A low groan left him as he kissed her. As he thrust his tongue into her mouth. As he molded his hands to her gorgeous tits, squeezing, massaging.

He loved it when she reached to undo his pants. Sweet Jenna, going for what she wanted. It made him even stiffer, if that was possible.

When his erection was freed, she moaned at the sight, then took him in her hand. Mmm, yeah—so good. He couldn't hold in a low growl.

And then he was leaning in, letting her pull his dick toward her pussy, until he thrust inside. Aw, God. So fucking tight. Wet. Even after all she'd been through tonight, she was so hot for him. He curled his hands around her ass and let her set the pace, find her rhythm.

As she undulated against him, tits to chest, belly to belly, he let that rhythm move through him and soaked up everything hungry and wild and female about her. He ran his hands over her curves. He listened to her hot breath in his ear. Then he molded his hands tight to her ass, squeezing hard as she swayed and moaned, clearly getting close—beautifully close—then whimpering, "Now, Brent, now—oh God . . ."

Fuck yes. She looked and felt so beautiful coming in his arms that he could barely hold back. But he did—because this was *her* moment, to climax, to free herself a little more, to feel everything he wanted her to feel. He watched the orgasm wash over her, stealing her senses, and loved it more than he ever had. The way her eyes fell shut, her mouth dropped open, slack and lost to passion. The way she sighed, replete, when it had passed.

Then and only then did he take over, once again feeling the urge to dominate, because he needed release so fucking bad. He pressed her back to the table and climbed on. Then he plunged into her fiercely, unrelenting, loving the way her body jerked and her tits bounced with each drive, loving the way she held on to the table with both hands to better meet his cock with her sweet cunt.

"Beg me some more, baby," he murmured against her breast, nibbling on the nipple. He'd had no idea how much it would excite him to hear that—Jenna begging.

"Fuck me," she pleaded without hesitation. "Please, please fuck me!"

And that was all he needed. To ram into her still more powerfully, to make them both cry out with every pummeling stroke, and then to explode inside her.

"Damn—I'm coming, I'm coming!" he told her as a violent climax drained him. He groaned with every burst of come he shot inside her. Then he collapsed gently atop her soft body, amazed by the whole night.

At first, Jenna was surprised to wake up in Brent's bed. But she instantly liked it there, a lot. And then she remembered the way the night had ended. He'd kissed her cheek and murmured, "Let's go to my place, get some sleep." She hadn't argued. So she'd put on her black coat and let him lead her from the dungeon to another luxury golf cart, and they'd proceeded here.

She hadn't been able to see much in the dark except the ocean—the small house rested high on the beach in a row with two or three others, all sharing sand and some palm trees for a yard. And to her surprise, the tiny community felt quite isolated from the rest of the resort.

Now she sat up in bed, peering out a window covered with sheer curtains to see a hammock stretched between two palm trees and another glimpse of the beach. She could hear the waves crashing from here.

Looking around, she found Brent's home completely . . . normal. She wasn't sure what she'd been expecting, but not this. The bedroom was bright and tidy, with a large teakwood bed and Spanish tile floors. The open bathroom door to the right revealed a large, modern shower and a wide vanity, with plush navy blue towels hanging from a bar in between. A glance in the other direction provided a glimpse of the living room, where she spied a leather sofa, expensive-looking end tables, and a large flat-screen TV.

"Morning, sunshine," he said, his voice raspy from sleep.

She gazed down at where he lay, not in the least embarrassed to be naked with him any longer. "Morning."

"How are you? Still doing okay after last night?"

"Sore," she said. The muscles in her arms and upper back ached, and in her thighs, too—maybe from walking so far in those ridiculously high-heeled boots.

"Sorry about that. But I scheduled a spa visit for you this afternoon with our best masseuse, Rhoda."

She tilted her head, remembering where she was—not his bungalow, but the Hotel Erotique. "So—is a massage here a massage? Or is a massage here a sex thing?"

He grinned softly against his pillow, and she liked the way he looked with messy hair, needing a shave. "We do some massage fantasies, but most of the time, sunshine, a massage here is just a massage. Rhoda is a sweet, older woman who'll give you the best massage of your life."

She couldn't help asking. "What is someone like *her* doing working *here*?"

"Her kids are grown and gone, she likes the beach, and we pay well," he replied with a lazy wink—after which he looked a little more serious. "But back to the point—how are you, besides sore?"

She hadn't yet thought about that. Mainly, she was focusing on the *last* round of sex, with Brent, and the fact that he'd whisked her back here as if it were the natural thing to do. "I think I'm okay," she answered honestly. "I . . . don't feel upset. I feel sort of like you said last night . . . like it was a dream or something." Then she tilted her head. "Are the rest of my fantasies going to be . . ." But then she drifted off, not exactly sure what she was asking.

"Not quite as intense," he replied, seeming to understand her concerns. "If your visit here is a hurdle in your sex life, then last night was the hurdle in your visit here. Now that you accept certain things and are less afraid, the rest should come easier." Then he propped himself up on one elbow. "Don't get me wrong, though. Don't start expecting those silk sheets and violins of yours. You'll still be experiencing new things and I'll still be stretching you to new limits."

"Okay," she said with a light nod, pleased enough by his answer. Last night had ultimately brought her many new and intense kinds of pleasure, but she wasn't sure she could do that again. "So . . . does this sleepover come with breakfast?"

He looked a little doubtful, then sheepish. "I'm, uh, not a big breakfast guy. I usually grab a muffin or something easy from one of the restaurants, on the way to my office. What did you have in mind?"

"Um, eggs? Bacon?"

"Nope, sorry."

"Donuts? Pastries?" she suggested.

"Nada."

"Cereal? Toast?"

His eyes widened happily. "Hey, *that* I've got. I can offer you a smorgasbord of Cheerios or Rice Krispies. And—don't get too excited, but I just remembered I might even have some cinnamon raisin bagels."

"A fine feast to restore my energy after last night," she teased.

After getting up, Brent slipped into a pair of white boxer briefs from a drawer, leaving Jenna to admire the way they hugged his ass—and his bulge, when he turned around. "Want a T-shirt?" he asked.

"Sure," she said, and he opened another drawer, soon tossing a faded aqua Miami Dolphins tee across the bed.

"Ah, look what we have here," he said as she followed him into the living room a moment later. Through the front door, which sported a long glass panel, she followed his eyes to a shopping bag on the front stoop bearing the Hotel Erotique logo.

"What is it?" she asked as he opened the door, admitting a salty sea breeze.

"I sent a text message to the front desk last night after we got here," he replied, pulling the bag inside. She'd remembered him playing with his phone, but had assumed he was checking messages. "I asked the clerk on duty to open the gift shop and send a few things over."

When Brent handed her the bag, she looked inside to find a cami, some cotton shorts, a Hotel Erotique thong with hot pink trim, and a pair of flip-flops.

"Just enough for you to get back to the room without feeling obvious this morning. No bra—but I figured you're a big girl now and won't freak out if anyone sees you without one between here and there," he added with a wink.

She couldn't help saying the obvious. "That was really thoughtful." Then what was *equally* obvious. "But is, um, that sort of request normal? To have clothes sent to your place?"

"No," he said simply.

"So, um, won't that mean whoever handled the request will figure out you brought a guest here after a fantasy?"

"Probably."

"Will you be in trouble for that?"

He gave a shrug, but she wasn't sure if he was as relaxed about the question as he tried to act. "Other employees might be pissed since it *is* against the rules—but I guess that's one perk of being an owner. They can *be* pissed without it really affecting me."

As Brent found cereal bowls and toasted the bagels, Jenna took the opportunity to explore a little more. She wasn't sure why—but this seemed like the best chance she'd get to see what made Brent tick, besides insatiable lust.

She perused the built-in shelves in the living room—which opened onto the kitchen—and other than some sexual psychology books, again found all typical stuff. Among the CDs, which ranged from the eighties to current music, she spotted some Stone Temple Pilots and a lot of Pearl Jam. Besides the sex books, she spied a few sports books, a world atlas, and several volumes on car repair—one specifically about classic Mustangs. "Do a lot of car repair here on the island, do you?" she joked.

Turning from the fridge with a small tub of margarine in his hand, he grinned. "I used to be into cars—before I came here." So he'd given up cars for sex. She supposed when push came to shove, most guys would.

Then her eyes fell on an old photo album, the kind with sticky pages. Checking to make sure he wasn't watching, she smoothly pulled it out and let it fall open.

Inside, she discovered snapshots of a younger Brent. She guessed him to be around twenty in most of them, and whereas he was a rugged, handsome man *now*, *then* he'd been a fresh-faced, just-as-good-looking boy. Quick glances told her he'd had a lot of friends—there were group pictures at parties, picnics, events she couldn't identify. In one, he had his arm around a pretty yet plain sort of girl and she noted how comfortable they appeared together. Jenna might have thought it was a sister, except they looked nothing alike. She was struck by the girl's simplicity—hardly the bombshell cheerleader type she would have expected Brent to hook up with at that age, or *any* age.

When she heard the toaster pop and Brent said, "Breakfast is served," starting to butter the bagels with his back to her, she quickly returned the album to the shelf and made her way to the kitchen—she didn't want to be caught snooping quite *that* much.

And as they ate and Brent started chatting about the other resort owners who were his neighbors, she was almost *sorry* she'd gotten this peek into his life, into how normal it all seemed.

Because being with him had been . . . well, *easier* when she'd thought he was so different from her. She was already in major lust with the guy, and she already felt way too much when she had sex with him. Or—hell—even when he watched her fool around with someone else. So she surely couldn't start feeling attached in *non*sexual ways, too.

She would be here for only another week, after all. And at heart . . . they *were* different. *Very* different. *You have to remember that. He's had sex with hundreds of women, maybe thousands. He's happy living here on an island doing nothing but creating sexual fantasies for people and having still more sex. He's no one to fall for. No matter how hot he is, no matter what crazily intimate things you've done with him—and* for *him.*

You have to see him as . . . a sexual conduit, nothing more. Do not get any more attached here.

So she resolved not to ask him about anything else in the house—not where he got the peaceful beach painting over the sofa, or where he'd traveled, or who the people in the album were, or *anything*. She had to do what *Brent* was so good at—keep this all about sex.

So when they both stood up a little while later to carry empty bowls and plates to the sink, she set hers back down, stepped close enough to him to feel his warmth, and said, "Fuck me again."

He lowered his chin, looking somewhere between amused and aroused. "Who's the master here, sunshine?"

"Maybe *I* am. Or would I be the mistress?" Then she slapped his ass through his underwear and tried to sound more dominating than playful. "Now do it."

It didn't work—she just wasn't the bossy type—but that didn't keep Brent from easing his strong arms around her, planting them on her bare ass, and lifting her onto the kitchen table. He stepped between her legs, kissing her—kisses she could easily get lost in—but she still managed to reach inside his underwear. He was only half hard, but still big in her hand, and stiffening rapidly.

He let out a hot sigh when she squeezed and began to massage the length in her fist. "Mmm, sunshine, that's nice. You're getting better at this all the time."

She didn't answer, simply took pride in the fact that his cock had just become a stone pillar in her hand. "God, you're so big," she murmured, always amazed by it.

"And you like it," he teased with sexy, half-shut eyes.

Why bother lying? "I *love* it. It scared me at first, but now I *crave* it."

"You've done very, very well, Little Mary Sunshine," he growled, "so here's a reward." And with that, he plunged the object of her lust into her waiting pussy.

As usual, she cried out. Mmm, God—she wasn't lying about his size or how incredible it felt inside her. She parted her legs as wide as possible to welcome his thrusts.

Soon, though, he wrapped his arms around her waist and she curled her legs around his hips, and he carried her to the couch while still inside her. He eased back onto the creamy brown leather, which left her straddling him. "Oh, Brent," she purred as hot lust rushed through her veins, "you feel even *bigger* like this."

He cast a cocky grin. "I know. That's why I brought you over here."

In fact, it was almost a challenge to ride him in this position, with all her weight on him. She grew used to it as she found her rhythm—but she couldn't help moaning deeply with every undulation, feeling truly impaled on his magnificent shaft.

"Oh God," she groaned as he filled her, as she moved on him. "Oh God, oh God."

"Work that sweet pussy, honey," he said low, his dirty talk intoxicating to her now.

Oh God, this was so good, so hot. Without kinky settings or special costumes or disciplinary roles. It was steamy and perfect just to fuck him, in a T-shirt, on his couch. Like normal people. Normal lovers. With that thought in mind, she shut her eyes, let her body guide her swaying movements, and came.

Moments later, he came, too, after which she sank against him—truly, utterly exhausted from so much sex in less than twelve hours. She still managed to smile into his eyes, though, to say, "This is the first time I've been on top with you."

His warm hands gripped the curves of her waist, under her shirt. "You look good up there, baby. Confident. Like a woman who knows what she wants."

"I do," she teased him. "Your big, perfect cock."

"Damn, I love to hear you talk sexy now. What a difference a few days make. You say 'cock' now like it's nothing."

"Oh, it's far from nothing," she assured him. "It's my favorite part of you."

He grinned, kissed her, and she wanted to melt in his arms. They rested together like that, until finally Brent said, "I'm afraid if we don't get up, I'm gonna fall back asleep, and I have work to do today."

Coming out of a sleepy comfort of her own, Jenna smiled into his eyes. "More fantasies to plan for me?"

He tilted his head. "You're not my only guest, you know."

Actually, she'd sort of forgotten that. He'd made her feel so special. "But the others are guys, right?"

"Right."

"And you don't take part in their fantasies, right?"

"Right again." Then his eyes narrowed slightly. "Why?"

She tried to slough if off. "You don't know by now that I'm nosy and inquisitive?"

"Crazy me—I forgot. And by the way, just so you know, no fantasy for you tonight."

Still snuggling with him on the couch, she tried to hide her disappointment. "No?"

"Last night was a lot. You need some downtime. You have that spa appointment today at two, but the rest of your time is your own until you get new instructions tomorrow. Enjoy," he said with a wink.

But she would have enjoyed it much more if her plans had included *him*.

They took turns in the shower, and while he was in the bathroom, she couldn't help herself—she went back to that photo album. Able to look a bit more slowly now, she found pictures of young Brent at some sort of formal dance, with the same plain girl as before, although she looked prettier here in a blue gown with her hair piled on her head. She saw what appeared to be family pictures at Christmastime: Brent and a teenage sister—who *did* look like him—with his parents, opening presents; Brent wearing a Santa hat, making a silly face for the camera. She also stumbled upon college graduation pictures: Brent in a cap and gown. But he looked sullen in them compared to his friends.

As she climbed back on the golf cart with Brent a little while later, heading back into the wild world of the Hotel Erotique, she kept up the playful small talk, even grilling him for some hint about her next fantasy, but he didn't budge. Yet when he let her off at her building with a kiss, as she walked away from him beneath the tropical sun, she began to feel . . . very worried.

Because yes, she'd come an amazingly long way. But . . . what if he was the only guy on the planet she could be this hot and wild with? What if she was healed . . . only with him?

And worse yet . . . despite her admonitions to herself this morning, she was beginning to think she'd made those resolutions far too late. Because parting with him just now had hurt, leaving her to feel ridiculously lonely. She still felt his kiss on her lips when she reached her room. And knowing she wouldn't see him again until probably tomorrow night . . . well, it sounded like forever. And to think that after another week, she'd never see him again? Her heart physically ached.

The horrifying truth was—she'd fallen for Brent Powers. She'd fallen for him hard, and she had no idea how to save herself.

Chapter 9

Jenna had allowed herself the luxury of catching up on sleep that morning, and even after waking to look out on another glorious tropical day, she hadn't felt inclined to venture out—so she'd ordered lunch in, then gone to the spa.

In addition to the massage, which had been fabulously relaxing and had indeed soothed her sore muscles, she'd gotten a facial and taken a mud bath. But after that, she'd felt a bit . . . bored, and remained out of sorts, all because of her newly acknowledged emotions for Brent. She suffered the insane urges of an in-love teenager—wanting to track him down, persuade him to spend time with her; time was so short, after all. And she'd resisted, of course, but she knew she needed to get her head straight about everything happening to her here.

Irritated with herself, she soon decided it would be wise to spend the evening much as she had her *last* evening alone. Rather than moping in her suite over her too-deep feelings for her guide, she pulled herself together and chose to continue soaking up the experience of being here as much as possible—even if in a more chaste way than usual. She put on a beaded tank and flowy skirt and went to dinner at the Paradise Grill.

She was slightly surprised to find the same calypso band playing, and she suffered mixed emotions. She'd loved their music, and she'd enjoyed the dance with her Blair Underwood look-alike, but she also felt a little embarrassed to see him again. Because she was unsure if any sexual vibes had passed between them—truthfully, she wasn't used to recognizing such things if they weren't as obvious as they'd been with Brent—and if something sexual *had* been there, would he think she'd come back because of him? And that brought up a familiar question: What did *he* think about the women who came here for sex? She was technically one of them now, no denying that. So did her handsome calypso singer think that made her a sex maniac, a slut, or maybe even worse—some lonely woman who couldn't get it anywhere else?

Yet when his eyes met hers across the deck as he sang, she quit asking herself those questions. He simply gave off an air of utter . . . respect. And just now, in these strange surroundings, in the body of this strange version of Jenna Banks, she appreciated that—deeply. So when he smiled her way and offered a wink, she demurely smiled back and decided to enjoy this man's simple, reverent attention. Maybe it was exactly what she needed to distract her from being so wrapped up in Brent.

Despite that, when the band eased into some soft reggae—"Is This Love," a Bob Marley song she knew only because Shannon had gone through a Rasta phase in college—she couldn't have been more surprised when the singer strolled slowly between the tables until he was crooning directly to her, the lyrics informing her he wanted to love her and treat her right. Her whole body went warm—partially with embarrassment, but the heat reached between her legs, too. When he lifted her hand for a kiss, her skin prickled, and the sensation skittered all the way down her arm and into her breasts. Oh my.

It was a relief when he moved on—even though she knew she had nothing to be self-conscious about. Sometimes it was hard to remember that everyone here had come for sex and was doing it with strangers—so having a handsome black man sing a romantic song to her was hardly a big deal.

Except that . . . well, this just shored up her fears. That she could be free and wild with Brent, but inside she remained the same old Jenna who shied away from sexual situations until she was deeply involved in a relationship. And now, after a few days and nights with Brent, she knew something else, too—what she'd thought was good sex for her entire adult life had actually been . . . pretty average. Even if, looking back, she could remember particular moments of glory, none held a candle to the level of pleasure she'd experienced here, with Brent Powers.

The band went on break when her food arrived, which bummed her out a little—her distraction was gone. Yet she'd already resumed being a little depressed, so she decided she'd just eat her chicken sandwich, then mope back to her room. Maybe she'd just be old Jenna tonight. Not that her old self moped—she never had, actually, because before coming here she'd truly been convinced she was happy with her sex life. But the old Jenna *was* content to spend an evening with a good book, and maybe that was the thing to do here. Quit pushing herself to stay "up" for every second of this. It was okay not to be immersed in sensuality every minute. In fact, it was probably *smart*. Soon life would go back to normal—so perhaps it was prudent to keep some aspects of it normal even while she was here, so the transition wouldn't feel so shocking.

She'd just lifted her wineglass for a final sip when she looked up to see her sexy Jamaican heading her way. Oh boy. Her heart beat too fast, but she met his gaze and tried not to be nervous. She wished she felt as brave with him as when they'd danced together, but it seemed her most recent emotions with Brent colored her reactions to this man, too.

"I'm happy to see you back this evening, pretty lady," he told her, his expressive brown eyes saying more. Sensing his honest admiration helped her relax a little.

Still, she tried to play it cool—since, in fact, she hadn't returned because of him. "I enjoy your music," she said, then gazed out over the setting sun and the blaze of colors it sent streaking across the sky. "And you can't beat the view."

When she looked back up, his eyes remained firmly planted on *her*. "The view is pleasant for me, too."

Oh boy. His smooth-as-silk voice made her chest spasm lightly.

Just then, he glanced over his shoulder to where the other band members were reconvening on the deck's small corner stage. "Ah, I waited too late to say hello—I must go, but you have a lovely night."

"Well . . . thank you. For coming over," she said, stuck for how to reply.

"The next song is for you," he told her in parting, and she thought, *Wow—okay, yes, there are officially sexual vibes passing between us.* Which felt a little weird. She'd never been attracted to a man anything like this one before. He was a musician. He was Jamaican. She suspected she understood even less about *his* world than she did about Brent's.

When the steel drums began again, she recognized the song—the reggae version of Peter Frampton's "Baby, I Love Your Way." Her calypso singer's voice delivered the sensual lyrics with a sexy lilt she felt in her panties, especially when their eyes met.

Jenna remained at her table for a while longer, enjoying the music and the night, and all in all, by the time she departed, she felt better—about everything. So she was madly in love with Brent—big deal.

Well, all right, yes, it *was* a big deal. Because whether it was love or just infatuation, it could still totally consume her. But she had to be practical here. She'd known Brent a week—which meant that when she went home, she'd get over him. That simple. And maybe her fears about being able to get wild only with him were wrong—maybe she'd find out she could be sexually open with other men, too. After all, she was suddenly attracted to a Jamaican singer; so maybe she'd soon discover she was attracted to all *sorts* of new guys, and maybe they'd be guys who would inspire true sexual freedom in her and who would appreciate and understand if she shared with them the things she'd done here. Maybe, maybe, maybe. It was all uncertain—but for now it was . . . hope. Hope that she'd leave here with more than wild memories and a broken heart.

So that was it. While she was at the Hotel Erotique, she'd indulge in whatever Brent wanted—she'd give him all of herself. And when it was over, she'd be sad—but ready to move on with men, and sex, and life itself.

When she awoke the following morning to find an envelope under her door, she was eager to learn about her next fantasy. What she'd found, however, was another handwritten letter from Brent that had nothing to do with that.

Dear Jenna,

Since I've left you with extra time on your hands, I thought of something you might enjoy. Think of it as a little reward for surviving the dungeon. ☺

You might have seen a location on resort maps called the Grotto. It's a small, private swimming area designed to look like a natural tropical pool with rock walls, a small waterfall, and thick foliage surrounding it. It was created for fantasies—being secluded, it's perfect for fucking. But when not reserved for that, we make use of it by offering it to a few guests at a time. It's a great place to relax and soak up the sun with more privacy than you get at the other pools. There aren't even any waiters—but you can pick up a carafe of rum punch at the main pool's bar on your way.

Only two other women have reservations this afternoon, both also single guests—and they might not even be there at the same time as you. Since a spot was open, I wrote in your name—the time slot starts at two and I'm enclosing a map. Feel free to indulge in some topless sunbathing or skinny-dipping if you want.

An invitation to your next fantasy will be coming soon. But for now, enjoy the Grotto.

Brent

P.S. I'm imagining you topless there, even though I know you won't be daring enough to do that. ☺

Despite the thoughtful invitation, Jenna couldn't help being disappointed. Having quickly gotten used to a steady diet of kinky fantasies, she was ready for the next one and didn't want any more recovery time. She wanted to see her man, wanted to see what he'd planned next for her.

But at least the letter meant he was thinking about her, too. Which, despite the differences between them, made her heart flutter in her chest. So if he'd been considerate enough to plan a relaxing afternoon for her, she'd certainly show up for it.

And if it was as lush and beautiful as he said, maybe it would be just the thing to take her mind off her emotions. After all, hadn't she come here to bask in the sun? Even if she'd ended up getting much more in the bargain, once she managed to clear her mind of sex and Brent for a moment, the Grotto actually sounded like a lovely place.

Of course, she was aching for him by the time she picked up the carafe of erotic rum punch he'd suggested. It was hard to believe how fast she'd grown accustomed to naughty sex.

But she would drink her punch and luxuriate by the Grotto, and . . . maybe be bold enough to go topless and surprise them both. Well, if the other women he'd mentioned weren't around, of course. She would love telling Brent later that she had, just to see the look on his face.

Brent waited patiently at the Grotto—although not out in the open. He'd dragged a lounge chair back into the bushes and wore a Hotel Erotique baseball cap, pulled low over his eyes.

A day had passed since he'd seen Jenna, but he was still reliving their most recent night together. The truth was—her dungeon fantasy had gotten out of hand. He'd gotten too caught up in the role, in the power struggle, and taken things too far. As a facilitator, he'd never lost control of a situation before, *ever*—so he wasn't sure how to explain it to himself. But she'd handled it like a trouper—she'd turned out to be so much stronger than probably either of them could have guessed. There was a lot more to Jenna Banks than he'd expected.

As for taking her back to his house . . . that part of the night also left him shaking his head. What the fuck had *that* been about? He concluded that he'd just been brain-dead after the dungeon scene. He'd followed urges without thinking. He'd simply . . . wanted to keep being close to her, not ready for the night to end.

Which was stupid, stupid, stupid. And he was getting stupider with her all the time.

He couldn't help wondering what the other facilitators had thought when there had obviously been more going on between the two of them than a normal dungeon fantasy. Would he lose their respect? Would everyone suddenly think it was okay to get involved with a guest?

So he was creating problems with her here, multiple ones. Damn it.

You have to stop this shit, once and for all.

Of course, he kept telling himself he was getting too close, feeling too much, but did he manage to get it under control? Not very well.

Yet he'd decided there was only one way to look at this. She had another week of fantasies, so during that time, he'd try to make the relationship less personal. And if he kept fucking up—well, it was only a week. And then she'd be gone and things would get back to normal.

God, why had Mariel had to be called away *now*?

But then he drew in his breath at the thought. If Mariel's father hadn't suffered that heart attack, Brent wouldn't know Jenna—she'd be just another girl by the pool. She'd have convinced Mariel she didn't want any fantasies, so he wouldn't even have encountered her as a facilitator. She wouldn't be growing, freeing herself, replacing those old, unhealthy perceptions of sex with new, better ones.

And as for him—well, for him the effects of her stay wouldn't be nearly as profound, but if things hadn't happened this way, he would have missed out on knowing someone whose company he enjoyed very much, and on a woman who, it turned out, excited the hell out of him. And after fifteen years here, that was saying a lot.

In fact, he was excited right now, his dick making a tent in his cargo shorts. Because it was time for Jenna's next fantasy—only she didn't know it.

Unlike her previous fantasies, however, he was simply here to privately observe and see how she reacted—not to take part. And though the opportunity for this fantasy had come up only yesterday, he thought the timing was good. This was a great point for him to step back, to let her spread her sexual wings without him there to push her.

Just then, a striking blonde in a pink bikini entered the Grotto area—and he could see immediately that she was just as beautiful as her pictures, and sexy as hell. He hoped Jenna would feel the same way.

He knew from Roxanne—the only female guide on the premises this week, who'd been too overbooked to take Jenna—that Chrissy was a twenty-eight-year-old lawyer on a fast track to the DA's chair who, despite being straight, had long fantasized about being with other girls. But her social circle didn't offer the opportunity, nor did she feel she could risk her professional reputation at home where so many people knew her.

She'd come here strictly for girl play, and so far had done very well in her first two fantasies. In one, Kirsten had guided her through some soft experimentation on the beach; then yesterday she'd lived out a courtroom fantasy, being seduced by two powerful women, the opposing counsel on a pretend case she'd just won, getting it on atop the judge's bench in the resort's on-site courtroom.

Now it was Chrissy's turn to seduce. She knew only that she was supposed to be at the Grotto in her bikini, that at least one of the other parties didn't know a fantasy was taking place, and that this was her chance to try her hand at tempting another woman into sex. Also on hand a little later would be Natasha, a facilitator who would keep things on track for both guests if required and also partake if it worked out that way.

As for *Jenna's* progress, there was no more discipline needed. She'd learned to give and to take when commanded, allowing Brent to acclimate her to wilder sex than she'd ever had, and teaching her to accept and follow her body's desires.

Of course, inducing her to obey him, while being a necessary evil that he'd personally enjoyed, had also reinforced her tendencies to please people, particularly him. So this fantasy—other than the added benefit of getting him out of the picture—was about encouraging her to be bolder, on her own. To respond to pleasure with ease. To *choose* to give it in return.

If she indeed followed her impulses, he'd know his tutoring was succeeding. After which he could advance her further, giving her new types of fantasies based more on her personal tastes—even if the actual *content* of the fantasies would be designed to continue expanding her limits.

And if more discipline came into play later, so be it. At least one of Jenna's future fantasies contained such elements because he'd been unsure where they'd stand at this point and he'd, frankly, underestimated how malleable she'd be. But for today, that didn't matter. Today was all about hoping Little Mary Sunshine was ready for a full-blown lesbian encounter. Hell. His cock was as hard as the rock walls of the Grotto, stiffening almost painfully when he envisioned what he hoped was about to happen here. Ah well—that was apparently how things would be for him until Jenna's stay was over. He was going to enjoy monitoring this fantasy far too much.

It was after Chrissy spread her towel at the edge of the pool, sitting down to dangle her feet in the water, that Jenna arrived. And Brent's heart nearly stopped. *Damn—hot bikini, babe.* He wished he could tell her. She looked fucking amazing. Not that the sight of her in a leopard-print bikini should get him that worked up, considering every *other* way he'd seen her. But there it was—Jenna just plain turned him on now.

As she lowered her carafe of punch onto the grass, then laid out her towel on a chair, all of Brent's senses heightened. It wasn't, by far, the first fantasy he'd monitored—guides sometimes watched fantasies to make sure everything went as planned—but it was probably the first fantasy he'd ever monitored with such intense, prurient interest. He was doing his job, but at the same time he was just another horny guy hoping to see some girl-on-girl action from the woman who'd been driving him to distraction the last few days.

Come on, Jenna, do this for me. Let yourself go. Let yourself play.

The Grotto was everything Brent had promised in his letter and more. Well off the beaten path, it was close enough to the beach for Jenna to feel the breeze and hear the calls of seagulls, but remained so isolated that it delivered the sense of being on some remote South Pacific island, as opposed to the grounds of the Hotel Erotique.

Only one other woman had arrived and, when Jenna approached, she turned to look up from her spot by the pool. "Hi," she said, flashing bright eyes and a friendly smile. She was extremely pretty, with long, blond, model-worthy hair.

"Hi," Jenna said, then looked around a bit more—toward the small waterfall Brent had mentioned, tumbling from a small rocky cliff built into the verdant landscape. The pool itself wasn't any larger than you'd find in the average backyard, but that somehow made it feel all the more like a secret utopia. Bright pink bougainvillea and other tropical flowers flourished near the waterfall and all around the area's perimeter, and though a few palm trees dotted the soft grass, the space was sunny and bright. "This place is beautiful," she heard herself murmur.

"I know," the other girl said, appearing just as in awe. "I've been sitting here taking it all in. I'm Chrissy, by the way." She gave her head a pretty tilt, leaving Jenna struck by how naturally vivacious she was.

"Jenna," she introduced herself, lowering herself to the edge of her lounge chair, then bending to pour some rum punch into a plastic cup.

"Yum," Chrissy said with a smile. "Lucky you. I just brought some water."

Given that she hardly needed to drink a whole carafe, Jenna said, "Want some? I even have an extra cup." The bartender at the main pool had given her two, in case one blew away in the breeze.

"If you're sure you don't mind. It looks delish."

Jenna widened her eyes as she filled the other cup. "You haven't had any erotic rum punch yet? It's great—I can't seem to stop drinking it and will probably be five pounds heavier by the time I get home."

Chrissy gave her a quick perusal and said, "With pretty curves like yours, five pounds won't hurt—you'll still look totally hot."

"Thanks," Jenna said softly, flattered but—even after her experiences here—not used to having girls compliment her body in a sexual way. When she stood to pass Chrissy's cup down to her, that's when she noticed the other girl's tattoo—a white and yellow daisy in the small of her back, just above her small pink bikini bottoms. She'd never seen a tattoo look at once so innocent yet sexy, and she thought it suited Chrissy well. "Nice tattoo," she said. Though she'd never felt much one way or the other about them, this one appealed to her.

Chrissy smiled over her shoulder. "Thanks. A gift I bought myself for passing the bar."

"You're a lawyer?" She didn't *look* like a lawyer. She *looked* like a swimsuit model.

Chrissy nodded easily. "Don't let the friendly exterior fool you—I'm a tiger in the courtroom."

"I'm impressed," Jenna said, leaning back in her chair, and—mmm, the sun felt incredible on her skin. There *was* something special about the privacy here—even in the presence of someone she'd just met, she felt completely at ease. She stretched out, even lifting her arms up over her head.

And when she glanced back to Chrissy, she almost got the impression her new friend was taking in her body—again. "Oh, come on—I'm sure you do something equally impressive and fabulous." Then she added, with a laugh, "You'd have to, to afford *this* place."

"Actually," Jenna informed her, "I won the trip in a contest."

"Wow—lucky girl."

"As for being impressive and fabulous, you'll have to be the judge. I write historical biographies for a living."

Chrissy gave her head a speculative tilt. "So you're an author?" she asked to clarify.

Jenna nodded. "But don't let the *occupation* fool you. I'm doing well, but I'm not living in a mansion or driving a Mercedes just yet."

Chrissy shrugged. "Still sounds pretty fabulous." Then she kicked up her feet, splashing lightly in the water, and leaned her head back. "Mmm, this is *so* nice."

"Is the water warm?"

"Just right," Chrissy assured her. Then she patted the grassy spot next to her towel. "You should join me."

Okay, so this wasn't going to be a *quiet* or *introspective* sort of afternoon. Jenna hadn't really planned on chatting, but she liked Chrissy and decided it could be nice to just . . . hang out with another girl for a while. In fact, it might be enlightening to get to know another guest—she'd hardly spoken to anyone here besides employees. The guests tended to keep to themselves or the people they'd come with, and she'd actually been very glad to discover it worked that way—but given her curiosity about the sort of person who paid to come here, and that Chrissy wasn't what she might have expected, maybe this would be interesting.

So Jenna moved her towel, smoothing it out next to Chrissy's.

And as she sat down beside her, Chrissy said, "I just have to tell you—that's a rockin' bikini. Your tits look amazing in it."

Jenna tried to ignore the blush warming her cheeks and hoped Chrissy wouldn't see it. Maybe it made sense that girls who paid to come to the Hotel Erotique were more comfortable talking openly about bodies than she usually was—so she would try to go with the flow. "Well, thanks. I was actually admiring yours, too." She punctuated the remark by dipping her feet in the water—the perfect temperature, as promised.

"My bikini or my tits?" Chrissy asked on a laugh.

Jenna caught her breath, but still tried to act as cool as she wanted to be. "Well, I meant your bikini, but your tits look pretty awesome, too." She hadn't really seen them before, but her new vantage point revealed that Chrissy possessed enviably perfect breasts—large, round, and so firm Jenna wondered if they were real. Real or not, though, they looked worthy of any men's magazine.

In response, Chrissy gave her chest a little shimmy, making her boobs jiggle provocatively. "Glad you like 'em," she said with another attractive smile. And for some reason, the move made Jenna aware of her *own* breasts, held snug in her Lycra top, and a surreptitious glance down revealed that her nipples were erect. Then again, they were *usually* erect these days, just as Brent had noticed earlier this week—the effect of him plus kinky sex.

"Oh, damn," Chrissy said, snapping her fingers. "I forgot to put on sunscreen." With that, she leaned back to reach for her beach bag, at the foot of another lounge chair just out of arm's reach. She ended up lying nearly all the way over on her side, stretching one shapely leg across Jenna's thighs. Jenna bit her lip uncertainly until Chrissy returned to the usual upright position, giggling. "Sorry—it was farther away than I realized."

For some reason, Jenna made a point of not watching Chrissy apply her sunscreen, but as the scent of coconut met her nose, she couldn't help observing from her peripheral vision: Chrissy smoothed it sensually over her arms, then her chest, including the round curves of her breasts. After doing her stomach, she rubbed more lotion across her thighs, massaging it in slowly and parting her legs to get the inner areas as well. Then she held the tube of lotion out to Jenna. "Do my back?"

If this were Shannon, it would be nothing—they'd been doing each other's backs since high school—but with Chrissy, it felt different. As Chrissy faced away and lifted her long hair, Jenna wondered how it would feel to rub the lotion into Chrissy's tan back as sensually as Chrissy had in front. So, with tiny butterflies fluttering through her stomach, she worked the fragrant sunscreen slowly and thoroughly into Chrissy's skin—although she hoped it wouldn't seem like she was . . . into her. "All done," Jenna said, snapping the cap shut and setting the tube down between them.

Okay, so she found Chrissy attractive. She'd learned in her time here that this was all right, that it didn't make her weird or anything. But as she'd applied the sunscreen, she'd also realized that she didn't feel compelled to . . . go further, to fool around with her. It was liberating not to be freaked out by her light sexual response to Chrissy—yet overall, she just didn't think she was that into girls. It had somehow been different when Brent was there—being with another girl, or more than one, had been so pleasurable because he'd wanted her to do it and it had clearly excited him.

"You didn't put any on, either, did you?" Chrissy asked.

Jenna remained distracted by her thoughts. "Huh?"

"Your shoulders are turning pink. You need sunscreen, too."

"Oh—thanks." Geez, clearly she was *too* distracted if helping Chrissy lotion up hadn't alerted her to do the same. She was usually smarter than that. "I keep forgetting the sun here is so much stronger than at home."

"You have to stay on top of it or you'll burn. And I bet that could really put a damper on a naughty fantasy. Here, I'll put some on you," Chrissy said, grabbing the tube.

Jenna offered her back, holding up her hair as well, as she said, "Good point." She'd hate to miss her next long-awaited fantasy with Brent.

She waited patiently as Chrissy applied the lotion—with just as much slow sensuality as when she'd put it on her *own* skin. Jenna bit her lip, absorbing the smooth, deep massage of Chrissy's fingers, and—mmm—despite herself, it *definitely* felt different than when Shannon did it.

Just enjoy it, she advised herself, remembering Serena's words from the dungeon and knowing Brent would tell her the same. Taking some pleasure in the sensation still didn't mean she was into the girl thing.

So as Chrissy's touch vibrated through her, Jenna let out a silent sigh, arching her back slightly. She became aware when Chrissy slid her fingers up under the lower strap of her top, and also when her new friend's touch glided downward, directly against the edge of her bikini bottoms.

"Hold your hair up higher so I can do your shoulders," Chrissy instructed, and as Jenna did so, she sensed Chrissy shifting behind her, turning more directly toward her back.

She rubbed Jenna's shoulders just as sensuously, her fingertips curling over Jenna's collarbone—and Jenna began to feel it in her breasts.

That was when Chrissy rose up onto her knees and extended her massaging motions down onto Jenna's chest. "You don't want to burn here, either," she said as if the move were perfectly natural, and Jenna bit her lip, pulled in her breath. Until finally Chrissy's fingers—sporting a French manicure—stretched directly down onto the bared inner curves of Jenna's tits.

She sucked in her breath as Chrissy worked the warm lotion into her soft flesh. Oh. My. It felt good. On her breasts. And in her bikini bottoms. She could barely reply to Chrissy's last comment, finally murmuring, "No . . . I don't." The words came out whispery, and her pussy tingled, yet she still remained unsure if she was into this. The physical response was certainly there and it would be easy to let herself enjoy some simple pleasure in such a sexy setting, but . . . something held her back.

Maybe because it felt simple *right now*, but she knew once things got started, it would be more complicated. There would be expectations, reciprocations. Things she wasn't sure she'd enjoy as much as these soft, easy touches.

Just then, another woman entered the area, and when Jenna turned to look, Chrissy automatically pulled her hands away. Jenna's heart skittered, as if they'd been caught at something.

But the new girl on the scene seemed completely unconcerned with them and looked almost frighteningly confident. The shapely, mocha-skinned woman wore a bright orange tropical-print bikini, cut very narrow and possessing much less fabric than either of theirs. She appeared to be bi-racial, and she was beautiful in a severe, almost intimidating way. Taking the lounge chair on the far side of the pool, she said in a slightly husky voice, "Hi, I'm Natasha. Do you mind if I take my top off?"

And as Jenna tried not to choke on her own saliva, Chrissy calmly replied, "No, of course not. This is the Hotel Erotique, after all."

"Thanks," Natasha said just as casually, reaching for the tie behind her neck.

And it was at that exact moment that Jenna saw something—oh God, it was *Brent*—in the bushes! Just his eyes, actually, beneath the brim of a baseball cap, but it was undoubtedly her sexy—and devious—guide!

She drew in her breath, her gaze locking on his. That sneak! This wasn't a casual afternoon at the Grotto, after all—it was another fantasy! Just one she wasn't privy to.

How dare he—not telling her! She flashed an irritated, scolding look in his direction.

But, upon moving slightly more into view, he only flicked his glance playfully back and forth between her and Chrissy a few times, then raised his eyebrows and mouthed the word, *Hot*—which left her more amused than angry, despite herself.

And then more . . . *aroused*. Because she could instantly see that he wasn't just teasing about it being hot. His gaze darkened on her and all playfulness faded as she understood he wanted this to happen: her and Chrissy.

Natasha was still busy shedding her top, and Chrissy was saying, "Wow, those are magnificent," which drew Jenna's attention briefly from Brent to take in the dark-skinned girl's enormous boobs, which *were*, she had to admit, pretty magnificent. But then she turned her gaze back to the man in the foliage, still unnoticed by the other two girls, who were now discussing the merits of Natasha's breasts.

She cast him another reproachful look, narrowing her eyes, and in reply, he simply grinned, shrugged, and spread his hands as if to say, *What's the big deal?*

She crossed her arms. *You know what the big deal is.*

His smile grew more lascivious again, and she read his silent challenge.

Especially when he darted his glance back to Chrissy—then gave Jenna a sexy wink just before sinking back into hiding.

She remained miffed—a little, anyway.

But she couldn't deny that now she was mostly . . . turned on. By Brent's very presence. And what he wanted her to do. And the knowledge that he was watching, waiting. Her pussy quivered anew.

"I'd love to see *your* tits, hon," Natasha was saying to Chrissy when Jenna tuned back in to the conversation. She nearly bit her tongue at the turn it had taken, but tried to calm down and get hold of herself. Because she could feel Brent's gaze. Nudging her. Prodding. It made her want to be sexy, made her *feel* sexier already.

Chrissy turned to Jenna with a friendly smile, then replied to Natasha, "Hell—why not?" Then she put her back toward Jenna. "Will you unhook me?"

And it suddenly seemed so much easier now.

To reach up and undo the bottom of Chrissy's bikini top.

To know where things were starting to go here.

Feeling how much Brent was enjoying this, she looked again in his direction as she said, "Here, I'll get the top tie, too," and gave the string at Chrissy's neck a long, slow pull.

Jenna watched as Chrissy tossed her pink top aside in the grass, then turned back toward the Grotto. She bit her lip as she peeked down at her friend's tits, her cunt pulsing.

"Girl, those are fantastic," Natasha said, her voice downright lust-filled.

But for some reason, it surprised Jenna when Chrissy turned to *her* and asked, "Are they all you hoped?"

Firm with hard pink nipples circled by wide areolas, they were . . . pretty damn stunning, no doubt about it. The triangular tan lines somehow heightened their appeal, perhaps reminding Jenna that she was seeing something usually kept covered. "And more," she admitted.

Chrissy cast a sensual grin. "Now you have to show us yours, too—it's only fair."

So it was. And truly, everything inside Jenna had changed now. Doubt had been replaced by daring, and she was completely into the game. Giving her lower lip a provocative bite and reaching behind her neck for the thick tie, she was taken aback to realize she actually enjoyed the sexy drama of revealing herself—she felt it in her clit as the top loosened and her excitement only grew as she pulled away the leopard-print fabric, even going so far as to lightly jiggle her boobs once they were freed.

"Mmm, *nice*," Chrissy said, biting her own lip as she studied them. "And we definitely don't want *those* to burn." She reached again for her sunscreen. "Can I? Pretty please?"

Jenna's pussy spasmed. A tiny part of her still remained nervous, but mostly, she was ready—ready to please Brent. So in reply, she simply sat up straighter, turned her body toward Chrissy, and once again reached to hold back her hair.

A naughty smile lit Chrissy's pretty face as she flipped open the cap, squeezed some lotion into her hand, then leaned in to oh so sensually rub the sunscreen into Jenna's breasts, massaging while running her fingers over and around Jenna's erect nipples, and leaving Jenna's pussy soaking wet. It felt, once again, as if she'd stepped into a porn movie—as if she were living someone else's wild life.

"Do mine, too," Chrissy said, passing the tube—and Jenna felt empowered now. So she didn't hesitate to fill her palm with coconut-scented lotion, then transfer some to her other hand. After which she lifted both palms to Chrissy's breasts.

Oh. God. So soft. Feminine. Strange but exciting, especially when Chrissy arched her tits into Jenna's grasp and moaned. She couldn't believe this was *her*, doing *this*—and yet she enjoyed every second of the sunscreen application, fueled by knowing Brent was probably going crazy with lust behind the tall bougainvillea across the pool.

When finally all the sunscreen had been massaged into her sexy new friend's bare tits, Chrissy cast a lascivious smile and said, "Come into the water with me." She took Jenna's hand and Jenna followed, rising to her feet, letting herself be led.

Perhaps oddly, her descent down stone steps into the sun-drenched pool made her think of baptism, but of an entirely different kind than you'd receive in a church. One more renewal here, one more new awakening that, in many ways, felt like a true rebirth.

Once both girls were in the pool, the water rising to just below chest level, Chrissy smoothly slid her arms around Jenna's waist and began to kiss her. Jenna returned the kisses, surprised but still emboldened, no longer afraid of new—even if alternative—sexual experiences. She continued to feel Brent's arousal somehow radiating from his hiding place as she sank cautiously but surely into the oddly pleasurable sensation of kissing another girl. As Chrissy shifted slightly, moving close enough to rub their tits together as they kissed, blood rushed to Jenna's cunt, everything around her feeling soft and sensual. Natasha watched from her lounge chair, but Jenna barely thought of her—she thought only of her body, her actions, and her guide: her master, the man who had transformed her and was, it appeared, transforming her still, using only his eyes now.

When Chrissy bent to tenderly kiss the sensitive tip of Jenna's breast, it shot through her like electricity, but—still practical, always—Jenna said, "What about the sunscreen?" Chrissy had definitely applied it well—right where she was kissing.

Yet her sensuous friend only smiled, softly murmuring, "Edible. Got it in the gift shop." Then she proceeded to lick and kiss Jenna's tits some more.

"Mmm," Jenna moaned, not even trying to hold it in. Brent wanted her to experience pleasure here, so she now would luxuriate in it. It vibrated through her in slow, hot pulses that made her cunt feel like a deeply beating heart between her legs. Chrissy fondled Jenna's breasts while she laved and sucked them, and Jenna's eyes soon fell shut as the sexy sensation consumed her. Oh God, it felt just as good as when a guy did it, only . . . softer, sweeter somehow. She leaned her head back as she grazed her fingernails lightly over Chrissy's shoulders, suffering the urge to make *her* feel good, too.

So when Chrissy finally lifted her head, licking her upper lip as she gave Jenna another seductive grin, Jenna didn't think twice before following her next inclination. She returned the favor, dipping to gently rake her tongue across Chrissy's left nipple.

Mmm, God—it was so taut against her lick. She instantly had to do it again—and again. Then she caught the pink bead in her mouth, gently sucking even as she swirled her tongue around it.

She heard Chrissy's light gasp of delight and relished it. She could pleasure a girl. A hot, gorgeous one. She had the power. *Yes*.

She suckled Chrissy's nipple in earnest then, loving the sounds the other girl made and still envisioning Brent's reaction. She soon moved to Chrissy's other ripe breast, again licking, sucking, nibbling, as comfortable as if she played with girls all the time.

When she rose back upright, they resumed kissing and pressing their tits together, moving sensually in the water until Chrissy's thigh slid between her legs. Within a second, their bodies were interlocked that way, each pushing one thigh to the other's crotch and beginning to grind, a position she remembered sharing with boyfriends in high school and college—simulated sex. Their motions were slow, sensual, Jenna's body heating wildly from the inside out, until Chrissy whispered in her ear, "I want to lick your pussy."

Jenna's breath caught. But she didn't argue. In fact, she didn't say anything at all. She simply met her pretty new girlfriend's gaze, gave her lower lip a hot little bite, then turned and walked up out of the pool.

As the water sluiced from her body, she reveled in it—even still wearing bikini bottoms, she'd seldom felt this gloriously naked, especially when the sun hit her breasts and she thought once more of Brent watching.

Looking back to the pool, she was surprised to see Chrissy not following, but when she caught the hungry look on her girlfriend's face as she instead neared the Grotto's edge, Jenna realized she should simply sit back down on her towel.

As she took a seat, though, her stomach lurched. This was getting serious. This was going to that place she hadn't been sure she wanted to go. But she was here, and her cunt pulsated madly, so she simply chose to forget her worries and go with the moment.

Situating herself at the pool's rim and lowering her feet in the water, she parted her legs and let Chrissy step between them—then released a hot sigh as Chrissy smoothed her hands up Jenna's open thighs. First Chrissy was gazing up at her, but then her eyes dropped to Jenna's leopard-print-covered crotch, so that when Chrissy whispered, "So pretty," Jenna wasn't sure if the compliment was for her or the mound between her legs.

When Chrissy reached for Jenna's bikini bottoms, Jenna drew her knees up, then planted her hands on the ground behind her and lifted her ass, letting Chrissy pull them down. She'd felt naked *before*, but this completed it. She'd never felt bolder than when she parted her legs *again*, this time putting her freshly shaven cunt on display.

As her girlfriend let out a low sound of lust, Jenna glanced down to see her pink folds glistening beneath the sun. That's when Chrissy molded her palms to the muscles stretching from the tops of Jenna's inner thighs and leaned in to lick her most intimate flesh. The pleasure burst through her like fireworks and a hot cry left her, unplanned. All she could do after that was bite her lower lip and watch.

She watched as Chrissy licked her pussy again, again, each time forcing a moan from Jenna's throat.

She watched as Chrissy sank her whole mouth over the pulsing pink creases in a sensual, openmouthed kiss that made Jenna instinctually part her legs wider, the small of her back arching involuntarily.

She watched as Chrissy thrust two fingers inside her as she laved and kissed and teased Jenna's clit with her mouth, leaving her to sink into a state of pure abandon. She leaned back on her elbows, still watching between her spread thighs and soon kneading her own breasts, needing sensation everywhere.

Oh God. The naughty sensations pumped through her like a whole new kind of blood in her veins. She felt so dirty—dirty *good*—knowing Brent watched her, imagining how long and rock-hard his cock was right now. She thrust lightly at Chrissy's eager mouth, the pleasure deepening, thickening, slowly becoming the biggest part of her. She took in the blue of the sky, the scent of coconut lotion, the slick moisture of her pliable breasts against her palms. She felt the grandeur of pleasure, pure physical pleasure, without attachment or commitment, just like Shannon and Kevin wanted for her, just like Brent wanted, too. And then she exploded into a hot orgasm that flowed up through her body like a volcanic eruption, covering her thoughts and senses so that all she knew was the buffeting, pounding release that washed away everything else.

Until she was coming back down, the upsurge receding—and even before the final pulses ebbed, she wondered, *What next? Do I have to return the favor? Do I* want *to?*

And then, like once before, Natasha saved her. The sound of a splash drew Jenna's eyes to where the topless woman had just entered the Grotto from the other side and now moved across the shallow pool, coming up to smoothly, confidently embrace Chrissy from behind. Her hands closed sensually over Chrissy's breasts, eliciting a fevered gasp from her the very moment she lifted her head from Jenna's crotch.

Almost immediately, Chrissy responded further, letting her head drop back in pleasure as she covered Natasha's palms with her own. Soon, though, Natasha's hands dropped, both of them grazing down Chrissy's slender stomach and into her pink bikini bottoms under the clear water. A low sob echoed from Chrissy's throat as the two women began to move together, Chrissy writhing against Natasha's touches, Natasha rubbing her shapely body against Chrissy from behind.

Weirdly, Jenna almost suffered a pang of jealousy—had Chrissy forgotten her that quickly? But then, as if reading her thoughts, Chrissy looked up. "Come back in and play with us."

Jenna instantly but politely declined, saying, "I just want to watch," yet felt better having been asked, silly as it seemed.

Not that she really wanted to watch—but she wanted to be *comfortable* watching. She wanted to be a woman who could lie here naked on an island, comfortable watching two other women pleasure each other. Or . . . did she mostly want to be that kind of woman for Brent?

Either way, she watched, feeling wild and free as they touched each other, soon kissing—but then she got up, putting on nothing but the wedge slip-ons she'd worn here, and began to make her way around the pool.

"Where are you going?" Chrissy stopped kissing Natasha to ask.

Jenna smiled lightly and replied, "Just taking a little walk—I'll be right back."

After which she left the two women to slink off into the bushes to find Brent—surprisingly comfortable, even happy, to stroll up to him naked in the hot sun. She discovered him reclining in a lounge chair in shorts, a T-shirt, and the baseball cap she'd noticed before. She put her hands on her hips, challenging him—even as she kept her voice low. "What's going on here, mister?"

She got a little wet again as his eyes roamed her body. "*You're* going on, honey," he said quietly. "Look at you—Little Mary Sunshine walking around naked and gorgeous, getting her pussy eaten by a pretty girl at the pool."

She simply arched one brow in reply. "I guess you think you're sneaky."

He gave his head a tilt. "I *did*. Until you saw me. That kind of ruined the sneaky element for me," he informed her with a grin.

She moved on to the heart of the matter. "Did you enjoy it?"

"Very much," he answered deeply. "I'm very proud of you."

His commendation warmed her. "Good."

"Did *you* enjoy it?"

She drew in her breath and answered honestly, as she always did with Brent. "More than I might have thought."

He continued appearing well pleased. "I'm glad. You looked amazing, by the way. Kissing her. Sucking her tits. And when she was eating you, I loved the way you massaged your breasts and didn't hide how good it felt."

Her cunt quaked lightly at his blunt words and she admitted, "I guess you've taught me something about that."

"You're a good student."

She cast a teasing look. "So I don't need any more punishment from Father Powers?"

He offered another grin in reply. "No, I'm afraid you're not misbehaving so much anymore, sunshine."

"Would *this* be considered misbehaving?" she inquired, then lifted one leg over his chair, lowering her naked body to straddle him. She pressed her palm to his hard-on, finding him gloriously big. *Mmm*.

A hot sigh left him just before he said with a dirty little smile, "Yes, honey, definitely. But you'd better get off me or you'll give me away."

"To those two? With all the noise they're making?" Chrissy and Natasha had gotten quite loud now and Jenna was, frankly, happier to be over here. "I want this," she told him, giving his erection a sexy squeeze.

Brent looked amused yet admonishing. "Well, sunshine, as the Rolling Stones once said, you can't always get what you want."

Which irritated her. "Why not?"

"Because this isn't that kind of fantasy."

"*What* kind of fantasy?"

"A cock fantasy," he said.

As more need welled in Jenna's chest, she leaned inward and whispered in his ear. "I hate to tell you this, but *all* of my *real* fantasies are cock fantasies." *Especially since meeting you.* Though she left that part out.

She saw him draw in his breath, his expression of humor beginning to edge into something more like arousal. Yet still he said, "It's not that I wouldn't love to, but I can't."

"Why not?" She didn't want to sound pouty, but she was starting to feel that way.

It surprised her when his face grew clouded, troubled. "Oh so many reasons," he murmured, perhaps more to himself than to her.

She blinked at him. "You're serious. You're seriously not going to fuck me?" She feared she might be talking too loud at this point, but she almost didn't care.

"Not now, honey," Brent told her, keeping *his* voice soft as he lifted one hand to her cheek. "Like I said, I'd love to, but you're not the only one in a fantasy right now, and if your girlfriend over there finds me here, it fucks up *hers*."

"It didn't fuck up mine. It helped it," she went so far as to admit.

"Don't say that," he told her gently.

"Why?"

He pursed his lips slightly. "You were supposed to do this without knowing I was here. You were supposed to do it just because it felt good."

She bit her lip, and gave him still more truth. "It did feel good. But it felt better after I saw *you*."

Brent narrowed his gaze on her, and she waited for some kind of admonishment, but instead he simply said, "So maybe we learned something new here. Little Miss Sunshine gets off on being watched."

By you. She nearly said it, but didn't. Instead she simply acknowledged, "Maybe."

"That's good to know," he replied—but at the same time, he began raising her off him, his hands on her ass, pushing upward.

She balanced on her knees, still astride him, and couldn't resist trying one last time. Dangling her tits near his face, she whispered, "You're really going to leave me here, soaking wet for you?"

He gave her a look. "Quit torturing me and get back to your fantasy." Then he proceeded to lift her further, until she had no choice but to stand.

To her surprise, he stood up, too.

"You're leaving?"

"I have a meeting in ten minutes."

She tilted her head. "What am I supposed to do about being, you know, turned on?"

"You have two perfectly capable partners over there, sunshine," he reminded her with a sly smile.

"You're evil," she replied, lifting her gaze to his.

"That's right," he answered. "I'm a very bad boy." And with that, he kissed her hard, deep, reaching down to stroke his fingers smoothly through her pussy. When he'd ended the kiss and backed away just slightly, he slid those same fingers in his mouth, quickly sucking them clean. "You're right, sunshine—you're soaking."

Then he reached around to smack her bottom, adding, "Be sure you put some sunscreen on this pretty ass," just before he walked away.

Jenna watched the rest of the fantasy, still not knowing exactly whose fantasy it *was*, but didn't get involved. Despite her poolside orgasm, she remained almost painfully aroused, but as she'd suspected, she just really wasn't all that into the girl thing if Brent wasn't there. The fact that he'd left her that way was both frustrating and infuriating.

When she returned to her room, though, she discovered a package on her bed—a narrow box of hot pink wrapped with a white ribbon. Upon removing the lid and pushing aside white tissue paper, she couldn't have been more stunned to discover—oh Lord!—a bright pink penis-shaped vibrator! Brent's gifts never ceased to surprise her, that was for sure.

Then she saw the note.

Pretend this is me, sunshine. Sorry I had to leave you that way. Tonight when I'm having an orientation dinner with my new guest, Danny, I'll secretly be envisioning you using this.

Brent

Holy God.

Jenna had never had a vibrator before. She'd had a longtime boyfriend, a few years ago, who'd occasionally been into using toys on her, but that had been her only experience with them before the glass dildo in the dungeon.

Her first thought: She didn't want to use it on herself—she wanted Brent to.

But God, she needed the release.

She stood staring down at the vibrator as if it were a rabid animal that might strike at any second. Then she realized how ridiculous that was and ran her fingers along the length of it, where the shaping was so exact that she found fake veins built into the thick, sturdy rubber. She picked it up, tested its weight, then grew bold enough to play with the knob on the end, filling her room with a low buzzing noise.

What would a naughty girl do right now?

Lie down on the bed and use it?

No. That seemed . . . too easy.

Take it to the shower with her? That sounded sexier, but who knew if it was waterproof, and God, what if she somehow shocked herself? Ugh—not a good thought.

She supposed she could be so daring as to take it out on the balcony, or even out on the beach tonight to use it *there*. But then—that only made her feel more lonely. Who was so desperate that they took a romantic walk on the beach with their vibrator?

Then an idea hit her. A really dirty one—so dirty she wasn't even sure she could bring herself to do it. But the moment that fear struck, that fascinated, curious sort of doubt—the "Can I?" question—she knew she had indeed figured out exactly what a truly naughty, nasty girl would do.

Her whole body tensed as she walked to her purse and drew out her cell phone. She'd barely looked at it all week—and had long forgotten about calling Shannon, unsure now that she could even share with her best friend all that was happening—but she was suddenly glad she'd brought it. Flipping it open, she set it to record video—then she propped it against her purse on the desk, pointing it toward the bed.

And then . . . she became a porn queen again.

Chapter 10

Brent sat at a table next to one of the resort's many pools, eating an orientation dinner of barbequed ribs with his newly arrived guest. Not every new arrival was greeted in the gazebo with wine and fancy food—Danny Gibbs was a Georgia construction worker who'd just inherited a lot of money, and barbeque by the pool was more his style.

Danny's needs and desires were par for the course here, especially for guys like him who didn't have much luck with the kind of girls he wanted—gorgeous model types. So his first fantasy would be a beach tryst with a beautiful bikini-clad babe, progressing from there to a multiple cheerleader fantasy and other similar scenarios. Compared to Jenna, guiding Danny was a breeze—Brent could practically do it in his sleep. But he did have a goal for Danny—he hoped by the time Danny left he'd be more confident, smoother with the ladies, and as they ate, he casually gave the guy some pointers without making it obvious that's what he was doing.

Just as he was schooling Danny on how to approach a woman, though, his phone vibrated in his pocket. "Just a second," he said, annoyed at the interruption. But given that the staff didn't usually bother guides during meetings, he thought he'd better check it.

Glancing down, he saw a text from the front desk: *Jenna Banks asking for your #. Says important. OK to give?*

Hmm. Never a dull moment with Jenna. She'd been on his mind all afternoon since her sumptuously sexy performance at the Grotto.

He sent back a quick *OK*, then returned to his conversation.

Fifteen minutes later, as Brent was going over some basic fantasy rules, his phone vibrated again. He paused to pull it out and take a look, surprised to see Jenna wasn't calling but *had* sent him something.

Was it . . . a video? He didn't use most of the fancy gadgets on his phone, so he wasn't sure, but when he clicked, it was indeed a video—of Jenna stretched out on her bed in only a pretty pair of lace panties, again caressing her breasts. His chest tightened instantly and he pushed the pause button, looking to Danny. "Excuse me," he said, trying to sound completely calm and professional. "I'm afraid I have to take this."

Brent hurried away across the patio onto a more private sundeck, empty now that night had fallen. Then he resumed watching the video of Jenna—in total awe.

She massaged her tits so sweetly, so sensually—he knew she wasn't just acting for the camera. She was truly making herself feel good. And though thoughts of her had kept him moderately hard all day, now he stiffened further.

Next, she reached beside her and—ah—drew his little present into the picture. He watched, utterly captivated, as she raked the pink shaft up over one nipple, then the other, playing, experimenting for him. As she let the fake cock glide down over her beautifully bare torso, she watched its progress, sensually sliding her tongue across her upper lip before she dipped the toy between her legs. *Yes, baby, that's so hot.* His erection grew.

He waited patiently—but also eagerly—until she set the vibrator aside and used both dainty hands to ease those sexy panties down her thighs, then off. *So, so pretty, Jenna. So sexy and hot.* Then she parted her legs—toward the camera. *Damn. Nice.*

With her moist tongue still poised against that soft upper lip, she positioned the vibrator's tip at her opening, and as she pushed the head into her sweet pussy, clenching her teeth and letting out a small groan, Brent's stomach contracted. *Fuck. He felt this too much.* Way *too much.* He had to move to a bench at the deck's edge and sit down.

When she pushed the toy all the way in with a heart-stopping sigh, Brent felt almost as if *he* were sinking into her. The sight stole his breath.

And then she began to slide the fake cock in and out, in and out, moaning softly with each inward drive, and he felt weak watching her pleasure herself for him.

Soon she turned the vibrator *on*, and those moans grew deeper. His cock ached and he began to sweat despite the sea breeze. He'd selected a toy that came with a nub at the base, designed to stimulate her clit with each deep thrust, and it was easy to tell it was working, especially when she stopped the in-and-out strokes and instead just left it all the way *in*, simply working the base of the cock against her clit now.

As Brent watched, his focus moved gradually from her cunt to her face. The screen was small, of course, but he could still see how much she had opened herself to him, in every way. The blood drained from his cheeks and his dick felt like it would burst from behind the zipper of his khakis as she moaned and groaned—until finally she came, in a barrage of hot little breaths and then the longer, higher sobs he'd heard from her before.

When the video ended, he simply sat there for a long minute.

Damn—she was so dirty now. Truly a bad girl. He could barely fathom the difference in her from when she'd first arrived.

Except that . . . her surrender, her sexuality, were still too attached to *him*.

He'd felt much more in control of the whole situation after managing to keep his cock in his pants today at the Grotto, but then—shit—he'd had to go writing that note, telling her he'd imagine her using the toy. If she'd simply used it by herself, on her own, he'd have felt one step closer to making her newfound naughtiness independent of him—but as it was, just the opposite had happened.

Well, he'd have to think about how to change that—but for now, the horny guy in him just played the video again and got a monster hard-on as he watched it a second time.

After which he finally returned to Danny and cold barbeque with an apology—but no matter what he did after that, he couldn't stop thinking about Jenna.

Hours later, Brent lay in the hammock next to his bungalow, listening to the waves crash on the shore and watching as Jenna fucked herself over and over again with the toy he'd sent her. He felt like an eighteen-year-old kid seeing his first porn movie—for some reason, he couldn't get enough. She was so . . . innocent. And yet not. She somehow straddled both ends of the spectrum.

The truth was, he wanted to call her, or just go to her room. He wanted to fuck her brains out. He wanted to give her what she'd begged for today. *Begged. Jenna.* She'd gotten so good, so fast, at expressing her desires. "My dirty, dirty girl," he whispered toward the tiny screen on his phone.

He wanted to fuck her tonight—but he couldn't. Just couldn't.

Tomorrow she'd have another fantasy. And he'd be involved—yet so would others, so at least it wouldn't be . . . intimate.

Then again, somehow the harem fantasy had turned intimate between them, and even the dungeon fantasy, by the time it was over, had felt very much like they were the only two in the room. But he'd at least *try* to make tomorrow's fantasy different. He was giving her something he thought would appeal to everything inside her—but in the end, this time, he wouldn't give her . . . him. He'd just decided that part, right now. He wouldn't fuck her tomorrow. He'd keep reinforcing that this wasn't about *him*—it was only about *her*. Even if it killed him.

And it might, he decided as he finally unzipped his pants and took out his straining cock.

Dick in hand, he watched her again, fucking herself to ecstasy—the only difference now being that he came *with* her this time.

And then—hell, he knew he shouldn't do it, shouldn't respond at all, but she *had* opened herself to him, *so* much, *so* completely. She'd put herself out there in a way that . . . well, it had to be scary for her, and he was so enormously proud of her for pushing her fears aside time after time. So he sent her a simple text message:

Thank U, baby
I just came with U
Goodnight

But this had to be the end of the personal stuff between them. It had to.

. . .

You Are Invited to a Fantasy

Where: Castaway Beach (map included)
When: Today, 4:00 p.m.—but the year is 1715.
You are the only survivor of a shipwreck and are stranded on a desert island.
Fortunately, a trunk of clothing has washed up on the beach with you,
and you've found ample fruit to eat.
Rescue is imminent—if you are agreeable.
Ultimate pleasure and freedom will soon be at hand
for a woman bold enough to accept the price.
(Your safeword is Cleopatra.)

Jenna sat on the isolated beach at the far end of the island, her pussy humming with anticipation. Wearing the emerald green colonial-style dress she'd found in the trunk, she pulled up the skirt to keep from getting too hot, then glanced back down at the invitation she'd received earlier. She wasn't exactly sure what would happen here, but she was already entranced. This was the first fantasy she'd faced without fear—only excitement. The eighteenth-century was one of her favorite time periods, and she was particularly immersed in the era right now—back in real life—while she penned her pirate anthology. Had Brent planned something piratical for her? She didn't know—but couldn't wait to find out.

And she also just plain couldn't wait to see him. For hours last night she'd worried he wasn't going to respond to her naughty video and she'd even begun to regret how audacious she'd been. But then her phone had finally rung, and she'd gotten that delicious text that had made her hot and wet all over again.

She really felt a bit like a colonial castaway in her fancy frock. Although no underwear other than a corset had been provided, she was well able to imagine that if she were shipwrecked, she'd quickly abandon most of the heavy undergarments of the period anyway. The antique-looking corset shoved her breasts upward, but didn't cover them, leaving deep cleavage atop the dress's low-cut bodice. Trimmed in white lace, the dress wasn't completely accurate for the time, but close enough, with a black ribbon crisscrossing down the front. Buttons spanned the back seam of the dress and she'd been unable to do them all the way up, but the dress still held together well enough, albeit loosely at the shoulders. Narrow sleeves extended just past her elbows, from which several inches of white lace drooped prettily.

It felt odd but somehow exotic to be wearing such a formal gown while barefoot, digging her toes into the sand. Sitting in the shade of a large banyan tree, she reached for a banana from the pile of fruit next to the trunk, also containing plums, mangoes, and oranges, along with a knife—which made her grin, wondering if she'd also been so fortunate to have *that* wash up onto shore with her. Her convenient shipwreck luck had also provided an open, corked bottle of wine, so she washed down her banana with it.

It was as she took a last sip that she glanced up to see the most amazing vision—a dark wooden pirate ship had just come into view in the distance, complete with the Jolly Roger flying high! The sight sent chills skittering up her arms and down her spine—this suddenly felt much more real, as if she'd truly stepped back in time.

As the pirate ship slowly neared the shore, her heartbeat kicked up—she wasn't sure if it was due to seeing pirates or . . . seeing Brent. Not being with him—*really* being with him—for two days had felt like an eternity. Even if last night had helped. She bit her lip, remembering his message and picturing him getting himself off while watching her. The emotions that had rushed through her had run so much deeper than a mere physical attraction.

Oh God, I love him.

She knew it was true—because she felt both giddy and miserable when she thought about it.

But as she'd been telling herself for the past couple of days, now was not the time to brood over it. Now was the time to enjoy him—every inch of him. *Do not sulk. Instead, soak him up. Take him inside you, both physically and mentally.* She was simply in too deep here to run from the feelings or push them away now—her emotions were tied up intrinsically with everything else taking place at the Hotel Erotique.

Her heart was in her throat by the time anchors were dropped over the sides of the ship. And wow, it was just hitting her that the resort had its own real, full-size Spanish galleon! A moment later, a smaller rowboat was lowered to the water for bringing the passengers—in this case, her pirate!—to shore.

The galleon was anchored far enough away that she couldn't clearly see the smaller vessel's inhabitants until it came bounding over the waves breaking just off the beach. And then her heart *really* did flip-flops in her chest. Oh my. The boat held three hot, sexy men all in pirate garb, and one of them was indeed Brent. She rose to go meet them as the rowboat glided up onto the sand, and soon all three pirates marched toward her.

Brent wore a long navy blue captain's coat, no shirt underneath, with historically accurate-looking breeches and leather knee boots. A strip of red cloth was tied around his head and he sported a day's dark stubble on his chin; a long dagger hung from his belt as he strode up the beach with authority. And *mmm*, Brent did pirate very well.

She barely even looked at the two men flanking him, but as they grew close, she recognized the long-haired one as dangerous Zack from the dungeon and was pretty sure she'd seen the other—with dark, messy hair and a profusion of muscles—somewhere here, but she couldn't quite place him.

Only once they got close enough to make eye contact, however, did Jenna remember that they were *pirates* and that, in terms of the fantasy, she probably shouldn't be tramping so happily toward them. Unless . . . "Have you come to rescue me?" she asked hopefully, falling into her character with sudden and shocking ease.

Brent's eyes narrowed on her darkly, and she sensed—with still more excitement—that she would soon be ravished. "What have we here?" he asked, looking downright predatory. "We come looking for treasure and get a comely wench in the bargain." He spoke with a light pirate's accent, and—oh boy—even that made her cunt weep with lust.

"A wench, sir?" she asked, acting offended. "I will thank you to remember you're addressing a lady."

Brent let out a hearty pirate's laugh, but she could see in his eyes his true amusement over how she'd warmed to her role, even embellishing it. But the dress had told her she was surely a member of upper-class society.

"A lady, are you?" he asked, sounding insultingly skeptical.

She added more details to her persona. "Indeed, sir. I was sailing to meet my husband at his sugarcane plantation in Jamaica. He is very wealthy and will reward you handsomely for my safe delivery there."

"Well, *my lady*," he said, injecting sarcasm into the words, "be a good wench and we may consent to drop you in Jamaica, but I can't promise you'll be *safe* in our hands."

She pressed a palm to her chest in faux shock. "Why, whatever do you mean?"

"We've been at sea a long while and there's something we're in far greater need of than gold or silver right now."

She played dumb, but also began to act uneasy. "Well, whatever form of payment you desire, my husband will gladly give it. Name your price."

"Our price, wench, rests between your creamy thighs."

At this, Jenna's pussy swelled and her breasts heaved lightly against the tight corset shoving them upward. Gasping, she feigned pure horror. "You—you cannot mean . . . to defile me."

Brent's gaze sparkled on her beneath the hot sun. "Depends on how you look at it, I suppose. What you call defiling we see as pleasuring. And we do indeed intend to pleasure you, *deeply*, my lady. With all the cock you can handle."

When Jenna sucked in her breath this time, she wasn't faking it. She'd just *had* to tell him yesterday how much she craved his cock, tossing around the word like it was light and casual, hadn't she? In an instant, however, she understood that she was to get way more than just *his* cock in this fantasy—and that remained daunting. *Very* daunting. Her tight corset was making it difficult to breathe.

"What do you say to *that*, my lady?" he finally asked, his expression threatening. Even though she knew he was simply playing a role, her stomach churned lightly—because he'd been playing a role in the dungeon, too, but it had also seemed very real. She had to wonder—her trepidation returning, damn it—what her commanding guide had in store for her now.

When she didn't reply, he went on. "My crew and I will gladly deliver you to your husband—all *you* need to do is spread your legs."

"No," she said, "I cannot." Then she turned away. She didn't exactly mean the words yet she wasn't sure she wanted what he had planned for her here, either. Meaning . . . more than him—other guys, too. Inside her. And she'd ultimately reaped pleasure from that in the dungeon, but it hadn't come easily. Perhaps it had been stupid of her to look so merrily forward to this—thinking only of Brent, Brent, Brent. She'd somehow forgotten to see the big picture here.

"Well, my lovely wench," Brent said, "if that's your decision, so be it."

She spun to face him again, surprised.

That's when he added, "What you do not choose to give, we'll simply take."

Their eyes locked just before he moved toward her in a rush. Instinctively, she lifted her arms in front of her and Brent grabbed tight to both wrists. She found herself struggling, not against Brent but against the lusty pirate he'd become. Before she knew it, she'd toppled to her knees and he came down with her, pushing her to her back in the warm sand.

Pinning her arms to the beach on each side of her head, he kissed her—hard. And whatever strange combination of reactions she felt in that moment—worry, lust, intimidation, nervousness—it all fell away and she suffered nothing but the joy of being beneath him, taking his hot kisses and returning them with everything inside her.

When he shoved his knee between her thighs, she let out a moan and sank deeper into every sensation. Soon he freed her wrists, and she ran her fingers through his hair, digging them into his broad shoulders. At the same time, he captured her breasts in his grip, making her cry out at the rough caress—then he yanked the dress from her shoulders, where it was already loose, until her tits were on display. A growl erupted from his throat just before he latched his mouth on to one tightly engorged nipple, sucking deeply, wildly, making her sob as she wriggled beneath him, her pussy flooding with heat.

He moved hungrily to the other breast, the stubble on his chin abrading her soft flesh, but she didn't care—it compared nothing to the powerful need he sent spilling through her.

One moment he'd nearly doused her arousal with his threats of multiple lovers—the next he'd completely restored it, driving her even wilder than she'd been to begin with.

"Oh! God—yes!" she heard herself cry as he sucked her tit almost painfully. Her delight overrode that, and as the intense sun burned down on them, all she wanted was more—more of whatever Brent wanted to give her.

Finally, when he released her tender nipple from his mouth, his breathing labored, he peered down at her. "You've become more agreeable, I see."

She was just as breathless, admitting, "So I have."

When Brent looked deep into her eyes she felt it everywhere, moving through her like hot liquid. "Have you been a long while without a man, my lady?"

Continuing to meet his gaze, she thought of the last two days without him inside her. "It . . . feels that way."

She knew his next deeply spoken words were about more than his role—they were about what was coming, about preparing her for it. "Then give in to your body's needs and think of nothing else."

Rolling off her, he bent to scoop her into his arms. With her dress still falling off, revealing her higher-than-normal breasts, he carried her a short distance across the wide beach until lowering her to the sand, on her feet, next to an old fallen tree. The sun had bleached its trunk nearly white, the remaining remnants of branches nothing but snarled twists of wood. The other pirates joined them and given that her tits were visible, she probably should have felt more embarrassed—but clearly her stay here was having an impact, since she was much more concerned with the need coursing through her now.

Not bothering to be gentle, Brent pushed her against the thick tree stretching across the beach and growled, "Bend over, wench."

She did so, at the waist, resting her stomach on the smooth tree. She was rewarded almost instantly by the sensation of his hard-on pressing into the center of her ass through their clothes. The sound of her harsh breath mingled with the crash of the tide as she waited—silently begging, *Please, please!*—for Brent to fuck her.

She let out an almost gleeful sigh when his strong hands pushed up under her dress, sliding smoothly up her thighs and onto her bare bottom.

"Lift her skirt," she heard him tell one of the other guys. She couldn't even see which one obliged but felt the sea breeze waft over her skin as the weight of the long dress settled around her waist. In response, Brent let out a small groan and said, "Mmm, look at this pretty, round ass." When he resumed rubbing the rock-hard column of his shaft there, she wiggled against him, unable to help herself.

Seconds later, he leaned forward, warming her back with his front, until he whispered in her ear. "Ready yourself for pleasure, my lady. *Deep* pleasure." And when he began to massage her rear, she couldn't hold in her moan. Her swollen pussy pulsed and her breasts ached, and any touch helped fill the rough need he'd built in her.

"Now fuck her," Brent said.

And just as she was registering that he'd made the demand of someone else—new hands molded to her hips and a hard shaft plunged inside her. Despite herself, her body arched, her head dropped back automatically, and pleasure roared through her as her long, low sob echoed through the air. Oh God. So hot, so filling. Brent had primed her, aroused her, and now—oh Lord, it truly seemed any cock would do!

Jenna caught her breath—adjusting to having another man inside her, adjusting to the strange satisfaction it brought—just as that man began to move in and out, pumping, pumping. And God help her, she moved *with* him, fucking him back.

Just then, Brent appeared in front of her on the other side of the dead tree. Closer to standing upright than bent over now, she still leaned forward into the wood, holding on to it for balance—so she only had to lift her gaze to meet his eyes. She tried to read them, but all she could decipher with certainty was passion.

When his hands rose to her breasts, she sighed and whispered, "Yes." And when he leaned in to kiss her—deep tongue kisses that permeated her soul—while another man drove his cock into her cunt, she'd never felt so utterly consumed with heat.

This was different than the dungeon. There, she'd been fearful and worried, fighting everything so hard—but now, she very quickly accepted the pure, overwhelming pleasure of the fantasy. She sank into it fully, meeting the cock that fucked her from behind, meeting the warm mouth that kissed her lips in front. Since she was standing, each stroke bored into her more intensely, stretching all through her.

She moaned into Brent's mouth as he caressed her tits and lightly pinched her nipples. Sensation pulsed through her whole body, out through her fingers and toes, up into her scalp, and soon she struggled to stay on her feet. When her knees gave way, Brent caught her in his arms, as did the unseen lover behind her. And even just that, being in the arms of two men, felt so bizarre and wondrous that she quit thinking and simply went with utter abandon wherever Brent wanted her to go.

"Turn her around," Brent instructed, and she felt her body being rotated, then Brent's able grip at her waist as he hoisted her ass onto the sun-washed tree. It gave her a chance to see that the man so capably fucking her was Zack, who'd done so in the dungeon as well. He made a hot pirate, wearing a flowy white shirt, open across his chest, and through his long hair she spied a silver hoop in one ear. His erection remained upright, sprouting from undone pants, near the cutlass strapped to his side. Now Jenna knew what she'd felt pressing against her thigh—which told her the knives were fake, even if impressive visually.

The other pirate stood nearby, and she got a longer look at him now, too. He appeared to be of Latin descent, also sporting an earring. He wore only a black vest over tan breeches and black boots, and tattoos spanned his biceps. His dark eyes were as lust-filled as her own surely were, and a large bulge stretched upward at his crotch.

"Eat her pussy, Rico," Brent demanded, and the Latin man came toward her. And then it hit her—Rico! Their waiter that first night in the gazebo. But he looked . . . well, different now, to say the least.

One of Brent's arms was anchored around her waist, but he used his free hand to gather the skirt of her dress, pulling it briskly up. "Spread," he whispered darkly in her ear, so she parted her legs.

Rico stooped down and leaned in, immediately devouring her—and she cried out, not expecting him to start out with such hungry eagerness. In fact, she wasn't sure she'd ever been eaten with such bold gusto before—she seemed to feel his tongue, teeth, and lips everywhere at once, stretching from the bottom of her cunt to the top.

Broken cries left her throat as her body responded involuntarily, her pelvis lifting, contracting in a jagged, unsteady rhythm she couldn't control. Brent held her tight from behind and she clutched at his arm and relished the feel of his masculine body supporting her. Soon she lifted her feet onto the smooth log, allowing her to spread wider, feel it all more intensely. She bit her lip as she watched her new Latin lover go down on her.

She'd never even spoken to him, but that didn't impede the hot pulsations echoing through her body, growing wilder each second. Wet sounds rose from where he worked and she met his tongue with her clit—again, again—moaning at each new burst of heat. Brent massaged one breast, then the other, kissing her neck, gently biting her shoulder.

She gasped when she knew orgasm was approaching. "Mmm, yes," she murmured, nearly breathless, eyes falling shut, her head dropping back to Brent's chest. And then—"Oh. God. *Now,*" she murmured just before the tumultuous climax hit, rocking her body, again taking all her control—but Brent still held her as she screamed her release.

When finally it passed and limp exhaustion came, the delicious pressure between her legs ceased and she loved recovering in Brent's embrace. He let her rest that way for a long, tranquil moment—before saying, "Lie back on the tree, sunshine."

She opened her eyes and peered over her shoulder at him, aware he'd broken out of character. But he didn't seem to have noticed—he was easing away from her, yet still supporting her, helping her recline until her head rested against a large branch, broken off only inches above where it began, providing a good headrest. Her dress remained pulled to the top of her thighs and falling down over her breasts.

"Zack, let our pretty wench feel your cock on her tits." She was just processing Brent's words when he added, "And Rico, climb onto the tree and fuck her." Jenna drew in her breath as a passing breeze set her skin tingling all over.

And yet . . . no Brent? Apparently not, right now.

But somehow he'd finally done it, filled her with enough brazen desire that it didn't matter anymore.

Rico, the Latin now *technically* becoming her lover, boosted himself onto the log with the agility of a cat. This time, she didn't even have to be told to spread her legs—she simply did it, letting them drop over the sides of the tree so that she straddled it, waiting while rough and sexy Rico unbuttoned his period-style breeches and an impressive phallus popped free. She bit her lip at the sight—thick and slightly curved, it was smaller than Brent's but ample indeed.

As Rico knelt between her legs, Zack stepped up beside her and their gazes met. She remembered him whispering dirty things to her the other night and sensed he might be recalling the same. When his hand cupped her breast, she tensed—but again, all she felt was pleasure, pure and thick, washing through her. And when Rico lifted her thighs, bringing them across his own, then smoothly slid his hard cock into her cunt, that pleasure increased tenfold, nearly swallowing her.

Low moans left her with each even stroke he delivered and she lay content to soak up the filling sensation. A hot, "Ohhh," echoed from her when Zack leaned in to do what Brent had said, running the length of his stiff shaft over her breast. She watched both cocks pleasure her, acceptant and grateful, aware that her entire body felt cradled in a warm, dirty delight she'd never experienced.

A few feet away, Brent observed, and though she tried to keep her focus on Zack and Rico, she knew she reaped far more joy from the same source as yesterday—Brent's eyes on her. It was almost as if his gaze touched her, caressed her, supported her, reassured her. In a strange way, it was almost as good as if *he* were inside her, as if *he* were teasing her tits with his erection. Not quite, of course—but not a bad substitute.

So she alternated between watching the thick phallus filling her moist, tight opening below and studying the other erect cock caressing her nipples or sliding over the softer part of her breasts—and she found it utterly hot when Zack positioned his body to lay his shaft flat between her tits, then used his hands to push them up around it, fucking her *that* way. But the thing that thrilled her most of all was the constant sight of Brent in her peripheral vision, taking it all in, experiencing it *with* her.

Both Zack and Rico growled and groaned their pleasure and she thought it made a lovely little erotic symphony—reminding her how wild she was now; that she was with two men at once and being watched by a third; that she had suddenly become a dirty, dirty girl and—to her shock—she liked it. But when another male sound echoed from her left, she turned her eyes past Zack's firm body to Brent, whose face now filled with deep want, and whose dick was freed from his pants, in his hand.

Oh God, that was hot. To see him touch himself—for her. It was what his message last night had made her envision and was nearly enough to make her come, even without direct attention to her clit. She bit her lip, watching *him* watch *her*, and loved letting it send a whole new hot, naughty sensation vibrating through her body.

Soon her gaze focused tight on his big, masterful cock, so stiff and huge in his fist. Mmm, God, she wanted it. In an entirely different way than she wanted Rico's or Zack's. This ran deeper, like she imagined an addiction might feel.

She heard her breathing increase, becoming more rapid—and that changed the pace of the sex. What had been, for a time, moving slow and hot now grew faster, rougher. Rico's thrusts drove deeper and came with small, heated grunts. In turn, Zack kneaded her breasts with more intensity, then rubbed his rigid length more brusquely over one tit.

The change fired more pleasure through Jenna's body, escalating her arousal to a fever pitch—it took only a moment given all she'd been through today, this week—and when she looked over at Brent again, their gazes locked in torrid lust. Oh God, how she wanted him! How she wanted that cock of his!

Dropping her gaze to it again—oh, oh Lord . . . with one penis in her pussy and another at her tits, she actually longed for a third. Found herself *hungry* for it. *Truly* hungry—she wanted it in her mouth. She felt wild for it between her lips, desperate for it to fill her, be inside her, however or wherever it could go. With her eyes on his majestic erection, her lips parted, wider, wider, from pure instinct and need. And, mouth still open in bold invitation, she cast him a look of pure yearning, silently pleading with him to put his cock inside.

Brent appeared just as desperate, his eyes half shut, his jaw lax, as he gazed at her gaping mouth, then her eyes—just before he lightly shook his head, refusing her unspoken appeal.

Jenna closed her eyes, crushed and left feeling amazingly empty given the erection still thrusting between her legs. *God, why didn't he want to? How could he say no to her—now?*

That's when his deep, lusty voice broke through the other sounds around her. "It's so hot to watch you be fucked, my dirty little wench," he said, dark, seductive, still affecting just a hint of his pirate accent. "I love to see your wet cunt swallow that cock, to hear the way you purr and moan."

And somehow, just *that* helped. Again, not a physical touch—but now it was as if his voice reached out to her instead. "You make my cock so fucking hard, my lady," he added with a sexy glint in his eye. And she had no idea why *he* wasn't fucking her—or touching her, or *something*—but, incredibly, just the dirty words he spoke so warmly were enough to make her feel close to him. She knew he'd felt her need, and this was how he was feeding it.

"Put the wench on her hands and knees on the beach," he said, and she wondered what he had in store for her next. Jenna didn't fight or resist as the other two men lifted her down from the fallen tree trunk and gently pushed her to her knees in the soft, hot sand. She planted her hands in front of her, bending over, thinking—*Please, Brent, fuck me. You, not anyone else. It's you my body craves.*

"Very good, my lady," Brent said, fully back in character now. "Such cooperation may get you to Jamaica yet." And when he moved near her, she was sure her silent begging had been answered—but Brent merely bent down to lift the long emerald skirting back up over her ass.

How obscene must she look right now? But it didn't bother her; it only made her feel like an object of erotic desire—in a *good* way. She'd always believed being objectified was horrible, but she was slowly learning that, sometimes, it was exactly what she wanted: to be desired solely for sex, for her sexual self. It made her feel free of all the mental chains that had kept her from fully enjoying her own sexual nature up to now.

"Zack, fuck that pretty pink pussy," Brent said, stepping back to one side of her. "And Rico, fuck her soft little mouth."

Part of Jenna's heart broke. He *really, truly* wasn't going to be with her in *any* way? What was wrong?

Yet then she sensed pirate Zack kneeling behind her in the sand, his hands at her hips. Pirate Rico then dropped to his knees in front of her. And Brent stood to the side, again just a vague image in her peripheral vision—but oh God, for him, *suddenly, again*, she *wanted* this. Whether he was really a part of it or not. She wanted to be that dirty, that filled. She wanted him to watch. She wanted to feel it for him.

She cried out as Zack plunged inside her from behind—and, oh Lord, the position made him feel bigger. She bit her lip, adjusting. Then she saw Rico's sturdy cock before her eyes, in his hand—ready.

Releasing a hot breath, she opened her mouth and let him slide inside. He went slow, gentle, clearly understanding that this was a lot for her to take. She wanted it to be Brent. Just as she wanted the man behind her to be Brent, too. Impossible as it was, that's how she thought of it in a way. Neither man was Brent, yet they did his bidding, responded to his commands. They fucked her because he said to.

And oh God, how the two pirates filled her. It was almost overwhelming, and at moments, she forgot all about Brent because her senses were on overload—her body was being pummeled from front and back, top and bottom, and all she could do was take in the sensations and endure the way they echoed through her. Sex, she had learned here, was about so much more than certain body parts—at times, she truly felt it everywhere at once, as if her entire *being* was getting fucked.

But, of course, the longer it went on—oh hell, she was back to feeling Brent again. His gaze, his intent interest, the sexual aura that radiated from him. And—mmm, God, yes—coming back to him, emotionally, made it all even better. When she felt him studying her every move and reaction, her pleasure grew still more intense.

She shut her eyes and threw herself into the acts of sucking and fucking. She listened to the sound of the crashing tide mix with her own deep sounds of pleasure as her hands and knees sank deeper into the gritty sand. Her face felt flushed, her stomach sweaty beneath the corset. It all felt so overpoweringly good, and she needed Brent to see that, feel that. She wanted desperately to make him come.

"You're doing so good, honey," he said deeply, his voice nearly making *her* come instead. "That's right, Jenna. Suck that cock. Feel everything that's happening to you. Don't think about anything else."

Even you? Impossible. I tried. But you're all I see.

"Zack," he said then, "rub her clit."

When the pirate behind her did as Brent instructed, she nearly collapsed in the sand. But somehow she stayed up on her hands and knees, even weak as she'd become. Fresh, new, wild pleasure expanded rapidly through every inch of her body and she cried out around Rico's erection. Her body rocked and her tits swayed beneath her. And, oh . . . mmm . . . nothing mattered but coming now. She screamed louder. Sucked deeper. Thrust harder.

And then—oh God, oh God—she came. *So, so* hard. Screaming and sobbing around the cock in her mouth, letting it all flow through her in hot rivers of pleasure that energized and drained her all at once.

Until finally it was done.

And she automatically released the erection from between her lips.

Brent didn't object, saying only, "That was good, honey—you did *so* good."

But then Rico's cock was in his fist and he was looking to Brent for direction—and much to Jenna's surprise, Brent simply said, "In the sand."

And Rico didn't exactly look thrilled, but said nothing, simply turning toward the ocean, working his erection madly—until finally he groaned and shot three arcs of white semen into the air.

"You, too, Zack," Brent instructed, again catching her off guard. Zack still pumped into her, grunting and groaning—but on Brent's command, he cursed softly, went still, then slowly pulled out. A moment later, she saw him yards away, on his knees, taking care of himself the way Rico just had.

The next thing Jenna knew, she lay on the beach exhausted, physically replete. Oh Lord. It was over. Over. She didn't see her two lovers anywhere and wondered how they'd disappeared so fast and if she was suddenly alone here—when she found Brent towering over her.

His cock was back in his pants—but he still looked like a pirate who might ravish her. Which she wouldn't have minded at all. Only . . . she knew now, that wasn't happening. He'd worked too hard to *keep* it from happening. And she still didn't understand why.

Brent scooped Jenna up and carried her the few yards back to the sun-washed tree. Lowering them both to the sand, he leaned back against the trunk, keeping his arms wrapped around her from behind.

This was a fantasy originally planned to be about submission, and even though she'd advanced beyond needing that anymore, he'd proceeded anyway, knowing she'd enjoy the historical aspects. It had also turned into a good opportunity to have her be with other guys, without *him* being one of her lovers.

He'd felt her delight in imagining herself at the mercy of pirates, and it had pleased him greatly, especially when she'd so quickly invented her own role in the game. But his gut had pinched with knowing she wanted him and wasn't getting him. And he'd loved how she'd thrown herself into the sex with utter abandon—but he had a feeling, again, that even without fucking her, his presence had influenced her pleasure. Shit.

And when both guys had needed to come . . . hell, usually, he would have let Zack finish the normal way, inside her—and he might have instructed Rico to ejaculate on her tits, or her ass. But something in him had frozen when the time for that had arrived.

Somehow, even as he wanted her to be with other guys—he'd discovered very unexpectedly that he hadn't wanted another guy to come *in* her, or *on* her. He'd simply had the feeling that . . . it wasn't the right thing to do. For her. Or for him, either. Double shit. What the fuck was *that* about?

It didn't even make sense. Except that . . . for a guy like Brent, whose whole adult life had been spent at the Hotel Erotique, coming in a woman's body, or even on it, was maybe the one truly intimate part of sex.

He hadn't even known he felt that way until this insane moment—but he'd felt that way with her before, hadn't he, when he'd come on her tits in the harem room? It was leaving part of him *in* her, whether that meant inside her pussy or being rubbed into her skin. And hell—he just hadn't wanted anyone else to do that with Jenna.

Worse still—damn it—his response had felt, startlingly, almost like . . . jealousy. He wasn't sure, though, because he'd never actually experienced that before. At least not since . . . high school, maybe. It was all a vague notion in his mind.

"Doing okay, sunshine?" he finally whispered down to her. Sand covered her dress, but the way it still fell from her chest was hot—she looked so much like a woman who'd been *taken* that he yearned to be the one who'd done the taking.

She nodded up to him, appearing understandably tired, and maybe a little sad. "I'm only disappointed you didn't join us."

He held in his groan, but damn it . . . he wanted her. So fucking bad. He didn't usually have this trouble—he was skilled enough to get a good hard-on but not fall apart if he didn't get to come. Sometimes that was part of providing a good fantasy—sometimes not everyone *got* to come. You just hooked up with another facilitator later or took care of it yourself. Only, right now, his dick throbbed like crazy and it was all he could do not to shove her to her back in the sand and finally give her what she longed for.

Still, he found a way. Because he had to be strong here, do what was best for her in the long run. So he simply replied by saying, "Tell me *your* pirate fantasy."

She bit her lip and lowered her lids slightly. "Having the captain ravish me."

Aw, God. The expression on her face nearly buried him. So hungry now, his Jenna, so aggressive—in her own lovely way. His cock physically hurt—each pulsation so strong it became an ache. He wondered if she could see the pain on his face when he simply said—perhaps too quietly, too honestly, "Jenna, I can't."

Her face crumpled in distress and it made his *heart* hurt now, too. "*Brent,*" she pleaded. She said nothing more, just his name. But he felt it in his gut. How bad she wanted him, too. He'd let things go too damn far, and now she was hurting for it.

But this was no time to give in. He was a guide and facilitator. He did not get emotionally attached to guests. No matter how brutal the ache between his legs—or in his chest.

She turned in his loose embrace to peer up at him—and he simply closed his eyes to try to block it all out. "I'm sorry, honey. I want to, but I can't."

"Why?" she demanded.

"I think you *know* why."

"Tell me."

He let out a sigh. Fine, maybe it had to be said. So he'd say it, if that would start to *fix* it. "I've gotten too involved with you. You know that." Shit, his voice still sounded way too pained.

"It's only another week," she argued, her tone conveying a desperation he felt in his gut. "Why not just let it play out?"

Another sigh left him. He hurt for her. He hurt for *him*. "It's not a good idea."

"Why not?"

God, why wouldn't she let it drop? "You won't leave here with what you need," he replied a bit more forcefully.

She simply looked at him for a long moment, her green eyes soft and gentle—and unyieldingly sure. "Maybe this is one time when you're wrong—when *I* know what I need. And it's you. Inside me."

His cock physically lurched in his pants at her words. Damn it. He didn't know what to do, how to make her understand.

But he had to. He had to make her see. This was how things had to be.

"I'm sorry, Jenna," he finally said around the lump in his throat.

Then he pushed to his feet and walked away.

Chapter 11

Jenna lay on the bed in her room, trying not to cry. *Oh God, you're probably the only woman in the history of the Hotel Erotique who was dumb enough to fall for her guide, and now weak enough to shed tears over it.*

But then she bolstered herself, remembering: Other women hadn't been given a sexy male guide, asked to confide in him and trust in him in such an intimate way. So maybe this wasn't her fault at all—maybe the blame fell on Brent.

Not that it made her any less crazy about him. No, instead she was just hurt and upset.

Did his refusal to be with her this afternoon mean her future fantasies wouldn't include him, either? Or that he'd take part only as a spectator? Well, if that was the case, then . . . maybe she didn't *want* any more fantasies. And she'd tell him that the next time she saw him. She'd use her safeword if that's what it took. She knew they didn't have a real *relationship*—she knew this would go nowhere . . . but for now, here, it *was* what she needed: sex with a man she was completely crazy about.

She was jarred from her despair by a knock on the door. God—what now?

Rising cautiously—because she'd learned surprises lay behind every door, sometimes even her own, at the Hotel Erotique—she twisted the knob and opened it to find no one there; yet another gift box rested at her feet. This one looked more innocent than some of the others she'd received—it was a simple white box tied with a thick lavender ribbon.

Of course, she hurriedly brought it inside and opened it up.

She discovered, nestled in lavender tissue paper, a lovely yet surprisingly old-fashioned peignoir set—a long white nightgown of silk and lace, and a matching robe that tied under the bust and possessed lace-festooned sleeves much like the dress she'd worn today. The set also came with a pair of white lace string bikini panties—certainly the most modern part of the ensemble.

A card lay in the box as well—another written in Brent's jagged handwriting:

Put this on, sunshine. Then go for a walk on the beach.

That was it. Not even a signature this time.

Jenna pulled in her breath, wondering what this meant.

But as it was already fairly late—after ten—she quickly decided to quit wasting time and just do what the note said. She only hoped that whatever was happening here, it would include the man she craved. If not, she wasn't going to play these games anymore.

Ten minutes later, Jenna left her room in the dainty, antique nightgown and robe, her heart beating in her throat. In one way, it felt odd to be going out like this, but on the other hand, it was demure nightwear to say the least, especially with the robe—and as she often had to remind herself, this *was* the Hotel Erotique, so she'd have to be seen in a lot less to make a passerby even blink.

Still, she was relieved not to encounter anyone as she followed the main path, barefoot, across well-manicured grounds lit by tiki torches. Crossing a wooden boardwalk that spanned the dunes, she stepped down into the cool sand and into another world.

The beach was empty, stark yet peaceful tonight, and it was easy to forget a trendy sex resort lay just behind her. A bright crescent moon guided her toward the shoreline, casting a ribbon of light across dark water. For a moment she forgot to wonder why she was here and simply soaked up the soft, salty breeze as it blew her satin gown up around her thighs, making her skin ripple lightly.

Leaning her head back, she took in the stars above—countless millions of them twinkling in an inky black sky. Would she see people fucking out here, experiencing *their* fantasies? Somehow, tonight, the very thought seemed ludicrous—because since reaching the beach, it *did* feel as if she'd been transported someplace else, someplace . . . simpler, quieter, more remote.

A glance to the sea at her right revealed . . . hmm, a few lights. Did this mean—was the pirate ship still anchored offshore? Like this afternoon, the sight whisked her back to another time.

It was at that very moment that she saw the vague shapes of people running toward her . . . a white shirt . . . a man . . . *two* men. She tensed automatically, but before she could think, one of them grabbed on to her arm, almost hurting her. She gasped, pulling back, but it was too late—the other man held her opposite wrist now and was soon jerking her hands together in front of her. The harsh scrape of rope tightened on her skin.

Looking up, she found herself gazing into the shadowy stare of someone familiar—Zack. Her first thought: *Oh God, I can't believe I've had sex with this guy twice but barely exchanged a word with him.* Her second: *Damn it, I'm being tied up.*

"Thought you could get away, did you, wench?"

Brent was angry with himself—for his weakness. And he was angry with *her*—for making him this way. He'd have never dreamed the woman he'd met a week ago could affect him like this. Little Mary Sunshine? Not anymore, that was for sure.

Except . . . maybe *part* of her still fit that description—the guilelessly honest part, the openly inquisitive part. And maybe it was the combination that was getting to him, and the way she'd yielded to him sexually . . . so very deeply.

But it was the anger that surfaced when the wooden door to the captain's quarters banged open. He lay across the bed watching with a strange mix of desire and resentment as Zack and Rico brought her inside, her wrists bound before her in thick rope.

The rear of the Spanish galleon reproduction was small and dimly lit by kerosene lamps, and for a moment, it was almost easy to believe he was his character—a ruthless pirate ready to slake his need between the legs of the nearest wench. Except the girl in front of him, looking lovely and innocent in white satin and lace, wasn't just any wench. And despite himself, he liked that she appeared just a little frightened when she saw the look in his eyes.

"The wench, captain," Rico reported.

"Leave us," he said, shooing the other men away. He liked the darkness surrounding them, liked knowing that as soon as Zack and Rico took one of the rowboats back to shore, he and Jenna would be all alone, floating isolated, away from anything and anyone. Tonight, he needed to believe the Hotel Erotique didn't even exist. Tonight he needed to fuck her—man to woman, not guide to guest or teacher to student. If he was going to surrender to his needs, he was going to surrender hard.

And he wasn't inclined to make it remotely soft for Jenna, either. He knew none of this was her fault—but his anger toward her right now was real. No one weakened him this way—*no one*. Well, once, maybe, but that had been different, and sex had . . . sex had *saved* him in a way then. And no one had ever made him feel sexually out of control—until now. He couldn't help it—he wanted to punish her for that. If she wanted him so damn bad, well, she would have him, all right. She would have every inch of him, every way he wanted to give it to her.

He wore a white, billowing pirate's shirt now and the same breeches and boots from earlier. Rising slowly to his feet, he reached in the scabbard at his waist and drew out his dagger.

Damn, she truly did look pretty—so very innocent. Somehow it made him want to conquer her even more. Despite everything he'd told her today about why this couldn't happen, he'd given in to his own desires and now here they were, both about to pay for it.

Stepping close to her, he curled his hand over her bound fists and lifted them firmly up over her head. Then he slid the dagger down inside the front of her nightgown and robe, aware that she was beginning to tremble, and—cruelly—liking it. She'd clearly picked up on the fact that the blades on the beach today weren't real—and had now realized this one *was*. Carefully, he pressed the curved dagger flat between her breasts. "Does the blade feel cold against your skin, my lady?" he leaned nearer to ask.

Her answer sounded shaky. "Yes."

He was hard as a rock, had been that way all afternoon, even after getting himself off in the shower, and now he pressed his aching hard-on against her hip. "And does my big cock feel ready to impale you?"

She lifted her gaze to him and he saw the stark desire residing there as she responded breathily. "Oh, *yes*."

With care, he turned the dagger so that the sharp edge pointed outward—then he sliced through the fabric, all the way down, until both the gown and jacket fell open across her breasts and torso. She gasped, and he groaned—because he'd just gotten a little stiffer, damn it. He couldn't wait much longer.

So he wasted no more time. Slipping the dagger carefully into the side of her pretty lace panties, he cut those, too, leaving them to fall about one thigh. She let out another gasp and he whispered hotly, "Do I frighten you, wench?"

"Kind of," she replied softly. And it moved all through him like liquid—her voice, her fear.

"Good," he said, low and dark. "Because right now, sunshine, I'm scaring *myself* a little, too."

And with that, he tossed the dagger aside, picked her up, and threw her to her back on the bed.

She landed with a small cry of surprise and struggled lightly against her ropes. Meanwhile, he briskly undid his pants, reached in to free his aching cock, and promptly nailed her to the bed with it. It happened that quick—one fluid set of moves and he was in her, deep, hard, and she was crying out at the entry. He felt it low in his belly, that hot little cry—in it he heard her fear, her surrender, her pleasure, her need, and he loved all of it, more than he could understand; he loved being the man who made her feel so many things, so very profoundly. *Feel me, sunshine*, he thought as he began to drive into her warm, tight cunt. *Feel me, feel me, feel me.*

She moaned at every hot, hard plunge—and he fucked her relentlessly, like a madman. He grabbed on to her ass, pulling her to him so he could thrust to the hilt, make her take it, make her take *him*. He grunted and growled as the dark delight of fucking her so roughly vibrated inside him.

What would happen after this? He didn't know. He hadn't thought that far ahead. He only knew he couldn't resist fulfilling her fantasy—even at the emotional peril of them both.

It took a few minutes to realize that despite how hard he was giving it to her, she was fucking him back—meeting his strokes, slamming her pelvis into his again and again. They groaned together, and her bound wrists circled his neck. Even afraid, she wasn't fighting him.

Finally, he pulled out, pressed her body back to the bed, and moved to straddle her shoulders. Then he held his cock down to her mouth and said, "Suck me."

She opened wide, willing and beautiful, and he fed her his length. And a part of him wanted to go just as hard there, be just as brutal, but . . . he couldn't. She looked too defenseless with her bound arms stretched over her head, giving in to him so fully.

And—damn, it felt good to go slow anyway. Her warm mouth hugged his erection, snug and wet, making him curse under his breath as he tried to keep from coming. Shit—when *had* he lost control with her? He didn't even know. He only felt himself succumbing more and more.

"Dirty girl," he whispered down to her. "With such a hot, dirty little mouth. That's so good, honey—suck my cock. Keep sucking it, dirty girl." He'd never thought a woman looked exactly beautiful doing this—he'd thought they looked hot, nasty, obscene, and a host of other descriptors—but despite himself, he thought Jenna somehow indeed looked beautiful, even if in a really naughty way, taking his cock deep into her throat.

But when he again feared he would come, he withdrew. He wasn't done here yet—no way. Not even close.

Catching his breath, he began to back slowly over the length of her body, letting his erection glide over her chest, between her breasts, onto her slender belly, and when he lifted his gaze back to hers, right below his now—hell, he had to kiss her. Just had to.

His hands cupped her face and his mouth sank over prettily swollen lips. He didn't kiss her gently, though—he kissed her like a man who was starving for her. Still tied, she kissed him just as ravenously and it made his heart beat harder, his cock pulsing madly.

Needing still more, he kissed his way briskly down her body—raining kisses over her breasts and tummy, placing one next to her belly button, and then pressing his mouth into her open slit.

Damn, she tasted good—the sweet, salty, feminine taste of her instantly permeated his senses. And as he licked at her folds and delivered openmouthed kisses to her beautifully engorged clit, she let out the hot little whimpers and cries he adored. She appeared lost in abandon—eyes shut, lips parted—except for when her teeth clenched in sweet agony each time he focused tightly on her turgid little nub. He found himself licking at it harder, wanting to drive her toward climax, loving the way she began to fuck his mouth then, loving the sex-hungry woman Jenna became in his arms.

And that's when he realized he needed to give her *more* right now, something extra, something new. No normal orgasm seemed good enough for her at the moment. So, still licking at the top of her pussy, he smoothly inserted two fingers where his dick had been a few minutes ago. A ragged sigh left her at the small intrusion, after which he began to stroke his fingertips deliberately along the upper wall of her vagina.

This didn't work for every woman, but it did for most, given that he knew what he was doing. He found the spot he was seeking easily, where the surface of the flesh was just a little softer, smoother—then he stroked some more, curling his fingers toward him, like one might scratch a cat's chin.

Above, her breath began to catch and his whole body turned hot at the gentle yet unsettled sounds of pleasure as he returned to suckling her clit in earnest. She began to tremble amid her whimpers so that they came out shaky, uncontrolled. "Oh . . . Ohhh," she began to moan.

He stroked the inner wall of her cunt more intensely, faster now, as he sucked her clit deeper between his lips—and at the moment he felt her climax start to break, he closed his teeth over her distended nub and rubbed her wildly inside.

"Oh! Oh God! Oh God!" she cried. And then she began to yowl like a

wild animal, her pelvis bucking against his face in a jagged response he could tell was involuntarily—her body was jerking the powerful orgasm out of her with or without her consent. It went on a long while, pleasing him deeply, making his cock harden further.

He lifted his head only when she went still, quiet. His Little Mary Sunshine looked utterly spent, her chest heaving, her arms still stretched over her head. When she opened her eyes, she tried to speak, but her lips still quivered. "Wh-what was . . . ?"

"It was your G-spot," he whispered.

Her green eyes grew big and round. "That really exists?"

He tried to keep from chuckling. Still innocent in some ways, his sunshine. "Hell yeah, it exists. You just felt the proof."

"Holy shit," she murmured. Then let her eyes fall shut again.

Brent gave her a minute to recover—he knew she needed it—by rising from the bed and finding the dagger he'd tossed aside earlier, ready to free her wrists. When he returned, she looked much more feral than frightened now, even with her wrists bound, even with the cut remnants of her white nightgown still falling away from her otherwise naked body.

He carefully sliced through the rope between her fists. Then he gave her his pirate look again—the look that said, *I'm going to take you rough and hard*—even though he wasn't thinking about being a pirate anymore. He was only thinking about the fierce urges still driving him.

Planting one palm on her bare hip, he rolled her to her stomach on the bed. Then, sweeping the white fabric aside to reveal her round ass, he gave it a slap and said, "On your hands and knees."

She obeyed, looking at once pretty and obscene—and he decided he needed her *all the way* obscene. So without warning, he used the dagger still in hand to cut down the *back* of the gown and robe this time, letting it fall away in the other direction to leave her enticingly naked. "I'm gonna fuck you so hard," he breathed over her like a threat—but her only response was to arch her ass higher for him. "Good girl," he said, low, deep.

Then he grabbed her ass with both hands and plunged his aching shaft back into her slick, enveloping pussy. She cried out, and he groaned, too—mmm, she was still so tight, even after a week of hot fucking. He rammed into her with all the power he possessed, as rough as he'd promised, making them both cry out at each stroke. And he smacked her ass, simply to provide another bit of sensation for them both. At some point, he bent his body over hers, anchoring his arm around her waist, to deliver shorter but still intense thrusts, and felt like a rutting animal.

Her sobs of pleasure fueled him and he knew he still hadn't gotten enough of her. She was wet and willing and perfect, she was sexy and beautiful and dirty for him, she was everything a man could want—but tonight, he was driven to a point of needing still *more*.

Rising back upright, he continued to fuck her, drive after wild drive, now kneading her soft ass. His fingers dug into her flesh; so did his thumbs. Each time, his thumbs parted her bottom just a little, giving him a clear view of her tight, tiny asshole—which contracted, just slightly, with every stroke he delivered. Shit.

He knew what he wanted in an instant. He wanted in her ass.

But he also knew he was surely too big, even despite the glass toy she'd taken there the other night. That part of the toy was designed specifically for anal play, after all—his cock definitely was not. He'd fucked women in the ass before, but not many—and only girls who were well accustomed to that kind of sex.

Still, as he moved in Jenna's moist passageway, relishing the hot slide, his thumbs moved farther inward, playing around the tiny fissure, soon stroking it in rhythm with his drives. The weak, lusty sighs that now came with her sobs told him she felt it, liked it. He couldn't resist slipping the tip of his middle finger inside.

"Oh!" she cried, leaning her head back, arching invitingly.

Brent slid the rest of his finger inward, all the way, listening to the deep moan it tore from her throat. And he began fucking her ass with his finger as he fucked her cunt with his cock.

Her responses grew more wild and he felt strangely desperate to make her wilder still. And oddly compelled to get into her ass. More than just his finger. His cock. If her pussy was this tight, how compact would that sweet little ass feel around his erection?

He wouldn't hurt her, of course—he couldn't risk that. But he knew, in sex, when there was a will there was often a way. And if he prepared her well enough, and if her body wanted it the way his did, he might indeed get into that tiny opening.

He inserted a second finger without warning, making her howl in pleasure. Damn, she was hot. He still fucked her cunt, slowly, but concentrated more on her anus now, moving his fingers in small circles, trying to gradually expand the flesh there. He couldn't remember the last time he'd been this deeply, hotly aroused, a sensation that grew in his gut. He wanted to possess her in a way no one ever had; he wanted to *own* her right now.

Withdrawing his fingers and cock, he whispered, "Rest a second, baby," then retreated from the bed to a set of drawers built into the cabin. Given that this wasn't a real pirate's ship, he found an array of unpiratelike articles: fur-lined handcuffs, *real* handcuffs, an enormous black vibrator, some condoms, a silver cock ring—and then, finally, *yes*, a nearly full tube of lubricant! Thank God.

Returning to the bed where Jenna leaned forward, resting with her shoulders on the mattress but her knees still tucked up under her, Brent smoothly reinserted his fingers in her ass. A strangled cry erupted from her, pleasing the dominant side of him.

He moved his fingers again in circles, gently stretching her, his arousal compounding at the sight of her widening asshole. "So hot, honey," he murmured instinctively—and she only let out a weak, whimpering sigh in response.

Mmm, God, he was so ready for this. So ready to take her where no one else had. He'd done that many times already, of course, but this felt different from all the other fantasies—even more intense, more personal.

Upon withdrawing his fingers this time, he squeezed a generous portion of the lubricant into the slightly opened fissure. He knew, because it was the Hotel Erotique's signature lube, that it would feel cool and tingly—and he heard her surprised gasp.

Feeling urgent now, he applied the lubricant to his cock, rubbing it over the whole length but concentrating on the head—and was forced to let out a small gasp of his own.

His gut clenched in anticipation as he leaned in from behind, then bent to whisper in her ear, "Your safeword is still Cleopatra."

She turned her head to look at him, eyes questioning.

"In case this hurts," he explained, low. "Don't let me hurt you, Jenna."

Too late for that, Jenna thought. But she had no time to think about that kind of hurt at the moment—the current threat felt much more immediate. And still, she wanted it. She wasn't even sure why, but she yearned to have him inside her in this new way.

At her rear, the tip of his erection nestled in that oh-so-sensitive spot, and she shut her eyes, bracing herself, as he began to push.

Oh God. It hurt. He was too big—he'd never fit. She clenched her teeth, and her fists, wanting this to work.

"Relax," he said gently. "Try to relax your muscles."

She did, focusing on the task. And then it hurt less. It was still tight as hell, stretching her there, forcing her to bite her lip—but she never said Cleopatra. Because she didn't want him to stop.

Behind her, Brent's breath came labored and thready, and she knew he was partly inside her anus now. He massaged her ass as he worked, clearly trying to comfort her and stretch her more at the same time. She bit her lip and willed her body to open to him there.

"Aw . . . aw, fuck yes," he muttered—and then she felt his thick cock make the painstakingly slow glide into her ass.

She sucked in her breath at the overpowering sensation. Although she was aware of being stretched to the max, it no longer hurt—exactly. Or maybe it did, but at the same time, it filled her with . . . gloriously overwhelming pleasure. "*Oh God*." The words came straight from her core.

"Does it hurt?" He sounded barely able to talk.

Did it? Crazy as it sounded, she wasn't sure. "Yes. And no. I . . . I . . ."

"Tell me, damn it—am I hurting you?"

"N-no. It's . . . amazing."

"*You* are," he whispered deeply. "Fucking amazing."

She could only sob in response. Because the sensations this position produced were growing, multiplying, spreading all through her body. It felt like his cock was *everywhere*, pervading her entire being. She'd never imagined any sexual experience could be *this* consuming. More than two cocks. More than surrendering to everything he'd inflicted on her in the dungeon. More than *anything*. It filled her. It saturated her. It owned her. Sweat began to pour from every part of her body as she clenched her teeth against the strange, hot pleasure, at once frightening and glorious.

And then he began to move.

Short, gentle thrusts in that tiny, narrow tunnel. And she lost all control.

As Brent slid into her, growling his pleasure with every stroke, Jenna found herself crying out through clenched teeth, pounding her fists on the bed, besieged with sensation. "*Oh God, oh God, oh God!*" she heard herself scream. All the blood drained from her face and her body grew weak trying to absorb it all. She heard the deep sobs and cries echoing uncontrolled from her throat and could barely fathom anything but the huge cock in her ass and her own incredible response—she'd never been this crazed.

And even after the most powerful orgasm she'd ever had—oh Lord, the G-spot was real!—she felt on the edge of another, wildly hungry to come again. Her clit ached—she craved friction there.

Behind her, Brent growled ferociously and she became aware of one more important thing—*his* pleasure. It felt as intense as hers, roaring through her almost as forcefully.

Soon, her limbs grew so shaky that she sank to the bed completely, flat on her stomach—still with Brent fucking that tiny fissure that felt so huge right now. And almost as soon as her clit touched the woven bedspread, the orgasm hit like an earthquake.

Her heartbeat pounded in her ears as it echoed violently through her—her body thrashed about and she screamed through the raging pleasure pumping from her cunt. And just when it ended—as mind-numbing and earth-shattering as the previous climax—Brent let out a deep groan, said, "Jesus, I'm coming in your ass, baby," and thrust into her, spilling himself.

Then he sank on top of her and they both fell into an exhausted sleep within seconds.

Jenna woke a little while later to the rocking motion of the ship, astonished. Wow, she'd discovered her G-spot *and* been fucked in the ass, all in the same short span of time—no wonder she felt so replete yet drained.

Brent lay next to her, still in his sexy pirate clothes. Sexy, but she wanted them off now—especially since her own lay in shreds around her.

Just then, his eyes opened. "You okay, sunshine?" he asked softly.

She bit her lip, feeling sheepish about her reply. "More than okay," she admitted. "I have been . . . *thoroughly pleasured.*" Then she let out a small sigh. "Although . . ."

"Yeah?" He lifted his head slightly to peer down at her.

"Well, my—um—anus feels kind of odd, like it's . . . uh . . . sort of more open than usual right now. Which felt better, frankly, when there was something inside it."

He cast an indulgent smile. "That'll go away in a little while."

He said it with such confidence that she wondered how he knew, but then remembered who she was talking to—he wasn't just *her* lover. He'd likely been having this same discussion for years with *other* girls he'd fucked this way. Ugh—unpleasant thought, so she pushed it aside and tried to ignore the senseless jealousy pulsing through her veins.

As Brent scooted toward the head of the bed—they'd ended up sideways across it—he reached for her. "Come share a pillow with me," he murmured, still sounding sleepy.

She replied by joining him but giving *him* a command, too. "Take your clothes off. The pirate thing is hot, but naked is hotter."

Brent said nothing, just agreeably removed the white shirt over his head to reveal the muscular chest and arms underneath, then shed his boots and pants as well. Together, they wordlessly pushed down the covers and crawled underneath.

Then it hit her—what did this mean? Was she spending the night with him here? Or was this just a temporary rest period before they went their separate ways for the evening? Given his declarations this afternoon about not being able to get close to her anymore, she was pretty confused by this whole night.

So she propped up on one elbow and looked down at him. "I thought you said we were getting too involved."

"We are," he answered simply, without quite meeting her gaze.

"Then why . . ."

"Don't ask me."

"How come?"

Now he looked at her. "Because I don't know the answer. I just did it. Because I wanted to. And because *you* wanted to."

Hmm. Wow. He'd wanted her just like she'd wanted him. Enough to break more of his own rules. She couldn't help it—she leaned down and kissed him, a move that left her scalp tingling. "You've . . . changed me so much. In such a short time."

He nodded. "That's my job, sunshine."

And her stomach pinched lightly. But, deciding this was no time to start holding back, she asked what was on her mind. "When I leave here, Brent, will I . . . mean anything to you? At least be someone you remember fondly?"

"Honey, let's not go there."

Damn it. "I need to. *Need*, Brent." She knew that was a word he well understood.

He sighed, looked slightly troubled, but then met her eyes once again, looking calmer, more acceptant. "Okay, yes," he admitted. "I will remember you . . . very fondly." He reached up to gently stroke her hair. "Today on the beach—my God, I loved your . . . recklessness. You've gotten to be amazing in bed, Jenna."

She lowered her gaze briefly, ready to make a confession of her own. It was obvious, but she felt the need to tell him. "I never could have done it without the freedom you've brought me. And . . . maybe I'm beginning to understand that those, um, occurrences in my youth *did* color my opinions of sex. So . . . thank you. For pushing me to do these things."

Beside her, he used his elbow to raise slightly, as well, giving his head an inquisitive tilt. "So tell me, did you really not like being with girls?"

She shrugged, amused with the question. Guys were always so obsessed with that. "I *kind of* liked it. But I told you—I like it more when *you're* there." Then she smiled, teasing him. "Why do guys always think girls secretly want other girls? After all, have *you* ever been with other *guys*?"

"Yeah," he said easily—and her jaw dropped.

"Oh." His answer left her utterly stunned—and then, for some reason, it kind of aroused her. "Do you . . . like it?"

He lowered his head back to the pillow. "Sometimes. Does that turn you off?"

"No. I mean, I never thought about it, but . . . to tell you the truth, I don't know why, but it's kind of getting me hot right now."

He grinned up at her. "Good." Yet then his expression changed. "Though maybe it would have been better if it turned you off."

"Why? Isn't all this about me becoming more and more open about sex?"

"Yeah, but . . . it would be best if it stopped having to do with . . . me."

Oh, hell. They both knew the situation, but hearing him say it made her feel like some "guide groupie." So she simply chose not to reply. Instead she lowered her head to the pillow, too, bringing them face-to-face. "Tell me," she said softly. "About being with other guys."

The request hung in the air for a moment before he said, "What about it? I've been here for fifteen years—there's not much I haven't done, sunshine."

Another harsh reminder, but since she was thinking of him with other guys instead of other girls right now, it didn't sting so much as simply remind her that she was practically still a virgin compared to Brent Powers. "Tell me . . . what you like. With another guy," she asked, cautiously. Because yes, she was weirdly turned on by the idea, but she wasn't sure how much, or what she wanted to hear, or if his answers would transform her arousal to something else.

When he hesitated, she realized maybe she wasn't the only one uneasy with the topic—maybe he was embarrassed to talk about it with her, afraid of her reaction. It was the first time she'd ever seen Brent uncomfortable with any aspect of sex—he was usually so confident and smooth. But maybe it was because of the weird divergence in current society—straight girls playing at bisexuality had somehow become socially acceptable, but straight guys experimenting with other guys? Not as much.

Finally, he replied, speaking more softly than normal. "Sometimes . . . I like that it's harder than sex with a girl—I mean, I like feeling a harder body against me."

His answer made her heart pound. Possibly because it meant he truly understood—through experience—something a *woman* liked about sex? Or perhaps just because it clearly wasn't easy for him to say and yet he was telling her anyway.

"What else?" she asked, fascinated. "What else do you like about it?"

He met her gaze squarely, as if about to confide in her. "Honestly, sunshine," he said on a slightly awkward laugh, "if I'm in the right mood, *everything*."

Everything. Wow. Did he really mean that? "Sucking another guy's cock?"

He nodded simply.

"Having yours sucked by another guy?"

Another nod.

Her chest tightened at the images forming in her mind. "Do you . . . you know, fuck them?"

"Yeah, honey, I do." He looked a little less embarrassed now, like he was coming back to himself, to his normal confidence. In fact, he sounded much more amused than worried when he asked, "So, are you . . . not liking me yet?"

She shook her head. "I'm actually . . . *amazed* by you. This means you're not all talk."

He cast a typical Brent grin. "Nope, afraid I walk the walk, babe."

"And you've . . . been fucked? By a guy? In your . . ."

"Ass?" he finished for her. "Yeah."

Whoa. So *that's* how he'd known the odd feeling would go away—and it had now, mostly.

"What are you thinking?" he asked when she said nothing.

She didn't respond immediately. There were too many new, impossible pictures in her head. But the answer, she realized to her surprise, was, "That I'd kind of like to see it. You with a guy."

"Oh," he said, back to sounding unsettled again.

"Can I?"

"I don't know."

"Why?"

"Well, because that doesn't have much to do with my plans for you. And trust me, we've already sailed far enough off course without drifting farther."

She couldn't help smiling. "You're talking like a pirate."

He laughed softly and said, "No, if I was talking like a pirate, I'd be . . . asking if you want to see my yardarm or . . . saying you've got the nicest booty I've ever seen."

She giggled in reply. "You were much smoother as Captain Powers."

He shrugged, grinned. "I'm not in character right now, so you have to settle for the goofy stuff."

Just then, her eyes fell on the tattoo on his arm. She noticed it often when they were together, but only now did she feel bold enough to bring it up. She reached to run her fingers over the initials. "Did pirates have tattoos?" she asked inquisitively.

"Probably."

"So, who *is* D.L., anyway?"

"An old girlfriend," he said with a slight shake of his head, as if it was nothing.

"I didn't think a guy like you *had* girlfriends," she said, half teasing, half serious.

He grinned in reply, but his eyes looked sad. "It was a long time ago."

"She must have been special," Jenna speculated. "I mean, to warrant a tattoo, a permanent reminder."

He shrugged, still managing to sound totally blasé even as he said, "Yeah, she was."

She couldn't help wanting to dig more. "What was her name?"

"Deena," he answered softly then, his voice sounding different, lower, as he said it. "Deena Little."

She *had* been special. *Very* special. Jenna could tell. "Did you meet her here? Another guide or something?"

Brent shook his head. "It was back in college. We were in love."

Oh. Wow. The girl in the photo album? The plain one. "But it ended?"

"Yep." He rolled to his back, looking like he didn't want to discuss it anymore.

"Did you ever get over her?" Jenna pressed anyway.

"Of course." He peered toward the ceiling as he spoke now. "It was more than fifteen years ago. Why?"

Now it was Jenna's turn to shrug. "Well, like I said, she warranted a tattoo. That just seems . . . important. Permanent. Like maybe you thought *you and she* would be permanent."

He glanced her way. "Once upon a time, I did. But you know how life goes—you fall in love and think it'll last forever, but it doesn't always. That simple."

Hmm—sure didn't *sound* simple. "Have you ever been in love again?"

When he looked at her this time, he gave her a sexy grin. "No, Miss Inquisitive. Now go to sleep, my little pirate wench, and maybe I'll tup you again in the morning."

So they *were* spending the night here. On the pirate ship. Breaking rules. Already planning more forbidden guide-and-guest sex in the morning. It was, as he'd surely planned, enough to take Jenna's mind off Deena Little and make her snuggle against him in the captain's bed, back to feeling sexy and thinking about all the naughty pirate fun he'd given her. "Thank you, by the way," she said. "For the whole pirate thing. I'm sure you knew how much I'd like that."

Slipping his arm around her, he raised his eyebrows playfully. "I did, but I was still surprised to find out you were the wife of a wealthy planter."

"I'm unpredictably quick on my feet sometimes."

"And your husband would have been shocked, my lady, to see you getting your brains fucked out by two guys on the beach today."

"And now, too. Don't forget—I just let the captain fuck me in the ass."

He chuckled and said, "I must be the luckiest buccaneer on all the seven seas to find such an accommodating wench."

"Well, keep giving me orgasms like that and I'll . . ." Oh crap, she'd started to say she'd forget the planter and become the captain's wench for good. But under the circumstances—being a "guide groupie"—she stopped, and fumbled for a conclusion. "I'll . . . let you . . . play in my treasure chest anytime."

He laughed at her silly attempt at more pirate talk, then smoothly slid his free hand onto her ass. "Honey, I've got news for you—you couldn't keep me *out* of your treasure chest if you tried."

Chapter 12

You Are Invited to a ~~Fantasy~~ Masquerade

Where: The London home of the Duke of Sexingham
When: Tonight, 9:00 p.m.—but the year is 1650.
The most raucous soiree of the season offers a grand buffet
of sumptuous choices amid the cloak of anonymity.
Appropriate apparel—and a mask—will be provided upon your arrival.
Come ready to indulge.
(Your safeword is Oprah Winfrey.)

Jenna sat in her room, reading the invitation. Other than the historical aspects, she had no idea what to expect, but the fantasy's content—hard to believe—was not her main concern.

Oh God, please let him be in this fantasy—please let him have given up the idea of my being with other people without *him.*

She just didn't want that. And she saw it as her choice. She was the guest here and she'd played by most of his rules—but this was one time she would insist he do things her way. She didn't much care if he knew how she felt—it was clear he knew she'd gotten too attached, and in some respects, yes, that made her feel vulnerable and even a little silly. But when he was fucking her, she didn't feel silly. When she was screaming her way through the craziest orgasms of her life, she didn't feel silly. And when he'd held her in his arms all night and indeed "tupped" her again this morning, she hadn't felt silly.

After the morning sex—a hot but tamer liaison like the one on his couch a few days ago—Brent had called shore and had someone send out a light breakfast and another outfit from the gift shop for Jenna to wear back to her room. "I knew I was forgetting something when I put this plan together," he'd told her teasingly when she'd pointed out that he'd sliced her other clothes to ribbons. She hoped he'd just been too caught up in heat to remember every detail.

After two full fantasies yesterday, Jenna was still tired and knew it would probably be wise to crawl under the covers of her own bed and get some extra sleep. After all, she had a masquerade to attend this evening and something told her it might require some stamina.

Yet her mind—or maybe it was closer to her soul—felt too energized right now. She didn't feel like hiding away in her quiet room today. More than ever since her arrival here, she had the urge to be out among people, basking in the tropical beauty of the resort, enjoying her life to the fullest. She could only attribute the feeling to the astounding sex last night. It had left her feeling as if . . . she knew herself better. As if she knew the whole *world* better. It had left her feeling *alive* and like she didn't want to waste another moment not soaking up that wondrous sensuality that floated in the air here. She'd never felt more fully aware of her body, her thoughts, her desires—and she'd never felt more *comfortable* with all those things, either.

Just slipping on her bikini was a sensuous experience, the fabric hugging her most intimate body parts—she relished showing off her figure in a way she never had before. And rather than steal away to some secluded spot on the beach, she went to the main pool and found a lounge chair, which also provided a view of the ocean. She luxuriated in the fruity scent of her sunscreen, in the lush warmth of a sea breeze wafting past, in the sweet flavor of the erotic rum punch as it slid down her throat. She found herself stretching out in her chaise, one leg slightly bent, her arms stretching languorously up overhead, and she didn't hide the small, dreamy smile she felt coming over her—instead just delighting in the full measure of her femininity. And if anyone wondered if her smile was the result of wild, uninhibited sex in a Hotel Erotique fantasy—unlike a few days ago, she didn't care. In fact, she almost *wanted* people to know. A small, brazen-but-happy part of her wanted to climb to the thatched rooftop of the tiki bar and shout, "I discovered my G-spot last night!"

Each sexual experience here had changed her, moved her to a new place both mentally and physically—but somehow, last night, when it had been only her and Brent, *that* encounter had affected her more profoundly than any other.

Of course, Brent would probably tell her it was some sort of cumulative effect. And maybe he was right. But at the moment, she still felt just as pleasured, relaxed, and happy as she had after coming last night, and her thoughts kept returning there.

She let herself bake in the Caribbean rays, her tan skin making her feel all the more exotic and sexy, until she decided it was time for a dip. And even *that* felt sensual—the cool water on her warm skin, her body moving smoothly through it. And as she emerged up through the surface to feel the hot sun on her face again, as she pushed her hair back over her head and began gliding toward the steps leading back out of the pool, she remained utterly aware of her body, her sexuality. Her breasts felt plump and her pussy softly engorged with a pleasant level of desire that would build through the day and lead her into the evening with growing hunger.

It was as she climbed the stairs, water sluicing off her skin, that she saw Brent—he sat watching in the lounge chair next to hers in a pair of red swim trunks, hands comfortably behind his head. His sexy gaze roamed the length of her body as it came into view, adding to every other sensation already assaulting her.

"Well, if it isn't Captain Powers," she quipped, strolling toward him.

"You'd have been wasted on that planter, babe," he said, adding with a wink, "Good thing you found *me*."

"Speaking of finding—am I under surveillance or something?" She pushed the book in her chair toward the end of it and sat down on her towel, leaning back to dry in the sun.

Brent grinned in reply. "Believe it or not, this is a coincidence. It's my day off, so I came to the pool—and when I saw a Civil War book, I knew it had to be you."

She'd still managed to read very little, but she'd brought it with her just in case the urge struck. "You know me too well," she said, thinking the words were all too true, in so many ways. How could she *not* be attached to a man who'd seemed so very concerned for her well-being from the very start, and who seemed to understand her so innately? "So you have *days off*?"

"I'm into my work, sunshine, but everybody needs some time to themselves." It was then that she noticed a book *he'd* brought: A paperback copy of *Catch-22* by Joseph Heller lay on the ground between their chairs. And if she hadn't been completely in love with him before that moment, she was *now*. The sex doctor with his life full of meaningless physical encounters cared about other things! He liked to read! She *loved* guys who liked to read. And a classic, too!

"Great book," she said.

"Yeah—I'm going back through some I didn't appreciate when I had to read them in school. They're much better now." Oh wow—she nearly swooned. And she'd thought the pirate outfit was sexy? For her, *this* was the ultimate turn-on.

"You look damn fine in that bikini, by the way," he said, reminding her that he *was* still obsessed with sex.

But right now, she didn't mind. The compliment warmed her pussy even as she pointed out, "You've seen me in much less and in ultimately more revealing positions."

He cocked a slight grin in her direction. "Never underestimate the power of a rockin' bikini, babe."

Just then, a horrible thought hit her. "So . . . are you taking the *whole* day off?"

In reply, he lowered his chin and flashed a knowing look. "The day, sunshine, not the night." Then he shifted his gaze back toward the ocean, adding, "Don't worry—I'll be there. And not just watching."

Thank God! Though rather than let him see her extreme relief, she instead said, quietly, "Thank you for that. Believe it or not, sometimes I really do know what's best for me."

"Fair enough," he answered. "Besides, it's not my goal to make you unhappy. Just the opposite. I only hope you agree by now that sometimes *I* know what's best for you, too."

Jenna pulled in her breath, then let it back out. She'd been doing a lot of thinking about that, and in addition to what she'd told him last night—about the events of her past—something more specific had hit her. "You know, you've made me revisit some memories I hadn't for years, and . . . the truth is, maybe there are even more of them than I put in my questionnaires. Nothing huge, but just more little things that might have built up inside me."

"I kinda knew that," he said softly. "I could tell."

"*And* . . . my experiences this week have forced me to realize something." She lifted her eyes to his, glad no one else was in earshot. "You remember that incident with my cousin?"

He met her gaze. "Of course."

She took another deep breath. "Well, I'm just now understanding that what he did made me feel ashamed, as if I'd done something bad—even though it wasn't my fault. And the reason I'm just now seeing this is because—oddly enough—nothing I've done *here* has made me feel that same bad way. Here, I've . . . questioned my actions at times, worried about the morality of them or wondered if they made me a slut—but all that has been more about questions than actual feelings. I've just never felt bad inside, here, the way I did then."

The warmth in his expression made her feel all the more close to him. "That's because everyone here respects you, and one another, and sex. It's all in how it's approached, sunshine. It's *people* who sometimes make sex bad—whether they misuse or abuse it to exert power over someone weaker than them, or whether they insert a double standard, or whether they simply send negative messages about it, forcing their own morality or fears on others. But there's nothing inherently bad about sex on its own. It's just pleasure."

She found herself nodding as his words enlightened her. They lived in a culture that portrayed sex in extreme ways. Whether society was hammering into people that it was bad, wrong—or, more recently, overly glorifying it as something everyone should be seeking, all the time—it kept people from looking at sex with their own minds and forming their own opinions on it.

"But . . . I'm still not one hundred percent sure I agree on that last part," she couldn't help arguing.

"Why?"

She started to tell him sex couldn't be "just pleasure" because she still felt a connection with people she fooled around with—yet, that quickly, she realized it wasn't completely true. She'd felt a *temporary* connection—with the other pirates, the dungeon dwellers, the harem girls—but, in fact, the only *real* connection she'd experienced was with *him*. And she surely didn't want to say *that*, even if they both knew it. So finally she replied, "I'm still not keeping the emotion entirely out of it."

"Well, that's okay," Brent surprised her by saying. "I told you in the beginning, that's how you're wired—you can't really change it. Most women are physiologically programmed that way. But you're doing a great job of pushing that aside and finding what I wanted you to find here—how to free yourself, how to enjoy sex to the fullest."

Only she *wasn't* pushing it aside. With every liaison, she felt more and more tied to him. And, again, she *knew* he knew that. So was this Brent still trying to distance himself from that connection—one she knew he'd felt, too? She didn't want to squabble—she wanted to keep basking in the afterglow of last night—so she simply responded, with a smile, "Well, I definitely *am* enjoying sex more than ever before."

"That makes me happy, Jenna. You make me feel like my work here really matters. I mean, I've *always* felt that way, but given your hesitation at first, it's been more gratifying than usual to see the changes in you. Thank you for that."

Again, she felt him building that distance—wanting to claim their relationship was mostly about work for him and not the raw lust she'd witnessed in the dungeon, the fierce desire that had created last night's pirate ship fantasy. But if he wanted to pretend, so be it—she suspected she'd see his real feelings for her again tonight at the masquerade.

"So," she said, "how *did* you get into this line of work? And don't tell me again that it's just because you like sex."

Her lover and guide cast a wolfish grin. "It is. That's the truth. I came here the summer after graduation thinking it would be temporary, but I never got tired of it. It felt right to me to do this, long term."

Hmm. His answer made her want to dig for more, just like when she'd been in his home, or last night, talking about his tattoo. Who *was* Brent Powers and what really made him tick? "How does your family feel about your job?" she asked, trying to make the question sound more casual than prying.

Yet his face changed instantly—becoming guarded, and he answered matter-of-factly, as if it were no big deal. "Well, that's the one *bad* thing. My mother thinks I'm a gigolo, and I guess I kind of am. And my sister hasn't let me see her kids since they were little. I have a nephew, Cody, who's sixteen now, and my niece, Tiffany, just started her freshman year of high school. And it kinda sucks that my sister thought I wasn't . . . any more than my job, that she thought I'd somehow corrupt them and not be a good uncle—but that was her choice, and that's life."

It took Jenna a second to catch her breath. It all made sense, she supposed, but she hadn't imagined the ramifications—or the losses—a job like Brent's might involve. "How long since you've seen them?"

When Brent sighed, she sensed him trying to decide how much emotion to show, how much of that mask of practicality to keep wearing. "Ten years now," he said—and Jenna's heart sank for him.

If he *was* still trying to hide his pain, it was leaking out through his eyes. "I ask my mother to send me pictures now and then, and even though she doesn't like it, she sends them. I can't believe how old they are and that I've missed out on most of their lives. Their dad took off after Tiff was born, so for a while, I was the closest thing they had to a father. I didn't see them a *lot*—I was usually here working—but I flew home to Pittsburgh for a few weeks here and there and spent a lot of time with them when they were little.

"My mom and sister didn't know then what I did for a living," he went on, and Jenna could scarcely believe he was confiding so much. "My dad knew, though, and he didn't like it—but he thought I'd outgrow it."

"What did your mom and sister think you were doing?"

"They only knew I was working at a resort. They thought I was waiting tables, which I was, but they didn't know about the rest. A couple of years after my dad died, though, my mom pinned me down and asked when I was gonna put my degree to use. I'd just decided to further my studies, specializing in sex, so I figured the time had come to tell her the truth and hope she understood. She didn't. And neither did Kim, my sister, and that was that. Now I send the kids gifts at Christmas, but I'm sure they barely remember me and wonder why I'm not around anymore."

Whoa. Jenna had never even imagined Brent sounding so . . . vulnerable. His voice stayed strong, sure—but she could feel his pain anyway. It was a side of him she'd never seen. "Is it worth it?" she asked quietly. "To lose your family—for *this*?" Her tone implied the Hotel Erotique was nothing worth sacrificing for, but she didn't care.

"I must think it is," he told her simply.

"Yet you sound so sad about it."

He met her gaze squarely. "You can't let anybody, not even your family, choose your life. And I know what I've chosen is controversial, so if they want to cut me out, I figure that's their right. I don't like it, but I respect it."

She supposed he made a good point. Whereas *she'd* let *her* family's negative views of sex color her perception of it, Brent had ultimately stood up and done what he believed was right for him. "Well," she said softly, "I'm still sorry it has to hurt you."

He tilted his head, gave her another insightful look. "Hey, no one's life is perfect. And don't worry about *me*, Little Mary Sunshine—at the end of the day, I'm doing just fine. Now let's get in the pool," he concluded with a grin.

"I just got out," she reminded him.

"But looking at you in that leopard print got me all hot and bothered. Come help me cool down."

And when Brent pushed to his feet and held his hand out to her, it was invitation Jenna couldn't resist.

As Brent prepared for the elaborate fantasy that night, he couldn't get Jenna off his mind.

Maybe that's because you spent the whole damn day with her.

He really hadn't planned it—he really *had* gone to the pool only to catch some rays and relax. And it would have seemed pretty shitty, all things considered, to see her there and not hang out with her. Never mind the instant joy that had come over him when he'd spotted that Civil War book and realized she was there.

But why the hell did you tell her the whole melodrama about your family?

Hell, he had no idea. He could only attribute it to a lack of sleep. And that it was October, which meant Christmas was coming, and sometimes he got a little lonely at that time of year. But he handled it fine—he had plenty of friends here to spend the holidays with; the Hotel Erotique was good for turning people into adult orphans, it seemed.

Now he regretted opening up to her because, like so much else he'd done with her, it was just a bad idea—it reinforced the escalating emotions between them. *Idiot*, he chided himself as he selected another period dress for her to wear tonight, this one a more elaborate ice blue brocade trimmed in ivory lace.

Of course, he'd also told her about having had sex with other men—since she'd asked. Even upon realizing it wasn't as easy for him to talk about as other sex. There, at the resort, it was commonplace—sex was sex was sex and there was no judgment. But with her, maybe he'd feared there *would* be. Still, given how much honesty and openness she'd shown him, he'd felt he owed her the same.

When she'd been surprisingly cool about it, even wanting to see it, the reaction had shocked him—and made him like her that much more. It seemed he uncovered new layers of Jenna with each passing day.

So hell—who knew?—maybe *that* was why he'd spilled to her about his family. Maybe it felt good to share it with someone so nice, so sweet.

Turning to a large chest in the historical section of the wardrobe building, he located a pair of ivory fishnet stockings with a satin bow at the top of each. They weren't totally period, but they'd look delectable on her—and he found himself getting a little hard already just thinking ahead to what would take place in a few hours.

Damn, he loved her newfound appreciation for sex. He loved how trusting she'd been about letting him in her ass last night. He loved everything about her.

Except—shit—love wasn't a word he should have on his mind with Jenna or any other Hotel Erotique guest. So he pushed the thoughts aside and found a corset that would give her some insanely hot cleavage—then laughed at himself for being in a position to know so much about women's clothing.

Tonight's fantasy would be the grandest she'd taken part in—with more than thirty participants. Most would be facilitators, but this was a rare occasion when seven guests would enjoy the same highly structured fantasy. He'd not originally planned on her being involved in the masquerade, but it fit well with where she was on her journey.

In one sense, he saw it as a reward for her, for all the trust she'd put in him this past week. But it would also serve a greater purpose. The goal moving forward was to give her more power, more choices, to slowly retract and reverse the submissiveness he'd created in her. Before her time here was through, he would even prod her toward the other extreme, pushing her to be dominant, aggressive, to take what she wanted. But tonight's fantasy was simply about giving her options and opportunities. And he was growing impatient—both professionally and personally now—to see what choices she made.

Of course, giving her so much new freedom would also allow her to regress, to reject the sexual smorgasbord he laid before her, and if that happened, he'd deal with it. But he didn't think it would.

Jenna had followed the map provided with her invitation and now found herself in another of those small changing rooms that seemed to be the gateway from normal life into fantasy.

As promised, her wardrobe had been provided and she was almost giddy about it. The dress was very Marie Antoinette—not completely authentic, but close enough. The extremely low-cut bodice nearly revealed her nipples while the ivory satin corset underneath shoved them high, making her feel like a sumptuous courtesan. Otherwise, the frock's shape was much like the green one she'd donned on the beach yesterday, yet with wider skirting and a few lace panels sewn into the ornate brocade.

Beneath the dress, she wore only stockings with ivory bows at the front of each thigh, and ivory shoes that matched the period. According to the note with the dress, "You have decided to forego undergarments tonight as the weather is warm and you are feeling a bit naughty." True, and true, she decided merrily enough.

Just as she stood before the mirror in the small room admiring her dress—and her breasts—a woman attired as an English maid came scurrying through the door. "Sorry to be so tardy, m'lady," she said, sporting a thick cockney accent, "but 'ave you a seat and we'll fix up your hair right nice."

One thing she had to say for the Hotel Erotique—they understood the value of details. She couldn't hide her smile as she sat down at a small dressing table to the right of the large mirror and let the maid begin working. With no mention of the modern curling iron and pins being used, the maid chattered about how the party was well underway and how fancy all the ladies looked.

"And oh, them 'andsome lords in their tight breeches!" the maid screeched, fanning herself. "Some of 'em looks like they got a lot to offer a lady, if ya knows what I mean." Meanwhile, she styled Jenna's hair into an admirable seventeenth-century coif, complete with tightly ringed sausage curls falling over her shoulders.

"Off ya go now," the maid said with a shooing motion when she'd finished. But before Jenna could even get to her feet, the maid held up one finger. "Wait! I've gone and forgot the most important thing!"

"What's that?" Jenna asked.

The maid stepped to a cabinet across the small chamber and pulled out a glittery ice blue mask adorned with a clump of fluffy ivory feathers. It was so beautiful Jenna gasped—and the maid smiled. "Can't very well go to a masquerade without this, now can ya?"

"Definitely not," Jenna said, warming to the fantasy even more.

Then the maid carefully fit the mask over Jenna's head, securing it with the attached elastic band, which she hid beneath certain locks of hair, and ignoring that the elastic was a modern addition.

The mask covered only the top part of Jenna's face, and her eyes shone vividly through, but it still made her feel sexy and mysterious. She smiled at her reflection in the mirror as the maid resumed her previous shooing. "Go now. Ya don't wants to miss the merriment. But ya best be careful," she added, winking, "for I 'ear there's a rascally rogue or two what might try to have his way with ya."

When Jenna stepped through the door that led to the fantasy, she found herself immediately immersed in seventeenth-century London! Like last night, the sense of being swept back to another era was instantly more profound than in yesterday's beach fantasy and nearly took her breath away. To one side of the ornate room, a string quartet played, filling the air with classical music. Candles in ornate wall sconces lit the space, drawing her gaze to intricately carved woodwork and brocade-covered walls where period paintings hung. The large parlor buzzed with people in costumes similar to hers—they stood in groups talking, maybe flirting, drinking wine and snacking on fancy finger foods. Some women and even a few men wore tall powdered wigs; others, like her, simply had their hair styled in a suitable way. If she wasn't mistaken, she spotted Zack beneath a simple black mask, his long hair drawn back in a queue—he was busy charming a woman in a yellow gown and looked surprisingly debonair in a doublet and breeches.

Just then, a hand touched her elbow and she looked up to find Brent, and—oh my—talk about debonair. She wouldn't have believed he could make the showy men's fashions of the mid-1600s look so . . . masculine. The dark fabric of his short doublet fell open across his chest to reveal the high-collared linen shirt beneath, and his breeches—tucked into leather boots—were fitted enough to hint at the bulge between his thighs. The small gray mask he wore did little to hide his identity, at least from her. "Lord Sexingham, I presume," she said with just a hint of playfulness, amused by the silly name.

His eyes returned the emotion. "I am delighted you could come to my little soiree this evening, Lady Jenna."

"Ah, so my mask does not hide me any better than yours does you, I see."

He gave his head a dashing tilt. "I would know your beauty anywhere, my lady."

To her surprise, Jenna felt a blush color her cheeks, and turned away, both utterly smitten and embarrassed by it.

"I trust," he went on, "that you will find this a most *pleasurable* gathering."

"As do I," she replied, and even as she spoke, she realized that, already, the mood of the room was beginning to change slightly, feeling a bit more . . . tawdry than she'd noticed upon first walking in. On a divan across the room, a woman sat perched on a man's lap, kissing him as he fondled her breast through her dress. And the quartet had begun a new piece of music that somehow felt more sensual as well.

"Come—have some wine," Brent said, taking her hand to lead her through the mingling crowd. A moment later, she was sipping on a sweet chardonnay that went down easily. And suddenly, she had the odd feeling she should drink enough to get relaxed. She wanted very much to be a part of what took place here tonight, whatever that might be—and like earlier today, she began to suspect something extreme.

As she drank more wine, she spotted another couple—two girls—beginning to playfully touch one another, putting their arms around each other's waists, starting to kiss. It looked stranger than usual, given the costumes, yet somehow all the more erotic for it.

"You should feel free to follow any whim that strikes you tonight, my lady. After all, we are all safe behind our masks," Brent said with a wink.

She lifted her eyes to his with a grin, starting to feel the wine a bit. "What happens in 1650 stays in 1650?"

Brent let out a loud laugh and she liked having shaken him from his role—even if he plainly wasn't as deeply in character as he'd been as a pirate. "Something like that, Lady Jenna. You have quite a keen wit," he added.

"Thank you. And *you* look quite handsome in your late-Renaissance clothing, Lord Sexingham," she heard herself say. Damn wine.

Just then, an attractive girl with blond hair, ample curves, and an extravagant beaded mask came scurrying up to Jenna and Brent. Funny how the mask made Jenna focus on the parts of the woman she could see: lush pink lips, seductive brown eyes, and plump, uplifted breasts that appeared ready to burst from the tight laced bodice of her lavender gown at any moment. Leaning into Brent, but with her gaze planted provocatively on Jenna, she said, "Pray, what have you here, Sexingham? I hope you won't keep this tasty morsel to yourself all night."

"The lady is most free to dally with whomever she chooses," Brent replied to the slightly raucous but pretty girl.

"That is happy news indeed," the lady said, her voice thick with lust—then she boldly reached out to slide her fingertip along the top edge of Jenna's bodice, just above her nipples, all the way from one uplifted side to the other. "You have scrumptious tits, my lady," the woman said, leaving the objects of her affection to tingle madly as she dashed gaily off into the crowd.

When Jenna lifted her eyes to Brent's, his had turned heated—his arousal visible even through his mask. "It would seem the masquerade element of the party is loosening my guests' inhibitions, Lady Jenna. You cannot be offended by the other lady's impropriety, however, since she speaks only the truth about your tits."

The dark desire that had just deepened his voice made Jenna's breasts heave slightly, and she suddenly wondered if *hers* would be the ones to spill from her dress.

When a sensual female moan met Jenna's ears, she turned to see a blond man sucking the breast of a woman in a tall powdered wig. The bodice of her cornflower blue frock had been drawn down to reveal just one small but perky tit, and her eyes were shut, jaw lax, as she sighed and groaned her pleasure.

The quartet's music now quickened, becoming lively, playful, yet expressing an urgency Jenna began to feel in her bones as she observed the debauchery starting to infest the lavish room. She caught sight of another couple on a chaise lounge—a handsome man in a small powdered wig playfully shoved his hand under the lady's dress, making her squeal in delight, and then purr with pleasure. A moment later, another woman—a redhead in an even redder gown, alit on the lounge on the other side of the lady, soon reaching up to begin massaging her breast, then kissing her lips.

Brent's warm voice in her ear made her shiver. "Is your pussy getting wet, Lady Jenna?"

She looked up, meeting his gaze behind the gray mask. "It's been wet all day, my lord."

"I hope to make it wetter," he promised.

Jenna bit her lip as hot desire trickled all through her. She kept her eyes on Brent's, letting him know she was ready—for anything.

When next he spoke, though, he was more Brent than Lord Sexingham. "Tonight, Jenna, no commands, no submission. But I hope you'll let yourself be free. No doubts or worries. I want you to do what your body urges you to."

What her body urged her to, huh? That sounded so easy now. So easy that she said, "If you insist," then pressed herself against him, breasts to chest, cunt to cock. *Hard* cock. A warm purr left her throat as that hardness filled her with pleasure. "Mmm, so big," she breathed, curling her hands into his ass through his breeches.

"And your pussy feels so fucking soft, my lady," he whispered deeply in her ear. "Is it hot? Swollen?"

She let out a small moan. "Yes, and yes."

At that, Brent led her to a plush divan upholstered in burgundy velvet and gently pushed her down onto it, stooping in front of her. She'd just begun to wonder what he was planning when he reached beneath the hem of her beautiful dress, his hands closing warm around her ankles, then smoothly slid his touch upward, to her knees, taking the skirting with him. Her spine tingled as his palms glided still higher, soon revealing the playful ivory satin bows at the front of each stocking, halfway up her thighs. She sat with her legs demurely together, feeling at once innocent and naughty.

Until Brent pushed her legs apart, wide. Then she felt only naughty. Delightfully so. She bit her lip as he studied her cunt, appearing enraptured, and her entire body pulsed to realize that, around them, more and more people were breaking into couples or groups, touching, kissing, pulling down bodices, raising skirts. She sensed *their* eyes on *her*, too—on her slit, which surely glistened in the candlelight, and it made her all the more eager.

"Lady Jenna," Brent said from between her knees, "your pussy looks delectable."

She sucked in her breath, felt her breasts lift slightly within the tight confines that held them, and offered her most inviting expression. "You should taste it."

When Brent's warm mouth sank over her cunt, she cried out from the abrupt pleasure. She couldn't have held in her hot sighs if she'd tried—so she didn't try. As the classical music swirled around her, as the elegance blended with decadence, Jenna sank fully into the strange ambience of the gathering: the sex, the atmosphere, the fantasy. Brent feasted on her vigorously—licking, kissing—and she relished the way he looked between her stocking-covered thighs, the tightness of the corset, all the finery and rich fabrics, everything. She felt glorious, alive, and indeed, free.

Just then, a pretty woman in a powdered wig sat down beside her, peering longingly at Jenna through a glittery pink mask. The girl was altogether feminine and sexy, from her moist pink lips to the watered pink silk of her gown, trimmed in mounds of white lace and tiny pink bows. "I must kiss you, my lady," she said, sounding eager and almost demure at the same time.

Without even thinking of Brent for a change, Jenna, caught up in the moment, murmured, "Yes, please." Then she sighed softly in response to Brent's continuing ministrations below.

Gently cupping Jenna's jaw, the girl leaned in for a soft, tender kiss, heightening every sensation rushing through Jenna's body. Quickly, however, the kisses deepened—when the girl's tongue pressed between Jenna's lips, Jenna met it with her own, after which she simply quit thinking, shut her eyes, and kissed her the same as she would kiss Brent. Soon the girl in pink was leaning over Jenna as they made out, their breasts pressing, rubbing together.

When the girl's lips left hers, Jenna watched in awe as the other woman slowly tugged at Jenna's bodice, finally revealing her nipples.

"Oooh," the pretty girl moaned at the sight of them, beaded and hard, jutting overtop the laced edge of the fabric. She smiled as she bent to lick one of them, and Jenna bit her lip, watching. She trembled as the effects arced through her, combining with the continued pleasures from Brent at her cunt. Meeting his gaze, she knew, even through the mask, that he was well-pleased—and she tried to part her legs still further, wanting to open herself to him, and to this experience, more and more.

Jenna's female companion continued to kiss and lick at her turgid nipples, sometimes gentle and playful, at other moments starting to suckle and nibble more roughly—a sensation that shot straight to Jenna's engorged clit. She began to feel completely devoured by her lovers. And she soon wanted to return the favor.

So even as her new girlfriend licked and teased her tight nipples, Jenna reached to caress her breasts. Like Jenna's, they were pressed upward in a corset, leaving Jenna unable to truly cup the globes in her palms as she wanted—so she played around the bared upper ridges with her fingertips, teasing the flesh just above the bodice.

Finally, the other girl's kisses ceased as she sat upright to encourage Jenna's touches. Jenna leaned in to kiss her soft upper breasts as Brent's lengthy feasting continued below. Mmm, God, her cunt hummed beneath his mouth, and to make sure he knew it, she paused to peer down at him. "Keep eating me, my lord," she purred.

Then she looked back to her lady in pink, bit her lip as another last inhibition dropped away, and pulled at the silken bodice until her breasts were freed—not only from the fabric, it seemed, but the corset had lowered, too, so that the other girl's tits tumbled freely from the dress, tipped with pale pink peaks.

"Oh, kiss them, my lady," the girl begged, and Jenna obliged. She raked her tongue gently over one nipple, focusing on the feel of the pearl-like bead—then she followed the urge to run her tongue around it.

Moving to the other lovely tit, Jenna closed her lips over it, sucking lightly, delighting when the girl moaned—a sound she felt between her legs. She pumped softly at Brent's mouth as she suckled the pretty girl's nipple, then raised slightly to brush her own bared breasts against the other pair. Both girls sighed, rubbing their tits together.

The light play of hard, pointed nipples against Jenna's breasts sent such a burst of pleasure exploding through her that she could scarcely believe she hadn't yet come. The sensations were intense, spreading through her whole body now, and she could only attribute her staying power to wanting to make this last.

When her pretty girlfriend leaned back on the divan, a move that sent her medium tits pointing upward, Jenna returned her tongue to the breast nearest her, again licking, teasing, pleasing—as she molded the girl's other tit in her palm.

It was when an unexpected warmth came near Jenna's hand that she looked up to see a masked gentleman with dark, unkempt hair had joined them, leaning in to suck on the spare nipple. Jenna didn't stop, instantly intrigued by sharing the girl the same as Brent had shared *her* so many times. And even when the man's hand reached out, closing around one of *Jenna's* exposed breasts, she didn't stop. She felt wild. Free. Delightfully dirty. Ultimate pleasure was hers. Ultimate sexual freedom.

Just then, a deep groan echoed from Brent's mouth—vibrating through the deepest part of her pussy—and she looked down to see . . . oh—oh God.

Brent was no longer alone. Another masked man held Brent's erect cock in his hand.

Chapter 13

Jenna had lifted her right foot to the divan at some point and now Brent shifted as well, angling his body to one side, even as he ate her pussy. He moved from his knees to his ass, legs spread, knees bent, breeches open, his beautiful cock jutting like an obelisk through another guy's fist.

Such warmth permeated her at the startling sight that she abandoned her girlfriend's breast. The move led her to rest her head on the plump mound she'd just deserted—but her playmate seemed undaunted, simply looping her arm around Jenna from behind to begin tweaking and twirling one of Jenna's nipples between her fingertips.

Jenna watched in awe as Brent's new companion—younger, clearly sexy—bent to take his cock into his mouth. Her pussy jolted at the sight, almost violently—but she still managed not to come. Brent lifted his head, his face wet with her juices, to meet her gaze.

"So hot," she breathed, and immediately saw the heat and relief mingling in his eyes—he'd obviously cared if this aroused her; he'd obviously worried it would not.

As if in reply, Brent smoothly inserted two fingers into her cunt, making her sob—just as the man who'd caressed her breast before now did so again, still suckling the other girl's tit. Thus both of Jenna's breasts were fondled as Brent fucked her with his fingers—but for the moment, he turned his eyes on what took place between his legs.

Jenna had never seen one man sucking another's cock before and the vision transfixed her—especially since Brent's low groans told her how deep his pleasure ran. And as the younger guy slid his mouth capably up and down Brent's erection, it hit her: Good Lord, could that be

Ryan, the cute waiter she'd met early in her stay? But before she could ponder it further, Brent turned suddenly back to her parted slit, burying his face there with a wild fury that made her cry out.

She watched Brent pump his rock-hard column into that male mouth as, at her pussy, he latched on to her swollen clit, sucking deep and rhythmic. Still mesmerized by the cocksucking, she writhed brazenly against Brent now, getting closer and closer—oh God, yes, it was coming—and then finally she was screaming as the orgasm rocked her body involuntarily, as the whole scene seemed to collapse around her in a glorious, replete climax she couldn't have imagined.

The moment the waves of intense pleasure faded, Brent released her clit and let out a hot, low groan, whispered the words, "Fuck—*now*," and thrust harder into his male lover's mouth, coming. She'd never gotten to see that before—Brent coming with someone other than her—and it was an amazing, arousing sight that made her skin prickle and her pussy pulse anew. She practically wanted to come again herself, just witnessing the obscenely hot vision.

When it was over, Brent's cheek came to rest on her bare thigh. She stroked his hair and let her head fall back against the divan, eyes closing, and sensed their other companions drifting away to seek greener pastures now that they'd both reached orgasm.

But Jenna needed to be closer to him now, and since, all around them, half-clothed bodies sprinkled not only the furniture but the carpet as well, she eased herself to the floor with Brent to lie down, drawing his head to her chest.

When Brent opened his eyes after a short, orgasm-induced sleep—which he didn't usually fall prey to, but he'd been more sexually active this week than usual—he found "Lady Jenna" curled up in his arms, her bodice still pulled low. His cock flopped lazily from the opening in his pants, reminding him: She'd watched Ryan suck him off. And she'd loved it. He couldn't have imagined such a response from Jenna even a few days ago and simply recalling the look in her eyes made his dick begin perking back to life.

Around them, the sex party raged on—they lay in the middle of what had become a tangled mass of bodies and hands and revealed private parts.

As he shifted to take in the rest of the room, Jenna stirred, soon lifting her head, peering down into his eyes. He reached up to pull her sparkly mask back into place—it had gotten skewed in sleep. "We can't have you revealing your identity, can we, Lady Jenna?" he whispered teasingly.

Instead of replying to what he'd said, she simply rasped, "I want more," and reached down to slide her cool palm over his cock, now nearly half hard.

The touch, and her need, took away all his amusement. "Then more you shall have. Take whatever you like."

And then Jenna began to kiss him. He'd gotten far too attached to that simple affection with her, but for now, he indulged fully, meeting her tongue with his, letting her feel his desire.

Soon she was pulling him to sit upright in the middle of the floor, then lifting her brocade skirt to straddle him. His erection was stiff and full now, and he released a low growl when she skimmed her wet slit provocatively up and down his length, just before—God yes—she lowered herself onto him. They both groaned and her head fell back, and he liked knowing he felt bigger inside her in this position.

"Am I huge in you, sunshine?" he asked throatily near her ear.

She drew back slightly, bit her lip, and sounded lost in passion. "Impossibly so."

She began to ride him then, purring and moaning as she found her rhythm. He molded one hand to her ass under the dress; the other he used to knead her breast—before bending to suckle it. He loved her tight nipple on his tongue, between his lips—the sensation stretched straight to his groin.

Couples, trios, and other configurations fucked all around them—the string quartet could barely be heard above all the moans and groans and dirty whispers—but for Brent, there was only Jenna, looking beautifully naughty and eager as he pumped up into her. "Ride me, baby," he growled, and she ground her pussy on him harder.

Damn, she was so sexy, his Little Mary Sunshine gone bad—and he yearned to give her more and more pleasure.

Just behind her stood Zack with two girls—both guests, Brent thought, since he didn't recognize them—who knelt before him and took turns going down on him. And Brent knew Zack well enough to know his overriding sexual preference was, indeed, having his cock sucked. So as the two girls began kissing one another, seeming to forget the large phallus in their midst, Brent met his gaze, silently summoning him.

When an erect, veined cock suddenly appeared at eye level next to Jenna, she glanced up, looking slightly taken aback. So Brent was glad when Zack briefly lifted his mask to give her a quick wink hello, knowing it would put her at ease for what he hoped would happen next.

Lowering her eyes back to Brent, her expression was a charming mix of daring and sheepishness. So he would help her along.

As they fucked, he reached up, took hold of Zack's hard-on, and drew it toward Jenna's mouth.

He couldn't decide whether or not to be surprised when she parted her lips willingly—but as they closed over Zack's cock, it was all Brent could do not to come.

Above, Zack groaned, beginning to glide gingerly in and out, and Brent's limbs actually grew weak watching her suck another guy this way, just a few inches from his face, while he moved in her below.

A few minutes later, Jenna extracted the shaft from her swollen lips—then guided it toward *Brent's* mouth.

He didn't hesitate. What Jenna wanted tonight, he would gladly give her. He opened wide, let her feed Zack's erection to him. He welcomed the fullness in his mouth, no stranger to the sensation—and he kept his eyes on Jenna as he worked, pleased with how awestruck she appeared. Her eyes, her lips, were incredibly close, and just like when it was *her* mouth being fucked, something about the nearness made it ultimately more intense.

"I want him to come in your mouth," she said, undulating on him wetly. And everything inside him clenched at sharing this fresh, new dirty lust with her.

He sucked Zack with more vigor, and within seconds, Zack was thrusting, sliding his length roughly toward Brent's throat. Jenna looked enthralled, growing more and more excited, and Brent only hoped Zack exploded before *he* did, since he was having a hard time holding back now.

He sucked harder, deeper. Felt dirty, dirty, dirty—all for sweet Jenna, *with* her, in *response* to her. She moaned, clearly entranced and on the edge herself. While, above him, Zack began to emit a low groan, murmuring, "Shit, yeah, almost, almost," and Brent reached up to gently squeeze his balls.

"Hell yeah," Zack bit off—then shot his come to the back of Brent's mouth. Brent swallowed, again, again, taking it all in, his eyes shutting in the heat of the moment—after which he heard Jenna sobbing and knew she was coming on him, too.

Oh God, oh fuck—he couldn't hold it in anymore, either, and just as Zack fired a last arc of semen into his throat, Brent erupted inside Jenna's body, moaning around the erection filling his mouth.

Jenna could barely process all that had just happened. As Zack pulled his wet shaft away, she stared at Brent, thinking—*Oh my God, I've never experienced anything so intense in my life.* And she'd done it with *him*, and she knew, whether or not he'd admit it, he felt the same way. She'd seen it in his eyes, felt it in his kiss.

"Doing okay, honey?" he asked softly.

And that's when it hit her—*Oh Lord, I've just taken part in an orgy. A real, true-life, freaking orgy!* But she had no regrets, because she'd been with Brent. And somehow that made everything—*anything*—okay. "Yeah, I am. I can't believe it, but I really am."

Yet she suddenly didn't want to be here anymore. The rest of the room writhed in raucous abandon, but she felt . . . well, that she'd experienced the full measure of what she could here. "Can we take off, though? Go to your place or something?"

To her relief, he didn't show the slightest reluctance. "Yeah, let's go." And a moment later, he was taking her hand, whisking her past the pulsing mass of bodies toward the door.

Once outside in the warm tropical air, they made their way to the nearby beach, where Jenna stopped to shed her period shoes. They walked hand in hand, Brent holding both their masks, until Jenna looked up at him to say, "Is it all right for Lord Sexingham to leave his own party?"

He let out a light laugh, looking as if the thought hadn't occurred to him until now. "Not really, but they'll get by without me."

"I'm sorry to make you break so many rules," she said.

He grinned down at her in the moonlight. "No you're not," he scolded. Then he stopped, dropped the masks to the sand, lifted his hands to her face, and kissed her for a very long time.

They lay in Brent's bed, snuggling. Upon reaching his bungalow, they'd said little—both tired, she guessed—but they'd undressed each other very slowly, then wordlessly crawled beneath his sheets. She still wore her stockings, though, and she sensed that Brent especially liked them.

"Did I do okay at the masquerade?" she asked against his broad chest.

Above her, he let out a deep, throaty chuckle. "You have to ask, sunshine? You were fucking phenomenal." Then he used one bent finger to lift her chin so that she met his gaze. "But this fantasy was about doing what *you* wanted, not what *I* wanted you to do. It was about total freedom."

"Then it worked, because that's exactly what I felt."

As was so often the case, he looked pleased. "Good."

"That said," she reasoned, now that the excitement was over, "I'm not sure how this is going to translate into my real life. I don't see many more orgies in my future."

The corners of his mouth turned up in just a hint of a smile. "I'm not suggesting that this would even be *wise* in real life. But I wanted you to experience it, to know that you can. And I . . . wanted to see you that way," he admitted. "That part was selfish."

"I don't mind," she whispered.

Cuddling back up to his warm body, she noticed the initials on his arm once more. And the closer she felt to him, it seemed, the more she longed to know about the one woman Brent Powers had ever fallen in love with. Biting her lip, she reached out to gently run her fingertips over the tattoo. "What happened with Deena?" she asked.

But he didn't respond.

She waited for a long moment, yet he still remained quiet, eyes on the ceiling, as if she'd never asked.

Given that the two of them *had* grown close, whether he liked it or not, she didn't hide her disappointment. "You're really not going to tell me?"

"She died," he said.

Oh no. "Oh. God. I'm sorry, Brent." Then she whispered, "How?"

This time, when he hesitated, she didn't dare press him—she could see how hard it was for him to share this, but that he was trying now. "An accident. On the highway. A semi lost control."

Jenna's heart constricted. "God, that's awful."

"Yeah," he agreed. "They say it was quick, though—no pain." Yet then his eyebrows knit.

"What?" she asked.

He gave his head a short shake—but then he confided in her further. "We'd fought that day. About sex. She was . . . kind of like you."

"Like *me*?"

He met her gaze briefly. "She'd had some bad experiences growing up, and she wasn't very comfortable with sex. But I wasn't mature enough to get it at the time—and I was mad she was always rejecting my advances, always acting turned off." He stopped, sighed. "So we argued. And so I've always known she was mad at me—*hurt* by me—when she died. And worse, she had every right to be, because I was acting like an asshole."

Jenna blinked, shocked, putting pieces together. At the risk of over-estimating her importance to Brent, she whispered, "Is that why? Why you insisted on fixing my problems?"

His face changed then, going dark, looking even sadder somehow. "I don't know. I never thought about it." Then he let out a rough breath, appearing disgusted with himself. "Shit—I kind of wondered why it was so damn important to me, so . . . hell. Maybe."

"Maybe you wanted to . . . give me what you weren't able to give *her*?" Jenna suggested cautiously.

Brent's only response was to close his eyes—and then she saw a tear leak free, rolling down his cheek.

Oh God. Oh God, her heart broke for him. "I'm sorry. Maybe I shouldn't have said that."

Yet then he seemed to shake off the more brutal emotions. "No, it's okay," he said, reaching up to wipe the wetness from his face. "I just hadn't realized it, but you're probably right."

Despite herself, Jenna still wanted to know more. She wasn't sure she should keep prying at this point, yet . . . "When did Deena die?"

"The April before I graduated from college."

Oh, wow. That explained a lot. Like why he'd looked so unhappy in those graduation pictures. And could it also explain . . . ? "That was . . . right before you came *here*. Right?"

He nodded against the pillow. "I came that summer."

She simply looked at him, wondering if he truly couldn't see what *she* suddenly saw. She raised on one elbow to peer down at him. "You came here to get away from her death," she said.

Yet he only shrugged. "Sure I did. It was a good distraction. A different lifestyle, a different world."

"But you never left, Brent. You came here to hide from it and you never stopped."

This finally got his attention. He arched a brow and she felt his muscles tense. "Okay, who's the psychology major here?"

Jenna wasn't sure how to proceed. She didn't want to be hard on him, but the fact was—his girlfriend had died a very long time ago. He should be over it by now. So she was as honest with *him* as he'd been with *her* about confronting her issues. "Maybe you should quit trying to dodge this, because I think I'm right. I think you've been . . . hiding here all this time."

"Hiding from what?" he snapped.

She tilted her head and didn't let his tone deter her. "I'm not sure. Love? The fear of loving somebody that much again and losing them? The fear of hurting somebody and never having the chance to fix it? The fear of living the life you'd planned with her—*without* her? Maybe *all* of that? Am I getting close?"

He didn't say anything for a minute, and she knew she'd pissed him off. He still held her in a loose embrace, but the tenderness of it had faded. Finally, he looked her in the eye and said, "I don't hide from anything, Jenna. You should know that by now."

"I should know that just because you're all big and tough and sexy?" she asked, still feeling bold. "Talk about being in denial. All I can say is . . . sex doctor, heal thyself."

Brent knew there was truth in her words. He'd always known it. He'd just chosen not to think about it. Now he had only himself to blame for getting so close to someone that they could see it.

"Jenna," he quietly explained, "there are times when it's possible to . . . recognize what you're doing, and know why, and even realize that maybe it doesn't seem like the best thing . . . but if you function fine that way, maybe you decide it *is* the best thing—for *you*. I'm happy here, so why would I change that—no matter what brought me here?" Maybe that would shut her up.

Unfortunately not. "I could ask you the same question about *my* issues. I was fine, happy, content—but you insisted on fixing me anyway. And I feel better about myself inside than I have in years. I thought I was fine when I came here, and I could have lived that way forever without any real problems—but you made me *better*. Better than I knew I could be."

"Apples and oranges," he said decidedly.

"I disagree," she replied. "I think . . . you're afraid of the world beyond this island. I think you're afraid of all the ways there are to hurt and get hurt if you indulge in a relationship that goes deeper than sex."

Okay, that was it. He'd tried to be nice about this, but she'd just pushed him too far. Still, he tried to keep his voice calm as he said, "*I* think *you're* butting into something that's not your business, sunshine."

"Maybe I care about you," she shot back at him.

Shit. "Don't go there, Jenna," he warned.

"*What*? Why?"

So he'd have to explain this, too, huh? Fine. "Because that was my exact fear all along. It's why a guide should *not* take part in your fantasies. And I fucked up a lot more by . . . by all this talking and getting to know you. You're not *supposed* to care about me."

She spoke more softly. "What if it's too late for that?"

His chest tightened. He'd been trying to ignore the ramifications of getting close to her, trying to just ride it out like she'd said—and that's exactly what he was going to keep doing now. "You need to push it aside," he told her unequivocally. "Just like all the other emotions you've needed to push aside this week to free yourself sexually."

She let out a sigh, pursed her lips, and said, "What if I . . . haven't really pushed them aside very much?"

Hell. He had no choice. He had to lower the boom here, once and for all. He didn't want to hurt her, so he spoke gently—but the words would still wound her. "Jenna, let me say this plainly. I've enjoyed being with you this week, and yeah, I've taken some special satisfaction in helping you overcome your issues. But I never should have talked so openly with you. And I shouldn't have you in my bed right now. Because despite enjoying your company a great deal, this is still my job."

She looked tougher than he might have expected—more challenged than hurt. "Right now?" she asked. "Having me in your bed is your job?"

"Kind of. Because you needed extra attention, extra prodding—you *know* that. Getting closer to you helped me find out what you needed."

"Oh," she said, her voice coming out too soft. It made his stomach pinch, but he had to ignore that and go on.

"And, if you recall, you would only consent to going through with the fantasies if I took part in them. So I didn't exactly have a choice if I wanted to help you."

Next to him, she bit her lip and looked down, clearly embarrassed to remember that part.

And shit—he felt like an ass. "Don't be mad at me," he said. "This doesn't mean we're not friends."

"Friends," she repeated, as if the word were ridiculous.

And she was right—it was. Hell.

So he flashed an irritated look of concession. "Okay, yes, damn it, I care for you, too—but . . . I can't care in a way that goes beyond *this*, right here, this island. Because this is my world, my life, what I do. And in a few days, you're going back to the world *you* know, the world where you belong. All this will, I hope," he said gently, "be a pleasant memory, for us both."

It relieved him when she nodded and said quietly, "Yes, it will be."

"I'm sorry," he told her then, "if everything I just said hurt you. I don't mean to be harsh. I just needed you to know."

"It's all right," she said, her voice soft but stronger now.

Good. Maybe they could get back to normal here. "Now—can we cut out all the damn psychoanalyzing for a while and just fuck?"

She blinked. "You still want to—after all this? You aren't going to suddenly . . . push me away? Worry that I can't handle it or something?"

He shook his head and spoke the truth. "I wouldn't do that. I want this to be . . . what it's been up to now—a good, satisfying thing for us both. Okay?"

"Okay."

"Now, come here," he said, "and let me nibble on your pretty tits."

And nibble he did, while she purred and sighed—but the whole while he knew with brand-new certainty that things *had* to change here. She'd left him no choice—she'd shown him there *was* no riding this out on its current course.

He'd meant what he said—he wouldn't suddenly abandon her; he'd continue to be her guide *and* her lover. And he'd probably continue to feel way too much while he was doing it. But plain and simple, he'd have to make it so that her sexual world no longer revolved around him.

The conversation had left Jenna stunned. To find out Brent's first and only love had died so tragically was heartbreaking. And to further discover that the event had—in effect—trapped Brent here for fifteen years? Wow. She *had* felt presumptuous playing psychologist with him, but it had seemed so obvious once she knew the facts.

As for what had followed, about his relationship with her, the things he'd said *had* hurt her, but they hadn't *surprised* her.

In fact, what had surprised her was how . . . normal things felt afterward. They'd had slow sex, him moving in her deeply, making her feel connected to him all the more. They'd slept snuggled together beneath the sheets and woken with the sun. He'd seemed happy to see her, kissing her good morning with a drowsy smile, then asking if she wanted Cheerios.

"You're a charmer in the breakfast department, Powers," she'd teased him. "Do all your other overnight guests put up with Cheerios and bagels?"

He'd just shrugged, looking as if there was something he wasn't saying.

"Well?" she prodded.

"There aren't all that many, sunshine," he said matter-of-factly, shocking the hell out of her.

"Um, why?" She'd assumed his bungalow would be worthy of a revolving door.

"Think about it. I don't get sexually involved with guests outside of their fantasies."

"Except me," she pointed out.

He ignored that. "So that leaves Hotel Erotique employees."

"Of which there are plenty. And they're gorgeous. And I'm sure they're happy to share your bed."

He shrugged again. "I used to indulge in that more when I was younger than I do now."

"Why?"

"Guess it got old," he said shortly. Then changed the subject. "Come on, or I might eat the last bowl of cereal and *then* where would you be?"

Over breakfast, Brent had told her she wouldn't be having a fantasy today. And, of course, that had disappointed her, but she understood—last night's had been a doozie, and the night before that had been a double dose for them both. And even though she still wanted to soak up all the sex with him she could, maybe a day off to absorb everything she'd learned last night wasn't a bad idea. Since she couldn't stop thinking about it.

"I scheduled you a seaside massage, though," he said. "Two o'clock."

"Seaside?"

"Just outside the spa—under an awning—with a view of the ocean," he explained. "It's nice—you'll like it."

Now she lay on a massage table on her stomach, resting her chin on her hands to take in the scenery until the massage began. The bamboo awning sported four stone arches emerging from the soft lawn—and the only sound was the rolling tide in the distance. Brent was right—while the spa was luxurious and serene inside, for Jenna nothing beat the tranquility of being outdoors in a peaceful setting. She hadn't spent much time thinking of the Hotel Erotique as peaceful, but her time sunbathing at the beach had indeed been that, the perfect contrast with all the wild sex. And today, it provided a nice sense of calm, offsetting the shocking new facts of Brent's life that still swirled in her head.

"Hi, I'm Courtney."

Jenna looked over her shoulder to see a tall, Norwegian-looking blonde in a white spa coat. "Oh, hi. No Rhoda today?"

"No Rhoda," the girl said with a smile. "Her day off, so you're stuck with *me*."

Jenna returned the friendly smile. "Oh, that's fine. I just assumed—since I had Rhoda a few days ago."

"Well, I promise to take good care of you," Courtney said. Then she reached for a bottle of massage oil on a teakwood cart. "You can rest your head in the headrest or enjoy the view, whichever you like. Just let me know if the pressure is good, or too hard, or if anything I do feels uncomfortable."

Jenna nodded, then settled in for relaxation. She sighed in pleasure as Courtney massaged warm, fruit-scented oil into her shoulders, which had gotten a little sore lately—maybe from the times her arms had been bound. "Mmm, that's nice," Jenna told her.

"Good," Courtney replied. "People often get more of a workout here than they expect, so a few massages during your stay can keep you limber and comfortable during recreation." She said it as smoothly as if Jenna had come here to play tennis.

Courtney proceeded working her magic slowly down Jenna's back, and eventually folded down the white sheet covering her to begin kneading her ass. Rhoda hadn't done that. But it felt nice, so Jenna didn't protest.

The massage progressed down her legs to her feet, and then back up—to her ass again. She bit her lip as she began to feel the response in her pussy and anal area. Was she *supposed* to be feeling it there?

Up to now, the massage had truly relaxed Jenna, and despite the new sensations, she remained *mostly* relaxed, so she decided to go with the flow—for now anyway.

As Courtney's skilled hands worked, her fingers seeming to stretch closer and closer to Jenna's cunt, she asked, "Does everything I'm doing feel good?"

Jenna didn't lie. "Yes."

"Do you want to turn over?"

Oh. Okay. Now Jenna got it. This was just like at the Grotto—another unannounced fantasy. Maybe it was a fantasy meant to relax as well as titillate her, or maybe Brent was stuck on convincing her she liked sex with girls as much as with guys. Either way, knowing he was somewhere watching, as he'd been at the Grotto, instantly increased her arousal, and her sense of adventure.

"Sure," Jenna replied easily now that she understood the situation. As she carefully shifted to lie on her back, she found herself peeking around the area beyond the awning, wondering where Brent might be. She didn't see him, but for all she knew, he was doing a better job of hiding this time, with binoculars—or maybe even watching through a secret video camera somewhere.

The move left her uncovered by the sheet, naked and exposed on the table. Courtney smiled easily down at her, the same as if this were a normal massage, and said, "Shall I take my coat off? I'm wearing pretty lingerie underneath."

"All right," Jenna said.

And Courtney smoothly pulled at the placket, undoing all the snaps at once, then let it fall to the ground behind her. She wore a lacy bra and thong in a pale shade of peach. Her body was predictably thin, her breasts medium and high, and a tattoo of an elaborate, multicolored butterfly decorated the skin just below her navel.

"I'll take off more if you like," Courtney offered in a friendly manner when she saw Jenna checking her out.

But Jenna wasn't in the mood for a full-blown lesbian encounter today—not even for Brent—so in just as pleasant a tone, she replied, "No, the lingerie is good, thanks."

Courtney nodded in response, then squeezed more oil into her hands. "Relax," she breathed as she bent over Jenna, firmly yet gently massaging Jenna's tits. Jenna closed her eyes and sucked in her breath, allowing herself to feel the pleasure spreading through her. She thought of Brent watching somewhere and let out a soft, "Mmm . . . ," both content and aroused.

Courtney worked the warm oil into Jenna's breasts for a long while, until Jenna's pussy had turned equally as heated. Finally, her firm, kneading touches moved down over Jenna's belly and onto her hips. Jenna bit her lip when Courtney reached her upper thighs—she felt that part of the massage deep in her cunt, soon releasing a small moan.

When she opened her eyes, Courtney smiled gently down on her, still moving her palms over Jenna's legs. She found herself smiling back as a light, salty breeze washed over her. It was shockingly easy to let Courtney make her feel good, mostly because . . . she could so easily imagine Brent's gaze on her. Just like at the Grotto, just like every other fantasy where someone else had been touching her or fucking her. If Brent wasn't the one directly pleasuring her with his hands or cock, he pleasured her in another way—with his eyes.

Courtney continued the deep yet tender massage, and Jenna didn't hide her physical response—as Courtney's touch echoed between her legs, Jenna moaned appreciatively and envisioned how hard Brent was getting.

When Courtney's kneading edged its way down onto her *inner* thighs, Jenna let her legs part. Her moans came louder as her pussy began to pulse. She felt open to the experience because Brent had taught her to be, and because she knew he was enjoying this, probably even more than she was.

Courtney turned away from the table to return a few seconds later with a vibrator the color of orange sherbet. Like the one Brent had sent her, it was shaped like a penis, only it also came complete with balls, and the bump near the base designed for clit stimulation was larger and more protruding.

Jenna thought Courtney would insert the toy in her cunt, but instead, after turning it on to create a light buzzing noise, she ran it in a circle over one of Jenna's breasts.

"Oh, it's warm," Jenna said, surprised.

Courtney's expression stayed as calm and pleasant as before. "It's been heated."

"Mmm," Jenna purred at the strange sensation as Courtney rubbed the vibrator over Jenna's other tit.

Soon, she glided the vibrating phallus slowly down Jenna's stomach—and then she pulled it away, squeezing oil onto it and rubbing it in with her free hand. "Remember, it'll feel warm," Courtney cautioned—then she smoothly slid the fake cock into Jenna's pussy.

It went in with slick ease and Jenna gasped at the sudden fullness, along with the promised warmth. Heat spread through her cheeks as she adjusted to the size as well as the riveting vibrations.

"Good?" Courtney checked.

"Mmm hmm," Jenna breathed, but it came out sounding a bit excited.

When Courtney began to slip the toy in and out of Jenna's wetness, Jenna's arousal grew, and soon she was biting her lower lip, softly meeting each warm thrust. She shut her eyes, wondering about Brent's exact view—could he easily see the vibrator moving in her pink folds?—as she grew aware of the fake balls pressing against her perineum, as well as that pronounced bump jutting into her clit with each inward drive. It was hard to believe this was her, Jenna Banks, letting another woman fuck her with a vibrator—but Brent had truly transformed her.

She loved knowing he was witnessing her pleasure—which increased quickly, given the angle of that naughty nub against her clit. Her body began to meet Courtney's plunging toy harder, harder, needing it deeper, her clit longing for still more firm pressure. Until soon Courtney switched motions—no longer sliding the vibrator inward but instead inserting it to the hilt and simply grinding the bump against Jenna's needy clit. Mmm, yes, that was good—and she realized she'd ended up using a similar action with the toy from Brent when she'd videotaped herself.

Her breath came labored, shakier, as she neared climax. And then she heard herself moaning—lightly, but then louder—and then the orgasm struck, and she fucked the humming toy in Courtney's hand, aware that the soft, gentle pleasure from moments before had turned raw and intense and completely unrestrained. She gripped both edges of the massage table as she propelled her torso against the toy cock with abandon, her body urging her to absorb every ounce of hot delight.

When finally she went still, she felt a bit strange. It was over, and where was Brent? Even at the grotto, when she'd come, she'd known exactly where he was. Without him right here, she suffered an unsettling loneliness—but she had to push that away.

Because she was at the Hotel Erotique where sex was an emotionless sport. And because Brent *was* watching, experiencing this with her, even if she couldn't see him.

Courtney extracted the vibrator, turned it off, then smiled down at Jenna—looking more aroused to her now than she had before. "I hope that was as enjoyable as it looked."

Jenna felt numb, still coming down from the orgasm in what suddenly felt like a foreign environment without Brent. "It was," she managed honestly. "Thank you."

Courtney leaned over her closely then, her breasts nearly spilling from her bra as she said, "It was truly my pleasure. If there's anything else I can do to please you, I'm happy to. Anything. Just name it."

Courtney was pretty, and clearly excited now. Jenna knew she could prolong the game, lengthen the fantasy, if she desired. Part of her was tempted. Having turned Courtney on left her feeling hot, and a little bit curious where such an invitation might lead. And yet, again . . . where was Brent? If she could see him right now, she'd gladly move forward with this.

But because he was the necessary ingredient here, she mainly felt the need to find him. See his reaction. Maybe fuck his brains out.

"That's an enticing offer," Jenna admitted to her newest Hotel Erotique playmate, "but I'll have to decline."

Courtney looked disappointed even as she kept her pleasant expression. "Are you sure? I thought we were getting along so well."

"We were—are," Jenna promised. "And you're beautiful. But . . . I have to go now."

A few minutes later, Jenna exited the spa in a pair of her new Hotel Erotique shorts and a cami. She found herself watching for Brent at every step, waiting and hoping for him to appear from behind a potted plant or a palm tree. When she'd arrived at the main pool with still no sign of him, she reached in her bag and pulled out her cell phone, dialing the same number to which she'd sent her naughty video.

"Hello?" he answered, sounding totally casual. Not like a man who was . . . well, fighting a massive hard-on or anything.

"It's Jenna. Where are you?"

"Uh, home."

"Home?" she asked. She couldn't have been more surprised.

"Yeah, I'm working from my home office this afternoon, going over the profile of a guest arriving in a few days. Why?"

Jenna sank onto the nearest available lounge chair. All around her, people luxuriated in the sun, bartenders mixed drinks in the nearby tiki bar, and music played, but she felt . . . isolated, as if she were suddenly somewhere very far away from it all, completely alone. "You're working right *now*?" she managed.

"Yeah. Why, sunshine? What's wrong?"

Jenna's heart rose to her throat. "I just came from my massage," she informed him.

"Ah," he said, suddenly sounding playful, amused. "Did you enjoy it?"

Her chest tightened until she could barely speak. "I . . . thought I did."

"Uh . . . what does *that* mean?" He suddenly sounded as confused as she felt.

"It means I assumed . . . you were there. Somewhere. Or watching through a hidden camera or something. Are you telling me you weren't?"

He stayed silent for a moment and Jenna's chest hurt so much she feared it would burst. "No, honey, I wasn't."

"I see."

"It's not customary for your guide to be at or observing *all* your fantasies."

"You always have before. Even at the Grotto," she reminded him.

"I was at the Grotto to see how things went, to gauge your progress. I never actually meant for you to know I was there—I just fucked up and didn't stay out of sight well enough."

"Hmm," she said. Because it was all she *could* say. Other words completely eluded her, trapped in her throat by the anger beginning to spread all through her. He'd done this on purpose. He'd just reminded her last night, after all, that she'd only agreed to all of this on the condition that he would be part of her fantasies—it was very clear to them both that she wanted, *needed*, him there. He'd done this to remind her she was only a job to him, a project.

"Jenna, are you okay?"

She suddenly found her voice. "Other than the fact that I feel completely betrayed and abandoned? Sure—I'm just fine."

She heard him blow out his breath on the other end of the line. "Jenna, please don't feel that way. This was the same as any other fantasy—meant to bring you pleasure and expand your horizons in a new direction. Nothing more, nothing less. If it brought you the intended pleasure, then mission accomplished and you should be happy about that."

"Don't tell me how to feel," she snapped. Then, as the full measure of his betrayal hit her, she simply pushed the disconnect button.

She couldn't bear to talk to him any longer if he was going to argue with her about it, tell her she was wrong to have the emotions she did. She'd done something sexual with Courtney that she *wouldn't* have—plain and simple—if she'd known Brent really wasn't involved in any way. It made the experience feel . . . empty. No, worse. She almost even found it a little repulsive.

Because she just wasn't like the other people here. Try as she might, she hadn't come here for the sole purpose of getting off. After *all* of this, sex, to her, still meant more. At the very least, it meant sharing something intimate with someone she trusted. And she'd trusted Brent so, so much. She'd trusted him with . . . everything, with all of her—her emotions, her thoughts, her past, her body, her pleasure. She'd trusted him and he'd just . . . abandoned her.

I hate him.

No, that was a lie—she *wanted* to hate him, but she couldn't, because she *loved* him.

Yet she hated what he'd done to her, and she was going to make damn sure it didn't happen again. She was done with *this*, done with *him*! And she was getting the hell out of the Hotel Erotique, once and for all.

Chapter 14

Jenna marched up the sunny beach. Because the moment she'd decided to end her experience here at the resort, she knew she needed to see Brent one more time. To finish this.

Her heart pounded against her ribs as she trudged through the hot sand toward his house. When she reached the bungalow, she didn't bother knocking; instead, she yanked open the door and barged right in.

She found him standing in his living room, cell phone pressed to his ear. He looked fairly frantic. "I've been trying to call you back—why did you hang up on me?"

She didn't answer, though. Instead, she said, "Susan B. Anthony! Marie Antoinette! Cleopatra!"

"What?" he asked, shaking his head in confusion.

"Oprah Winfrey!" she continued. "Amelia Earhart!"

Then he stood up a bit straighter, his expression telling her he suddenly understood.

"That's right," she confirmed. "I want out of this—now!"

He simply met her gaze for a moment, and she kind of wanted to cry—because seeing him again made her chest contract, because she was so crazy about him and only wished he hadn't misled her. "Tell me why," he finally said, his voice gentle.

"You *know* why. I just engaged in a sexual act under false pretenses."

"How false could it have been if you came?" he protested.

"I only came because I thought you were watching me. If I'd known you weren't, I would have declined everything beyond the regular massage. I was only into it because . . . I thought I was sharing it with *you*."

Brent pulled in his breath, let it back out. She couldn't read his face.

"It's my responsibility, at this point, Jenna, to . . . prepare you for sex without me. Surely you can see the logic in that."

Jenna blinked, sighed, feeling sad. Sure, she could see the logic. But what she *mainly* saw was that nothing had really changed for her here, after all—she still couldn't have casual sex. Somehow Brent had made everything feel intimate, like a connection, something deep and emotional as well as physical.

When she didn't reply, he went on. "You've had sex with *lots* of people here. Why is what happened today so different?"

But Jenna simply shook her head in response. "No, I haven't," she explained. "I haven't *really* had sex with anyone but you."

"What?" He didn't get it.

And she was determined to make him understand. "I've had sex *you've* ordained. I've had sex *you've* orchestrated and demanded and urged and encouraged. I've had sex with you *physically*, and sex with you *mentally* when you were there watching. It all felt like having sex with *you*. All of it. But today was the first time I really had sex here *without* you."

Brent sat down on the leather sofa, ran his hands back through his hair. It was small comfort that his reply came out sounding guilty. "Jenna, I thought you needed today's fantasy. I'm sorry, but it's what seemed best to me."

"I'm so tired of hearing what you think I need," she told him, not so much angry now as exasperated, weary. "The fact is, *you* needed this fantasy—not me. You needed to . . . start erecting walls between us. So you wouldn't care so much about me. So you won't miss me when I'm gone."

"I just did what I thought made sense," he replied calmly.

The non-response sliced through Jenna's chest like a knife. "Well, screw you," she said, full-blown anger returning. "I don't want any more of your stupid fantasies! I'm done with this place—I'm going home!"

She turned to go, only to hear him say, "Wait."

Looking back, she saw that he'd pushed to his feet and moved toward her.

"You have the power now," he said gently.

"What?"

"No more submission for you—now you're the powerful woman in control."

"Damn right I am—and I choose to go home."

"No, Jenna," he said, shaking his head. "Don't you want more mind-opening experiences here? What happened just now was only one fantasy—I wasn't planning on backing out of your fantasies for good. Don't you want to know what else I've got planned for you?"

Oh God, did he think it was that easy? That he could lure her back under his spell with offers of more sex? "No," she answered simply.

"I wanted to make you into a powerful Tudor noblewoman," he went on, "who chooses which of her peasants must pleasure her. I wanted to take you to the Wild West and make you a powerful, in-demand saloon girl who can choose any man she wants. I wanted to take you back to the dungeon, Jenna, but this time you'd be the dominatrix, calling the shots." He offered up a weak, pleading smile. "*You* can punish *me* this time, and I'm guessing right about now that sounds good to you."

"*No,*" she said again, adding some bite to the word.

"Then what about a beach fantasy?" he asked, speaking more softly. "Something sexy, simple, like you put on your questionnaire. I'd love to give that to you, Jenna."

Oh, hell. But . . . "No," she said once more, even if that one held an enormous amount of appeal.

And yet he still didn't give up. "Jenna," he whispered, reaching out to take her hand, "why don't you tell me about the massage fantasy—tell me everything that happened. Then it'll be like I *was* there with you. I would *love* for you to tell me."

Wow, part of Jenna was tempted. She knew it would excite him to hear about her encounter with Courtney. And they would start kissing, and touching—and she'd get to have him inside her again, the most glorious feeling she could imagine.

Maybe he'd finally admit he had feelings for her.

Maybe she'd find a way to feel good about letting this continue.

Maybe he'd promise to be with her every step of the way from now on, and she'd believe him.

But conservative Jenna tended to protect herself. She'd always been a once-bitten-twice-shy kind of girl—once someone hurt her, let her down, she never gave them a chance to do it again. She just wasn't capable of feeling the same level of trust once it was breached.

So no matter how nice it sounded to let Brent fuck her on the beach or how hot it sounded to turn him on by telling him about the massage, Jenna knew it would never feel the same to her, never feel right to her, again.

Taking a deep breath, she drew her hand away from his. "No, Brent, I can't. It's time for me to go."

Then she turned around to walk out of his house, and out of his life, heading up the beach feeling stalwart and strong. She even managed to get halfway back to the resort before she started to cry.

Within an hour, Jenna had booked a flight home from Miami and called the front desk to arrange for her transport there—Gabe would pick her up from the open-air lobby at noon tomorrow.

Every time she thought of Brent, her stomach hurt. She wasn't sure what had happened to her here. Was she truly stronger, freer, more in charge of her sexuality? Or was having fallen in love with her guide going to leave her weaker than ever?

As she sat on her balcony trying to read—clearly, she'd have to immerse herself in the Civil War memoir somewhere else, since it just wasn't working for her at the Hotel Erotique—she felt almost . . . conquered somehow. And she didn't like it one bit. In fact, she had no intention of leaving here feeling worse off than when she'd arrived.

So she needed to perk herself up. And she decided a pretty sundress and a late dinner at the Paradise Grill—one of the few *normal* things she'd done here—would be a good start.

As she tied a yellow and orange multiprint halter dress behind her neck, she hoped like hell Brent wouldn't show up there as he had the last time, but if so, she could always leave. And it was far past most people's normal dinnertime, so maybe he'd already be in for the evening.

Since she hadn't heard from him in the hours since she'd left his house, maybe that meant he'd accepted her decision to go. Or—hell, for all she knew, he was deeply immersed in some *other* guest's sex fantasy right now, fucking someone else the same way he'd fucked her, and she was the last thing on his mind.

Upon being shown to a table not far from the stage, she looked up to see her calypso singer just about to break into song—but he gave her a smile, punctuated with a sexy wink, before he began.

As usual, she enjoyed the island music, the warm night air, and the tiki torches burning in the darkness. Heartbreak kept her appetite light—she ordered only a salad and fruit cup—but the meal and everything around her provided a nice distraction from what had happened today. This was much better than moping in her room.

When the band took a break, her debonair Jamaican singer made his way to her table. "I was pleased to see the pretty lady had returned."

"I . . . needed a pleasant evening with some good music," she informed him with a slightly strained smile.

"I hope you're getting what you came for, then," he said, the sentiment somehow holding an air of sensuality.

"Very much so," she assured him.

He gazed down at her, looking speculative, maybe hopeful—until finally he spoke. "I'm soon done for the night, so . . . I wonder if the pretty lady would consent to a walk on the beach with me."

The request caught Jenna off guard. It was one thing for a singer to flirt with someone in the audience, another to suggest more. Her first impulse was to decline—but . . . why? He'd been so respectful of her each time they'd met, and he'd made her feel attractive, and special. Why not let him do it some more? And . . . well, if she couldn't even take a walk with a handsome man when invited, she *definitely* hadn't gained any freedom here. She needed to find out she was wrong about that—she needed to prove to herself she *could* be more carefree than when she'd arrived.

"That sounds lovely," she finally replied, and he smiled.

"What's your name?" he asked as they stepped down into the soft sand. Both carried their shoes, and he had rolled up the cuffs of his tan pants.

"Jenna," she said.

"Ah, I should have known—a pretty name for the pretty lady." He cast a gentle smile in her direction. "I'm Andre."

As they reached the shoreline, the tide washing up over their toes as they walked, she returned the smile, then asked politely, "So, do you do this often, Andre? Invite women here for walks on the beach?"

"No. This is, in fact, the first time."

She found herself casting him a look of doubt, teasing—yet wanting to protect herself again.

"I tell no lie, pretty lady," he said. "My band has played here only a few weeks. We work in Miami, mostly. But this place pays well, so I find myself back on an island for a month—then we'll see what happens."

Hmm—so maybe he really *was* just as respectful as she'd thought. She couldn't help wanting to know more about someone so different from her. "Tell me about your life, Andre. Are you . . . married or anything?"

He gave his head a quick shake. "No, I'm not the sort of man to cheat. I *once* had a wife, but . . . she didn't feel the same way."

"I'm sorry," Jenna told him, sincerely.

Yet he only shrugged. "I married too young. It was after leaving her that I left Jamaica, too."

"And have you been happy since then?"

Another shrug. "The world is a big place and it's good to see much of it. Broadens the mind. But I miss home sometimes. I visit, but it's not the same as living there."

"Will you *ever* go home?"

He gazed at the moon shining down on the water. "Could be. I think of myself like a palm frond in the wind—I go where the sea breeze blows me. Right now it's blown me here, to this beach, with a pretty woman named Jenna. So right now, I'm happy to be exactly where I am." And with that, he gently slipped his hand into hers.

And she let him.

"What about you, Jenna? Married? Single? Someplace in between?"

"Very single," she assured him.

"And adventurous."

It was a statement, not a question, and at first she wondered why he assumed that—but then she realized, and the warmth of a blush blossomed in her cheeks. "Oh, you mean because I'm here, at the Hotel Erotique."

She could see he was instantly sorry to have made her uncomfortable. "It's not my business—don't be embarrassed. I'm a great fan of freedom, and I admire the freedom I see in people here."

"But . . . I'm *not* like other people here, and despite what I might wish, not all that free." It felt important to make him understand she wasn't the average Hotel Erotique guest, although she kept the explanation simple. "I won the trip—without really understanding what it was about."

Andre turned toward her as they strolled, his eyes going wide. "A big mistake."

"You can say that again," she muttered, adding, "but I came anyway."

"And are you glad?"

"I'm . . . undecided about that right now," she admitted in complete honesty.

"Oh?"

And maybe she *was* a little freer than she thought, since right here, in this place and time, with this handsome Jamaican man on an island somewhere in the Caribbean, she saw no reason not to *keep* being honest. "I discovered that . . . it's easy to get caught up in the mood of this place, easy to become someone you're not. I'm not sure . . . who I'll be now, when I go back home."

"The way I see it," he said, "is that wherever you go, you're still you. Some places allow a person to . . . find new parts of themselves. Yet . . . *new* is not the right way to say it—no—because I believe all the parts were already there. So I should say that some places allow a person to . . . *release* parts of themselves." He nodded to himself. "Yes, that's better."

Jenna was unsure if she agreed. "So you're saying a place can't change you?"

"Like I said, seeing new places expands the mind. It can only open you up, help you see some of yourself you maybe didn't see before—but

I don't believe it can change you. Whatever you are, you are. People are complex, pretty lady—no? I think you're complex, too."

Hmm. "Maybe . . . more than I thought," she confessed. "But I'm still not sure I'm happy about it."

He smiled at her. "Ah, that is not wise. Celebrate what you are." He gave her a solid once-over. "I see a lovely lady who turns sad, and I'm sorry if I made you that way."

Jenna shook her head, quick to absolve him. "Oh, no, it's not you. It's something else. And I'm more than happy to walk on the beach and try to think of other things."

"And *I* am happy to give you something else to think of." He still held her hand, so when he stopped walking, she did, too. Then he took her other hand in his, his eyes sensual and suggestive in the moonlight—after which he leaned in to gently kiss her.

The kiss left her stunned at first—she'd never kissed a black man before, and she found the experience powerful, different, deep. Because it was new to her? Or was it simply the way Andre kissed?

She kissed him back, and soon he lifted one hand to her face. His mouth was firm yet tender, and she sensed confidence there, knew he was a man with experience seducing women. It felt easy to drift from one kiss into another . . . until he sank smoothly to his knees in the sand, pulling her down with him.

He'd just begun to kiss her again when she understood . . . oh God, she was entranced by the differences between them, by the exotic romance of making out with a Jamaican calypso singer, and she was charmed by his thoughtful personality—but she wasn't . . . aroused. She wasn't *driven* to kiss him.

In fact, it felt wrong. Because he wasn't Brent. And he wasn't in a fantasy that Brent was watching or had even created. And only sensual acts sanctioned by Brent, it seemed, moved her now. Oh Lord, it was awful—but true.

The realization made her lift her hands to his chest and push him gently back. "I'm sorry. It was very nice kissing you, but I'm afraid I can't."

"No?" Andre sighed. "That is a disappointment, Jenna."

"For me, too," she confided, shaking her head lightly. "I mean, you're so nice, so strong and sexy—I must be crazy."

"You, crazy? No," he said with certainty. "Just . . . perhaps this is the wrong place, the wrong time."

She nodded. "That's it." *And you're the wrong guy.* Oh God, she was doomed. "I'm sorry," she said again.

Rising to his feet and reaching down to help her up, he shook his head. "Please do not apologize. I got a lovely walk with an equally lovely lady. And a few kisses, too. Come, let me walk you back," he said, motioning in the direction from which they'd come.

"You're a good man," she told him with all sincerity.

"And you're a sweet woman. May I give you some advice?" he asked as they began heading toward the resort lights.

"All right."

"Whatever happened here to upset you, don't . . . let it change the way you view yourself. Because everything I see in front of me right now is good, all the way through. You've got a good heart, a good soul—I can feel that. So promise me you know just how good you are, Jenna."

His kind words nearly took her breath away, and compelled her to more honesty. "I do know," she promised him. "But I also think I'm . . . foolish. It's not so much what I've done here that's hurting me—it's that I've . . . come to care for someone here who doesn't care back. And I'm realizing it's no one's fault but my own."

"Ah, a broken heart," Andre said with consoling eyes. "Well, no wonder kisses weren't enough to fix it. Hearts take time to heal. And it has to come from within—no one can do it for you."

"Did *your* heart heal?" she wondered aloud. "After your wife?"

He seemed to be considering her question as they moved back up the beach, the tide still washing in around their feet, until he finally answered, "Very slowly. Now I am only sad to think what could have been. But I also appreciate what is. I take advantage of every goodness that comes my way—I appreciate every warm breeze, every sunny day, every smile, every walk on the beach with a pretty girl. Don't let your heart stay broken for long, Jenna. Life is too short to spend it suffering. Instead, live it. Enjoy it."

She let Andre's words sink in as they walked; she tried to analyze what they meant to *her*, right now. Wouldn't living life, taking advantage of it all, mean enjoying the last fantasies Brent offered her? Wouldn't it mean enjoying her last times with him, despite the hurt?

And yet, she simply didn't think she could do that. Sometimes it was best to cut your losses and move on.

Still . . . somehow coming home from this—from Brent and the Hotel Erotique—and getting back to real life, sounded impossible. She knew it *was* smart to move on from this—she just wasn't sure how to.

When Jenna returned to her room, she opened the door to find an envelope had been slid underneath. She leaned back her head with a sigh, then stooped to pick it up.

On Hotel Erotique stationery, she found a handwritten note from Brent.

> *Please don't go yet. Come see me tomorrow. There will be no one else there, just you and I, Jenna. I just need to see you, talk to you. I'll be waiting for you at 10 a.m. at the spot marked on the enclosed map. Please come.*

Jenna looked at the map of the grounds and found the indicated spot was labeled GARDEN OF EDEN. She'd never even noticed it on the map before and the very name made her suck in her breath. So Brent wanted to meet her in paradise, huh?

She had no idea what he could want at this point.

Maybe to apologize?

If that was his intention—God, it would be embarrassing in a way, since she'd laid herself so bare before him, both literally and figuratively. And what happened today had proven that even if he cared for her, he surely didn't care as much as she did for him. And she really *shouldn't* see him again—it would only increase the gnawing ache she suffered in her chest, stomach, and between her thighs, every time he came to mind.

Still, if he wanted to tell her he was sorry . . . maybe she should let him. It would begin . . . the closure. She'd gotten *some* closure by going to his beach house this afternoon, but not as much as she'd hoped. And letting him say whatever he wanted to would be better than running away from him and everything she'd let happen here.

And so she would go. Tomorrow. Ten a.m.

As she lay down to sleep a few minutes later, Jenna found herself thinking back over all her experiences at the Hotel Erotique. From nipple rings to shaving her pussy, from stripper shoes to vibrators to orgies, Brent had . . . stripped down every sexual idea she'd had about herself and replaced it with something shocking and new.

And maybe Andre had been right—maybe such wildness had been hiding inside her all along. If it hadn't, she surely couldn't have done such things so easily, let herself go so completely. And despite her hurt, some of the encounters she'd had on this island had felt . . . glorious, at least at the time. And she had Brent to thank for that. So *that* was a reason to go see him tomorrow, too—another bit of closure.

Tomorrow she would say goodbye to him—then she would go home and begin finding out if this had changed her life for the better or the worse.

She barely slept. Too much had happened.

All that remained was recovering from it.

And seeing Brent one last time, of course.

The Garden of Eden appeared, on the map, to be at the far end of the island. So after a room service breakfast, Jenna dressed in the casual skirt and lace-edged tank she'd chosen to travel in and set off, following one of the many shrubbery-lined trails that seemed to crisscross the grounds.

Having seen only a handful of the Hotel Erotique's fantasy settings, she could only imagine everything she'd missed, every other exotic or historic scenario the guides here created. No wonder Brent had retreated here from his heartbreak and never left. It was truly a fantasy world, where little was real. Despite knowing she wouldn't want to live in a world this utterly kinky all the time, she could see the appeal of moving to an island where every day was a fantasy, where existence was about pleasure and nothing more.

Finally, she reached the end of the winding path she'd taken across the island's interior to find an arched opening cutting through a tall hedge of bougainvillea, a sign labeling it as the entry to the Garden of Eden. Taking a deep breath, trying to prepare herself for whatever she was about to discover, she stepped inside.

Only . . . *nothing* could have prepared her.

She found herself on the edge of a pristine island meadow flourishing with lush flowers and enormous fruit trees. Colorful birds played among their branches, flying from one to another. Nearby lay a gorgeous natural island pool, a sizable waterfall tumbling into it from the hillier land just beyond—and although the space felt enclosed and private, a soft breeze wafted through the air, cooling her after her long walk. She'd never been anywhere that, indeed, felt closer to paradise.

Yet it was only when her gaze traveled lower that what she saw stole her breath. In the shade of a large banyan tree, Brent lay naked and gloriously erect on a brass bed festooned with flowering vines and draped in white satin sheets. The moment her eyes met his, violins began to play.

And tears came to Jenna's eyes.

Brent had finally given her what she'd wanted all along—satin sheets and violins. But it meant so much more now than it could have then.

The logical, self-protecting part of her wanted to stand strong—to make him find a way to fix what had happened yesterday, or to at least admit he was wrong.

But the Jenna she'd discovered here at the Hotel Erotique, the Jenna who loved sex and got weak in the knees every time she saw Brent, the Jenna who couldn't resist romance . . . simply went to him.

"Hey," he said, soft and low, wearing a small, sexy smile as she approached the bed. The only other sounds were the distant waterfall and the soft violins playing . . . somewhere.

"Hi," she gently replied.

He looked briefly like he might apologize to her or say something profound, but she could almost feel him thinking the same thing she was—that maybe none of that mattered right now in this moment that felt truly magical. Finally, he simply rasped, "Come to me, Jenna."

She responded by removing her top over her head to reveal a lacy yellow bra underneath, then let her skirt fall to the grass, uncovering matching panties. Brent growled at the sight of her as she approached the bed.

Things could have gone fast then, yet they turned . . . painstakingly slow. Brent took his time, touching her face, kissing her lips, letting his hands glide over her body. Every caress skimmed across her skin like velvet.

She touched him, too, just as slowly, exploring his body more thoroughly than ever before. She slid her palms across his broad shoulders, the firm muscles of his arms. She curled her fingernails into the smattering of dark hair on his chest. She kissed him there—over and over—tasting the salt on his skin. They were no Adam and Eve, and this was far from being original sin—and yet, as they touched each other, it felt . . . new.

When Brent finally peeled away her bra and began to rain kisses onto her breasts, she basked in the soft pleasure. And as he kissed his way tenderly down her stomach, she ached for him in her very soul.

Watching Brent draw down her panties as violins played, Jenna tossed her head back in abandon, soaking up the island breeze, luxuriating in the moment. Then she met Brent's dark gaze and parted her legs for him.

He kissed his way slowly up her inner thigh, and by the time he lowered his mouth gently to her clit, she thought she'd die from anticipation. She let out a moan, lifting, offering herself to him.

Brent met her gaze as he licked deeply into her, wanting to taste her, wanting to make her feel his tongue more intensely than ever. For him, this wasn't fucking—it was making love. And maybe it had been that way for a while now with Jenna, but suddenly he understood.

He understood that she'd been right about why he'd been so committed to freeing her this past week. He'd wanted to save her from what he'd never been able to save Deena from: a mediocre appreciation of sex.

But he also understood that it had quickly become much more than that. As he delivered passionate, openmouthed kisses to her glistening pink folds, he felt the same profound connection he'd experienced with her soon after that first night in the gazebo. The more time he spent with Jenna, the more that connection grew.

He understood that she was honest and outspoken, smart and funny, entrenched in history and her work, and extremely practical and logical—and he loved it all. But he loved just as much how cute and playful she could be, how hot and sexy she became when aroused, and how she'd learned to open herself up to daring new sex with him.

While he might have compared her to Deena in the back of his mind upon first meeting her, she'd turned out to be very different—*and*, he now had to admit to himself, so much more compatible with him than Deena had ever been. He'd genuinely loved Deena, but that was long in the past—and now he wondered if perhaps that hadn't been more of a . . . youthful love. He knew sometimes that lasted and sometimes it didn't, but either way, he found himself drawn to Jenna from a more secure position of experience and maturity.

He made love to her with his mouth, soon suckling on her beautifully engorged clit, enraptured in her sounds of pleasure—until he heard her moans growing deeper, more desperate, and just when he knew she would come soon, she did. She exploded into orgasm, sobbing her joy so emphatically that it made his aching cock even harder.

Rising up, he was just about to slide it inside her—when she surprised him by lifting onto her knees as well and playfully shoving him to his back on the bed. "Remember when you told me I was a woman in control?" she asked.

"Of course."

"Well, I'm taking it—now." And with that, she captured his stiff dick in her hand and went down on him, all in one swift move.

A startled, pleasured groan erupted from his throat as he watched her. Jesus God—she was shockingly good at sucking his cock. He let his eyes fall shut, lost in the hot delights her warm, wet mouth delivered. "So good, baby," he breathed. "So damn good."

And then she shocked him even more. Upon releasing him from her mouth, she ran the tip of his shaft over her prettily pointed nipples, wet-ting them that way, clearly lost in pleasures of her own, which thrilled him to the core. She used his cock to caress her ample breasts further, raking his length across the soft pillows of flesh, and then—mmm, yes—she let it rest in the valley between her tits, using her hands to wrap them around it.

"Jesus," he growled—and then he couldn't hold back; he fucked her tits.

And she responded by angling her mouth downward so that the head of his cock concluded each hot drive just within her lips.

God, she was astounding. He knew that already, but she kept proving it over and over. "So fucking hot, honey," he rasped. "Such beautiful tits. Such a soft, wet mouth. Such a perfect lover."

They moved together that way, Brent floating in a heavenly obscene bliss, until finally she released his shaft—but wasted no time straddling him, then impaling herself on it.

"Oh God," Jenna groaned, taking him deeply up into her pussy. Like this, it always felt as if his majestic cock stretched through her whole body. "So big," she purred. And then she began to ride him. She wasn't sure what had come over her—but somehow Brent's willingness to give her what she'd asked for today was inspiring her, making her wilder than ever.

They writhed together in a hot, grinding rhythm that made Jenna feel like the naughty girl Brent had taught her she could be. She didn't hesitate to caress her own breasts when the urge struck, meeting his gaze to see the fire there. And she didn't hesitate, moments later, to bend over him in the bed, dangling her tits in his face to say, "Suck them—hard."

The moment he obeyed her breathy command, the pleasure blasted from her breasts straight to her cunt and she rocked against him, grinding harder, deeper—until, oh God, another bright, flashing climax overtook her. She cried out as the mind-numbing pulses radiated from her clit out through her arms and legs, fingers and toes.

"Mmm," she moaned when it was done, letting herself rest on his chest, his erection inside her.

"Was it good, baby?" he asked low in her ear.

"*So* good," she whispered—then she rested there for a long, idyllic moment, listening to the birds and the waterfall, and the violins. "Where are they?" she asked then. "The violins?"

"The quartet from the masquerade is on the other side of those bushes," Brent said softly, pointing in the distance. And she smiled into his chest, thinking he truly was a man who knew how to make fantasies come true.

Once she got her strength back, she lifted her head from his chest and continued being this most aggressive version of herself—and loving the freedom Brent had given her to do so. "Now I want something you've taught me to appreciate far more than I ever did before."

"Name it, sunshine."

"Please fuck me hard, Brent," she said. "Make me scream."

As the words left her, she felt unashamed, simply joyful, cherishing the pleasure this man brought her. And then—wow—a more profound truth struck. Before Brent, feeling so free and unashamed *had* been something she could only fantasize about, or maybe wish for in a dark, hidden part of her mind. But Brent had made it real.

In response to her request, Brent turned her away from him, on her knees, instructing her to hold on to the curving brass headrails. When his hands molded to her hips, she braced herself, and then—*yes*—the hot, hard entry made her cry out. Mmm, God, he always felt especially big in this position, too, and as he began to fuck her, indeed making her sob with every pummeling stroke, she could barely stand the shocking joy of it.

Both of them moaned as he drove into her slickness, again, again, leaving Jenna replete with pleasure—full with it, as full as she could be—until Brent began to rub one fingertip over the fissure of her ass and she realized she was wrong; there was still more pleasure to be had.

Her face flushed and her whole body perspired as Brent slid his finger into her ass. *Oh God, yes.* She heard herself yowling, felt herself begin to tremble.

"I love to fuck you, baby," Brent was murmuring, his voice deep and raspy. "I love to fuck this sweet little pussy. And I love to fuck this tight little ass."

"*Yes! Yes!*" she was screaming. It was all too much. Too much sensation to bear. Every cell of her body throbbed, and she needed to come like she needed to breathe. "Rub me," she begged. "Please, Brent, rub me!"

"Aw, baby," he growled at the request, and the next thing she knew, the fingers of his free hand pressed between her legs.

"Oh! Oh God!" That was all it took to send her into an explosive orgasm that utterly consumed her. After that, there was only screaming and thrashing and pulsations that stretched outward through every limb, the climax rivaling the one when Brent had found her G-spot. She couldn't think, could barely breathe—her whole world in that moment was about coming.

It was as Jenna's wild climax finally faded that Brent's low groan met her ear. "Oh, fuck, honey—me, too." Then he nearly nailed her to the brass rails with the ferocious drives of his cock, moaning and growling with each powerful thrust.

Jenna's body went limp and she found herself in a tangled heap with Brent among the slick satin sheets. When she recovered enough to open her eyes, she found his head on the pillow next to hers, his dark gaze pinning her in place. "I love you, sunshine," he said.

And Jenna's heart nearly stopped. She'd adored what had just happened between them, but she'd had no idea it was leading to *this*.

"What?" she breathed.

"I love you," he repeated, sounding amazingly sure, "and I'm an idiot because I tried to fight it."

Jenna lay staring at him, aware that at some point her jaw had dropped. "I love you, too," she said, still shaken.

"I know," he said, reaching up to touch her face. Then he closed his eyes, tight, and Jenna realized he was—oh God—fighting back tears. He opened them again to say, "I know, and . . . I forgot how nice that feels. To be loved."

"Oh, Brent," she said, touching his face now, too.

"I don't like admitting this," he went on, "but . . . I *have* been hiding here. It was easy, simple. And I never expected anyone to come along and call me on it, or make me suddenly start wanting something more, *needing* something more." His eyes filled with more emotion than she'd ever seen in them. "I need you in my life, Jenna."

"So now," she said, stopping to draw his hand away from her cheek and kiss it, "it's not about what *I* need—it's about what *you* need."

He nodded, completely contrite. "That's right, sunshine. With you, I have needs."

"I'll meet them," she promised.

He blinked. "Just like that? It's that easy? I mean, you know I've lived a very different sort of life than you, so . . . I'd understand if you want to take some time to figure this out."

Yet Jenna simply shook her head. "We'll figure it out *together*, but I already know—I want to give you whatever you need, Brent. Because *you* gave that to *me* when I didn't even know I needed it."

He hadn't given her the freedom to have casual sex with strangers, like she might have been seeking in the beginning. No, he'd given her something much more important—the freedom to have wild, uninhibited sex with the man she loved. And now he'd given her that love in return, too. What more could a girl need?

Epilogue

One year later

"So, what would I have to do to get the keys to the ship?" Kevin asked Jenna.

She simply rolled her eyes at him from her lounge chair next to the main pool. "It's a *ship*. It doesn't have keys. So I'm thinking you'd need to learn to sail before Brent would trust you with it."

"So he knows how to *sail*, too?" Kevin asked, sounding a little jealous.

Jenna just shrugged. "What can I tell you? He's a man of many talents."

"Well, if I can't have the ship, how am I gonna give Shannon her pirate fantasy?" He motioned to where Shannon floated on a raft in the pool in a lime green bikini.

"Let me talk to Brent," Jenna said, taking mercy on him, "and we'll see what we can work out."

He grinned. "Thanks, Jenna."

"I suppose it's the least I can do," she admitted. "Without your know-it-all interference, I wouldn't be the happiest woman alive right now."

"Damn straight," he agreed, now that she'd reminded him.

And Jenna wasn't exaggerating—she could barely believe all she had to be happy about.

Brent had decided to give up working at the Hotel Erotique, but he still retained partial ownership, including his beach bungalow. And that had allowed him to reunite with his family. It turned out his mother had been missing him deeply, and she and Jenna got along great. And it was clear to Jenna how much it meant to Brent to have his niece and nephew back in his life.

Brent had just started teaching a few psychology courses at a small Miami university, where he was also furthering his own education, pursuing other areas in the field. His hope was to earn a full professorial gig in a few years. Not only had he discovered he really enjoyed teaching, but his schedule left time to work on restoring the 1965 Mustang his dad had given him for college graduation—and it left summers free for island getaways. Although the Hotel Erotique was close enough to the mainland that even weekend trips were easy, like the one they were on now.

Fortunately, Jenna could write her historical biographies anywhere. Her current project focused on figures with notorious sexual pasts, such as the Marquis de Sade, Lady Godiva, and Caligula—and Brent was helping her with the psychological issues likely involved with each. She'd found it especially fulfilling to discover they *worked* together just as well as they *played* together.

Just then, Shannon came walking up the pool steps. "Is it time yet?"

Jenna checked her watch. Oh God, it was. "Yeah, come on, let's go."

The two of them were off to the spa for the afternoon. Afterward, they were having their hair done, and then they were going to a wedding: Jenna and Brent's. Despite the protests of both their families, they'd decided they wanted something private and secluded that reminded them of when they'd first met—and a barefoot ceremony on the beach fit the bill. Shannon and Kevin had come to serve as witnesses—and to partake in a few of the hotel amenities while they were here, although they'd decided to keep it a game of one-on-one.

And so had Jenna and Brent. Despite the pleasures Brent had shown her through multiple partners, now Brent was the only lover Jenna desired. Brent's life was no longer an escape into sex and Jenna's life wasn't an escape *from* sex—but there was still *plenty* of sex. They, too, never tired of enjoying what the resort had to offer—frequently spending private time together in the harem room, on the pirate ship, in the Tudor castle Jenna had only gotten acquainted with after her first visit—and when Brent was feeling especially dominant, he summoned her to the dungeon.

For their wedding night, however, they were returning to the Garden of Eden.

In the end, he'd healed her—but she'd forced *him* to heal, too, and she'd shown him he didn't always have the answers to *everything*.

All in all, life was grand, because *she'd* been daring enough to go to the Hotel Erotique, and because *he'd* been pushy enough to give her what she needed.

"I don't need a man. I don't need a man. I don't need a man."

Usually, Brenna did her morning affirmations at home, but the alarm had gone off late, and just like breakfast, her affirmations had been forced to wait until she got to the office. Fortunately, she was stealing a few minutes alone in the break room with a donut and the self-help book she'd been reading, aptly titled, *You Don't Need a Man to Be Happy*.

She lowered her voice even further for the next set. "I don't need a penis to pleasure me. I don't need a penis to pleasure me. I don't need a penis to pleasure me."

Maybe she should drop that one from her repertoire, though. Saying it only made her think about penises.

"I am responsible for my own pleasure. I am responsible for my own pleasure. I am responsible for my own pleasure." Which, of course, meant masturbation. And she had nothing against that—it could get a girl through many a long and lonely night. But to tell herself it would be *enough, forever*—well, that was challenging. She'd have to work on *feeling* that one more as she said it.

Still determined, however, she started the first repetition. "I don't need a man. I don't—"

"Spoken just like someone who needs a man."

Flinching, she looked up to find her friend and coworker, Kelly Mills—blond, fairly glamorous, and someone with plenty of men in her life. Kelly did PR for Blue Night Records, the indie music label that employed them both, and she also held a degree in psychology, which she claimed she needed in her line of work.

"I don't," Brenna reassured her about needing a man. Despite having little in common, the two had been good friends since Brenna had moved to L.A. three years ago, so if someone had to intrude on her affirmations, she was glad it was Kelly.

Kelly gave her head a scolding tilt. "People who don't usually *don't* need to say it."

"Huh?"

Kelly crossed her arms beneath ample breasts. "Take my next-door neighbor, Ms. Freeland, for instance. She's seventy-five and never been married. She's an artist, she traveled the world in her youth, she loves her Scottish terrier, Fiona, and she's never needed a man. She's never told me that, but it shows in everything she does. It's simply a part of her. She doesn't feel the need to go around explaining why she's not married or that she doesn't need a man—because she's so truly comfortable not having one.

"On the other hand, there's Ms. Nelson, three doors down." Kelly dropped her chin derisively and shifted her weight from one pointy red pump to the other. "She's forty-five and clearly lonely. She tells me all the time how she doesn't need a man to fulfill her, but what ruins it is how darned bitter and angry she sounds every time she says it. She might not *want* to need a man. But she obviously needs one."

"Your point again?" Brenna asked, eyebrows raised.

"Saying you don't need a man over and over indicates that, like it or not, you do. And there's no crime in that, by the way. Most women are wired to desire love and commitment."

Brenna only rolled her eyes. "Love and commitment—bleh." She didn't have to say more since Kelly knew all the nasty details about her cheating husband and recent divorce. "The last thing I'm interested in is commitment. And that's the truth."

Kelly nodded. "I believe you. You have trust issues. But I'll tell you what you *do* need."

"What's that?"

"To paraphrase the immortal words of John Mellencamp, you need a lover—who won't drive you crazy."

A lover? Brenna had had relationships, and guys she'd dated, and of course, a husband, but she'd never been the confident, carefree sort of woman who could have someone she thought of as a *lover*. So she pointed to her book. "According to this, a good vibrator will provide the same fulfillment."

Kelly raised her eyebrows matter-of-factly. "Do you have one?"

"No."

"Why not?"

Brenna pursed her lips. "Besides the fact that I'm too shy to go into one of those stores? Well, because somehow an evening with a vibrator just sounds a little . . . empty, as in boring. I know some women talk a good game about it, but—"

Kelly held up her hands in a *stop* motion. "Say no more. And listen to me. You *need* a lover. How long has it been since you've had one, by the way?"

"Does Wayne count?" Her smarmy ex.

Kelly grimaced. "Don't tell me he's the last? I mean, you've been divorced for, what, six months now?"

Brenna sighed. "And separated for a year before that."

Kelly looked as if Brenna had just announced the death of a loved one. "Oh dear God, you poor girl. Stand up."

Brenna blinked her surprise at the command, but the imposing look in Kelly's eyes pushed her to her feet. Placing her hands on Brenna's hips, Kelly positioned her in front of the small mirror above the sink in one corner of the break room. Reaching around her from behind, Kelly deftly undid the top two buttons on Brenna's blouse, then firmly cupped the undersides of her breasts to hoist them higher. "We've got to get you a man, and we're going to start by showing off your assets a little more."

Sadly, it had been so long since anyone had touched Brenna intimately that even Kelly's unexpected grasp aroused her a little, sending a tingling sensation shooting straight to her panties.

But she still had no desire for some meaningless affair. Or some meaning*ful* affair. Which pretty much cut out affairs. And brought her back to the book. "I don't know, Kel. I just don't think men or sex is on my personal menu anymore. That's why I'm doing these affirmations. I want to get them out of my system."

Kelly stepped back to the table, peering down at the books still lying open. Then she let out a huge *harrumph*. "Oh my God! Trust me, honey, you *do* need penises. We *all* need penises. Penises are one of God's gifts to women. Sure. He gave us labor pains. And periods. And kept us oppressed for centuries. But He did give us the penis, and that makes up for a lot."

Brenna simply sighed. Then buttoned up her blouse, hiding the cleavage Kelly had just revealed. This was pointless—the cleavage *and* the conversation. "Did you come in here just to harass me or did you have a purpose?"

"Oops, sorry—I almost forgot. Your moratorium on men totally sidetracked me. Jenkins wants to see you in his office." Their boss and the CEO of Blue Night. "Word in the halls is that he's got some big announcement to make, but no one knows what it is. So go check it out and end the suspense for all of us."

An announcement, huh? It was the first Brenna had heard of it, and being Jenkins' right-hand gal, she usually knew what was going on around here. So, after wiping away donut crumbs with a napkin, stowing her book in her desk drawer, and checking to make sure she'd rebuttoned her blouse correctly, she grabbed up a notepad and pen and headed toward Jenkins' office, knocking gently on the open door as she peeked inside.

"Brenna, come in," he said with what she thought was a rather devious smile. "And close the door."

Carl Jenkins was exactly the kind of man people commonly referred to by his last name. Smart and calculating, no nonsense, all business—more the kind of guy you'd expect to work at one of the majors than a small indie label. That said, Blue Night had grown fast the last few years, in no small thanks to him. Sporting slicked-back hair and rather beady eyes, he was also the kind of guy you never felt completely comfortable with, and Brenna still didn't, even after three years as his administrative assistant.

After pushing the door shut, she eased into the chair across from him, wondering exactly what the big news was. "Kelly said you wanted to see me. There's some sort of big announcement afoot?"

Her boss's gaze widened as he chuckled lightly. Clearly, he was surprised but not startled to hear his employees suspected something was up. "An announcement? Sort of, dependent upon this conversation. But first, a secret. And I know I can trust you to keep a secret—right, Brenna? Especially when it's in your best interest professionally."

"Of course," she said, hoping he didn't see her nervous swallow. Brenna *hated* secrets. Professional, personal—either way, she just didn't like them. She'd gotten *divorced* over a secret, after all—a secret affair. But it sounded as if she was about to have one dropped on her anyway.

"I've watched you grow in this business the last few years, Brenna. You're a quick learner, smart, responsible, and people like you. Plus, you're nice. In a city like L.A., you don't always *find* a lot of nice, and that makes you a commodity."

She was a commodity? When had *that* happened? But no matter—maybe this meant she was getting a raise. Maybe a *secret* raise no one else was getting? A secret like that she could probably keep. "Thank you, Mr. Jenkins. I've really loved learning about the music business since coming to work here."

"You may not realize this, Brenna, but you probably know the ins and outs of this company better than most people in this office. I hear you on the phone with everyone from our artists to our distributors, and you know what you're doing. To a degree that I think it's a sin to keep you in your current position."

At this, Brenna blinked. This wasn't just a raise?

"I want to groom you to be Blue Night's next A&R rep," Jenkins said—and she struggled not to let her jaw drop.

He wanted to give *her*—little Brenna Cayton from Centerville, Ohio—the most coveted position at the label? Most of the people who worked there, from the mailroom guy on up, had taken jobs at Blue Night with the aspiration of someday advancing to the glamorous post of artist and repertoire representative, scouting for and signing new talent. She, on the other hand, had not. She'd simply needed a job, gone on an interview. She found it fulfilling enough just to work at a cool record label. But to be that cool label's A&R person—wow, talk about a head rush.

Then it hit her. "Is Damon leaving? Going to one of the majors?"

Damon Andros *was* Blue Night Records to the industry—and the paparazzi. His heart-stopping sex appeal combined with his rock star persona to make him deliciously photo-worthy, especially when out partying with rock bands or on the arm of the latest female pop sensation. He was also Blue Night's sole A&R rep—so successful and well-known in the biz that there was no need for anyone else. Brenna attributed the label's accomplishments just as much to Damon Andros as she did to Jenkins.

Whose smile stayed in place but stiffened. "That's where the secret comes in."

"Oh?" Brenna held her breath, waiting.

"It's like this," her boss said, tilting his head. "Despite Damon's obvious success, over time he's started to . . . become a liability. If you don't believe me, just ask Kelly—she takes the calls from the reporters, fields the rumors. But I'm sure you don't *have* to ask her—because everyone knows."

Brenna nodded shortly, sighing. There *were* rumors. That Damon Andros ran a modern-day casting couch—signing women only after they'd slept with him. That he partied illicitly hard with the musicians he hung out with. He was the L.A. music scene's official bad boy. "I just didn't realize Damon's behavior had any significant impact on Blue Night's business." After all, it was a rock-n-roll lifestyle and this was La La Land.

"Fortunately, it's been a slow-coming thing. But now I've got Claire Starr threatening to sue us, claiming he wouldn't give her a contract until she had sex with him." Starr was a recent Blue Night one-hit wonder whose bad attitude had gotten her ousted from a label that usually nurtured performers and stuck with them through ups and downs. "Could be sour grapes since we dropped her, but on the other hand, it's the kind of publicity that could kill us, and whether or not it's true, his general behavior makes it plausible." A hopeful smile slid back onto Jenkins' face. "So, would you like to hear my proposition?"

Sadly, despite how exciting it was, this whole thing was suddenly making Brenna break out into a sweat. Still, she said, "Sure."

"I want to announce that we're adding you as an A&R rep due to our growth over the last couple of years, and I want Damon to begin training you—starting on his scouting trip to Vegas next week. You'll shadow his every move. He'll show you the ropes, introduce you around, teach you how to spot a star as opposed to a flash in the pan.

"As for Damon's fate, I'm holding steady until we see what happens with Claire. But the minute she sues, he's gone. That might be next week, next month, or never—we'll have to let it play out. Either way, I want you ready to take over. And . . . if it works out that Damon can clean up his act and put a more professional face on Blue Night, I won't leave you out in the cold. If I end up keeping Damon on the payroll, it's safe to say we'll continue making good money, and I'll need you *both* out there finding new talent."

"In the meantime, everything I've told you about Damon stays between you and me. To the rest of the world, you're training for a *new* position, not Damon's existing one. Got it?"

She drew her lips together, again trying to hide the nervous swallow. "And that includes Damon? He has no idea he's going to be grooming me to take his job when you fire him?"

Jenkins answered with a succinct but conclusive nod.

Okay, regroup. Your boss has just offered you the opportunity of a lifetime. And to get it, all you have to do is lie your ass off to the sexiest guy you've ever encountered. For a week. Maybe longer. Oh, and you have to lie to everyone else about it, too.

Her stomach churned.

"Can I count on you, Brenna? Are you on board?"

For a dream job? "Definitely." What else could she say?

About the Author

Lacey Alexander's books have been called deliciously decadent, unbelievably erotic, exceptionally arousing, blazingly sexual, and downright sinful. In each book, Lacey strives to take her readers on the ultimate erotic adventure, and she hopes her stories will encourage women to embrace their sexual fantasies. Lacey resides in the Midwest with her husband, and when not penning romantic erotica, she enjoys studying history and traveling, often incorporating favorite destinations into her work.